DEVLIN'S DESIRE

'You're mine. You've always been mine and no matter how you fight it, Holly, you'll always be mine!

Holly had been an innocent girl when Devlin had taken everything she had to give—and more. Then, after walking out on her, he'd proceeded to destroy her and everything she'd ever loved. Now he was back and what was more, he was making it quite clear that he still wanted her and was determined to prove that Holly still wanted him. Holly had vowed never to forgive him, but she had forgotten that passion and love were a more potent mixture than revenge and hate ...

Please note: *This book contains some sexually descriptive matter which may not be suitable for all our readers.*

Devlin's Desire

by

Margaret Callaghan

Magna Large Print Books
Long Preston, North Yorkshire,
England.

British Library Cataloguing in Publication Data.

Callaghan, Margaret
   Devlin's desire.

   A catalogue record for this book is
available from the British Library

   ISBN 0-7505-1278-4

First published in Great Britain by Scarlet, 1996

Copyright © 1996 by Margaret Callaghan

Cover illustration © Len Thurston by arrangement with P.W.A.
International Ltd.

The right of Margaret Callaghan to be identified as the author
of this work has been asserted by her in accordance with the
Copyright, Designs and Patents Act, 1988

Published in Large Print 1998 by arrangement with Robinson
Publishing

Magna Large Print is an imprint of
Library Magna Books Ltd.
Printed and bound in Great Britain by
T.J. International Ltd., Cornwall, PL28 8RW.

PART ONE

PART ONE

CHAPTER 1

'Hello, Holly. Long time no see.'

She froze, goose bumps erupting on her warm, sun-kissed skin. Caught without her sun shades, the world was a blur, the reflected glare of the sand dazzling, distorting. She raised her hand, planing the droplets of water from her face in an attempt to bring the man into focus. Not that she had need to. She knew that voice, would scent that musky tang of aftershave at a hundred paces. Only she hadn't, had she? she realized, damping down the panic. She'd spent years and years scanning crowds, aching for a glimpse of that arrogant profile, afraid her eyes would lock with his across a sea of heads, more afraid as the months passed that they never would again. Though she'd never lost the pain, time had dulled the ache, the want, the need, had foolishly allowed her to drop her guard, let Devlin Winter catch her unawares.

'Hello, Dev,' she responded coolly, amazed her voice didn't betray the inner turmoil. And needing time to think, she picked up her towel, rubbing furiously at her skin in an unconscious bid to instil some self-control. Why? Why now? she wondered, squeezing the excess water from her unruly mane of hair, and since Dev would know she was stalling, she took a deep, calming breath before turning back to face him.

7

'Seven years,' he murmured, a quizzical smile playing about the corners of his mouth. 'Who'd have believed it? And you don't look a day older.'

I'll bet, she derided silently, the pain of seeing Dev, being unnervingly close to Dev twisting the knife blade. And how ironic, yet another of Fate's cruel tricks, allowing Holly to stumble blindly from the sea and walk straight into Dev. Devlin Winter. Six feet two inches of sun-bronzed dynamism. Six feet two inches of sheer masculinity. And as the memory flooded back to taunt her Holly closed her eyes, closed her eyes but not her mind, every word, every gesture, each and every touch so real it might have been yesterday: strong arms closing round her, the whispered words of reassurance, the warm flutter of breath on her cheek as hungry lips moved down to nibble at the corners of her mouth. Man and woman, alone on a beach. Then and now.

And steeling herself to meet his sultry gaze, she raised leaden lids, subconsciously logging the legacy of time: the hint of grey in the jet-black hair, laughter lines fanning from the corners of his eyes. But still the most devastating man it had been her misfortune to meet. Oh, yes, she conceded bitterly, time had been kind to handsome Devlin Winter.

She licked her salt-baked lips, a nervous response that was unwittingly provocative and Dev swore lightly under his breath as he reached out, long fingers closing round her shoulders. Holly gasped, reacting, responding, for an unbelievable moment responding to a need so right, so true that the mere thought of denial was obscene. And then she remembered. Seven years. Seven lonely years. Seven years of hate.

'Don't,' she protested, beginning to pull away, but iron fingers tightened their grip and she was shockingly aware that nothing had changed. Until Dev was ready to release her, Holly was trapped.

'Don't? Don't what?' he countered softly. 'Don't hold you, Holly? Don't touch you, caress you? But why?' he challenged, completely unperturbed. 'I'm not going to hurt you. I simply want to hold you, to remember. I want us both to remember.'

And *yes*, Holly remembered, Dev's words, touch and devastating presence just eloquent reinforcements. Because they belonged, they'd always belonged. Past tense, she emphasized, stiffening, but Dev simply smiled, shook his head, black eyes dancing. 'Oh, Holly,' he chided softly. 'You know better than that. You can't fight the truth, Holly. So why not relax, relax and enjoy?'

And the voice was pouring over her, relentless, soothing, hypnotizing, so much remembered, so much she'd never forgotten, every touch, every word, every nuance a replay of the past. Holly was losing the battle, had never stood a chance against Dev, the blood turning to water in her veins as long, slender fingers began their soft, rhythmic kneading of Holly's naked shoulders. And, sure enough, she felt her knees give way and she slumped against him, the searing body-to-body contact driving the breath from her lungs.

'Oh, yes!' Dev crooned, pulling her even closer. 'Much, much better,' he purred. Yet, despite the urge to bask in his approval, somewhere in the fog of Holly's mind common sense stirred.

Approval! This man had destroyed her, for heaven's sake, had walked out of her life with never a second glance. Was she mad? Allowing him to walk back in as if they'd parted only yesterday? Oh, no! She'd grown up. Long days, lonely nights and the cruel realization that Dev had been using her had finally left their mark. Trial by fire. And damn Devlin Winter, but Holly had survived. All she had to do now was find the strength to fight him.

'Holly. Oh, Holly,' he murmured, chipping away at her resistance as he slid his hands down her back and over the swell of her buttocks. 'God, how I've missed you,' he groaned. 'Missed you. Wanted you. Needed you.'

'No!' With a massive surge of will, Holly twisted free. Oh, yes, the *need* was there, she acknowledged silently. A physical need. Nothing more, nothing less. But Devlin Winter's needs were nothing to do with her. 'Come off it, Dev,' she castigated coldly, grey eyes oozing scorn. 'Don't lie. Not now. Not ever. Seven years, Dev. You didn't need me then, you sure as hell haven't wasted a moment since with idle thoughts of gullible Holly Scott.'

'Haven't I?' he queried softly. 'Oh, Holly, if only you knew.'

'Only I don't, do I?' she snapped scornfully. 'And I don't want to know. I don't want anything, *anything* at all from you.' And swallowing the pain, she swung away, a gesture of dismissal she wasn't sure she really meant, but she had to do something, anything, to break the spell of Dev's disturbing presence.

Sharply aware of the sand burning the soles of her feet, she was even more aware of the man standing much too close for comfort. Black eyes seared her body as his gaze swept the length of her, tracing the curves, fanning the flames, lingering on the rapid rise and fall of breasts that tightened with an ache that only Dev's touch could salve. Heaven knew, trying to wipe away the stain of Dev's brand with a string of men she hadn't loved, hadn't wanted, hadn't enjoyed, was a shame she'd have to carry for the rest of her life.

Unlike that first time, it was busy on the beach, thank goodness, the rows of tented parasols pockets of shade in the glare. In another half-hour, the happy family groups would be heading for the air-conditioned bistros, scorning the mad English habit of frying in the sun at the hottest part of the day. And since Holly was beginning to overheat, the idea of a drink was suddenly very appealing—something long and cool to quench her thirst, followed by a large and out-of-character brandy. Dev. Why? Why, after all this time? And how dared he walk calmly back into her life and behave as if nothing had happened?

She blinked back the tears. 'Fool,' she berated herself softly, viciously, and, ignoring Dev completely, began to rummage through her holdall simply for something to do. Fingers closing thankfully around pocket mirror and comb, she tried to restore normality, the outward signs at least, as she raked the tangled, salt-dried locks. Convinced she must look a mess, she risked a glance at her reflection. Panic. A panic she did her best to mask as she angled the mirror and just as she'd feared—hoped?—Dev's solemn gaze filled the tiny square.

'Still here?' she murmured flippantly, donning her sunshades, the dark lenses a welcome layer of protection. 'Nothing better to do, Dev? Nothing to claim your attention for the next seven years or so? Dear me. Things must be bad. If I had the odd five minutes to spare,' she tagged on cattily, 'you could tell me your life story.' And dropping the comb and mirror back into the bag, she flashed him a bright, brittle smile before snatching a bottle of aftersun and giving it a vigorous shake. It was another dismissive gesture yet, just as before, Holly knew that if Dev turned and walked away now she'd be more hurt than she cared to acknowledge.

Only he didn't. 'Here. Let me,' he insisted.

'I can manage, thank you,' Holly snapped but Dev ignored her, taking the bottle and spinning her round, moving in behind, close, dangerously close, tiny hairs on the back of Holly's neck prickling out a warning.

'Stand still, woman,' he commanded huskily,

the rich velvet tones sending shivers of heat the length of her spine.

Stand still? With Dev's hands on her body? Some hope. Holly was a tingling, quivering mass, aware of nothing but the touch of skin on skin, of magic fingers gliding across an expanse of naked flesh, and sure enough she began to melt, the soft, gentle rhythm of swirling fingers lulling, soothing, disarming. Madness, she told herself with a secret little smile. Sheer insanity.

But Holly was powerless, was putty in Dev's hands, because clever, clever Dev knew exactly what he was doing. As the cream-laden hands moved down, tracing the ridge of her spine, she sent up a silent prayer of thanks, because it could have been worse. Think of the chaos he'd create if he spun her round to face him! And since the thought was enough to set her on fire, she felt her cheeks flame, was beginning to glow, aware of nothing but Dev and the magic touch of fingers, hands moving down, down and onwards, sweeping round into the curve of waist and hip, round again and down before pausing at the waistband of those briefest of briefs.

And Holly didn't breathe, didn't dare breathe. Waiting, wanting, knowing, the thrill running through her as Dev's fingers slid beneath the waistband.

'Dev!' she protested, pulling away, although her mind was screaming its denials. Because, oh, God, she didn't want him to stop.

And Dev laughed, a rich deep sound that was music to her ears as he drew her back, featherlight touches filling her with heat, filling her with dread and dredging up longings she'd thought were dead and buried.

'Oh, Holly!' he murmured, dipping his head, and his lips were nuzzling the stem of her neck, creating havoc.

Holly went rigid, suppressing the urge to lean back, to feel the length of his body against the length of hers, because instinct told her how Dev would react. His hands would move round and up, would close round her straining breasts, cupping, cradling, caressing, and public beach notwithstanding, he'd nudge aside the flimsy scraps of fabric, exposing her dark, swollen nipples to Dev's hungry gaze. And she wanted him. Oh, hell, how she wanted him!

But it was worse than that, she realized, balling her fists in an effort to stay in control. Because Dev was a craving she would never overcome and, like an addict mad for the taste of wine, Holly couldn't risk so much as a sip. Touch Dev, kiss Dev and she'd never be free.

You're not free now, she taunted herself silently. Maybe not, she allowed, but she'd moved on, had battled through the bad years, had proved she could live without him. Oh, yes, she *could* live without him. And she wasn't about to risk a second trail of devastation when Devlin Winter grew tired of playing games.

She pulled away, hugging her arms to her chest, suddenly cold despite the sweltering heat, and, gazing round in wonder, was shocked to find that outwardly nothing had changed. She was on the beach at Houlgate, waiting for Meryl and Jon.

For once, Meryl's total disregard for time was a blessing, because they musn't meet. Ever. Holly couldn't bear it. Allow Devlin a glimpse of her life, allow him back into her life? Not a hope in hell, she vowed, vaguely aware that families were beginning to disperse as fractious children, tired from the sheer hard work of having fun, were coaxed from the water's edge. Another five minutes and she'd be alone, alone on a beach with Dev in the full heat of the day. Mad dogs and Englishmen. Her lips twisted. Mad. That just about summed her up. She shivered.

'You're cold!' Dev accused, black eyes narrowing. 'Too much sun, you little fool. Come on, you need a drink.' He didn't wait for a reply, reaching for her bag with one hand, tugging at her wrist with the other. Like a child, Holly obeyed, too drained to deny him, aware of nothing but the touch of skin on skin, of the need, the shameful, naked, aching need she had of Dev.

Only she musn't. She halted, pulling him up short, and Dev swung round, raised a quizzical eyebrow.

'What is it?' he queried softly.

Holly licked her lips. 'I promised to meet someone. On the beach,' she added carefully. 'My—'

'Your—?' he interrupted tersely, and unbelievably Holly sensed fear in the half-formed question.

15

For the first time in what seemed like hours, Holly was back in control. 'Just Jon,' she murmured matter-of-factly. 'Jon and—'

'Jon! Ah, yes!' Dev growled, his face darkening and, though it hurt like hell to deceive him, Holly was glad.

'So—' He flung the bag down with a gesture of contempt, the grip on her wrist tightening. 'Tell me. Tell me about this...Jon, this...man who dares to leave you alone on a crowded beach.'

'He's—'

'Tall, dark and handsome, I suppose?' he interrupted savagely.

'Tall? Oh, yes,' she acknowledged indulgently, smiling despite herself. For his age, at least. 'And handsome too.' A very handsome little man. 'But as for being dark... No, Dev,' she informed him confidentially. 'But two out of three isn't bad for a guess.'

'And is he good?'

'I beg your pardon?' she murmured, stiffening at the fury in his tone.

'You know. Good. In bed,' he stated baldly, black eyes smouldering with hate.

'Better than you, you mean?' Holly needled him, wanting to hurt him, to pay him back for the years of pain, for the gaping void of his desertion.

He swore softly, savagely, and, snaring her free hand, he pulled her round so they were standing face to face and much too close for comfort.

'Better than me?' He shook his head, his lips

16

curling in contempt. 'No!' he growled. 'He could never be that. But good enough, hey, Holly?' he added insultingly. 'Good enough to keep you happy, satisfied, maybe. But good enough to make you beg for more and more and more...?'

He smiled—that is, the gleaming flash of teeth bore the hallmarks of a smile. 'No, Holly,' he stated matter-of-factly, pushing her away in disgust. '*I know* he could never do that.'

'But you'll never know, will you, Dev?' she heard herself goading him. 'You might think —hope—assume,' she informed him, saccharine-sweetly. 'But you can't be sure, not like I can.' And she raised her head, angling her chin in defiance. 'Now let me see, Devlin Winter, marks out of ten...' And she held his gaze, stretching the moment with tantalizing cruelty. Then it was her turn to shrug. 'Sorry, Dev,' she conceded carelessly. 'It's been so long I can barely remember.'

'You're lying.'

'Am I?' She smiled, aware of Dev's pain, equally aware of her own. She'd hurt him, touched a nerve, had aimed the insult squarely where it hurt. At his manhood. That and his pride. And yes, Devlin Winter was full of pride. And arrogance. And self-assurance. And fun and laughter and love, she remembered, not wanting to weaken. She had to stay strong.

He'd loved her, taken her innocence, taken everything she had to give and more. And not content with walking out, he'd ruthlessly destroyed Holly and everything she loved. For

17

that she'd never forgive him. If lying helped to keep him at a distance, then fine. She'd play her part like a puppet on strings, only this time it wouldn't be Dev who was pulling them.

'But of course.' The Dev she remembered was back in control, arms folded casually across his naked chest as he continued to regard her. Catching the gleam of speculation he didn't bother to hide, Holly backed away, putting space between them easily enough, but powerless to prevent his smouldering gaze from bridging the gap.

Sure enough, black eyes travelled the length of her, assessing, caressing; a long and leisurely perusal of Holly's body, down and up before reaching the swell of her breasts where he paused, lingered, a tangible touch that seemed to burn through the flimsy material of her bikini top.

Holly held herself rigid, fighting the urge to fold her arms in a giveaway gesture of protection, her breasts tightening despite herself, nipples hardening, straining at the fabric, the heat of wanting Dev to look, to taste, to touch almost more than she could stand.

And then he smiled, because Devlin Winter had his proof: Holly's thrusting nipples were an eloquent betrayal. She wanted him. She could lie till she was blue in the face but Dev knew, as Holly knew, that she wanted him.

'I—think I'd better go,' she stammered, desperate to escape the calculated scrutiny.

'Running away?' he taunted softly. 'From me?

Surely not? How ill-mannered when we've only just met. And besides, you've forgotten the absent Jon.'

'I'm sure he'll manage to find me,' she retorted coolly, darting eyes searching for her bag. She found it where Dev had carelessly tossed it but, since she'd have to pass dangerously close to Dev to retrieve it, the urge to walk away and leave it almost gained the upper hand. A luxury she couldn't afford, she realized, for if make-up bag and towel could be dispensed with, the passport and purse couldn't, not to mention the minor matter of her clothes.

If she did summon the nerve to walk half-naked through the streets, there was nothing to stop Dev sifting through the contents for her holiday address and then turning up on her doorstep. Since she didn't have a choice, the sooner she made a move, the sooner she'd escape. Escape? Some hope, she groaned. Physically she'd be free, but deep inside where it mattered, there was no escape from Dev. Ever.

Bracing herself, she stepped forwards, pulling up sharp as Dev second-guessed her intentions. 'Ever the gentleman,' Holly scorned, taking the bag from his outstretched hand and careful to avoid any skin to skin contact.

'But of course. Unlike the absent Jon,' Dev sneered, 'I know how to treat a lady.'

'And what makes you so sure Jon doesn't?'

'He's late. Assuming he turns up. Also assuming he exists, in fact,' he tagged on slyly.

19

'Meaning?'

'Meaning simply that. You find yourself alone on a beach with me and suddenly you're afraid. How easy to invent a companion, a male companion, a conspicuously absent male companion.'

'Sorry to disappoint you, Dev, but Jon's as real as you are.'

'A full-blooded male, no less.'

'If you say so,' she demurred, tiring of the game of verbal ping pong. Besides, her head was beginning to ache, the glare of the sun on the white shelly sand more than a match for her polarized lenses. And it was hot, unbearably hot.

'As a matter of fact, I don't,' he retorted, eyes narrowing as they swept the length of her, another cold and calculated invasion of Holly's body. 'No full-blooded male would leave you alone for long—not in that state of dress.'

'It's a perfectly decent bikini,' she pointed out coolly.

'That, my dear, is a matter of opinion.'

'It's also none of your business,' she spat, his smug expression galling.

'Wrong, Holly,' he contradicted coldly, black eyes boring through the lenses, surely seeing to the centre of her soul. 'You *are* my business. Because you're mine. You've always been mine, and there's nothing you can say to change it. Face it, Holly,' he urged without emotion. 'You're mine!'

'And you're mad,' she retorted. 'I don't

belong to you, to any man. I never have, never will.'

'Fine. In that case, Holly, you won't mind proving it.' He moved, quick as a flash. Belatedly aware of the danger, Holly stumbled backwards, tripping over her bag in her haste to get away, and would have gone sprawling but for Dev's hands shooting out to steady her, the grip fleetingly harsh. Then he was reeling her in, drawing her nearer and nearer to the solid lines of his near-naked body, the touch a featherlight restraint, but Holly was caught fast, powerless to resist. Because she wanted him, ached for him, needed him—oh, God, how she *needed* him!

And, having tugged her tantalizingly close to his gleaming, sun-kissed flesh, Dev paused, holding the moment. Holly didn't move, didn't breathe as Dev's words washed over her, gentle as a breeze yet creating havoc deep in mind and body.

'You want me,' he stated simply, his thumb caressing her cheek, a soft and gentle movement intended not to startle. 'You can fight it, you can fight me. You can scream your denials from the rooftops and the rest of the world can be fooled, but you'll be lying. Admit it, Holly,' he insisted relentlessly. 'You want me. Don't you? *Don't you?*'

And though Holly shook her head, Dev smiled his contradiction, reaching for her sunshades, her last flimsy defence. As her startled eyes collided with his the rest of the world retreated, would always be a blur with Dev around, his sharply focused presence filling her mind, a mind that needed to scream her denials. She *had* to be strong. She *had* to resist. She *had* to deny him.

'Please, Dev,' she pleaded, grey eyes dark with fear.

'Oh, Holly, Holly,' he crooned, shaking his head and smiling, 'don't fight me.' Powerful hands spanned her waist and urged her close, oh so close, yet stopping short of the searing body-to-body contact that Holly craved and feared—craved more than feared, she realized with dismay. 'You want me. You need me. We belong.'

No escape, she acknowledged, weakening. No escape from Dev whose smouldering eyes were fastened on her face, and Holly was melting, the flames licking through, consuming, igniting as Dev's sultry words washed over her.

'You were made to touch,' he insisted. 'To touch, to kiss, to love. And you're mine. You've always been mine. We belong. You and me. Mind to mind. Body to body. We belong.'

Holly's mind soared. He loved her. Every glance, every breath, every touch told her that he loved her, that he'd always loved her. 'All the tomorrows,' she remembered as the pain scythed through. And fool that she was, she'd believed him. Only, not this time.

'No, Dev!' she cried, attempting to pull away, but he out-thought her, iron fingers tightening their hold.

'Oh, but yes!' And he laughed, a cold, harsh sound that grated on the air as he dipped his head, his mouth brushing hers, a fleeting touch but enough to ignite her. She swayed against him, her lips parting in eloquent invitation, Dev's tongue sliding through, a lightning exploration, a brutal invasion.

No, Dev, she screamed silently as he pulled away. But it was too late. Much, much too late. He'd kissed her, she'd responded. Devlin Winter had his proof.

She took a step backwards and, swallowing hard, forced herself to meet that mocking, black gaze. 'Marks out of ten, Dev? Is that what this is all about, trying to prove that you're irresistible?'

'Trying—and succeeding, Holly,' he stated matter-of-factly.

'Really?'

'Yes, really. I look, your body responds. I touch, your body explodes. Deny it if you must, but...'

'But nothing. Leave me alone,' she hissed, darting forwards, her open palm slicing the air, Dev's lightning reflex denying her.

'Don't even think it,' he snarled, twisting her arm behind her back and pulling her close into his body.

Holly gasped at the contact, felt the strength of his arousal as he ground his hips against hers.

'Or else, my fiery love,' he growled, hands sliding into the curve of her waist as he urged her even closer, 'I could be driven to prove how badly you really want me.'

'Will you please let go of me,' Holly rasped, 'before you get us both arrested?'

'And would you care?' he asked, erotic thumbs stroking the soft underswell of Holly's straining breasts.

'Of course I'd care. I've my family to think about.'

'Not to mention the absent Jon.'

Jon. Holly stiffened. They could arrive at any moment, Meryl and Jon. She had to escape. She had to get away.

Only Dev, being Dev, caught the scent of panic and pushed her away with a snarl of contempt, the hate in his eyes almost more than she could take. He was wrong, about Jon at least. But as for the rest... Holly felt the anger die.

If she was honest, he'd come unnervingly close to the truth. There'd been so many men, too many to count, too many to want to remember—waves of disgust swept back to haunt her. She'd turned into a tramp, and all because of Devlin Winter, who had taken her, used her, tired of her, left her, destroyed her. But only once, she vowed. Never again. Never again would she let Dev—or any man—close enough to bruise her heart.

She turned her back, rifling her bag for her clothes, tears hovering dangerously as she shrugged herself into T-shirt and shorts. Then, crumpled but decent, she swung round, praying that Dev would have taken the hint and gone, would have walked away never to return. But her eyes collided with his and the contempt he didn't try to mask came blazing back at her.

'Why, Dev?' she asked tonelessly. 'Why? Why

can't you leave me alone? After all this time, everything you've done to hurt me, why can't you leave me in peace?'

'Because *I'm* not at peace. I'm living in torment. Every hour of every day, every night for the past seven years I've been in torment.'

'You've been in torment? You should have been in hell, Devlin Winter,' she informed him bitterly. 'I don't want you. I'll never want you. I don't need you in my life. I've rebuilt my life and I'm happy, damn you. I don't need you. Not any more. I've had seven long years to prove it, and believe me, Dev, I simply don't need you.'

'And if I take you in my arms, kiss you, touch you, lay you down upon the sand...'

But he didn't need to finish. Holly knew. She remembered—God, how she remembered! She dropped her gaze, flinching from the truth, Dev's low laugh grating in her ears.

She began to walk away, closing her mind.

'Holly—'

'Go away, Dev,' she murmured wearily, bare feet dragging through the sand.

She reached the pavement and paused, aware that, if the sand was hot, the hard-baked road would be more so. But with Dev just a step behind, she couldn't risk stopping to rifle her bag for sandals so, spurred on by panic, she urged herself forwards. A stupid mistake, she realized at once. The road wasn't just hot, it was scalding, not to mention dusted with grit.

Then, fool that she was, she tripped, stubbing her toe. She cried out in pain, and the tears that had never been far away to start with began to stream. Only it wasn't the pain of her stupid foot, of course. 'Fool! Fool! Fool!' she muttered, sniffing loudly as she limped on, alone, irrationally hurt that Dev had gone, that the moment she needed him most, he'd finally taken her at her word.

Only he hadn't. When had the arrogant Devlin Winter ever done as he was told? she recalled belatedly, hysterically, as he swept her off her feet, into his arms and carried her across to the other side.

'Put me down!' she protested, her cheek against his chest, not skin to skin this time because somewhere along the way Dev had slipped into his clothes. 'Will you please put me down?'

Amazingly he did, but the moment her feet touched the ground, he cradled her face in his hands, smiling, banishing the tears with soft, stroking fingers.

'Oh, Holly,' he murmured, dipping his head. She braced herself for the kiss she hadn't the strength to resist any more, raising her face, grey eyes cloudy as they locked with his, searched his, trembled at the unexpectedly tender expression that came back at her. And, in a blinding flash of instinct, Holly knew he musn't kiss her. Not like this. Anger and contempt she could handle. But anything else and she'd be lost and seven years of hell would have been in vain.

CHAPTER 2

'Holly! Ho-lly. Look what I've bought.'

The sound of the childish treble broke the spell and Dev swore eloquently before he released her.

Jonathan! Oh, thank God, Holly prayed, completely forgetting her earlier need to keep her family and Dev apart. She crouched, opening her arms and laughing as the small boy flung himself at her, and she swung him off the ground with a whoop of delight, twizzing him round and round till the world spun dizzily.

'So this is where you got to,' she observed laughingly, setting him down on his feet and admiring the bucket and spade that was duly held up for inspection.

She didn't glance at Dev, didn't see the flash of pain that crossed his face, immersing herself in Jon, stalling, she realized, but using the precious few moments it gave to pull herself together.

'Mummy says it's too hot for the beach now, but if I promise to be good, you'll take me later. You will, won't you, Holly? Please, Holly. Please, please, please,' he chanted, brown eyes cloudy.

'You bet!' she reassured. 'But lunch first, hey? I don't know about you, but I'm starving. And champion sandcastle builders,' she informed

27

him solemnly, 'have to keep their strength up.' Straightening, and as much in control as she'd ever be as Jon's hot and sticky hand slipped into hers, she glanced around, looking anywhere but at Dev. 'Now, where's mum?'

'Here I am,' Meryl murmured, coming up behind, waving a clutch of bulging carrier bags. Holly swallowed a smile. She might have known. Like a bear to the honey pot, Meryl had homed in on the boutiques. 'Sorry, Holly,' she acknowledged with a bright, disarming smile. 'I didn't realize how long I'd been. You know me...'

'Luckily for you,' Holly murmured drily, and better late than never, she added with a silent prayer of thanks.

Unlike her passion for clothes, Meryl's approach to time was casual. An irritating trait, Holly could allow, but since Meryl could charm the birds from the trees with little more than a flash of her wide, blue eyes, it was difficult to stay cross with her for long. Besides, having stood by Holly in the bad times, the dark months following Dev's desertion, Meryl could be forgiven far worse faults than tardiness.

'Oh!' Meryl breathed, those wide blue eyes now flicking from Holly onto Dev, silent but imposing just behind. 'I didn't realise you had company. Holly, my love, *do* introduce us.'

'Devlin Winter, an old—acquaintance,' Holly explained, half-afraid Meryl would recognize the name, would link Dev with that long hot summer and his role in her father's death. Unlikely, she supposed, since the two had never met and, despite the front-page coverage, Dev had somehow managed to keep his name out of print. 'This is Meryl Scott. My stepmother,' she tagged on drily, awaiting the inevitable, the flash of amazement, the garbled words that never failed to follow.

Only it didn't happen. Trust Dev to be the exception that proved the rule! 'Delighted to meet you,' he said instead, smiling broadly. 'Holly forgot to mention you'd gone shopping. Here, let me,' he insisted, taking charge of the bags.

Meryl preened. 'Thank you,' she breathed, long, curly lashes fluttering.

On the outside looking in, Holly stiffened. Ridiculous, really, since Holly knew Meryl was simply being Meryl; the devastating effect she had on the male of the species a private source of amusement to Holly, who'd long realized that Meryl was an unashamed flirt. She enjoyed the company of men sure enough, but wouldn't dream of taking things further. In that case, why the pang, the touch of the green-eyed monsters? Holly mused, seeing Meryl and Dev lock glances.

'I'm hungry,' Jonathan wailed, cutting through the tension.

'Are you, poppet? And what would you like to eat?' Meryl ruffled his curly blond locks.

'A Big Mac,' he replied promptly.

'No can do,' she informed him with a smile. 'Sorry, honey, this is Houlgate, remember? The nearest McDonald's must be miles away.'

'Not an awful many miles away, is it, Holly?'

he asked, tugging at her hand, brown eyes pleading.

'Afraid so,' Holly murmured, and then she bent, whispering in his ear.

Jonathan's expression lightened at once. 'Promise?'

Holly nodded. 'Scout's honour,' she agreed solemnly.

'I don't know what you're plotting with my son, Holly,' Meryl put in drily, 'but you can count me out. A burger bar is not my idea of food. When in France, I'd rather do as the French do.'

'An excellent idea,' Dev approved warmly. 'And since I was about to kidnap Holly, why not join me for lunch? There's a first-class restaurant just around the corner.'

'Dressed like this?' Holly scorned, appalled at the thought of spending a single moment more in Dev's disturbing company.

'It's a bistro, not Maxim's,' he teased. 'Red-checked cloths and plain scrubbed floors. But if madam's tastes are too upmarket these days...'

'Mine aren't,' Meryl countered pertly.

Dev grinned. 'Good. It's a date. Two of the loveliest ladies in Normandy and this handsome little chap who I guess must be Jon.' He crouched, bringing his face level with Jonathan's. 'Holly's told me all about you,' he explained confidentially. 'So how about you and I get together and treat your mum and Holly to lunch at McDonald's in Caen tomorrow?'

'Yippee!' Jonathan yelled as Holly's heart sank.

'Oh, what a shame,' Meryl trilled, the idea of missing out on the trip, if not the food, clearly disappointing. 'If it's tomorrow, you'll have to count me out.'

'There's a good range of shops,' Dev pointed out, shrewdly assessing Meryl's Achilles' heel.

'They'll still be there next week,' she observed coyly. 'So if a girl's allowed to take a rain check...' And she shrugged as she smiled, the sort of devastating smile that could floor the average male at a hundred paces. Sure enough, Holly noticed with another prickle of alarm, Dev preened.

'Fine.' He ruffled Jon's hair. 'It's settled then. Look out, McDonald's, here we come.'

'Yippee! Yippee! Yippee!' Jonathan repeated as Holly's sinking heart settled somewhere near the floor. A day out with Dev? Even allowing for a six-year-old chaperon? Yet how to refuse without disappointing Jonathan?

'Shall I take back some of those bags?' Meryl suggested before they could begin to move off.

Dev shook his head. 'Leave them with me. They'll be safe in the boot of the car for now.' And he dashed across the road to a dusty Citroën that Holly had been too upset to notice earlier, but which now explained the mystery of the lightning change of clothes when he'd followed her off the beach.

'He's nice,' Meryl mused, and Holly turned her head, catching a gleam of speculation in her stepmother's eyes and not sure what she was reading. Self-interest? she wondered. Or

31

an uncharacteristic spot of matchmaking? But since neither thought was particularly reassuring, Holly closed her mind.

The idea of food wasn't reassuring either, an overwrought Holly convinced she'd choke on every mouthful. Not that it seemed to worry Dev, who'd engineered the invitation. Invitation? She stiffened. He'd hit the nail on the head in the first place—kidnap was nearer the mark—and though Maxim's it would never be, there was no doubting the warm and friendly atmosphere. The restaurant was crowded—local families judging from the voluble barrage of French—but since Dev was clearly a regular, in a matter of moments they were cosily installed at a corner table, well away from the pungent blue haze hanging over the rest of the room.

'The *plat de fruit de mer* is always worth a try,' Dev suggested, nodding at the chalk board with its display of daily specials.

'Horsemeat? Yuk!' Jonathan pronounced as the grown-ups swallowed smiles.

'Not horse, shell fish,' Meryl corrected. 'Mussels and prawns and oysters and lots of lovely things like that.'

'But French people do eat horse. Peter says its just like beef. And *he* said mare,' he insisted, pointing at Dev. 'And a mare's a horse, isn't it, Holly? A lady horse.'

'It certainly is. But not in French. And it's rude to point and call people "he".'

'Oh! Sorry,' he murmured, with a shamefaced glance at Dev. 'I'm Jonathan Scott. What's your name?'

32

'Jon!' Meryl protested, but Dev simply laughed.

'Devlin Winter. But you can call me Dev,' he offered confidentially. 'And since horsemeat is definitely off today's agenda, how about some pancakes?'

An excellent idea, Holly decided, following Jonathan's example and choosing a galette, a mouth-melting pancake filled with home-cured ham and creamy rich cheese and just light enough to swallow without it sticking in her taut, dry throat. Nerves, she acknowledged, courtesy of Dev's disturbing presence just a knee's-width away, though the cause of all the turmoil, she couldn't help but notice, had no such qualms

But it was Meryl who provided the real surprise. Conscious of her figure, she rarely touched food in the middle of the day, which made the bowl of steaming *moules* she chose seem even more exotic. Out to impress Dev, Holly decided sourly, equally amazed to see Meryl shun knife and fork.

Catching Holly's reaction, Meryl grinned. 'When in France...' she explained, using the half-shell to scoop out the tender mussels and soaking up the poaching stock with freshly baked bread. 'Thank you, Dev,' she enthused, once her meal had been reduced to a pile of empty shells. 'I enjoyed that.'

'I thought you might. And seafood's a sensuous experience. I'm glad you felt you could try it.'

For a moment, a horrible, nauseating moment

to Holly watching from the sidelines, there was no one else in the room, just Meryl and Dev, her stepmother's wide blue eyes locked onto Dev's, Dev's solemn gaze fastened on Meryl's face.

And it hurt, it hurt like hell, the tension mounting, the atmosphere thickening, electricity crackling on the air, till Holly couldn't breathe, couldn't look, couldn't bear not to look. And then Dev switched his gaze, treacherous black pools focusing on Holly.

'How about you?' he asked.

'H-how about me?' she stammered, her voice seeming to come from miles away.

'Have you had enough, he means,' Jonathan supplied matter-of-factly. 'I haven't, so may I have some ice cream, please?'

It broke the spell, but did little to soothe Holly's nerves. For the second time in the space of an hour she'd felt excluded, would have given her eye teeth to know what was running through Meryl's mind. Just a harmless flirtation, Holly supposed, willing herself to believe it, an innocent bit of fun. And why not? Meryl was young, barely ten years older than Holly; close to Dev's age, in fact, she realized sickly, aware that in the eyes of the world Meryl was a 'catch', her stunning, silver-blonde looks combined with the 'wealthy widow' tag spawning a stream of would-be suitors—fortune hunters, Meryl scathingly acknowledged. And each and every one wasting his time.

And Dev? Holly probed. Would Dev be wasting his time too? But her mind skittered away, the idea of Dev with Meryl, Dev with

34

any woman, more than she could stand.

By the time the grown-ups had finished their coffee and Jonathan a second ice cream, the afternoon was well advanced.

'Time for the beach,' Jonathan reminded them as they emerged blinking into the sunshine.

'Time for your nap,' Meryl contradicted. 'But you can come down later, if Holly doesn't mind.'

'Oh, Holly doesn't mind,' he pronounced airily. 'She promised.'

'So I did,' Holly agreed, that sinking feeling around her heart again. It was the last thing she felt like doing, especially with Dev on the loose. And what exactly was he doing in Houlgate? A holiday, she mused, or work? Work. Her lips tightened.

Devlin Winter's approach to work, she recalled all too clearly, left a lot to be desired. He was a parasite. The lowest of the low, choosing a victim and preying on their weaknesses. Choosing Holly. Using Holly. Destroying Holly and everything she loved. Oh yes, she remembered each and every bitter moment.

They paused at the car. 'Climb in. I'll run you back,' Dev insisted, holding the doors.

'There's no need,' Holly scowled, her mind locked in the past. 'It's barely a footstep away.'

'Maybe so,' Dev agreed, ignoring the flash of ill humour. 'But it's hot, Jonathan's tired and Meryl's weighted down with bags. And it's no trouble.'

Maybe not to Dev, but to Holly the five-minute journey was a trial she'd have happily

35

done without, especially as Meryl climbed into the passenger seat, disconcertingly close to Dev, leaving Holly to scramble into the back with Jon. And stifling a sigh of relief when they pulled up on the drive, Holly couldn't believe it when Meryl flashed Dev yet another bright smile and invited him in for drinks.

'Thanks. Another time, maybe,' he demurred, allowing Holly's heart beat to go back to normal, though normal, with Dev around, was hardly the word to describe it. Palming his keys, he switched his gaze to Holly. 'Till tomorrow then. I'll pick you up at ten.'

He didn't ask, Holly noticed, suppressing the urge to make a smart salute. Simply assumed. Devlin Winter snaps his fingers and, yes, sir! the whole world jumps to attention. Well, had she got news for Dev. He'd better make the most of it, because things had changed and Holly Scott wouldn't be pushed around—not by any man, but most of all not by Devlin Winter. Not any more.

'So, where are we going?' Holly enquired once Jonathan's eager chatter had subsided.

'It's a bit early for lunch, I thought we'd go for a run first. Is there a problem?'

'Being cooped up in a car isn't much fun for the average six-year-old,' she pointed out primly. 'And this is supposed to be Jon's treat.'

'Six?' Seated behind the passenger seat, her eyes trained on his familiar, arrogant profile, Holly caught the frown. Disconcertingly, Dev turned his head, his piercing gaze holding hers

36

for the briefest of moments before switching back to the wheel.

Left to its own devices, Holly's mind went into overdrive. She could almost hear Dev's thoughts ticking over. He'd been surprised, and why not? Jonathan's size *was* deceiving. Head and shoulders above his friends despite his shaky start in life, Jonathan was clearly on course for breaking a few hearts. Ten or twelve years at the most, Holly decided, and he'd be a knockout. Just like Dev.

No, not like Dev, she insisted fiercely. Never like Dev. Holly wouldn't allow it. Turn out like ruthless, heartless Devlin Winter, who'd cashed in on his time with Holly, used Holly to get close to her father and then sold his story to the gutter press? Not a cat in hell's chance, she vowed grimly, attempting to block the pain. So much remembered, so much never forgotten. Her father's death, Jonathan's premature birth. All thanks to Dev.

'Can we go to the beach first?' Jonathan asked, unaware of the tension swirling all around.

'I don't see why not,' Dev agreed, his gaze flicking briefly, enquiringly to Holly. 'I hope you've brought your swim suit.'

Jonathan had, but Holly had judged it wiser to leave her own itsy-bitsy bikini at home.

'Chicken,' Dev pronounced with a much too knowing look when they piled out of the car.

'Not at all,' she countered primly. 'In case you've forgotten, Dev, I can't take too much sun.'

'Ah, yes.' He smiled, his fingers looping

a strand of her long, fair hair, a delicate restraint she was powerless to break. His face was suddenly dangerously close, black eyes unfathomable as they locked with hers, and Holly held her breath, afraid he was going to kiss her, more afraid that he wasn't. 'My delicate English rose,' he teased, his lips brushing her mouth, a featherlight touch that sent her pulse rate soaring. 'You just need to take things slowly, that's all.'

With you around, I intend to, Holly vowed, averting her eyes as Dev peeled off T-shirt and shorts to reveal his own skimpy beachwear. Very slowly. Exceedingly slowly. Stock still, in fact, she added silently, afraid she was overreacting, reading hidden meanings into everything Dev said and did. And then she remembered. Everything Dev said and did *was* for a reason, a calculated reason, and only a fool would choose to forget it.

'Race you to the water,' Dev challenged Jon, and Jonathan squealed in delight, setting off across the golden sands, Dev in steady pursuit, just near enough to spur the child on, to allow him to 'win' without suspicion. Safe from Dev's disconcerting presence, Holly could feast her eyes.

She curled up on a towel, knees drawn under her chin, arms hugging her legs, a hundred and one emotions running through her mind while man and boy splashed in the shallows. Jonathan's excited treble drifted back along with Dev's deeper tones of encouragement as Jonathan dipped his bucket over and over into the water in vain search for fish. Man and boy, heads close together. To anyone watching, they were just another happy family, could so easily have been a family that Holly felt the tears sting. Seven years. Seven years of loving Dev. Seven years of hating him. Oh, God, how she hated him! Why, why, why, after all this time, was she allowing him back into her life as if the past had never existed?

'What are you doing in France, Dev?' she challenged bluntly when Jonathan, sensibly covered in T-shirt and hat, joined a newfound friend in the serious business of sandcastle building.

'Would you believe, the same as everyone else?' he replied evasively, stretched out beside her, his bronzed body gleaming and inviting. 'Having a break. Taking a holiday.'

'Clearly a long one,' Holly needled, and when Dev raised a puzzled eyebrow, 'Your tan. You didn't acquire that overnight.'

'Ah, yes. Well spotted. I've—been here a week or so,' he admitted with just the slightest hesitation. 'And you?' he enquired politely.

'Like you, just a holiday,' she agreed. 'We arrived last week and decided to take things slowly. Jonathan's not used to the sun, and since he's so fair—' She pulled herself up short.

'Yes, an unusual combination,' Dev mused. 'Blond hair with brown eyes.' And he raised himself up on one elbow, his thoughtful gaze switching from Holly to Jonathan and back again. 'Still, eye colour and skin type normally match,' he conceded, after the longest pause of Holly's life. 'He ought to tan well. You're probably worrying over nothing.'

'Maybe,' she agreed, reaching treacherous waters and refusing to be drawn.

'He's a nice kid,' he surprised her by admitting. 'It can't have been easy for Meryl coping single-handed.'

Thanks to you, Holly remembered, the bitterness back with a vengeance. 'She had me,' she reminded him tersely, achingly aware that it was the other way round, that it was Holly who'd gone to pieces: Dev's betrayal, his disappearance, her father's death signalling the end of her world.

It had been a nightmare, Jonathan's birth the only glimmer of hope, and even his tiny life had hung in the balance—thanks to Dev. He had such a lot to answer for, Holly railed inwardly, and with the pain suddenly too raw to allow polite conversation with the cause of it all, she sprang up, stumbling blindly down to the water's edge. Alone and never more lonely she stood quite still, her long, muslin skirt swirling round her ankles as the sea lapped at her feet, the occasional large wave plastering the flimsy material to her legs and exposing shapely calves beneath the fleeting transparency of the fabric.

It wasn't as busy as Houlgate, nor as pretty. Riva-Bella was too near the ferry port to have developed a separate existence, but the stretch of pale, golden sand was dotted with people and parasols. Sun, sand and sea. Another five weeks of sun, sand and sea. And though the holiday in France had seemed a good idea at the time, Holly was having second thoughts.

It hadn't needed Dev's shock arrival to whisk her back to Tenerife. Sun, sand, sea and the flotilla of tiny yachts had managed that already. No. Dev was simply the final ingredient, a poignant reminder of everything she'd lost. First Dev, then her father. Death by drowning. An open verdict. An accident. And Holly had willed herself to believe it. Only she'd known from the moment the story broke that Gregory Scott had simply lost the will to fight the allegations, couldn't bear to live with the shame. Hurt. Shame. Betrayal. All thanks to Dev.

'Somebody's miles away,' Dev observed quizzically, breaking the barrier of Holly's isolation.

She swung round, eyes wild. 'Where's—?'

'Don't worry, Jon's perfectly safe,' he said soothingly, his hand on her arm sending currents of heat spreading out from each and every point of contact.

Her darting eyes found him, happily engrossed in his task, and though she allowed herself to relax, she was too aware of Dev's touch to lower her guard completely.

'So—are they worth a penny, Holly? Or shall I hazard a guess? The same sun, the same sand, the same sea. The same erotic thoughts, maybe,' he tagged on slyly.

'Hardly,' she countered waspishly. 'The same sun, maybe, Dev, but Tenerife's half an ocean away and the past is over and done with.'

'Is it?' he queried softly.

'Too right it is,' Holly said bitterly, pointedly shaking free.

'I don't agree. The past shapes the present, points the way to the future.'

'How very profound,' she heard herself sneering. 'I didn't realize you were such a philosopher, Dev.'

'There's a lot you don't know about me,' he replied coolly.

'None of it good, I'll bet,' she hissed. 'Save it, Dev. I really don't want to know.'

'Don't want to, Holly—or simply can't face it?'

'Take your pick,' she invited coldly, stepping ankle-deep into the water. It was a gesture of dismissal and she moved slowly along the shoreline, hampered by her skirt, eyes peeled on Jon, her wayward mind locked in the past.

Paradise. The most wonderful summer of her life, the secluded villa at Los Cristianos, lazy days at sea on *The Ilex*. And with her father caught up in business, jetting back and forth to England, and Meryl involved in the busy social round of drinks, dinners and parties, Holly had been left to her own devices. A whole summer with Dev. Sun, sand, sea—and what she'd foolishly taken for love.

Love. The images flashed unbidden—the sun-baked sand, her naked body writhing beneath his, Dev's lips trailing hungry kisses from her mouth to her throat and back again, and then down, from the pulse spot in her throat to the tip of each ripe breast. Dev, raising his head, molten eyes locking with hers as he allowed the

42

golden sun to warm her, touch her, caress her, just as he did. Hands, fingers, tongue, mouth, they were made for each other.

And seven years on, Holly's breasts hardened at the thought of Dev's tongue inciting, Dev's teeth nibbling, Dev's lips caressing her straining, tingling nipples.

Dev. She pulled up sharp, Dev's solid form blocking the way. And she raised her eyes from the ripples she'd created, her gaze drawn against her will the length of his bronzed, muscular body, slowly, ankle to knee, knee to groin, and the shock of his manhood straining against the flimsy swim suit sent hot floods of desire pulsing through her. She wanted him. Even now, she wanted him. Desperate for control, she clamped her hands to her sides, the urge to reach for him, hold him, touch him so fierce that she almost cried out with the pain. She loved him. And God help her, Dev had betrayed her.

Dev's black eyes locked with hers, his expression unfathomable. 'We ought to make a move,' he said at last. 'Jonathan—'

'Yes.' Holly nodded, swung round, felt Dev's touch on her arm and halted.

'Holly?'

'Dev?'

'I never had the chance to say I was sorry.'

'For what?'

'Your father. I know how close you are.'

'Past tense, Dev, since he's long dead. Why, Dev? Why?' she railed, grey eyes dark with accusation. 'Why push an innocent man to his death?'

43

'You make me sound like a murderer, Holly.'

'If the cap fits,' she reminded him bitterly.

'No!'

'Yes!' she hissed, and Dev flinched at her eloquent flash of derision, and for a moment his pain became hers, though Holly's mind was quick to deny it.

'I didn't break that story, Holly,' Dev stated flatly.

'No? So why didn't you stick around? Help me to pick up the pieces?' Offer the love and support he'd promised for all the tomorrows, she tagged on silently, bitterly. And seeing Dev about to speak, she cut him off with an imperative slice of her hand. 'No—don't bother to explain.' she castigated coldly. 'I really don't want to know.'

Because she already had the answer. Dev had been using her. An old-fashioned, cold-blooded seduction of an innocent girl so that Dev could worm his way into her life and gain a ringside view of her father's. And fool that she was, she'd let him.

They drove into Caen, heading straight for McDonald's, the 'Happy Meal' on offer putting the seal on Jonathan's day. Then the tense journey back, just Jonathan's tired voice breaking the silence, till he too fell quiet, slumping against Holly as his eyelids closed. And Holly stared stonily ahead, determined to avoid meeting Dev's troubled eyes in the driving mirror.

Sweeping into the drive, Dev brought the car gently to a halt. He was out in a flash, opening the rear door before Holly could move, and slipping his hands beneath the sleeping child's body, cradled him in his arms. Straightening, he raised an enquiring eyebrow and Holly nodded, leading the way into the house and up the stairs to Jonathan's bedroom.

She drew the curtains against the glare of the afternoon sun, a lump forming in her throat as Dev lowered him onto the duvet and brushed the fringe of hair from Jonathan's damp forehead, the image so much like the dream she'd had of sharing her life with Dev that Holly suddenly couldn't bear it.

She swung away before the tears could start, leaving Dev to make his own way down, pausing in the hallway, hugging her arms to her body, suppressing the urge to disappear into the garden without saying goodbye. Because Dev would know. He'd know Holly was afraid, was running away from him.

'Come and have a drink,' she urged politely instead, leading the way out onto the terrace. The day seemed never-ending but another ten minutes wouldn't hurt and Meryl was sure to keep the conversation flowing, which she did, leaving Holly free to lapse into brooding silence.

Small talk. Meryl had had her hair done and, of course, Dev simply had to notice. Meryl sparkled as brightly as the ice in Holly's glass of tonic and Holly felt cold, so cold, because she was jealous. She was jealous of Meryl, wonderful Meryl, who deserved so much more than life had thrown at her. A harmless flirtation, a bit of fun. Fun—with Dev. Only Holly couldn't bear it, was forced to sit and watch, sit and listen, sit and brood.

'It's a nice house,' Dev observed with an appreciative glance at the split-level gardens.

'Yes. We're lucky. We have it on loan from a friend,' Meryl explained. 'Talking of whom—oh, hell!' She broke off, blue eyes cloudy as she focused on Holly. 'Alex phoned. Something's come up and he can't make the weekend and can you give him a ring before five.' She checked her watch. 'Sorry, Holly,' she murmured apologetically. 'It's almost that now.'

'I'd better be quick, then,' Holly agreed, seizing the chance to escape.

'Pity,' Meryl acknowledged, her crystal-clear voice drifting across as Holly reached the open door. She paused, something in Meryl's tone sending prickles of fear running the length of her spine. 'That means we're a man short,' she heard Meryl bewailing.

Conscious she was being rude, listening in on a private conversation, Holly stood quite still, unable to tear herself away, the speculative, sideways glance Meryl trained on Dev yet another eloquent warning.

'I don't suppose,' Meryl mused with her most persuasive, wide-eyed smile, 'that you'd care to join us, Dev? Just a small dinner party—eight or ten at the most,' she explained. 'But with Alex letting Holly down...'

Say no. Please say no, Holly prayed, fixing her gaze on his arrogant profile.

'Seven for seven-thirty?' Meryl pressed him and Holly held her breath, praying to the God she was sure had long deserted her that Dev would turn the invitation down. Say no. Please say no, she repeated silently, fingers clenched, nails digging cruelly into the palms of her hands.

And Dev turned his head, his unfathomable gaze sweeping across and locking onto Holly's. Because he'd known—*how* had he known?—that Holly would be standing, watching, waiting. Torment, the pause never-ending. And then he smiled. 'Seven for seven-thirty,' he agreed solemnly. 'Nothing would give me greater pleasure.'

CHAPTER 3

'So—who's Alex?'

Holly jumped, spilling her glass of wine. Luckily it was white and wouldn't show, she realized, unlike the giveaway spots of colour in her cheeks. And she ignored the man, dabbing at the stain with a hankie, giving her racing heart time to settle down.

'Good evening, Dev,' she murmured at last. 'I didn't realize you'd arrived.'

'How could you possibly know I'd arrived,' he needled her, 'since you've hidden yourself away in the darkest corner of the garden?'

'Hardly,' Holly demurred, uncomfortably aware that she'd done exactly that. 'I was simply enjoying a moment's peace and quiet.'

'The lull before the storm?' he queried. 'Or a sneaky way of dodging my question? At the risk of sounding tedious, Holly, who is Alex?'

Who indeed? Holly whipped. She'd barely given him a thought—since Dev had walked back into her life, in fact, and the waves of guilt washed over her.

'He—owns the house,' she explained. 'We have it on loan for the summer. Didn't Meryl explain?'

'You know full well she didn't, since you listened in on every word.'

'Ah, yes. Rude of me, wasn't it?' she said

scornfully, her colour rising.

'Exceedingly rude. Someone—Alex, perhaps—ought to teach you some manners. I assume he is the current boyfriend?'

'Assume what you like,' Holly goaded him recklessly. 'I don't have to explain things to you.'

'Fine.' Dev shrugged. 'But don't be surprised, next time you overstep the mark, when you find yourself accountable to me.'

'Oh, yes? I'm not a six-year-old child, Dev,' she hissed. 'You can hardly put me across your knee.'

'I'll do precisely that, Holly, should the occasion demand it.'

'Are you threatening me?'

'Threatening, Holly?' Dev smiled. 'No, my love, simply stating facts. As you'll discover if you push me too far.'

My love. Holly swallowed the lump in her throat. His love. How good it sounded. Despite the lie. She gulped the rest of her wine.

'Drink?' she murmured over-brightly, raising her empty glass. 'What can I get you?'

'A glass of wine will be fine. But let me. Same again?' he enquired, taking her glass from her. 'A dry white? Or do you prefer something sweeter?'

'Dry,' she murmured. 'The sharper the better.'

'But of course,' he agreed, flashing her a smile. 'Razor-blade sharp to match your caustic tongue.'

He was back before she had time to miss him.

'Thank you,' she murmured, taking the drink he proffered and resisting the urge to drain it in one.

Dev flung himself down on the wrought-iron garden seat that Holly had vacated, patting the space beside him, eyes loaded with challenge. After a moment's hesitation, Holly regained her place, pushing herself into the corner, about as far away from Dev as she could manage.

She'd dressed with care, a beige linen jump suit that skimmed the contours of her body, the backless, cutaway style exposing the light golden tan of her bare arms and shoulders and emphasizing the swell of her breasts. She'd even taken time to make up her face, convinced from Meryl's startled reaction that she must have overdone it. Only Meryl's smile of delight had banished the fear.

'How do I look?' Holly had asked, suddenly nervous as a kitten.

'Perfect. Stop worrying. He'll love it. I take it this *is* for Dev?'

'Not exactly,' Holly had stalled and Meryl had smiled a knowing smile before going upstairs to give Jonathan his goodnight kiss.

Trust Meryl not to pry. And she hadn't once mentioned Alex, Holly recalled. But most of all, she'd given Holly something precious to hold on to. There'd been no rancour in her stepmother's reaction, so if Meryl *was* smitten with Dev, she was hiding it well.

So—just why *had* she taken so much trouble? The need to hide behind a mask of sophistication she was far from feeling? Or a pointed reminder to Dev of everything he'd rejected?

'You've crossed that ocean again,' he murmured drily.

Holly flushed, sipping her drink, refusing to take the bait.

But determined to force a rise one way or another, Dev closed the gap between them, dipping his head to kiss her exposed shoulder, and though Holly sat rigid, she was shockingly aware of the shivers of heat spreading out from the point of contact and rippling deep inside.

'Mmm. You smell nice,' he stunned her by saying. 'All clean, healthy, sunkissed skin.'

'You smell nice, too,' she riposted. 'But in your case, Dev, it's out of a bottle—an expensive bottle, at that. If I didn't know you better, I'd say you were out to impress.'

'Ah, yes, but as I told you earlier, Holly, there's so much about me you don't know at all.'

'But perhaps I'm no longer interested, Dev.'

'You're a liar, Holly, and a poor one. You're itching to know why I'm here for a start.'

'In Houlgate? That's easy. You're on holiday, just like me.'

'Exactly. But think, Holly, think. Remember what happened the last time I witnessed Venus emerging from the sea...'

Holly's cheeks flamed, and she was glad of the fading light to hide behind. 'Coincidence, Dev. Pure and simple. And believe me, lightning's not about to strike twice.'

'You mean, it hasn't already?' he challenged.

Holly didn't reply. She was playing with fire.

Simply being with Dev was crazy. Unbelievable though it seemed, in little more than twenty-four hours he'd managed to turn her world upside-down. Heaven alone knew how she'd cope if Dev stuck around for the summer. Only he wouldn't, she hastily reassured herself He wouldn't, he couldn't, he mustn't.

She risked a sideways glance. He looked—stunning, she acknowledged, swallowing hard. The white dinner jacket, taut on powerful shoulders, heightened the healthy glow of tan and contrasted starkly with the shock of black hair. And since the style and cut were impeccable, Holly couldn't help but wonder how he'd managed to acquire it at such short notice. And yet the fit was perfect—made to measure? she mused, aware that made-to-measure dinner suits didn't come cheap.

It was quite a revelation seeing him formally dressed—almost a revelation seeing him in clothes, she amended. They spent most of their time in Tenerife unashamedly naked. Naked. On the beach. In the sea. Man and woman. Body to body. Alone. Naked. Dev's beautiful body stretched out beside hers, muscles rippling beneath her touch, tightening at her touch, every inch of Dev's body branded by her touch.

And once she'd set the idea in motion, her mind raced on, remembering, savouring. Oh, God, how she'd wanted him. Oh, God, how she'd needed him. And just when she'd needed him most, he chose to walk away. Why, Dev? Why? she screamed. Why? Worse than that, how could she allow her traitorous body to override the pain of Dev's desertion? Because, Heaven help her, she wanted him. Even now she wanted him.

'Penny for *those* thoughts,' Dev offered, and though it broke the spell, Holly saw matching hunger in Dev's dark, brooding eyes and was suddenly afraid.

She shook her head, not trusting herself to speak, taking deep, deep breaths of the sweet night air.

It was warm in the garden, and since the house overlooked the sea, the lights from the tiny port of Dives were a sprinkling of jewels against a midnight-velvet cloth.

'Someone has taste,' Dev observed, cutting into Holly's thoughts.

She followed the line of his gaze. Alex. Alex had designed the house. Dear, sweet Alex who deserved so much more than Holly could ever hope to give. And if she'd been troubled with doubts before, how could she possibly go through with it now, knowing how she felt about Dev? Because she could bury her head in the Sahara Desert and it wouldn't change a thing. She loved him. Always had, always would.

Yet why should anything change? she asked herself, clutching at straws. Dev didn't love her. The only difference between today and this time last week was that Dev was present in body as well as in mind. Disconcerting, maybe, but nothing had changed. She *would* marry Alex. She had to marry Alex—for Jonathan and Meryl's sakes. And dear, kind, sweet Alex

53

was depending on her, too. A grand passion they'd never share, but heaven knew, she'd had her share of passion with Dev and look where it had left her.

'So, where are you staying?' she enquired politely.

'Would you believe a manor house, a typical French farmhouse beautifully restored, just this side of Branville, and complete with stables, pond and riding school.'

'And you really are on holiday?'

'Yes, I really am on holiday. Just like you.'

Only it wasn't like her at all, she could have pointed out, but didn't. She and Meryl were sharing Alex's home, Alex's hospitality: an ideal arrangement giving them a whole summer away and allowing Meryl to play hostess on a scale they couldn't match at home. Just like tonight, in fact, a houseful of guests en route to Paris or Deauville or the south coast resorts. And it was giving Holly a glimpse of what sharing a life with Alex would involve. Until yesterday she'd been sure she was doing the right thing. For everyone. Until Dev arrived, creating waves in her well-ordered world.

Hearing the tinkling chime of the dinner gong, Holly jumped thankfully to her feet.

'Whoa there, lady,' Dev crooned, his fingers snaking round her wrist. 'Haven't you forgotten the aperitif?'

'We'll be late for dinner, Dev,' Holly protested weakly, her legs turning to water as Dev reined her in.

'In that case, Holly,' he murmured solemnly,

kissing her mouth, nibbling her earlobes, his lips languidly trailing the long, long lines of her neck and down to the racing pulse in the hollow of her throat. 'Since I've no intentions of letting you go just yet, I guess that means we're going to be late.'

Unfair, Holly's mind screamed as she held herself rigid. A glance, a touch, a caress, just a smile or a word from Dev had always been enough to ignite her. Because Dev could bring her body to life. Only he musn't. Not now. Not ever. And, despite the need, the want, the traitorous trembling, as Dev's exploring lips reached the V of her cleavage, Holly clenched her fists, willing herself not to respond.

Only damn Devlin Winter, but he knew—the pause, the raised head, the eyes locking with hers in the subdued light of the garden a solemn underlining of that knowledge. Dev simply smiled and dipped his head. Another kiss, the tiniest, lightest brush of his lips, and Holly's blood began to boil.

'Please, Dev,' she murmured weakly.

'Please, Dev—what?' he queried softly, hands stroking the curve of waist and hip, sliding upwards, thumbs brushing the soft underswell of Holly's aching breasts. And then another tantalizing pause before he reached for the buds straining at the centre of each. More of a whisper than a touch, just the merest hint of a connection, and suddenly Holly couldn't bear it any longer, and she was pushing herself against him, shameless in her need, moaning deep in her throat, because she wanted him.

Dev, wonderful, mind-blowing Dev, was wreaking havoc with hands and fingers, and the barrier of clothes was just a temporary inconvenience as he slid his hands beneath the fabric. He found her straining, naked breasts and homed in on the rigid nipples, where yet another lightning touch carried her to heaven and back.

'Hell, woman, you drive me insane,' he growled, scooping her close. And then he kissed her, savagely, fiercely, but with breathtaking brevity.

'I think,' he murmured thickly as Holly's startled gaze collided with dark, smouldering eyes, 'that in the interests of propriety, my love, we'd better leave the next course till later. Later,' he vowed with another devastating touch of mouth against mouth.

Later. With an entire meal to get through. Food that might have been cardboard for all the notice Holly took. Small talk. She supposed she *must* have joined in since the people on either side seemed not to notice that anything was wrong.

Wrong. Drastically wrong. She'd allowed Dev to kiss her—worse, had wanted Dev to kiss her, and her cheeks flamed at the memory. And the night wasn't over yet by any means. Later. What exactly did that mean? Only Holly knew, of course. Dev, taking up where he'd left off in the garden, making love in the garden. Only he mustn't. Holly mustn't. And though the meal seemed interminable, the minutes were relentlessly ticking away.

But if the dinner was a nightmare, the consolation was Meryl, who sparkled like the wine that flowed the length of the table. It was good to see her at her best, surrounded by friends and enjoying every minute.

They led a quiet life in England, Gregory Scott's death having left his wife and daughter not so much in dire straits, as in need of a whole new lifestyle. In a strange sort of way Jonathan's birth had been a godsend, allowing the grief-stricken widow to go to ground with Holly and the baby.

If Meryl hankered for the bright lights, the exotic holidays, the trappings of wealth they'd once taken for granted, she'd never once betrayed it, just a wistful expression in her eyes in a few unguarded moments allowing Holly to guess. And it hurt. Because Meryl had been Holly's salvation and Meryl deserved so much more than life was prepared to give.

'So, what's happened to Lexy? I thought he was jetting in for the weekend.'

Holly wasn't sure who'd actually posed the question, the voice simply drifting down the table. But in her jumpy state of mind it sounded overloud—and loaded.

'Something came up,' Meryl explained. 'He sent his apologies, didn't he, Holly?'

'He—couldn't get away,' she supplied, darting a glance at Dev, thankfully deep in conversation with an attractive brunette. 'He was—just too busy,' she explained with an apologetic lift of the shoulders.

'Too busy making millions for the Courdrey

empire, you mean,' someone else piped in, raising a laugh.

'With wedding bells imminent, I don't suppose Holly's complaining, are you, Holly?'

'Courdrey?' Dev's voice sliced through the banter. 'You mean Alex Courdrey, the entrepreneur?'

'The one and only. Holly's a very lucky girl.'

'She is indeed,' Dev agreed. And his eyes flicked across to Holly who hadn't realized she was holding her breath until he raised his glass, then raised an eyebrow in silent, mocking challenge. 'My congratulations, Holly. And my apologies, too. It would seem I missed the announcement.'

'I—we—nothing's settled yet,' she stammered, blushing to the roots of her hair.

'Then more fool Courdrey,' he murmured, but softly, and for Holly's ears alone.

She lingered over the cheese, but should have known that trying to avoid Dev was a complete waste of time.

'Excuse me. Holly and I are old friends,' he explained with his best damsel-slaying smile once the coffee had been served and people began to drift back onto the terrace. And sure enough, the girl Holly had been talking to turned the brightest shade of pink.

'Such a lot to discuss you know,' he elaborated smoothly. 'I'll try not to keep her long.' And he snared Holly's wrist in another vice-like grip as he tugged her away from the house, down the steps and into the shadows of the garden.

'Will you please let go of me?' Holly demanded, stumbling in her heels and beginning to feel like a rag doll.

'All in good time,' he retorted, ignoring her feeble attempt to pull away.

'Dev, you're hurting me,' she hissed.

'Good! That makes us quits,' he shot back witheringly.

'What the *hell* do you think you're playing at?' she rasped when Dev finally released her.

'Strange, I was going to ask you the very same thing,' he countered, folding his arms and regarding her from under hooded eyes.

'I can't imagine why,' she spat out, unconsciously rubbing at the wrist where Dev's fingers had bit. 'I can't imagine why my behaviour, my life, should interest you in the least.'

'Oh, but it does. Call it the prerogative of an old friend, Holly.'

'Friend? Don't make me laugh. We were never friends.'

'Oh, Holly. Lovers make the best of friends, surely you know that?'

'Friends don't walk out when things get rough. Friends are there when you need them.'

'I'm here now,' he pointed out smoothly.

'Not by my invitation,' she cuttingly reminded.

'So—throw me out, ask me to leave.'

'Oh, and you'd go at once, of course?' she sneered.

'What do you think?'

'Knowing you? You'd probably do exactly that. And leave me to explain things to Meryl.

59

No thanks, Dev,' she informed him sweetly. 'Do your own dirty work for once. You decide.'

'My—we do have a warped view of things these days,' he drawled, the edge to his tone barely perceptible.

Only Holly's sharp ear caught it. Good. She'd ruffled his feathers. Progress indeed. Now all she had to do was keep him at that distance.

Join the others for a start, she decided, vaguely aware of voices on the terrace, music, laughter, the tinkle of glasses. They ought to go back, make a pretence of mixing. Not that Meryl would mind, but one or two others might find it strange that Holly had disappeared into the bushes with a virtual stranger. The idea caught her fancy and Holly smiled despite herself.

'Not warped, Dev. Simply realistic,' she explained as the anger retreated. 'I've grown up. I had to, you see,' she added without rancour. And though it hadn't been easy, Holly was aware she was giving him the truth. She *had* grown up. She'd picked up the pieces and had a whole new life ahead of her. And despite the threads of doubt, that future definitely didn't include Devlin Winter.

'Yes. It can't have been easy,' he surprised her by saying. 'For any of you.'

Holly turned her head, searching his face for a clue to his thoughts. She wanted to take the words at face value, but couldn't forget that Dev had been a journalist, might still be a journalist for all she knew. Easy words, an easy smile, an easy story. Oh, yes. Holly remembered it well. Clever Dev had played her like an expert and gullible Holly had swallowed the bait—once.

'It wasn't. But we coped.' Leastways Meryl had, she amended. And when Holly had gone off the rails, Meryl had been there, never judging, simply loving and supporting.

'Better than coped, surely, Holly,' Dev slipped in slyly, 'with Courdrey on the sidelines?'

She smothered a sigh. She might have known. Give him an inch and Dev would take a mile. 'Are you going to needle me all night?' she demanded, running her fingers through her hair in exasperation.

'Why not?' he challenged mildly. 'Someone has to make you see sense, point out the mistake you're making.'

'The only mistake that I ever made was you.'

'Ouch. And here's me thinking that you loved me,' he mocked.

'Past tense, Dev. Assuming I ever did. I was seven years younger—remember?'

'As if I could forget. Which brings us neatly back to Courdrey. Your age. His age.'

'It's none of your business.'

'But I'm an old friend. I'm concerned. I should hate you to make a terrible mistake.'

'Once bitten, twice shy,' she informed him. 'And this time, Dev, I know exactly what I'm doing.'

'Yes, I'm sure you do,' he agreed with un-expected anguish.

'And what's that supposed to mean?' Holly demanded, baffled by the lightning change of tone.

'Look, Holly, it's all right,' he said soothingly. 'I understand. I can see what you're doing and I do understand.' And he moved across, lifting her chin with surprisingly tender fingers, forcing Holly to meet his gaze.

'It's simple, Holly. You loved your father and you were little more than a child when you lost him. But marrying Courdrey won't bring him back. But that's what you're trying to do, Holly. Can't you see? Courdrey's a father figure. You're looking for a nice, safe, little-girl-lost, please-take-care-of-me relationship. But damn it all, Holly, the man's almost twice your age.'

'He's four years older than you,' she hissed, her body on red alert at Dev's nearness, Dev's touch, Dev's lightning change of mood. And since she was neatly cornered against an ivy-covered wall, she couldn't back away, couldn't escape, not without brushing against the powerful lines of his body, setting her own body on fire simply with the thought.

'Precisely. He's too old for you, Holly.'

'And you're not, I suppose?' she tossed out bitterly.

'What do you think?' Dev challenged, black eyes holding hers, refusing to allow her to look away. And in the half-light cast by the garden lamps, the effect was all the more disturbing.

'Age doesn't come into it,' Holly insisted, dodging the question. 'Five years, ten... It's all a state of mind. If I'm happy, why should anyone else care?'

Dev shrugged, releasing her, though he didn't move away. 'Fine. If Courdrey's not a father substitute, he's clearly not the man you love. You've given yourself away, Holly. Your body's betrayed you—and how. You want me.'

She gave a nervous laugh. 'You're mad.'

'Not mad. Logical. You want me. You need me. You've always wanted me. And since I haven't been around—'

'Exactly! You haven't been around. And guess what, Dev? I've rebuilt my life and, believe it or not, I've left you out of the picture. I had to, you see,' she explained tightly. 'Because you didn't want to stick around—remember?'

'It wasn't that simple, Holly.'

'It was to me. You used me, took everything I had to give and then you walked out, left me. Didn't even spare me so much as a second glance.'

'It isn't true.'

'No? No, I don't suppose it was,' she scorned. 'You'd remember Holly Scott all right—all the way to the bank, hey, Dev?'

'And what the hell does that mean?'

'You know. Don't pretend. I know the way Daddy's mind worked, and how easy it must have been to take what he was offering.'

'You bitch!' He snatched her to him, fingers digging deep into the skin of her upper arms as he jerked her close, black eyes raining hate. 'No one gets the chance to buy Devlin Winter,' he told her viciously. 'No one. Not even Gregory Scott. And if he had,' he informed her frigidly, shaking her, 'I'd have thrown it back in his face.'

'How very commendable,' Holly sneered,

63

subconsciously aware that she'd hit a nerve but too choked with anger to heed common sense. 'And how very easy to say.'

His thunderous face closed in, the familiar tang of aftershave catching at the back of her throat. And Dev was angry, furiously angry. She'd hurt him and he was angry. And it hurt. And she wanted him. Even now, she wanted him.

How easy to reach out, to touch his cheek, to have the familiar rasp of stubble beneath her fingers, and Holly knew instinctively that a single touch of skin on skin would be enough. The passion simmering beneath the surface would flare and the anger would be forgotten, the bitter words pushed aside as Dev captured her hand, nuzzled the palm with his lips, sent rivers of heat licking through her body.

And Holly responded to the thought, seemed to watch from a distance as she did exactly that, a tentative touch that Dev recoiled from, recoiled as if scalded, and yet moments later she was in his arms, had wrapped her own arms around his neck, wanting Dev, needing Dev.

'Dev! Oh, Dev!' she murmured between the kisses.

'Hush, sweetheart,' he soothed, the warm flutter of breath against her cheek sending fresh waves of heat coursing through her veins.

Madness, exquisite madness. And her mind pushed away the years of hate, remembering Dev, loving Dev, wanting Dev, her body craving Dev...

Dev's lips against hers, his tongue tracing

64

the outline of her mouth, and Holly was moaning, her lips parting in silent invitation. His tongue slid through, exploring the hot, moist recesses, while his hands slipped from shoulder to hip, pulling Holly hard against him, shocking Holly with his hardness. Her stomach muscles clenched, the need to touch, to taste, to savour filling her mind. The pain was forgotten. The man she loved was here, had never left her heart. They were together and they belonged, they'd always belonged.

And she was kissing Dev, her tongue seeking his, entwining with his, her lips hard against his mouth. And hip to hip, thigh to thigh, Holly felt the need he had for her and her mind soared. She wanted him, and Dev's low growl of approval as she pushed herself against him was all the proof she needed.

He wanted her, needed her, loved her; the barrier of their clothes simply heightened the tension, tantalizing, teasing, denying access to exploring, stroking fingers, and yet every touch was a brand, a brand of skin on skin because her body remembered, oh, how she remembered, and oh, God, how she needed him.

A lifetime passed before the frenzy began to calm, Dev's lips no longer demanding, simply caressing, his hands stroking the exposed skin on her back, sending shivers of heat darting up and down her spine. Holly raised her hands, running her fingers through the mass of black hair that brushed against his collar. Longer than she remembered, she noted subconsciously, yet silky smooth and tactile and—Dev winced, pulling away sharply, and seeing the grimace of pain, Holly gasped. She'd hurt him. How on earth—?

'It's all right, sweetheart,' Dev reassured her, pulling her back into the harbour of his arms.

'I—what is it?' she asked, aware that the smoothness of his scalp had been marred by a ridge of puckered skin.

'Just a scratch,' he explained lightly. 'Bit of a bump in the car. But having a shell like Humpty Dumpty, part of me cracked. Nothing for you to worry about, Holly, nothing at all.'

'But, Dev, I *hurt* you,' she whispered, horrified.

'You certainly did,' he agreed with a smile in his voice. 'But not in the way you mean. It's OK, Holly,' he added matter-of-factly. 'Everything's fine, but now and again the scar tissue's tender. You weren't to know.' He kissed her, a brief, reassuring touch of lips. 'Come on. I don't know about you, but I need a drink.'

Back to the crowd then. Holly swallowed the disappointment, allowing Dev to take her hand, tug her down the steps, and then the realization dawned. The way to the terrace was upwards.

'Where are we going?' she asked stupidly.

But Dev simply smiled, leading the way to the wrought-iron bench where she'd earlier taken refuge, and Holly went cold as she spotted the bottle nestling in its bucket of ice, the crystal champagne flutes on a snow-white table cloth. And the final touch—the single rose in a tiny silver vase.

'A slight matter of our unfinished business,'

Dev explained, uncorking the wine with a soundless, practised ease. 'Remember?'

Oh yes. She remembered. Foolish, foolish Holly. Allowing Dev to play with her emotions, allowing Dev to touch her, kiss her, rekindle needs she'd rather not acknowledge.

'Expecting company?' she challenged as something vital died. He'd planned it. Every word, every touch, every last caress. And he'd been so, so sure.

'Only you,' he murmured. 'Surely, you haven't forgotten my promise?'

'And what a dent to your ego that would be, hey, Dev?'

'If you say so,' he agreed, and though the words sounded pleasant enough, Holly's sensitive ear caught the thinly veiled edge.

'Well, I do. Goodnight, Dev. Good*bye,* Dev,' she pointedly added, folding her arms across her chest in a gesture of protection. 'I want you to leave and, if you care about me at all, you won't be coming back. Go, Dev. Get out out of my life.' Get out of my mind, she tagged on silently, bitterly.

'And leave you to throw yourself away on Courdrey? No chance.'

'Since he's twice the man you'll ever be, you've got a nerve,' she stated flatly.

'Ah, yes. But is it the man, or is the fortune?' he chided. 'After all, you are your father's daughter.'

'Meaning?'

'Money marries money, of course. With this fortune I thee wed,' he parodied coldly.

'Don't be so insulting,' she hissed. 'You know nothing about it.'

'No? Then prove to me you're not marrying Courdrey for his money.'

'And how can I do that,' she snapped, 'since you refuse point blank to believe me?'

Dev smiled—at least, his mouth did. In the shadows of the night, the expression in his eyes was unfathomable. 'It's really very simple, Holly. If it isn't Courdrey's money, then it must be something else. And since you've ruled out every other possibility, it all comes down to that quaint, old-fashioned feeling that goes by the name of love. So—' He paused, poured the champagne, offered a glass to Holly and merely shrugged when she refused it. Then, taking a sip from his own, he raised the glass in an awful mockery of a toast. 'Tell me, Holly. Just give me the truth and I'll walk out of here and never bother you again. Say it, Holly. Tell me you're marrying Courdrey because you love him.'

CHAPTER 4

Because I love him. Oh, yes, I love him. Fool, fool, fool to think I could ever escape. But he mustn't know. He mustn't know, mustn't guess. Because Dev would use the knowledge to hurt her, destroy her, destroy everything she'd worked for. Oh, yes. She loved Devlin Winter, always had, always would. But that didn't change a thing. She'd be strong, just like she had been for the past seven years. Oh, yes? Who was she kidding? And if she didn't face it now, she never would. Dev had destroyed her and, given half a chance, he'd do it all over again.

The tears welled, only a massive surge of will holding them back. Why, Dev? she silently implored. Why now, when she was so close to starting a new life, creating a whole new existence? Another few months and she'd be Mrs Alex Courdrey, and the future would be secure for Jonathan and Meryl. Why now, for pity's sake? And Holly was afraid, terribly afraid. Because she hadn't escaped. She'd never escape. Dev was inside her head and only a fool would refuse to admit it. And she'd tried. Heaven knew she'd tried—look where that had led her.

'Tell me,' Dev insisted relentlessly, black eyes locked onto hers, refusing to allow her to look away. 'Tell me, Holly. Say it. Tell me you're marrying Courdrey because you love him.'

She licked her dry lips, a nervous gesture Dev surely hadn't missed, yet he barely seemed to breathe, giving nothing away, his relentless gaze burning holes in Holly's mind.

Oh, what the hell! She swung away, needing to escape. Another futile gesture, as Dev's lightning response proved that once again he'd out-thought her, out-flanked her, as he pulled her up sharp. Holly flushed with part anger, part need, part fear.

'Oh, no! Not until you've given me an answer,' he growled, a band of iron fingers circling Holly's narrow wrist.

The anger surged then with a vengeance, swamping other emotions. 'Fine!' she spat out, resisting the urge to squirm. 'Are you listening, Dev? Because what I'm about to say, I'll say once and once only and believe me, that's more than you're entitled to. I'm marrying Alex because I love him. Happy now?'

'Liar!'

Holly flinched at the pain in his eyes, the pain in his voice, saw the muscles in his cheek tighten to reveal a pulse beating a wild tattoo at his temple and the pain hit her afresh. She'd hurt him. She'd hurt the man she loved and she had to fight the urge to give him the truth, because the truth would destroy her, destroy them all.

'You're lying, Holly,' he chillingly repeated, but there was doubt in his tone, little more than a nuance really, but enough for Holly to detect. Because she loved him. And she knew him. And Dev was afraid.

Holly smiled inside. For once, just this once, she had the upper hand and the knowledge was power, the power sheer intoxication. And she had to be strong—for Jonathan and Meryl, not to mention herself.

'Am I?' she challenged. And she moved her head from side to side in silent condemnation. 'I can't win, can I, Dev?' she pointed out coldly, pulling away. 'Since, whatever I say, you refuse to believe me.'

He didn't reply, simply stood impassive for long, tension-packed moments, the expression in his eyes such a curious mix of pain and disbelief that Holly could have cried, was suddenly ashamed that she'd had to lie to keep him at a distance. Dangerous thoughts, because Holly couldn't afford to weaken, and she stifled a huge sigh of relief as Dev broke the spell, moving wearily back to the table.

He tugged at the bow tie, impatient fingers snapping the top two buttons of the dress shirt, the dishevelled effect unwittingly appealing.

More pain, Holly acknowledged glancing down, vaguely aware that she was hurting, that in an effort to stay in control she'd clenched her fists, digging her nails into her palms almost to the point of drawing blood. She needed that drink, she decided, eyeing the glass that Dev had poured—hours ago now, it seemed. Though it took her dangerously close to Dev, she steeled herself, draining it in one, the bubbles barely hitting the back of her throat, and then she angled the empty glass in silent plea for more.

Dev refilled it, his eyes fastened on her face, all the time searching for the truth, a truth she had to hide. And her gaze didn't falter, the expression didn't waver. And she was lying, and deep inside she was dying.

As she raised the glass to her lips, Dev raised his own and Holly paused, waiting, simply waiting for Dev to speak, to deny her, to deride her.

'Another toast,' he mocked. 'To the past—and to the future, whatever that may bring. I'm too late, aren't I, Holly?' he conceded bitterly. 'Seven years too early, seven years too late. How the fates do mock.'

And suddenly the anguish and the pain were too much for Holly to take. 'Don't,' she implored, reaching out, the hand on his arm intended to console.

The effect was electric. 'Don't!' Dev spat, wrenching free, his eyes turbulent pools of hate. And the glass that he'd been holding shattered noisily at their feet. 'Don't touch me, woman. Not unless you're prepared to see it through. Because I want you. I desire you, and I'll take you. Are you listening, Holly?' he demanded harshly. 'I want you. And sooner or later you'll be forced to admit that you want me just as badly. And then I'll take you. And then you'll be mine—for all the tomorrows.'

All the tomorrows. The tears welled up and forced themselves out from under her tightly closed lids, trickling silently down her cheeks. Brushing them away with a gesture of impatience, she flung back the duvet. She'd get up. She might as well, given the night she'd just endured. Sleep. Holly's lips twisted. Not a cat in hell's chance. Not with Dev back in her life, back in her mind, destroying her fragile self control.

All the tomorrows.

And she'd believed him. For months she'd believed him, hugging the knowledge to her, starting each day with the belief that Dev *would* return, that he hadn't turned his back.

'Love? You don't know the meaning of the word,' her father had brutally declared, dismissing Holly's wonderful summer as a moment of madness with a beach bum.

But she'd closed her mind, not wanting to hear, not wanting to believe and, despite a mounting pile of evidence, refusing to believe that Dev had been using her, simply using her to gather copy. The cheque, the rumours, the sly insinuations in the gutter press that filtered back to Holly in her self-imposed exile—lies, all lies she'd convinced herself, loving Dev yet hating him, hating her father more. And when the story broke, plunging them all into the middle of a nightmare, still she'd refused to believe that Dev had betrayed her.

And then suddenly it hadn't mattered any more. Because her father had gone and the truth simply wasn't important. Dev was gone, Daddy was gone, and Holly and Meryl were left to cope alone. All alone. Oh, yes. She'd been all alone. But she hadn't coped, she acknowledged, checking her watch in the half-light and climbing wearily back into bed. Holly

Scott, tramp of the year, hadn't coped at all.

More tears, unheeded now as the memories closed in. And though she didn't want to remember, how could she possibly forget? She'd turned into a tramp. Hitting back at Dev, though heaven knows, he'd never known or cared. Hitting back at Dev by sleeping with another man, and another, and another, men she barely knew and sure as hell didn't want. Not deep inside, where the pain was festering. She'd wanted Dev, she couldn't have Dev, so Holly would have her revenge. Cold and calculating. Oh yes, she couldn't even plead a spur-of-the-moment weakness. One pregnancy was more than enough. This time Holly was taking no chances—with anything.

And she'd cried. Silently. Her heart had cried at every touch, every caress, every thrust of a body that wasn't Dev's. And strangely enough, she recalled, she'd refused point blank to let them kiss her. It was—more intimate, somehow. They could take her body and use her, the way Holly was trying to use them, and she could close her mind and imagine, for a fleetingly mad moment, that it *was* Dev in her arms. Then the truth would wash over her, the truth, the shame, the loathing. But it was separate from her mind, and Holly was passive. She simply wasn't there, not in mind. But kissing, an intimate touch of lips and tongue, was something else.

She punched up the pillows, drawing her knees up under her chin, remembering, hating, hating Dev for loving her and leaving her. Only he hadn't. He'd *never* loved her, Holly

74

acknowledged brutally. He'd never lied, never once pretended. He'd simply made love to her, with her. And then he'd gone. Just like that. Taken the money and run. Oh, Dev, how could you? Oh, God, how could I? Tramp of the year. And the tears were pouring down her cheeks, great silent sobs racking her body as Holly remembered that awful night when she'd finally come to her senses.

'Come on, sugar,' the man had urged. 'You can do better than this. Just wriggle your hips a little, huh?' And his heaving, sweating body had covered hers, ridden hers while the waft of stale cigarette smoke and the stench of strong spirits had stung her nostrils. Young, dark, handsome in a rugged sort of way, never Dev, but enough like Dev for Holly to glance down, see the shock of dark hair, want it to be Dev, believe it could be Dev.

She'd reacted to the thought, to the idea, the heat running through her like a flame. Sensing cooperation, the man had grunted, the thrusting frenetic now, but not for Holly. Because the truth had dawned. Not Dev, never Dev. And she'd hated it, hated him, hated herself more. And staring out over his shoulder, eyes unseeing, she'd emptied her mind completely. She simply hadn't been there.

And then the shock. The knock on the door an hour later.

'Jake says you're an obliging little lady...'

'I—'

'Sure you do, honey,' the man had insisted, pushing his way through. And he'd darted

75

a swift, assessing glance around the room, whistling softly under his breath. 'Looks like Jake was right. Rooms like this don't come cheap, lady. But my money's as good as the next man's,' he'd insisted, counting out a fistful of notes and tossing them carelessly down on the bedside table. And before Holly could even speak, he'd begun shrugging himself out of his clothes.

And then the truth had dawned. He was going to pay her—no—worse than that, he *expected* to pay her because Jake had given his personal recommendation. Which meant—oh, God! And now, as then, the waves of nausea began to swamp her, the shame, the loathing, the disgust. The disgust. Rock bottom. And she really couldn't sink any lower, she'd finally been forced to acknowledge. Because that man had been prepared to pay for sex with Holly. Brutal. But then the truth always did hurt.

But it was a turning point. Never again. Not even with Alex. Not until they were married, that is. And until Dev walked back into her life, turning it upside down, it hadn't seemed a problem. But sex with Alex, making love with Alex, making love with *any* man simply didn't appeal. Only Dev. And he'd ruined her once already. She'd be damned if she'd let him close enough to do it all over again.

'Telephone, Holly.'

Meryl's voice sliced through the pain. Alex? Holly wondered, vaguely alarmed. Eight o'clock on a Sunday morning, with London time set an hour behind? No. Holly's lips tightened. It couldn't be Alex, and if Meryl's knowing air was a clue, that only left Dev.

'Good morning,' she said briskly into the mouthpiece.

'My, my, we are up bright and early. Couldn't you sleep?' the familiar voice chided. 'And here's me, convinced you'd still be curled up under the duvet, dreaming wonderful dreams of me.'

'Those sorts of dreams are called nightmares, Dev,' she retorted waspishly, nervous fingers threading the plastic-coated telephone coil. 'And I haven't suffered those since I was ten years old.'

He laughed, a rich deep chuckle that was music to her ears. 'Don't knock it. Assuming you're telling the truth, you're a very lucky girl—either that or conscience-free. So, what exactly are you doing up at the crack of dawn?'

'Just enjoying the cool of the day,' she replied. And then something struck her. 'But what about you? What's your excuse? Don't tell me *you* couldn't sleep?' she queried slyly. 'Something on your mind, perhaps?'

'There certainly is, Holly. You!'

'I can't think why,' she demurred, her pulse rate leaping.

'I'm sure you could if you tried,' he retorted slyly.

Holly's colour deepened. So that's how he wanted to play it. Forget the anger, the heated words, the wild accusations. Dev was back to playing games. And how!

Catching sight of her reflection in the mirror at the end of the hallway, Holly stiffened. Because even from a distance, the body language said it all. She was afraid. Because Dev in playful mood was every bit as dangerous as Dev in any other. Dynamite, in fact. And she was rapidly reaching the conclusion that she was doomed.

Holly smiled grimly. Oh, yes? She'd had seven years without him when she'd coped, for heaven's sake. Why turn into a nervous wreck the moment he returned? Sorry to disappoint you, Dev, she silently berated, but Holly Scott's made of sterner stuff than that.

'Did you want something, Dev?' she enquired pointedly.

'Now there's a leading question,' he teased. 'Careful, Holly, you might get more than you've bargained for.'

'I doubt it.'

'Calling my bluff, hey? Hmm. The lady's got spirit, I'll grant you that.'

'Big of you,' she needled, but she was guiltily aware that she was flirting, courting danger, and she gave herself a thorough mental shaking. 'If you wouldn't mind getting to the point, Dev—'

'Because it's Sunday, and you're on holiday, and your diary's chock-a-block full for the next twelve hours?' he drawled, heavily ironic.

'Well, no-o,' she reluctantly conceded.

'Good. Because I'd like to stake a claim. An invitation to lunch. You, Meryl and Jonathan. Call it a thank-you for last night's hospitality.

How does two o'clock suit?'

It didn't. But how to convince such a stubbornly persistent creature? 'Thanks, Dev. But there's really no need. Meryl enjoys entertaining. And in case you'd forgotten,' she reminded him crisply, 'you were doing Meryl a favour by being there.'

'So I was, Holly. But as things turned out, the pleasure was all mine. And since I'm a man who likes to pay his way, you'll simply have to indulge me.'

'And if I don't?'

'Then I'll have to eat alone. And I just hate eating alone. Two o'clock. And no buts. I'll pick you up at quarter to.'

'I'm not sure we can make it,' she stalled.

'Oh, but you can. You see, Holly,' he informed her gleefully, 'knowing the way your mind works, I thought it wise to check with Meryl first.'

Meryl. Holly might have known. She skipped breakfast, the thought of having to share another meal with Dev playing havoc with her appetite, and slipped almost furtively out of the house and headed down towards the town, in desperate need of some peace.

There'd been no sound of Jonathan's eager chatter for once and Holly was glad that he was lying in. She wanted to be alone, alone with her thoughts. She didn't realize where her footsteps were taking her until she joined the crowd of people on the rue de l'Eglise. And even then, she found herself inside somewhere without making a conscious decision.

Organ music, the low murmur of voices an

unearthly echo. Holly pulled up short. She hadn't been inside a church since her father's funeral and, as the panic swamped her, instinct told her to bolt. Only she couldn't, a flurry of last-minute arrivals hemming her in, the heavy oak door swinging to before she could reach it. Though she could have wrenched it open again, some strange compulsion carried her instead to an empty back pew.

A rustle of paper as the mass sheets were unfolded. Holly smiled her nervous thanks as someone thrust one into her hand. Unsurprisingly, the words were in French. With her knowledge of the language almost non-existent, she struggled to make sense of it at first, then she stopped trying, simply drawing solace from the strange intonation, the hypnotic chant of voices raised in prayer.

Prayer. 'Let us pray for the soul of our brother departed...' Her mind slipped, seeing the ornate coffin as they'd lowered it into the ground. Strange voices, strange faces, so many staring, curious faces, drawn by the mountain of publicity. With millions of pounds missing from the pension funds, the speculation had been rife. Did Gregory Scott fall, or did he choose to slide into the water and simply drift away? Since he'd been alone on *The Ilex*, apart from a skeleton crew who hadn't heard a thing, no one would ever know the truth.

Except maybe, Holly, who'd earlier spoken to her father for the first time in months. And even then, she recalled with painful clarity, they'd managed to quarrel over Dev.

Dev! Holly gasped, her eyes widening as the familiar profile slipped into view. For an awful moment she was convinced that her mind was playing tricks, that she'd conjured him up from turbulent thoughts. But no. She wasn't dreaming, hallucinating, going mad. It *was* Dev, joining the shuffle of people in the centre aisle, a real, live flesh-and-blood Dev, and she followed his progress to the altar rails where he received the sacrament of bread and wine.

Holly was stunned. Devlin Winter in church, and not just in church but taking an active part in the service?

She stumbled to her feet. She had to get away, quickly, before Dev could turn and see her. She had no right to be there, felt unclean, sordid, as if she'd been caught spying on something very, very private. And she'd never known. But—how could she possibly have loved this man and never known about something as vitally important as his faith?

'So, like the condemned man, you ate a hearty breakfast?'

'I beg your pardon?' Holly stalled, blushing annoyingly. She'd been miles away and Dev had caught her unawares.

'Like the condemned—'

'Yes. I heard you,' she interrupted edgily. 'I heard what you said, Dev, I just didn't understand the question.'

His lips twitched, Holly's confusion a clear source of amusement. The more she tried to control it, the deeper the blush spread.

'So...'

'So?'

She smothered a sigh. Impossible man. Would he never tire of playing games? 'So, maybe you'd like to explain,' she suggested as evenly as possible.

The smile vanished and Dev stretched out a hand, Holly resisting the urge to snatch her own away as long fingers closed round it, the touch both soothing and stirring. And the lightly tanned skin of her arm, the deeper tan of Dev's with its dark covering of hair, stood out against the white of the damask cloth beneath.

'You didn't eat,' he said simply, the black eyes holding hers unexpectedly solemn. 'And since you didn't touch so much as a morsel last night either...'

'How very observant,' Holly said sharply, amazed that Dev had noticed. Lunch, yes—she could hardly hope to escape his scrutiny with just the four of them, Meryl to his left, Holly to his right and Jonathan proudly stationed at the head of the table. But as for dinner, *how* had he noticed when he'd been practically eaten alive by that much too attractive brunette, she recalled with an irrational stab of jealousy?

'Observant—and concerned,' Dev murmured softly. 'The prerogative of an old friend. Believe it or not, I'm worried about you.'

'Well, you needn't be,' she retorted briskly, swallowing hard. 'You were right in the first place. Too much breakfast,' she insisted, mentally crossing her fingers at yet another white lie, and though she tried to free her hand, Dev's grip tightened.

'Liar,' he replied, but there was no malice in his tone. Just concern.

Holly's gaze faltered. 'Sorry, Dev,' she murmured, dodging the challenge. 'I'm sure the meal was delicious but, like I said, I just wasn't hungry.'

He shook his head. 'Oh, Holly, what am I going to do with you?' he asked, his thumb brushing the back of her hand.

'Leave me alone?' she half-challenged, half-pleaded.

'Why?'

'You know very well why.'

'Ah, yes. The absent Courdrey.'

Not for much longer, Holly amended silently. Since Alex had been forced to cancel this weekend, he'd be sure to make the next. Another disconcerting thought, she realized, vaguely wondering why.

'It won't work, you know,' Dev cut in mildly.

'What won't?'

'You. Hiding behind Courdrey.'

'And what makes you so certain that I'm hiding?'

Expressive eyebrows rose. 'Oh, you know—this and that,' he drawled with heavy irony. 'Your behaviour last night for a start.'

'Positively saint-like, I'd say,' she told him waspishly. 'Given the provocation.'

'Provocation—or temptation?' he queried slyly.

'Where you're concerned, irritation is probably nearer the mark,' she snapped.

'A thorn in the side, huh? But since any

83

reaction's better than indifference,' he pointed out smoothly, 'I guess that means I'm winning.'

'The cad of the year award?' she heard herself needling. 'Too right, Dev.'

'Once, maybe,' he allowed, a shadow of pain crossing his features. 'But not this year, Holly. I promise you.'

'Quite the reformed character, hey, Dev?' she scorned, too late recalling his presence in church just a few short hours ago and hating herself for the cheap and nasty gibe.

'If you say so,' he allowed surprisingly mildly.

'I don't. But that *is* what you're implying?'

'And would it make any difference?'

'To what?'

'To us.'

'We don't exist, Dev. Never have, never will,' she reminded him.

'And Tenerife?'

'Was a mistake. The biggest mistake of my life.'

'But it did happen?'

'Unless I was dreaming—no, on second thoughts,' she sneered, hitting out at Dev, hurting Dev, hurting herself more, 'I remember it well. It was a nightmare, each and every moment.'

'So cruel, Holly.'

'I think honest is the word you're looking for, Dev. Truthful, honest, frank.'

'And hard as nails—on the outside, at least. Like I said, it isn't going to work. No hiding place, Holly,' he underlined intently, black eyes holding hers, pain, hope, need, a thousand and one emotions swirling in their depths. 'I'm back and this time I've no intention of letting you go.'

The door opened and Jonathan burst in, followed at a much more sedate pace by Meryl, who carefully brushed the dust off her heels with a moue of distaste.

'We've been exploring, Holly,' Jonathan confided, rushing straight across.

'Have you, poppet? And what have you found?' she enquired, seizing the chance to pull away and bending to hug him, acutely aware that she was hiding from Dev, using a six-year-old child as a shield.

'Horses. Lots of them. And ducks and geese and a really deep pool that Mummy says I've got to stay away from.'

'Pond,' Meryl corrected automatically. 'And you certainly must. You should have warned me, Dev. If I'd realized you were living on a farm, I'd have brought this little tyke a change of clothes. Correct me if I'm wrong, but didn't you call it a manor house?'

Dev laughed. 'And so it is, or would have been at one time. But thanks to complicated laws on French inheritance, the land's been parcelled off and the house is now a holiday home.'

'Well, it *is* lovely,' Meryl agreed doubtfully.

'But not quite what you expected? Not grand enough for madam's taste?' he teased.

'Just not my idea of a manor,' she allowed as Dev waved them through to have coffee in the lounge.

Manor or not, the half-timbered farmhouse, complete with thatched roof, uneven floors and low-slung ceilings that Dev regularly caught his head on, was impressive. And in contrast to Alex's modern design, just a ten-minute drive away, it had a homely feel, a lived-in feel, even down to cosy meals in the kitchen. Well, it should have been cosy, Holly amended, but she'd been too overwrought to see it at the time.

As for Alex, he'd have choked at the thought. Alex and Dev. Chalk and cheese. The one tall, blond, good-looking in a rugged sort of way; the other tall, dark and devastating. Similar age, similar height and build—and with a similar taste in women, she tagged on impishly. And then she stiffened, her strange sense of humour, she chided tersely, not the least bit amusing.

With the sofa beckoning anything but cosily, Holly settled for a chair, an almost imperceptible twitch of Dev's lips as he passed the coffee eloquent proof that he'd noticed. Though she tilted her chin in defiance, the rattle of her cup in its saucer was another sign of nerves that Dev would have logged, logged and understood. Because Holly was afraid. Despite the brave words, her stubborn insistence that she did love Alex, Holly was afraid. Of Dev.

No escape, she was beginning to believe. No hiding place, and using Jonathan's excited chatter as a cover, she lapsed into brooding thought. Because Dev was back in her life and Dev had no intentions of letting her go. Famous last words, she might have jeered, but she was shockingly aware that in Dev's mind at least, it was all just a matter of time. And Holly was afraid. Because she loved him. Because she'd lied about Alex, and Dev had known she was lying. Because Dev had kissed her, touched her, tasted her. And Holly had responded, just fourteen hours ago she realised, the scene in the garden etched on her mind.

In contrast to the dinner suit, Dev's look today was casual, tailored linen trousers and crisp cotton shirt open at the neck, sleeves pushed up to the elbows leaving his forearms bare. Bare skin. Arms and throat bare, the mass of dark hair at the V of his shirt screaming out for fingers to rake through it. Holly's fingers, she realized with a pang. And then Dev glanced up, catching her unawares and Holly went crimson. Because Dev knew. He could read her mind, the knowledge blazing out from his dark, smouldering eyes.

'You will take me riding, won't you, Holly?' a plaintive voice intruded.

With a massive surge of will, she switched her attention from man to boy. 'Sorry, poppet. What did you say?'

'I've asked Mummy but she can't ride. So will you take me riding, please? On a horse,' he added, as if explaining to a three-year-old.

'Well. Yes, I suppose so,' Holly agreed, her eyes crossing in silent enquiry to Meryl, who nodded her consent along with a shrug of apology. 'A pony, perhaps. You won't be ready for a horse for a while yet.'

Jonathan's face fell. 'But Peter says only babies ride ponies.'

'Who's Peter?' Dev enquired.

'He's my friend. And he's having a horse for his birthday. And it's this big,' Jonathan explained, jumping to his feet and stretching his arm as high as he could.

'But, darling, Peter knows how to ride already,' Meryl explained patiently.

'And I bet he learned on a pony,' Dev put in quickly.

Tiny mouth set hard, Jonathan was clearly not impressed.

'Tell you what,' Dev soothed, leaning towards him. 'How about coming across tomorrow and spending the day with me? We'll have the stable girls kit you out and then find you a horse that's just the right size.'

'Can't we do it today?' Jonathan asked, the scowl banished in a trice.

'Sorry, pal. It's Sunday, so there's no one around to teach you.'

'But you could watch me. And I'd be very careful,' Jonathan wheedled, dark eyes full of silent pleas.

'I know you would. But they're not my horses, you see,' Dev explained apologetically. 'And riding without a hat is dangerous. You might fall off, land on your head. And then all the king's horses and all the king's men would struggle to put you together again,' he finished on a light note.

Jonathan laughed, the disappointment tempered. 'But I'm stronger than Humpty Dumpty.

I'm a big boy. My head won't crack.'

'Mine did, and I'm much bigger than you.'

'Did you fall off a horse?'

Dev smiled. 'Lots of times. But that's not what caused the damage.'

'Oh?' Holly murmured, cutting in without thinking.

'I crashed the car,' Dev explained almost offhandedly.

'Nothing serious, I hope?' Meryl enquired as Holly remembered Dev's wince of pain the previous evening, the ridge of puckered skin beneath the shock of hair.

'It was serious at the time,' he admitted with a dismissive shrug of the shoulders. 'But I'm over it now. Apart from the occasional headache.'

'So what happened,' Meryl probed, 'if you don't mind my asking?'

There was a strange pause and as he glanced at Holly, tiny hairs on the back of her neck began to stand on end. 'I'm not really sure,' he began carefully. 'I was in France, as it happens, following up a story when I had some news about a friend. One minute I'm heading for home, the next thing I know I'm flat on my back in a hospital bed. I was driving too fast, at a guess, trying to get back to her. According to witnesses, I lost the car on a bend, and bang!'

'Wow!' Jonathan declared.

Holly went cold, an icy hand gripping her heart. A woman, she'd registered. Oh yes, there was bound to be a woman.

'It sounds like you were lucky,' Meryl observed.

'Yes. I suppose I was,' Dev allowed thoughtfully.

Jonathan's warm hand sneaked into Holly's. 'Come on,' he insisted, growing bored with the adult conversation. 'Come and see the horses.'

'Can I tag along, too?' Dev asked politely as Jonathan tugged Holly to her feet. 'If Meryl doesn't mind being left alone?'

'Don't mind me,' she insisted, waving them away with a smile. 'I'll just sit here and enjoy the peace and quiet.'

She should be so lucky, Holly railed as they emerged into glorious sunshine, but since Meryl's flirtation with Dev seemed to have fizzled out, Holly was too relieved to feel churlish for long.

Not surprisingly, Jonathan headed for the pond.

'No paddling,' Holly warned as he crouched at the edge.

'He's safe enough,' Dev reassured. 'It's barely deep enough to cover his ankles.'

Famous last words, Holly mocked, an unwitting echo of an earlier thought. And though Jonathan wasn't in any danger, Holly wouldn't want to be in his shoes if his best Sunday outfit took a ducking, and on the subject of ducks, surely six or seven yellow beaks could be seen peering out from the shade beneath the bushes?

Holly smiled. 'It's another world,' she observed, breaking into the silence.

'It certainly is,' Dev agreed, following the line of her gaze. 'And though the ducks add a pretty touch, Francine disapproves. They eat the flowers.'

'Francine?' Holly queried with another of those irrational stabs of jealousy.

'My housekeeper. The source of that delicious meal you've just missed out on. She's a treasure, as you'll discover for yourself'

Maybe, Holly conceded, but silently. No point in meeting trouble head on. Dev might not approve, but from now on she'd be giving cosy invitations like this a definite thumbs-down.

'And when the wind's in the wrong direction,' he added, grinning broadly, 'I could be sharing my home with the horses.'

'Except that it isn't,' Holly observed almost without thinking.

'It isn't, what?' Dev queried, frowning.

'Your home. It's a holiday let. A very pretty holiday let, but—' She gave an eloquent shrug. 'You surprise me, Dev.'

'Why? Because I prefer the peace and quiet of the country to the bright city lights? Don't forget,' he reminded her tersely, 'you don't know me at all.'

'No. But then I never did, hey, Dev? Not the real you, at any rate,' she added bitterly.

'What you see is what you get,' he reminded her harshly and, despite the warmth of sun, the temperature plunged. 'But if you go around with your eyes closed, Holly, don't be surprised when you miss all the clues.'

'Meaning?'

Dev shrugged. 'Meaning simply that,' he told her enigmatically.

Holly left it. She couldn't fathom his mood at all, didn't even begin to try. Since Holly had lapsed into brooding silence, Dev was left to make conversation, the fact that he was prepared to try surprising her all over again.

'What's wrong, Holly?' he asked finally, his hand on her arm as he turned to face her.

She glanced up, swallowed hard, felt herself beginning to drown in those deep velvet pools. Only, how could she explain when she didn't understand herself? And then the words were out before she could stop them. 'I saw you. This morning, I mean. I was in church.'

'*You* were at the service?'

She blushed. 'I—went for a walk, needed to think. I—just seemed to be drawn there.'

'And?'

Holly shrugged, afraid to put her thoughts into words, not even clear what she thinking. 'I don't know. I—'

'Couldn't believe what you were seeing?' he murmured drily.

'No! Yes! I don't know,' she retorted, her colour coming and going. 'I'm sorry, Dev.'

'For what? For being there? For needing solace? Ashamed, Holly? Of what, I wonder?'

'For getting things wrong. Somewhere along the way I misjudged you, didn't I, Dev?' She didn't know him then, she didn't know him now. And as for the future... Holly's mind skittered away.

'Maybe,' he conceded. 'But maybe you never stood a chance. You were young, Holly, and I was a fool.'

'For sleeping with a schoolgirl, Dev? I was sixteen. I knew what I was doing.'

'Exactly. Sixteen, damn it. And I was old enough to—'

'Be my father? Don't be so ridiculous.' she scorned.

'Old enough to know better,' he allowed.

'Ha! And just for the record, that first time, Dev, you didn't seduce me, we seduced one another.'

'Irrelevant, Holly. It shouldn't have happened, wouldn't have happened if I'd known.'

No. Holly felt the pain scythe through her. So much wouldn't have happened if Dev had known. Her wonderful summer in Tenerife and the string of disasters that followed. And yet she'd never lied, simply hadn't thought to mention her age. It hadn't been important. Making love with Dev had been the most natural thing in the world. But once he'd learned the truth, he'd been horrified.

Strange, really, the way things had worked out. Dev had been through his own private hell, surviving a serious accident and finding solace in God. And Holly? What had she done? she mused, meeting Dev's black eyes shadowed with concern. She'd been mentally hurt, not near-fatally wounded, she forced herself to face, and instead of facing life like an adult, she'd gone off the rails, turned into a tramp.

And if she'd felt sordid before, Holly was beginning to wonder how she'd ever lived with the shame.

CHAPTER 5

'Daydreaming, Holly?'

'Dev!' Holly jumped visibly, almost dropping her bagful of shopping, her confusion growing as Dev took the carrier from her without so much as a by your leave. 'Did you have to sneak up on me?' she demanded tartly, aware of the colour draining from her cheeks.

'Hardly sneaking,' he chided, lips twitching in amusement, 'in the middle of the high street in broad daylight. But there again, since you were clearly miles away...'

Yes. Four miles to be precise. Four miles too far, as it turned out, since the subject of her thoughts was less than four inches away, larger than life and, judging from his knowing expression, uncannily aware of her thoughts.

Holly flushed, snatching back her groceries and stepping out again, aware of Dev falling into step, and she wasn't sure which was more disconcerting, Dev beside her, or Dev overlooking her rudeness, or Dev annoyingly silent, perhaps. Taking her cue from that, she decided it was her turn to ignore his thorny presence at least, but it was easier said than done since he matched her step for step, an almost casual stroll alongside her own punishing pace. Still, he made no effort to speak, sticking like glue until Holly couldn't stand it any longer.

'Going somewhere, Dev?' she enquired, reaching the corner and pulling up short.

'Not especially,' he conceded, eyes crinkling at the corners. 'How about you?'

'The bank,' she said. 'The market, then home.'

'Time for a coffee, then.' He waved a hand to the café opposite. It was mid-morning, but the sun was already high in a cloudless sky and the pavement cafés were busy. Had it been anyone else, Holly would have been tempted, had been toying with the idea of lingering and spoiling herself—until Dev's sudden appearance drove the idea from her mind.

She shook her head. 'Sorry. Meryl's expecting me back and I'm running late already.' A feeble excuse if ever she heard one, but better safe than sorry.

'More haste, less speed,' Dev reminded. 'A ten-minute cup of coffee won't do any harm, then I'll give you a hand at the market and run you home. You never know, I might even coax an invitation to dinner for my pains.'

'And there again,' Holly snapped, 'maybe you won't. We're eating out,' she amended on a milder note, aware of overreacting. 'Otherwise, I'm sure you'd have done precisely that.'

'Pity,' he conceded, not the least put out. 'Anywhere I know?'

'Just—friends,' she explained warily.

'Here, in Houlgate?' he queried.

'No. Not Houlgate,' she admitted with a

tight smile. 'Cabourg. Some friends of Alex. Remember Alex, Dev?' she tagged on, with deliberate cruelty this time.

'I certainly do,' he conceded with an imperceptible tightening of a much too generous mouth. 'The absent fiancé. More fool Courdrey.'

'And more fool you for thinking he doesn't count. Goodbye, Dev. See you around some time—maybe,' she emphasized coldly, adding to herself as she flounced across the road, 'And maybe next time, Devlin Winter, I'll see you coming in time to change direction.'

It spoiled her mood, the brief encounter a storm cloud on an otherwise glorious day. She couldn't even shop in peace and was sharply aware that, absent or present, Dev played havoc with her thoughts. And since she'd swung away without thinking straight, she found herself in the market hall without the cash to pay for so much as loaf of bread, and whilst dinner wasn't a problem, it was Colette's day off and there were umpteen things needed for tomorrow...

'Damn, damn and damn the man,' she muttered vehemently under her breath as she retraced her steps. And sure enough, when she reached the bank, there was a queue. Holly stood and fumed. Half an hour ago she'd been early enough to linger, would have had time for that drink she'd been contemplating. Now she'd be lucky if she caught the market before closing time. And all because of Dev.

Emerging into the sunshine, she glanced swiftly left and right. Not a sign of him, thank goodness. She relaxed, and hooking the long strap of her bag more securely onto her shoulder, switched the plastic carrier to her left hand to balance. A moment later she was barged into from behind and was catapulted forwards, hitting the pavement heavily as the carrier split, scattering groceries in every direction.

She landed on her knees, was conscious of nothing but the breath leaving her body, and then Dev, appearing amazingly out of nowhere.

'Don't move. I'll be back in a moment,' he instructed urgently, bending down and giving her shoulders a reassuring squeeze.

Holly felt the tears sting, a sting that was matched by the grazes on her hands and knees. As a concerned crowd began to gather, Holly realized that in another couple of minutes she'd be blubbering like a baby. Needing a hankie, she reached for her handbag. Her bag! Oh, hell! What a fool she'd been, so caught up in thoughts about Dev that she hadn't noticed that the man in a hurry had been nothing but a thief, and a calculated one at that since she'd just left the bank.

The crowd parted, falling silent as Dev reappeared, dragging a boy—young man, Holly amended—by the wrist.

'Yours, I believe,' Dev murmured, dropping a navy leather shoulder bag into her lap, sharp eyes darting over Holly, assessing the damage. 'You'd better check the contents. If he was working alone, there's probably nothing missing, but you need to make sure before we call the police.'

'Police?' Holly glanced from Dev to the frightened boy—and he was just a boy, she decided—and back again. She nodded, made a swift mental inventory: passport, purse, travellers' cheques, the ubiquitous clutter of lipstick, comb, tissues and ancient till receipts. 'It's all here,' she told Dev, who'd retained a vice-like grip on the trembling boy's wrist.

The grim expression softened imperceptibly. 'Good. But how many others haven't been so lucky? It's a matter for the *gendarmerie*. I'm sure one of the shopkeepers would be happy to oblige.' He turned, addressing the crowd in fluent French, yet another revelation for Holly. Almost daily, it seemed, she was discovering facets to Dev she'd never suspected, and though she hadn't a clue what he was saying, she saw the nods of approval from the circle around, caught the flash of naked terror in the boy's eyes.

'No, Dev!' She stumbled to her feet, the grazes for the moment forgotten.

He turned, an eyebrow raised in enquiry.

'There's no harm done,' she insisted, her own eyes silently pleading.

'Not this time, maybe,' he conceded harshly.

'He's just a kid,' she pointed out softly. 'Look at him, he's terrified. He's not a hardened thief. Let him go, Dev. Please,' she added softly.

There was pause, a tense, electric moment when the rest of the world retreated and they were alone, Dev and Holly, the incident forgotten, the boy forgotten, and the messages flowed between them: hope, love, want, need, fear, like the flickering shadows of a magic lantern show.

Almost in a dream, Holly reached out, her hand brushing the side of Dev's face, the very touch electric, and Dev turned his head, nuzzled the palm with his mouth, the heat running through her like a flame. Suddenly afraid of the naked emotion, she snatched her hand away, breaking the spell, the flash of pain in Dev's eyes finding an echo in her heart.

'Please, Dev,' she repeated.

He swore softly under his breath and then switched his gaze from Holly to the boy, blasting him in voluble French. Holly stood rigid as the boy replied, a torrent of words that was stemmed by an imperative wave of Dev's hand. Shamefaced, the boy fished an ID card from a pocket of his tattered jeans, and Dev's contemptuous gaze flicked over it.

'You're a fool, Holly,' Dev growled, dropping his hold, and the boy scarpered under another barrage of French as the crowd began to move away, shrugging with Gallic insouciance at this example of English fair play.

Left alone with Dev, Holly became conscious of the sight she must present, hands and knees grazed, cheeks streaked with tears, her hair a wild cascade across her shoulders.

'You're hurt!' he accused mildly.

The tears welled again, and Holly shook her head, aware of her control hanging by a thread. And though the grazes were stinging it was—other things that caused the pain: the aftershock of the bag snatch, the dent to her pride that she could let it happen in broad daylight in a crowded street, and the fact that she'd been so wrapped up in Dev she'd been walking around in a dream. Dev. Oh, Dev. Would she never escape the pain, the need, the memory?

'Come on. You need a drink.'

Brooking no refusal this time, he led her to the nearest café, settling her at a table well away from prying eyes and despite her protests, ordering a brandy. 'Sip this, slowly mind. I'll be back as soon as I can.'

Five minutes, no more, which gave her precious little time to pull herself together, although the brandy certainly helped.

'This is going to sting,' Dev explained, producing cotton wool and a bottle of antiseptic from the pharmacy bag he placed on the table along with the basin of hot water supplied by the proprietor.

'Very resourceful,' Holly teased, achingly aware of the angle of his head as he bent to bathe first one knee then the other, though Holly winced, the warm trickle of water was soothing.

'Hands, please,' he ordered next, ignoring her muttered protests that she could manage. And with Holly's knees and palms finally a patchwork quilt of sticking plaster, Dev sat back, black eyes suddenly solemn.

'At the risk of sounding repetitive, Holly, you were daydreaming.'

'I was *not* daydreaming,' she protested, her sensitive ear catching the hint of disapproval.

'No? Well, if you say so,' he allowed, clearly not impressed.

She flushed, sipping her drink, watching warily from beneath a veil of lashes. He was angry. Hardly any wonder since Holly had snubbed him, had been deliberately rude when he'd suggested a drink. Having flounced off in a flurry of indignation, it would have served her right if her bag and its contents had been lost for ever. Only it hadn't. Thanks to Dev. Dev. Cause or effect? she wondered idly, smiling despite herself.

'Well, you look better now,' he observed on a lighter note, at the same time signalling for a coffee. 'Finish your brandy and then I'll run you home. And no buts,' he added before she could protest.

'But I haven't finished my shopping,' she pointed out sheepishly.

'No? Well, given the way you drifted up and down that street, it's hardly surprising, hey, Holly? And before you rustle up another denial, I saw you. You were miles away, damn it.'

'Spying, Dev? Bored? Nothing better to do?' she needled.

'As it happens, no. Luckily for you.'

'Yes.' She swallowed hard and placing her glass carefully on the table, forced herself to meet his accusing gaze. 'You're right. I'm sorry, Dev. I haven't even thanked you,' she conceded softly.

'All part of the Devlin Winter damsel-rescue service,' he quipped as his mouth softened. 'And a first-class service at that,' he claimed modestly as a young girl, laden with shopping, halted at their table.

'Damsel-rescue—or damsel-slaying service?' Holly queried tartly, logging Dev's winning smile and the girl's blush of pleasure as she backed away.

He shrugged. 'Take your pick,' he invited carelessly, waving a hand to the bags the girl had placed at his feet. 'Yours, I believe.'

Holly felt her cheeks burn. 'How on earth—?'

'Simple. When your bag burst, the shopping list was caught amongst the pile. And since madam was in no fit state to continue, and with half the town closing for lunch, yours truly used his initiative. Satisfied?'

'With the service? How could a girl find fault?' she stalled.

'Where this particular girl's concerned,' Dev reminded drily, 'believe me, Holly, very, very easily.'

It was a tense ride home. The brandy had helped but Holly was still in shock, Dev's larger-than-life presence honing the nerves.

Pulling onto the drive, he darted a shrewd sideways glance at her. 'I won't come in,' he explained, placing the bags of shopping carefully down on the doorstep. 'Meryl would take one look at me and another at your face and jump to heaven only knows what conclusion. See you around some time,' he murmured drily, blowing an airy kiss before spinning on his heels and sauntering back to the car.

Holly paused in the hall, the silence of the house unexpected and unnerving. Coming face to face with herself in the mirror, she pulled a wry face. No arguing with Dev's assessment this time. Her cheeks were a smudge of tears and that tangle of hair might never have had the benefit of comb.

Dropping the bags in the kitchen, she headed for the cloakroom, needing to make herself presentable, but out in the hallway she paused again, head on one side, listening. There wasn't a sound. It was unnatural. Something was wrong, she decided, and damping down the panic, headed for the stairs. She reached the top as Meryl appeared in Jonathan's doorway, a warning finger on her lips, and an icy finger touched Holly's heart.

'An ear infection, according to the doctor. Nothing serious,' Meryl reassured her down in the kitchen. 'But he's just this minute dropped off and I'd like him to get some sleep.'

'You called the doctor? But why didn't you tell me?' Holly demanded, running her fingers through her hair. 'I wouldn't have gone out if I'd known.'

Meryl shrugged. 'You know kids. Down one minute, up the next. And he was fine first thing. Just grew hot and tetchy as the morning went on. If you'd been here, Holly, there was nothing you could have done,' she insisted softly.

Maybe not, Holly allowed. But she would have been moral support for Meryl, could have nursed Jonathan, read him a story, helped to divert him. Only what had she done instead? Caused chaos in the high street, thanks to Dev. No, not thanks to Dev. Not even because of

Dev. Her own stupid fault for allowing Dev to creep under her skin and dominate her thoughts, reduce her to a near-nervous wreck. Ridiculous, really, after all this time, because Holly was safe. She was practically engaged to Alex and so she was safe.

All she had to do now was learn to cope with Dev in body as well as in mind. Easy. Easier said than done. Easier, too, if Alex were around. Easier, too, if the engagement were official, she mused, ashamed of the thought, of the need to hide behind a ring. And though Alex had been pressing her for weeks, she hadn't said yes. She hadn't said no, either, she argued, pacing the length of the terrace. With Alex expected for the weekend, what better time to give him an answer?

Holly's cheeks flamed. Use Alex, she meant. Use Alex to keep Dev at a distance. Could she really be so cold and clinical? Could she afford not to be? the demons in her mind pointed out. Could she go ahead and marry Alex, knowing she loved Dev? She hadn't said no, and she hadn't said yes. So why the delay? Even before Dev's reappearance, she'd been stalling. And, yes, she *liked* Alex, probably loved him in her own way, or as much as she'd ever love another man, any man, apart from Dev. But at least with Alex she'd be safe and Meryl and Jonathan's future would be secure. And put like that, the answer seemed glaringly obvious.

'I still think I should have cancelled, too.'

'And what good would that have done?' Meryl

104

chided softly. 'There's nothing you can do here, Holly, so you might as well go and enjoy the change of company.'

'But I won't know a soul. They're Alex's friends—'

'Exactly. Your friends now. And once you've broken the ice, you'll be fine. You're not even arriving alone, thanks to Amanda. She was perfectly sweet when I phoned to explain and offered at once to send a car. And since Jonathan's temperature is down now, there's nothing for you to worry about.'

'No.' Holly smiled. 'But it won't be the same without you.'

'Fiddlesticks. How many girls want their wicked old stepmother tagging along when they're out on the tiles? You'll have a much better time without me.'

'Wicked, maybe,' Holly allowed. 'But old? That's something you'll never be.'

Meryl simply smiled, pouring each a glass of wine. There was something wrong, Holly mused, sipping hers thoughtfully, something niggling at the back of her mind. Dev? she probed, swirling the ice-cold liquid round and round her glass. The aftershock of the day's events? It had been quite a morning, all things considered, and though she couldn't avoid giving Meryl an account of things, she'd deliberately played it down.

Meryl, being Meryl, had simply nodded. 'You were lucky. The boy did no harm and Dev was around to pick up the pieces.'

'Hardly pieces,' Holly had demurred. 'Just

bruised pride and couple of dented knees.'

'Which won't show, thanks to Dev.'

'No.'

They didn't show tonight in any case, since Holly had opted for trousers, a cream-silk pyjama suit which struck just the right balance between dressy and informality. At least, she hoped it did. In normal circumstances she'd have worn a skirt, but not with sticking plasters on her knees!

The doorbell chimed. Meryl glanced at her watch. 'It looks like your lift's arrived. And bang on time. And don't forget to enjoy yourself,' she reminded her as Holly kissed her cheek.

Holly pulled a wry face. 'I'll try. But my heart's not in it, and if Jonathan gets fractious—'

'He won't. But if he does, I'll phone. Now go. There's the bell again. Someone sounds impatient.'

But if someone wants to leave without me, Holly countered grimly, taking her time as she sauntered the length of the hall, these things can be arranged.

She forced a smile as she swung the door wide. 'Sorry to keep you—*you!*' She stumbled backwards, horrified.

'The very same,' Dev allowed, grinning broadly, and with a theatrical flourish, he swept a deep bow. 'And if madam is quite ready,' he informed her, the laughter rising in his throat, 'her carriage awaits.'

Approaching the lights of Cabourg, Holly broke the terse silence. 'I didn't realize you knew the

106

Cresswells?' she queried, the thought of arriving for dinner with perfect strangers daunting enough without the added strain of Dev and non-communication.

'It's a small world, Holly. And the English community abroad is always a close one. When you mentioned Cabourg, naturally I thought of the Cresswells.'

Oh, naturally, she echoed, irrationally annoyed that she'd let enough slip for Dev to pick up the clues, wangle an invitation. She'd had a fleeting moment of hope when he'd arrived, that Dev was simply the driver, the lift arranged by Amanda Cresswell. But one look at Dev, devasting in white dinner jacket, was enough to blow away that straw. And though the English abroad might be a tightly knit group, surely a couple of weeks on holiday didn't qualify? Clever Dev. Much too clever Dev.

'Strange, isn't it,' he mused, darting her a loaded sideways glance, 'the things we have in common?'

'As you say, it's a small world,' she retorted crisply. Despite the need to arrive on speaking terms, at least, she lapsed into silence. Besides, it was just beginning to dawn on her that Dev knew exactly where he was going.

Cabourg wasn't a large town, rather like a miniature Bournemouth, with its gabled house fronts and manicured lawns, but even so, Holly hadn't a clue where they were, unlike Dev, who seemed to reach a junction and signal almost without a pause. Of course, if he *did* know the Cresswells, he'd be bound to know the way, and

107

since Alex and Deric Cresswell had been friends for many years, the idea of Dev being part of the same circle didn't bear thinking about. To have to meet Dev socially, be polite to Dev, ignore Dev's part in her past? Oh, no! As Alex's wife she wanted to escape, not suffer daily reminders of the nightmare Devlin Winter had created.

'You're nervous.'

Statement, not question, Holly noted, and she moistened her lips before replying. 'I'm never at ease with strangers,' she admitted, climbing the steps to the imposing front door. Another legacy of the past, she thought bitterly. Over-exposure to the media at the height of the scandal and the prurient interest of so-called friends had left their mark. And as she and Meryl had led a quiet life since, Holly's skills as a social hostess were sadly in need of an overhaul.

'But as Mrs Alex Courdrey, you'd be meeting strangers daily,' Dev reminded slyly. 'He's an influential man, Holly.'

'I'll manage, thank you,' she said coldly, beginning to find Dev's sharp insights unnerving.

'No doubt. But if you find you can't face it, you could always stick with me. That way you'd never have to bother.'

'And how do you work that out?' Holly retorted as tiny hairs on the back of her neck began to prickle out a warning.

'Simple, Holly. You'd never be allowed out of bed long enough to dress.'

She flounced ahead, the front door opening almost on cue, but if she was annoyed with Dev, at least his thorny presence had a plus side.

Devastating. Far too good-looking for his own good, she decided, logging the impact he made on the roomful of people, the female half at least. And she'd been wrong. Dev didn't know the Cresswells any more than she did. Friend of a friend of a friend was how Amanda Cresswell phrased it, which threw Holly and Dev together as strangers in the crowd. Hardly a blessing in disguise, she conceded wryly, but...

'Quite a catch. If you can land him.'

Holly turned, hackles raised, goose bumps erupting as she met the woman's hostile gaze.

'I beg your pardon?' Holly murmured, eyeing the elegant redhead warily. She'd been seated next to Dev at dinner, had practically eaten him alive, Holly couldn't help but notice with more than a touch of the green-eyed monsters. And instinctively aware that this wasn't a social call, Holly stiffened.

'Cigarette?' the woman offered, tapping the box open.

'No, thanks. I don't,' Holly replied, watching with awful fascination as she drew on a cigarette, inhaled deeply and allowed a trail of smoke to escape from her nostrils.

'No.' Generous lips curled in contempt. 'That's obvious. Which is why you'll never hold him. Men like Dev Winter like a bit of spark in their women. Believe me, darling, you're simply too young to be of interest.'

'Unlike you, of course.'

Cold green eyes narrowed at once and Holly swallowed a smile. That had thrown her, and though itching to wipe the knowing expression from the woman's beautiful face, Holly resisted. Tempting, very tempting. Only she mustn't. Allow her to goad, give her the satisfaction of rising to her taunts? Oh, no.

The woman leaned across, the heavy scent of musk catching at the back of Holly's throat. 'My dear,' she crooned with her hand on Holly's arm, the vivid red talons that passed for nails incongruous against the pale silk material, 'bitchiness isn't becoming. But, like I said, you're young, you'll learn.'

Amanda Cresswell breezed across. 'Oh, good,' she beamed. 'I'm so glad you've managed to introduce yourselves. Alex will be pleased.'

'Alex?'

'But, of course, Lucy. Surely you've realized. Lucy Trent—Holly Scott.'

Trent? Holly wrinkled her nose. The name was vaguely familiar. And then she remembered. Alex's right hand. The indispensable Miss Trent.

There was a flicker of interest in Lucy Trent's eyes. 'Holly Scott? *That* Holly Scott?' she mused, suddenly alert. And when Holly nodded, 'And Dev?'

'An old friend,' Holly explained, with subtle emphasis on the second word. 'So—not so young after all, hey, Miss Trent?'

She swung away, an unpleasant taste in her mouth. She shouldn't have needled her. Lucy Trent wasn't so much an employee as an invaluable part of Alex's organization. And she was trouble, trouble with a capital T, not to mention hellbent on hooking Dev.

Since the dinner-table monopoly had merely been the opener, she sidled across to Dev at the first strain of music. Cheek to cheek, hip to hip, thigh to thigh, she and Dev were soon smooching round the dance floor as if the rest of the room had ceased to exist. And as for that flimsy dress... Holly's lips tightened. Full length it may be, it did little to disguise the voluptuous curves and with a neckline plunging halfway to her navel, was it any wonder male eyes were straining out on stalks?

Jealous? Holly mused, sipping an overlarge brandy. Hardly, she reassured herself tartly. Hadn't Lucy Trent been jealous of her, been warning Holly off in that less-than-subtle way? Only she needn't have bothered. Dev wasn't hers anymore and that's the way it was staying.

'Wallflower, Holly? Come now, this won't do. Imagine you're Mrs Alex Courdrey and this is your very first At Home. One simply must mingle with the guests, one should know.'

'One does,' she retorted, dismayed by the sudden surge of adrenalin, the rush of colour to her cheeks. And with Dev's vice-like fingers circling her wrist, she reluctantly allowed him to pull her onto the dance floor. 'But Devlin, dear,' she pointed out sweetly, 'you're the last person Alex would invite.'

'Maybe so,' he agreed, black eyes dancing. 'But luckily for me, I have this devastating effect on the female of the species.'

'Meaning?'

'That I'd simply work my charms on the lovely Mrs Courdrey—whoever she may be.'

'You're so sure, aren't you?' she challenged.

'About you?' Dev shrugged. 'Strangely enough, no, Holly. But I do know this. You might be hell bent on marrying Courdrey, but it's not because you love him.'

'And how do you work that out?' she snapped.

'Simple. You love me. Always have, always will.'

'Like I said, Dev, so sure. Always have been, always will be. But in this case, you're miles off the mark.'

'"The lady doth protest too much, methinks,"' he quoted lightly. 'Having trouble convincing someone? Yourself, perhaps?'

'Oh—go to hell!' she bit out, swinging away.

Eleven o'clock. The night was still young but she was tired, the events of the day beginning to take their toll. Being a guest, she was technically free to leave, but she was sharply aware that Dev had hit the nail squarely on the head again. As Alex's wife, she'd be the hostess, couldn't hope to escape until everyone else went home. But she'd learn, was learning fast already, coping with Dev, the sultry Lucy Trent. Trial by fire. But at least she'd have a say in her guest list, and if Devlin Winter were the last man on earth, he wouldn't get a look-in.

She checked the time again. She'd phone Meryl, a renowned night owl who'd be up for hours yet. Though Meryl had promised to ring if Jonathan turned fractious, she wouldn't want to spoil Holly's evening. Spoil her evening? Some chance, Holly railed, since Dev had managed that before it had begun.

A smiling Amanda waved her towards the study. Slipping inside, Holly found the darkness a welcome mantle of peace. And since she was still clutching the glass of brandy, she leaned back against the door, taking another tiny sip before closing her eyes. Peace, quiet—and escape from Dev. And then she heard a noise, her lids flying open in alarm. With the full-length windows open to the warm night air, someone else had slipped inside, and catching that distinctive whiff of musk, Holly froze.

Two figures, she identified, her eyes adjusting to the gloom. The predatory Lucy Trent, of course, and a man, his aquiline nose in profile. Dev. Holly went rigid. She couldn't bear to watch, couldn't bear to tear her gaze away, the woman's throaty laugh sending shivers of fear the length of Holly's spine. Powerless to move, to breathe, to banish the tableau, she looked on in awful fascination as Lucy raised a hand, caressed Dev's cheek before moving on, her fingers sliding round his neck, urging his head down to hers, mouth meeting mouth, body melding with body.

There was the sudden crash of glass, Holly's glass, as the brandy balloon exploded at her feet, and then a flood of light from a nearby table lamp.

'Well, well, well,' Lucy Trent drawled as Holly prayed for the ground to open up and swallow her. 'Look who it isn't. The little girl who never grew up,' she sneered. 'Spying on the grown-ups, Holly? I wonder what Alex would say.' And she moved, sliding her hand into

Dev's, the expression on her face a curious mix of triumph and spite as she glanced from Dev to Holly and back again.

But it was Dev's expression that hurt Holly most, the imperceptible trace of amusement in lazy black eyes.

'Like I said, my dear,' Lucy Trent underlined cruelly, 'it takes a real woman to hold a man.'

CHAPTER 6

'Hardly spying,' she pointed out tersely, 'since I was there first. I simply needed to use the phone.'

'Missing the absent fiancé, Holly?'

'If you must know, I wanted to call Meryl. Jonathan—'

'Is fine. I phoned myself less than an hour ago. He's sleeping like a baby, apparently.'

'But—why didn't you tell me?' she demanded. 'I've been worried sick all night, damn you.' And how had he known? she wondered, sinking into brooding silence. Dev hadn't mentioned Jonathan at all, hadn't mentioned Meryl either. And then she realized. Clever Dev. Wangling an invitation to dinner with strangers and then offering to accompany Holly. Hardly, she allowed as common sense returned. Even Dev couldn't have foreseen Jonathan's illness, had simply been quick to turn things to his advantage. But trust Dev to be in the right place at the right time.

Holly's mouth settled in a thin and angry line. Only it wasn't anger, she acknowledged sickly, that all-consuming emotion that filled her with pain. Anger she could deal with. Dev, flaunting that woman—any woman—she thought in anguish, was more than she could take. Why, Dev? Why? Why? Why? Why now?

Would she never be at peace? Stupid question, really, since she'd lived with the torment so long. And though she loved him, she hated him more.

Dev had had his chance seven years ago. Seven long, unforgettable, unforgivable years of hate. And sitting in frigid silence beside him, suddenly Holly was glad. Flamboyant Lucy Trent had done her a favour. She'd opened Holly's eyes. Dev was footloose and fancy free and could take his pleasure where he chose. Only not with Holly. Because Holly would be strong. Once bitten, twice shy.

Dev had brought the car smoothly to a halt. Only Holly had been too caught up in churning thoughts to notice that he'd left the main road behind and pulled in close to the beach—close to the beach and miles from home judging from the absence of buildings, she realized belatedly.

As Dev cut the engine, snapping off his seatbelt and twisting round to face her, Holly stifled the panic.

'Okay, Holly. Spit it out, whatever it is that's choking you.'

'What are we doing here, Dev?' she asked, hugging her arms to her body, suddenly cold despite the warm night air.

'Talking. Clearing the air. Getting things back onto an even keel.'

'It takes two to talk and I'm tired, Dev.' And I've nothing to say to you that you could possibly want to hear, she tagged on silently, bitterly. 'Take me home, Dev.'

116

'When I'm good and ready.'

'Oh, naturally, sir. Heaven forbid you do something out of the goodness of your heart, especially in your line of business.'

'And what's that supposed to mean?'

'Nothing. Anything. Anything you want,' she snapped. 'You're the journalist, twist it any way you like.'

'But you're the one making wild accusations.'

'Well, I guess that makes us quits,' she sneered.

'What is it with you? You're not making any sense, talking in riddles, freezing me out.'

'Good. Let's hope it stays that way.'

'Come on, Holly. You're not being fair.'

'And since when did fairness enter into anything Devlin Winter ever did?'

'You know something, Holly, you're turning sour. Heaven help Courdrey—'

'When I marry him? Only I'm not, am I, Dev, according to you?'

'If the little girl wants to play at dolls and houses—'

Holly felt the pain slice through her. 'Don't—'

'Don't what?'

'Don't drag my age into every conversation. I'm a grown woman, for heaven's sake—'

'Then it's high time you started acting like one—'

'With you? That is what you're implying, isn't it, Dev?' she queried icily.

'It's—crossed my mind,' he admitted with more than a hint of amusement.

Holly hit him. Pure reflex, she realized later.

At the time she was conscious only of the rifle-shot snap as her open palm connected with his cheek, the sharp hiss of Dev's indrawn breath. Horrified at her loss of control, she flung open the passenger door and scrambled out, kicking off her shoes as her heels sank into the soft sand.

She ran, blinded by tears, heading for the water's edge, half-afraid that he'd follow, more afraid as the minutes passed that he wouldn't, that he'd abandon her, leave her to make her own way home. Not that she could blame him.

The tide was in, had just about turned, judging from the yard or two of wet sand and Holly pulled up, staring out with sightless eyes, the tears pouring silently down her cheeks as she folded her arms and hugged her trembling body, drawing comfort from the sound of the softly lapping waves.

Hours later, it seemed, she sensed his presence at her side. 'Holly—'

'I'm sorry,' she said tightly, her self-control hanging by a thread. 'I shouldn't have done that. I had no right.'

'No.'

Her sensitive ear caught amusement in his tone and she stiffened again.

'But you and I never did play things by the book, hey, Holly?'

'All part of the price you pay for seducing sweet and innocent little me,' she retorted flippantly.

'Don't—'

'Don't what? Tell the truth, rub salt into the wounds? Guilty conscience troubling you, Dev? And to think,' she added hysterically, 'I never knew you had one.'

He pulled her round to face him, vicious fingers circling her wrist. 'You little—'

'Bitch?' she interrupted harshly, her head snapping up in alarm.

'I was going to say, fool. Oh, Holly!' He caught the glint of tears and swore lightly under his breath before pulling her into his arms, Holly stiffening at the contact, common sense and instinct battling in her mind. Then she melted against him, felt his arms close around her, was aware of his heart beating beneath her cheek, of his lips nuzzling her temples.

Suddenly, nothing else in the whole wide world mattered—not the past, not the future, simply the present, being with Dev, touching Dev, kissing Dev. *Yes,* she was kissing Dev, her body craving the touch of his lips against hers, her mind blocking out that other kiss in the darkness, the moment of pain in the Cresswells' study. She was here, now, alone with Dev and there'd been too many nights when she'd cried herself to sleep with just the bittersweet memory of his touch to console her.

And she hadn't forgotten. Her mind hadn't lied. Because she belonged, she'd always belonged in Dev's arms. As he pulled her roughly against him, the thrill ran through her like a flame. She loved him, wanted him, needed him, and Devlin Winter wanted her just as badly!

119

Somewhere deep inside Holly was moaning, because Dev was kissing her, touching her, tasting her. She moved her head from side to side as his mouth feathered the stem of her neck, then moved round to nuzzle the hollow at the base of her throat before sweeping upwards to claim her mouth again, and she closed her eyes, melting into the lines of his body, drowning, drowning in emotion.

'Wonderful, wonderful woman,' Dev murmured against her mouth and then his tongue was pushing through, sweeping on into its hot moist corners, dancing with her own, capturing her own.

Holly raised her arms, running her fingers through the silk of his hair, her breasts rising high against his chest, the contact searing, the sharp hiss of Dev's indrawn breath music to her ears.

Tugging her even closer, he ran his hands across the swell of her buttocks, urging her to meld with his body and the sudden contact with the hardness at his groin sent shivers of need pulsing though her.

'Dev. Oh, Dev!' she murmured, and in her mind's eye they were stretched out on the burning sand, the hot Tenerife sun blazing down on gleaming, glistening, naked skin. She'd been afraid that first time, too, the sheer depth of emotion catching her off guard, the raw, aching, all-consuming need taking her by surprise, the man's beautiful, naked body both compelling and awesome.

And now, as then, Holly didn't stop to

question. They were alone, man and woman, with a need primeval and true. As Dev's hands swept from her buttocks to the curve of her waist and up again, Holly swayed outwards from the pivot of her waist, aching breasts hardening at the first, featherlight touch of thumbs, her nipples standing out despite the constraints of jacket and bra.

'Please, Dev,' she begged as he laughed and skirted the soft underswell of her breasts before brushing lightly against them, an electrifying touch that triggered fresh currents of heat. Then it was Dev's turn to groan as he pulled her roughly back into his arms, hugging her fiercely, his mouth claiming hers, hard and demanding and driving the breath from her body.

Holly gasped as Dev pulled away, the scythe of pain followed by waves of pleasure as long, slender fingers snapped the buttons on her jacket and nudged aside the silky fabric, just the creamy lace bra denying them the contact that they craved.

Dev paused, smouldering black eyes fastened on her face in the soft silver light cast by a moon playing hide and seek among the clouds. 'I want you,' he told her thickly. 'Woman, you've no idea how much I've wanted you.'

'Oh, but I have,' she told him solemnly, smiling inside. Because she wanted him every bit as badly, always had, always would, and she was a fool to deny it, to deny them both. They belonged together. She stood perfectly still as Dev reached for the front fastening of her bra, snapping the catch with a single deft movement and allowing Holly's aching breasts to spring free.

'My woman!' he murmured reverently, his gaze switching from her face, to her breasts and back again. 'Oh, Holly!'

And Holly smiled, closed her eyes as Dev touched first one, then the other, with the lightest touch of a thumb. Then he dipped his head, his mouth closing round a nipple, lips sucking hungrily, teeth nibbling hungrily, and then he was kneeling at her feet, his hands pushing her breasts together, creating a valley tailor-made for his tongue, and Holly stood and trembled, her fingers raking the silk of his hair.

There was a pause, an electric pause, a moment, no more. His hands fastened on her breasts, he angled his head, his gaze compelling and the message flowed out between them: want, need, desire, love, most of all the love she'd never thought to know again, because Dev was here and he wanted her, loved her, needed her and nothing else in the whole wide world mattered. Just Dev.

He dipped his head again, his tongue sliding from breasts to navel, a delicious swirl of warmth and wetness that sent fresh currents pulsing through her, and then he was nibbling at the waistband of her trousers, the side-button fastening no match for deft fingers. As the flimsy fabric dropped away, it seemed the most natural thing in the world to step out of them.

'Oh, God! Holly,' he murmured, gazing up at her, and his eyes never left her face as he shrugged himself out of dinner jacket and shirt, the powerful muscles of chest and shoulders rippling like the waves upon the sand.

Holly smiled again, discarding jacket and bra with an offhand shrug of the shoulders, then she was standing proudly before him, naked but for the tiniest pair of briefs and that silver cloak of moonlight.

'You are wonderful,' he insisted thickly. 'The most wonderful woman in the world and I want you. I want you now. *Now*, Holly,' he growled, and he reached out, his hands caressing the backs of her knees before gliding across the soft, white inner flesh of Holly's thighs, slowly, oh—so slowly upwards, pausing for a single, tantalizing moment at the apex of her legs.

Holly held her breath, watching, waiting, needing, most of all needing *this* man. And as she watched, twin thumbs slid beneath the hem of her panties, plundered the curls, homing in on the pulsing, swollen bud at the centre of her existence, paused—an exquisite moment of hell—before sliding oh-so-gently backwards and forwards, creating a million tiny darts of pleasure. As the waves began, Holly began to tremble uncontrollably and Dev smiled up at her.

'I want you,' he said again, and he nodded, eyes full of knowledge, anticipation, love—

Love! Something vital in Holly's mind died. Love. Devlin Winter didn't know the meaning of the word. Now, as before, he was using her and, the moment she gave in, he'd toss her aside with never a backward glance. Oh, true, she'd have a night or two of pleasure, a week or two of pleasure if Dev was at a loose end, but don't kid yourself, Holly, she forced herself to face, that's all. Where Devlin Winter was concerned, that's all it would ever be.

She twisted free, took an unsteady step backwards. 'No, Dev,' she said simply, eyes full of silent pleas.

His head snapped up as if hit, the pain in his eyes almost more than she could bear and then realization dawned and smouldering hatred came back at her.

'Damn you!' He was on his feet in an instant, pulling her into his arms, his mouth a savage caress as he kissed her, slid his hands beneath the waistband of her panties, skin against skin as his palms cupped her buttocks. 'There's a name for women like you,' he bit out, raising his head, cold black eyes condemning her. 'An ugly name.'

He tugged her even closer, grinding his hips against hers, the strength of his arousal driving the breath from her body, but just as savagely he pushed her away, unzipping his trousers and peeling them over the long, powerful lines of his legs. For a moment, such a dreadful, heart-stopping moment, she thought that he meant to take her there and then. For an equally fleeting moment of madness she trembled inside and wanted him to take her, only Dev swung away, denying her, denying them both as his magnificent naked body headed for the water, reached the line where the beach fell away, and dived cleanly into the ice-cold sea.

Holly stood and shivered. She was cold, mind-numbingly cold, though the night was a mild one, a thin layer of cloud serving to trap the heat of the day. She wasn't sure how long she stood and watched those powerful arms slicing through the water as he swam parallel to the beach but, satisfied he was in no danger, she turned at last, retrieving her clothes and leaving Dev's in a neatly folded pile before heading back to the car. As she guessed, he hadn't locked it, and she dressed in privacy, sat and hugged her knees and watched and waited and wept deep inside.

'Why, Holly?' he asked simply on his return. He'd dressed at the water's edge, planing the water from his body with his hands before donning shirt and trousers. The dinner jacket, clearly ruined, was tossed like a rag into the back of the car as Dev climbed behind the wheel, making no effort to start the engine. 'Why?' he said again. 'You owe me an explanation, at least.'

'Wrong, Dev,' she replied in a voice devoid of emotion. 'I owe you nothing.'

'You wanted me—'

'I wanted you seven years ago,' she reminded him bitterly.

'And this is your idea of revenge?' he asked incredulously. And then, 'Like I said, Holly, there's a name for women like you.'

'Gullible, naive, foolish—' Where you're concerned at least, she tagged on silently. 'And don't forget slut, Dev. Not to mention that other choice epithet on the tip of your tongue. But just for the record, I don't go in for teasing.'

'No?' He turned his head, allowing his contemptuous gaze to flick the length of her body. 'I wonder. Pity help Courdrey if this is your idea of a joke.'

'But look on the bright side, Dev. It might have been you I was cheating on.'

'Not a cat in hell's chance,' he growled. 'No woman cheats on me—ever.'

'No. She wouldn't get the chance—hey, Dev?' Holly pointed out. 'Since you love them and leave with ruthless efficiency.'

'Meaning?'

Holly shrugged. 'Tenerife. Me. A wonderful summer of love, and then—nothing. Nothing for me, at least. Doubtless the payout made it worthwhile for you.'

'Payout? What the hell are you talking about?'

'The money, Daddy's money. It had happened before, you see,' she explained without emotion. 'Lots of times. And the sweet and innocent heiress would be safe from the clutches of men like you. Only Devlin Winter was clever, hey, Dev? You picked your time, waited till Daddy was safely out of the way and then you pounced. And gullible Holly Scott fell for your charms, hook, line and sinker.'

'And is that what you believe?'

'Since you've been conspicuous by your absence for more years than I care to remember, what else am I supposed to believe?' she challenged softly.

'Oh, Holly, if only you knew,' he murmured

126

wearily, running his fingers through the wet, plastered mass of hair and wincing involuntarily.

Something struck her. The scar tissue. She'd caught it earlier, her exploring fingers aware of the puckered ridge of skin at the base of his skull.

'Dev?' she questioned as he put the car into gear, coaxed the engine into life.

He paused, turned his head, the expression in his eyes unfathomable in the gloom. 'Holly?' he queried flatly.

'That woman. The one you were rushing back to when you had your accident. You must have loved her very much?' she probed with a sudden flash of insight.

'Yes, Holly. I did—and I do. She's—a very special lady,' he told her simply.

And beside him in the darkness Holly nodded, a single tear edging its way from under her lashes and trickling silently down her cheek. She was beginning to understand. He'd been hurt, and this was his way of coping. Love them and leave them and kiss goodbye to the hurt. And most of all, don't get involved. No commitment, no pain. Just an idle moment of pleasure. And though the logic couldn't be faulted, it was scant consolation. Dev needed Holly—any woman, she faced with brutal honesty, like a man with toothache needs an analgesic. Nothing more, nothing less. And only the biggest fool alive would ever imagine anything else.

'Someone looks peaky. A late night, Holly? Had a good time, I hope?' Meryl probed, having

127

reassured Holly that Jonathan had slept well. And since Holly had popped her head round the door on her way downstairs, she'd been able to see for herself that his temperature was down and he was clearly over the worst.

Holly shrugged, giving her stepmother a noncommittal smile. Night owl she might be, but there'd been no sign of Meryl when Holly arrived home in the small hours. A diplomatic retreat? Holly mused, blessing Meryl for the thought but wincing at the reality. Even without the scene on the beach, a night cap with Dev would have been the last thing on Holly's agenda. Common sense, she wondered fleetingly, or cowardice?

They'd driven home in silence, the atmosphere strained but no longer seething with hate. Because Dev had managed to temper his disappointment, and Holly was beginning to understand. It did little for the pain, but would help Holly face Dev when she took Jonathan over for his riding lesson on Friday.

'When's Alex due?' Meryl queried, changing the subject. Or maybe it was simply natural thought progression, Holly—Dev—Alex.

Holly almost smiled. Guilty conscience needling, she decided, aware she'd done nothing to feel guilty about, technically at least.

'Saturday morning. I'm meeting him at Deauville with the car. So don't go to any trouble over lunch, we'll eat out.' So much to catch up on, so much to conceal. It would be three weeks since she'd seen Alex last, and though nothing had happened, her whole world had been turned upside down. Would it ever

128

be the same again? she wondered, pushing the half-eaten croissant to one side and pouring another cup of coffee.

'It's decision time, isn't it, Holly?' Meryl challenged softly.

Holly's grey eyes widened. She flushed, meeting Meryl's solemn gaze full on. In her present state of mind, she wasn't sure what Meryl was implying—that guilty conscience sure had a lot to answer for, she acknowledged. And though Meryl might have guessed, might be giving Holly the chance to put her doubts into words, she took the coward's way out.

'Alex—'

'Needs an answer. Expects an answer. And unless I've read things wrongly, you haven't yet made up your mind.'

Holly stifled a sigh. 'No. At least,' she added unhelpfully, 'I have and I haven't.'

'As plain as that, huh?' Meryl observed, smiling this time.

'It's—a technicality,' Holly explained. 'As far as Alex is concerned, we're already engaged. All that's missing is the ring.'

'And a date for the wedding.'

'Yes.' Holly could just imagine it. A thousand and one guests for the wedding of the year. Because Alex would do things in style. Ironic really. Had her father been alive and things turned out the way he'd planned, the pampered only daughter of one of the richest men in the world would have starred in the wedding of the year. And though the wheel had turned full circle, Holly simply wasn't sure—not any more.

'Can I give you a word of advice, mother to daughter?' Meryl probed.

'Of course. But only if you make it sister to sister,' Holly insisted, smiling despite herself. 'You're barely ten years older than I am, remember.'

'Given a certain young lady's acid remarks when I married her father, how could I forget?' Meryl reminded her tartly.

'Ouch,' Holly countered, having the grace to look ashamed, but she knew Meryl was teasing, Holly's bitter accusations long forgiven if not totally forgotten. 'So?' she prompted.

'It's really very simple, Holly,' Meryl told her softly. 'Just do what I did. Ignore what the rest of the world thinks and follow your heart.'

Follow her heart. Marry Alex and make everything right for Meryl and Jonathan—or throw it all away on a man who would take her, use her and ultimately discard her. And though she loved Dev, would follow him to the ends of the earth if he asked her, Holly was achingly aware that Dev already had his own love and that, sooner or later, Holly would be surplus to requirements.

CHAPTER 7

'He's a natural. How come he's never had lessons before?'

Holly flushed. Dev was being polite but the tone spoke volumes. Why didn't Jonathan have a horse—pony—of his own, was what he really meant. And watching Jonathan trot around the stable yard, his body rising and falling in complete harmony with the pony, Holly could understand Dev's curiosity.

It was the first time she'd stayed to watch, was amazed how far Jonathan had progressed after half a dozen lessons. And since she'd been a good rider herself once, she hadn't needed Dev to point out the obvious. Something else Jon had missed out on, she realized with a pang. And though their's was hardly a hand-to-mouth existence, there'd been precious little to spare for the kinds of activity the youthful Holly had carelessly taken for granted.

'Oh, I guess he's never really shown an interest,' she stalled. 'Too many other things claiming his attention.' But not any more, she knew. If Peter was having a horse for his birthday, how long before Jonathan decided on the same?

Dev touched her arm and Holly glanced up in surprise. 'He'll be ages yet,' he pointed out logically. 'Come and have a drink.' And though

Holly didn't reply, he led the way across to the table and chairs set out beside the open kitchen door. 'Coffee? Beer? Fruit juice?' he offered. 'Or a glass of chilled white wine?'

The wine sounded tempting but it was barely midday; since Dev had walked back into her life, her consumption of alcohol had increased drastically. Fruit juice, then. Safer, though she was clearly safe enough out in the yard.

Spotting Francine at the open kitchen window, Holly raised a hand in response to her cheery, *'Bon jour.'* Small and plump and with a permanent smile on her face, the housekeeper spoke no English but her friendly manner had made Holly feel welcome the moment they'd been introduced.

Just like the master of the house, in fact, her wayward mind acknowledged impishly. It was the first time she'd seen Dev since their emotional scene on the beach, but if Dev's thoughts were following that tack, he was giving nothing away. And why should he? He'd been furious at the time, sure enough, but Dev was a virile man and wouldn't be short of offers, she allowed with an irrational stab of jealousy.

Having set the thought in motion, she gazed across the yard with unseeing eyes as a light breeze lifted the edges of her hair and stirred the leaves in the trees. Suddenly cold despite the heat of the day, she folded her arms, goose bumps puckering the lightly tanned skin. Three weeks. Three tense, emotion-packed weeks and, since Dev had clearly been here a lot longer, high time he was moving on. Unless he was working on a story in France? Logical, Holly mused, testing the idea in her mind, since he didn't seem in a hurry to go and hadn't dropped any hints that he'd be leaving soon. Yet he didn't seem to be working on anything in particular—the Devlin Winter hallmark, Holly remembered. He'd given exactly the same impression in Tenerife.

A shrill, squeaky noise pierced the silence, a wheel in need of oiling, and a youth rounded the corner of the house, trundling an empty wheelbarrow. He paused to talk to Dev; though Holly smiled, the boy regarded her warily, kept his head down, seemed reluctant to meet her gaze. And then it hit her.

'But he's—'

'He's?'

'The boy who took my bag,' she exclaimed. 'What on earth is he doing here?'

'Simple, Holly. He's working for me.'

'But—I don't understand. How? Why?'

'He needed a job, Francine needed a hand round the place. Leon works mornings for me and a couple of afternoons at the stables.'

'I'm surprised you would risk employing a thief at your home,' Holly exclaimed without thinking.

'He's not a thief, just a boy,' Dev countered coolly. 'And yes, he took your bag, but he was hungry. Give him the means to feed himself and the need to steal disappears.'

'I hadn't realized you had such touching belief in human nature,' she countered crossly.

'Hardly surprising since you don't know much about me—remember? And if you're so convinced that Leon's a thief, why didn't you turn him over to the police, press charges in the first place?'

Distaste at the thought of having him arrested? Holly wondered. Seventeen, eighteen at the most, he *was* little more than a boy. And since there'd been no harm done...

Holly shrugged. 'To give him a second chance?' she mused.

'Exactly. To give him a second chance.' Dev smiled, but the light didn't reach his eyes. 'Ironic, isn't it?' he bit out. 'You can give a perfect stranger a second chance, yet leave the man you love in hell.'

'I love Alex.'

'So you keep saying. But I'm still not sure who you're trying to convince, you or me?'

'My, my, the arrogant Devlin Winter admitting to having doubts.' She was forced onto the defensive.

'Why not? I'm only human, just like you. I have my hopes, fears, needs—'

'And what about my needs?' she interrupted sharply. 'The need to be left in peace—'

'Marry Courdrey and you'll never be in peace,' he told her harshly.

'Marry you and I'd be living in hell. Oh, but silly me, I almost forgot,' she whipped back. 'That's not what you're offering, is it, Dev? Now a frolic on the beach at midnight, or a tumble between the sheets, for old time's sake, of course—'

'And would you?'

'Would I what?'

'Marry me?'

'Since the question's hypothetical, it hardly requires an answer,' she scorned.

'In other words, no?'

'If you were the last man on earth, Devlin Winter,' she told him sweetly. 'The answer would be no.'

'So sure, Holly. Always so sure,' he castigated coldly.

Not where Dev was concerned. And he hadn't asked, she realized, swallowing the pain as she jumped up, crossing to the fence, her swimming gaze focusing on the horses trotting round the paddock. She spotted Jonathan, waved, watched heart in mouth as he wobbled, almost fell off, but Jonathan simply laughed as he regained control. So self-assured. Just like Dev. Just like Alex, for that matter. A male characteristic, Holly decided sourly. Arrogance.

'He's like your father.'

Holly turned her head.. Dev had joined her, the angry words for the moment pushed aside. Like Daddy? Different colouring, of course, but maybe seeing him through a stranger's eyes, Dev had a point.

'You miss him, Holly, don't you?'

'What do you think?' she muttered crossly.

'I don't think, I know. You were little more than a child when you lost him—'

'Hardly,' she contradicted him coldly.

'No. Given the wanton way you seduced me on that beach, I guess I'd go along with that.'

'And did I?'

'Did you, what?'

'Seduce you?'

'Someone did,' he conceded, lips relaxing in mellow recollection. 'Venus emerged from the waves, the most beautiful, naked woman, and I was lost.'

'Surely you mean child, Dev?' she challenged softly.

'Oh, no, Holly. Not a child. A woman, with a woman's mind, a woman's body, a woman's needs.'

'And yet you walked away. Why, Dev?' she asked, an icy finger touching her heart. 'All this time you've insisted that my age was the problem.'

'Not your age, mine,' he informed her. 'I was too old for you, Holly.'

'Don't lie, Dev. Not now.'

'And what have I to gain from lying?'

'Where you're concerned? Heaven only knows,' she observed bitterly. 'Not money, that's for sure. Not this time, at least.'

'And what's that supposed to mean?'

'Money. The truth, Dev. The real reason you walked away.'

'And I've told you, Holly, you're wrong. What else can I say to convince you?'

'Since the only man who knows the truth is dead—thanks to you—nothing. Nothing that I would care to hear at all.'

'For heaven's sake, woman!' He snatched at her arm, swinging her round to face him, and Holly winced under the sudden blast of anger. 'You're not being fair,' he bit out, black eyes blazing. 'What the hell do you want me to say?'

'Nothing. So save your breath, Dev, your plausible, persuasive, lying breath. Because I know. Because I spoke to Daddy the night he died and I know. He said—'

'Yes, Holly? Just what did he say?' he asked, oh so softly. And the fingers on her wrist tightened as Dev moved imperceptibly closer.

Holly licked her lips, was conscious of nothing in the world apart from Dev, saw the hatred raining down on her and cried inside. Love and hate, twin emotions, the dividing line in between stretched close to breaking point. She loved him, hated him, loathed him, wanted him. Even now she wanted him. No escape. Ever. Because heaven help her, she'd want this man until the day she died. Despite the past. But she'd be strong. She'd deny him, deny them both.

Cringing now under the blast of Dev's contempt, Holly almost laughed. Deny him? She wouldn't have to, she thought hysterically, because Dev hated her every bit as much as she hated him. Love and hate. And right now, hate had the upper hand.

'I'm waiting, Holly,' Dev reminded her icily. 'And I'm running out of patience. What did Gregory say?' he demanded with a dangerous lack of emotion. And he shook her, his hands slipping upwards, digging cruelly into the skin of Holly's upper arms. 'Well?'

'He—Oh, I don't know—'

'Liar!' He shook her again, brought his head in close to hers, and the smell of him, the touch of him, the need she had of him, made Holly go weak at the knees. She closed her eyes, shutting out the man, but not the need, but Dev simply tightened his grip, the sheer bite of iron fingers forcing Holly to open her eyes. 'What did your father say, Holly?'

And since the words were engraved on her mind, Holly told him, word for word, her voice almost as flat as Dev's had been. '"That beach bum,"' she quoted. '"The reporter. I was wrong. Money wasn't the answer. Or maybe it simply wasn't enough."' And she raised her head, tilting her chin in defiance. 'Satisfied now?'

He released her, thrusting her away in disgust, swinging round to face the paddock, leaning on the fence and staring out, defeat written into the lines of his body.

And fool that she was, Holly felt the sting of tears. She rubbed at her arms, soothed the skin that Dev had branded. She was crying inside. The hate had all gone, would only ever be transient where Dev was concerned. And she loved him. And she'd hurt him. He'd asked for the truth and she'd given him the truth, but she'd hurt him, hurt herself more. And she was wrong. She'd lashed out in anger, had used the one weapon guaranteed to keep Dev at a distance—the truth—and she'd hurt him. She didn't have the right to hurt him. Without thinking she reached out, touching his arm.

'Don't!' He shrugged her off as if scalded. 'Don't say or do anything,' he snapped. 'Just leave me alone. Are you listening, Holly?' he emphasized coldly. 'Just leave me *alone.*'

Leave me alone. Ironic, really. He walked back into her life out of the blue, caused chaos from the moment he appeared, and then *he* wanted Holly to leave him alone. Well, had she got news for Dev. Nothing would give her greater pleasure.

'I don't believe you've heard a word I've said.'

Holly banished the shadows, bringing the man back into focus. She smiled apologetically. 'Sorry, sweetheart. I guess I was miles away.'

'Anywhere I know?' Alex queried softly, reaching for her hand.

Strangely enough, no, Holly realized. The two most important men in her life had holiday homes just four miles apart and yet one was completely unaware of the other's existence. She shook her head. 'Just—one of life's little irritations,' she told him airily. 'Nothing for you to worry about.'

'But I do worry,' he told her solemnly. 'Where you're concerned, at least.'

'Yes.' Holly swallowed hard. Alex. Wonderful, caring Alex who wanted to take care of her, wanted to wrap her up in cotton wool and keep her safe and sound for the rest of her life. Not the grand passion that life would be with Dev, but a warm and loving relationship. Because Alex loved Holly, and Holly would make sure that Alex was never shortchanged. She'd be safe, and Jonathan and Meryl would never have to worry about a thing.

'...one or two friends for drinks,' Alex was saying. 'I did think about dinner but—'

'I'm sorry.' Holly blew away the cobwebs. 'Tonight, you mean?'

'Since I'm heading back to London tomorrow, it will have to be tonight, my love. Any objections?'

'To your going home? Too right, I have. Do you have to go, Alex?' she pleaded softly. 'You've only just arrived and it's weeks since we've been together.'

'And absence makes the heart grow fonder? Good.' He smiled, the expression in his eyes causing Holly's heart to skip a beat. 'Because there are times, Holly, when I've wondered if you're ready to commit yourself. You do know what I'm saying, don't you, sweetheart?'

It was Holly's turn to nod, to swallow the lump in her throat. He was waiting for his answer, an answer that was long overdue, and for a moment, a breathtaking moment, she was tempted. Say yes, Holly. Say it now. Kill two birds with a single stone. Make Alex happy and push Dev into the background. The right reason. And the wrong one. Because Alex deserved an answer. But he deserved something else as well, she realized starkly. When Holly finally said yes, she had to be sure that Dev wasn't the deciding factor.

'Soon,' she told him, forcing a smile. 'Very soon, I promise.'

'I'll hold you to that,' Alex replied, and there was something in his tone that sent a shiver of apprehension the length of Holly's spine.

Lunch over, they headed west, Alex's impressive Bentley Turbo lapping up the miles. Why

140

on earth he had to keep such a powerful car when a runaround for the town would have made more sense, Holly had long stopped asking.

She'd driven to the airport in trepidation, glad to relinquish the wheel to Alex for the short journey back, but was still a bag of nerves when they arrived since Alex drove hard, braked hard and paid scant regard to limits on speed. And as for piloting his own light plane... Holly swallowed a smile. He hadn't earned his pilot's wings yet, but he was working on it, and then heaven only knew how often she'd see him.

It would make life easier, Alex had been insisting, allowing him to jet around the globe without annoying delays for commercial planes and connections, but Holly wasn't convinced. Alex was a wealthy man, a self-made man, and expensive toys, she was beginning to think, were just an outward manifestation of Alex's success.

Jonathan met them in the hall, hands and face liberally smudged with crayon. 'Hi, Uncle Alex. Did Holly tell you I'm learning to ride?'

'She sure did. Glad to hear it.' Alex landed a playful punch on Jonathan's arm as he passed, kissing Meryl, who was framed in the doorway. 'Hmm. You look and taste wonderful,' he told her, and Meryl smiled at the cheerful words that Alex never failed to deliver. 'I called in at the house and picked up the mail,' he explained, handing Meryl a large brown envelope bulging at the seams. 'Mostly bills, by the looks of things. Sorry, Meryl.'

She smiled ruefully. 'Never mind. They were bound to catch up with me sooner or later. I'll look at them tomorrow when I'm feeling in the mood. In the meanwhile, I'll fix some drinks.'

As Alex flung himself down on the canopied lounger at the sunny end of the terrace, Jonathan settled on the steps at his feet. 'Look, Uncle Alex, I've drawn a horse,' he exclaimed, reaching for his sketch pad and upsetting the box of crayons. Holly bent to retrieve them. 'That's Holly,' he pointed out proudly, Holly's lips twitching at the stick-lady image that made the horse look like a hippopotamus. 'And that's me and that's Dev—'

'Dev?' Alex showed a flicker of interest.

'This great guy who lives at the stables. He says I'm a natural,' Jonathan revealed proudly. 'We could go across later if you liked. It isn't far,' he explained, his face bright with anticipation. 'And then you can watch me too. And Dev says—'

'Sorry, kid. Another time, maybe.' Alex cut him off, smiling as Meryl placed a tray on the table in front of him. 'Thanks, Meryl. But you shouldn't be waiting on me. Colette could have made the coffee.'

'She's busy preparing dinner. Which reminds me. Any guests? Holly wasn't sure when I mentioned it earlier.'

'Just you and Holly,' Alex conceded. 'But I've invited some friends for drinks later. You don't mind?'

'It's your home,' Meryl reminded.

'But it's your home for the summer,' he

insisted. 'So don't disappear on account of me. We need you here, don't we, Holly?'

'We certainly do,' Holly agreed, and it was there again, a shiver of apprehension trickling down her spine. That guilty conscience again, working overtime and giving her the jitters. Why else read strange meanings into everything that Alex had said so far?

'Deric and Amanda, of course, Brett and Katrina Shires, the Smithsons, the Bryants. Tom Clancy,' he added, grinning broadly at Meryl. 'Still footloose, fancy free and pining,' he revealed as Meryl turned an interesting shade of pink. 'Oh, and Lucy Trent. Did I mention Lucy was over here on holiday?' he asked, switching his gaze to Holly.

'We met,' she conceded, masking her dismay. 'At the Cresswells'.'

'Ah, yes. I'd forgotten.' He grinned again. 'No doubt she'll be bringing along her latest conquest.'

Poor Dev, Holly mocked silently. So easily forgotten, if he only knew.

Alex drained his cup. 'I'll pop up and change, slip into something casual.'

Holly hid a smile. Alex's idea of casual was a novel one. Sure enough, when he returned he was immaculately dressed in tailored trousers and an open-neck shirt. All part of his image, she decided, trying to picture him in faded jeans and a T-shirt. It didn't work and, disconcertingly, a picture of Dev flashed into her mind. Dev, naked and tanned on the beach at Los Cristianos. Dev, stripping off for his midnight swim.

Would Alex strip off on a beach? she wondered. Would Alex waste time on a beach? And the stark fact was, Holly didn't know, was beginning to find that, where Alex was concerned, certain thoughts were anything but reassuring.

'Alone at last!'

'Hardly,' Holly murmured as Alex patted the seat beside him.

'You know what I mean.'

Yes. As always Meryl had diplomatically disappeared, taking Jonathan with her, managing to merge into the background when Alex was around, afraid of playing gooseberry, more afraid of Jonathan being a nuisance.

'He's a nice kid as kids go,' Alex conceded, slipping his arm round Holly's shoulder and drawing her into the lines of his body. 'But...'

Holly stifled a sigh. The 'but' had sounded ominous. She had a sneaking suspicion that Alex didn't like children, that he tolerated Jonathan simply because he was Holly's brother. Half-brother, she amended. And Alex's future brother-in-law. Not 'Uncle' Alex any longer. Just plain Alex. It didn't sound right, she decided, swallowing a smile. Unlike Dev, which tripped naturally off Jonathan's tongue. Dev. Holly stiffened.

'Come on, Holly. Loosen up a little,' Alex whispered in her ear, and Holly was suddenly conscious of his mouth nibbling the stem of her neck as the fingers of one hand brushed the swell of her breast.

'Alex!' She tried to pull away, heard Alex's

low growl as he caught her to him, pulled her round to face him full on, and her grey eyes darkened.

Sky blue eyes danced merrily back at her. 'Look around you,' Alex invited, waving a lazy hand. 'We're alone. The garden's empty, we're shielded from the house and Meryl's far too well bred to stand at a window prying. So—' He paused, his gaze travelling the length of Holly, from her face with the twin spots of colour burning in her cheeks, to her breasts rising and falling beneath the flimsy cotton blouse, then lower, a long, lingering perusal of the curves and convolutions from which a frozen Holly instinctively recoiled. And then he smiled, bringing his gaze back to lock with hers.

'Since we haven't seen each other for weeks, Holly,' he reminded smokily, cupping her face in his hands and dipping his head to brush his lips against hers. 'I've decided that it's high time my blushing bride-to-be showed her fiancé just how much she's missed him—the real way...'

CHAPTER 8

Another spoiled meal, she realized, pushing the exquisite food around her plate. There was an enormous cloud hanging over her and she simply wasn't hungry. Dev? she mused, attempting a mouthful of fluffy salmon mousse and swallowing hard. Or Alex?

Alex. Why the panic? she probed, glancing up to find his surprisingly thoughtful gaze fastened on her face and forcing a smile. She'd known him for over a year now, was practically engaged, would be married within months once the announcement was made. And it was what she wanted, needed, for all of them, Meryl and Jonathan as much as Holly. Alex was security. A lifetime of security with Alex, or a few weeks of pleasure with Dev? No contest. And yet, how mercenary it sounded. Dev. It was all down to Dev. Until Dev reappeared she'd known she was doing the right thing. But now...

'Too many bones?' Alex queried, frowning.

Holly flushed. 'I—yes,' she lied, crossing her fingers and silently begging Colette's forgiveness. 'And I have to be in the mood for fish. My own fault, really, I should have asked for soup.'

'I'll speak to Colette—'

'No.' Holly smiled. 'Please don't. I should have realized earlier.'

'Well, if you're sure...'

Holly nodded. 'I'm sure.' Only she wasn't. Not any more. Not with Dev around.

But if the meal was a trial, thank heavens there were only the three of them. She'd have to mix later, Holly acknowledged. Standing beside Alex, she'd be expected to sparkle and fizz like the bubbles in a glass of fine champagne while Alex showed her off to his friends. But for now it was just the three of them and Meryl, wonderful, wonderful Meryl, kept the conversation flowing, just like a first-class hostess should. Just like Holly should, she realized guiltily.

The moment they finished eating, Holly slipped upstairs to give Jonathan his goodnight kiss. It was a warm night and he was stretched out on top of the duvet, following the picture story in the *Black Beauty* book that Dev had managed to acquire out of nowhere. Dev. Holly smiled wryly. No escape from Dev. Because, all of a sudden, all roads led to Dev—it really was most disconcerting.

'Can I go riding tomorrow?' Jonathan asked, sitting up as Holly appeared.

'Not tomorrow, poppet. The girls don't work on Sundays, remember? But if you're good,' she promised as his clean and shining face fell, 'I'll phone Dev, see if we can squeeze in an extra lesson before Friday.'

He climbed onto her lap, snuggling down into her body, and Holly allowed herself a five-minute snatch of peace. Since they'd eaten early there'd been no real reason why Jonathan shouldn't have joined them. Just an over-cautious Meryl, Holly sensed, ensuring some privacy for Alex and

147

Holly, making sure she and Jonathan didn't impose. Privacy. Time alone with Alex. And, if Alex had his way, she'd have a lifetime alone with Alex.

Holly smothered the panic. It was what she wanted too, she told herself, and allowing another man to come between them at this stage was lunacy. And not just any man. Devlin Winter, who'd already done his best to destroy Holly and her family and, directly or otherwise, had had a hand in her father's tragic death. Could she really risk her future happiness, not to mention Jonathan and Meryl's, all on account of Dev?

As Holly reappeared, Meryl made her escape, popping up to read Jonathan a bedtime story, a very long story, if Holly knew Meryl.

Left alone with Alex, Holly tensed as he patted the space beside him. 'Missed me?' he mused, pulling her down into the curve of his shoulder.

'You know I did,' she replied, aware that he wasn't referring to the time she'd spent with Jonathan. 'Like I said earlier, it's been weeks, Alex. You work too hard.'

'Maybe,' he conceded, nibbling thoughtfully at her ear. 'But maybe I simply want the best in life, for both of us.'

For both of us. How final it sounded. Decision time, Meryl had suggested, and whilst Alex seemed to be hinting, nothing had been said. So—Holly licked her lips. Was tonight the night that Alex finally popped the question?

His nibbling mouth moved round to hers.

'Mmm. You taste wonderful,' he told her, gathering her to him.

For a moment Holly froze, then she forced herself to relax, to allow Alex to kiss her. A grand passion it would never be, but Alex was a man of the world, knew how to kiss a woman, would know how to please a woman. As his tongue slid through into the moist corners of her mouth, Holly swayed against him, gave herself up to the moment, her mind blocking out the reality, and she felt herself respond, heard the man's growl of pleasure.

Suddenly it was Dev who filled her mind, Dev she was kissing, and for an unbelievable moment she really did believe it, her heart soaring skywards as the kiss deepened, tongue entwining with tongue as mouth against mouth, lips against lips, Holly slipped into another dimension.

And he was kissing her, coaxing, teasing, generous lips exploring, hands exploring, stroking, hands sliding upwards and brushing the swell of her breasts and Holly wanted him to touch her, wanted him, needed him, her nipples rigid with the need, craving the touch of Dev's hands, Dev's fingers and—No!

She pulled away, the shock registering in her eyes. Not Dev. Alex. An amused Alex, whose smouldering gaze now travelled her body, from the flushed cheeks and overbright eyes, down the long column of her throat to the deep V of her cleavage, where aching breasts were rising and falling, rigid nipples standing out against the flimsy fabric of the dress; a frank, appraising

149

glance that seemed to narrow in speculation as Alex brought his eyes back to lock with hers.

'Oh, Holly,' he murmured softly. 'Absence really has made the heart grow fonder, hey, my love?'

She nodded, forcing a smile, was saved from the need to reply by the doorbell chiming, and then Meryl popped her head round.

'I'll organize the drinks while Colette lets them in,' she insisted. 'And yes,' she added enigmatically, nodding at Alex, 'everything's ready.' And though alarm bells were ringing in Holly's mind, she was too overwrought to make sense of the secret smile that passed between them.

For once Holly was grateful for the crowd—safety in numbers, she acknowledged sickly, sipping her wine and determined to make it last. Since she'd met most of Alex's guests before, it was nothing like the strain it might have been, mainly thanks to Meryl, who glided from group to group, ensuring that glasses were well filled and everyone was happy.

Then she spotted Meryl in a corner, hemmed in by Tom Clancy, Meryl's silent but frantic signal for help ignored by an unrepentant Holly. Meryl could look after herself. It would do no harm to remind her that she was a young and attractive woman who deserved to have fun once in a while. A successful model with the world at her feet, she'd given it all up to marry Holly's father, for love, as it happened, though Holly hadn't thought so at the time, and, though things had gone drastically wrong, Meryl had

150

never once complained, simply accepting the hand that life had dealt.

'Just Lucy to come,' Alex observed, checking his watch and shrugging. 'Hellbent on arriving late and making a grand entrance, if I know Lucy. She's flying back with me tomorrow so she's probably making the most of the last night of her holiday. And talking of holidays, I'm keeping the last two weeks of August free for us. Have you anywhere special in mind?' he asked, threading his fingers through Holly's and tugging her outside.

'And what's wrong with Houlgate?' Holly asked, the fact that he'd chosen the shadowy corner of the terrace strangely disconcerting.

'Too crowded, of course,' he growled, and before Holly had time to realize his intentions, he'd taken the glass from her fingers, placed it on a nearby table and pulled her into his embrace. A moment later he was kissing her, his lips suddenly hard against hers, his tongue pushing through into the depths of her mouth, and though Holly froze, Alex seemed not to notice, the kiss lengthening as he urged her into the long lines of his body, and Holly gasped, aware of Alex's body responding to the contact with hers. Damping down the panic, she closed her eyes, closed her mind, emptied her mind.

She was passive, accepting the thrust of Alex's tongue, the touch of his fingers, just as she had with all those others. Acquiesing, pretending, hating each and every moment yet, heaven help her, this was the man she was planning to marry and—

151

'Alex—whoops, darling! Didn't mean to interrupt!' An amused female voice, Lucy Trent, Holly identified, springing guiltily away from Alex, who simply laughed as he tugged her possessively back to his side.

Bracing herself, Holly raised her head, met the other woman's gaze, the scorn apparent even in the shadows. Her glance slipped over Lucy's shoulder and onto the man beyond, their eyes locking, the expression in his hooded in an instant. But not before Holly had time to log the pain, the disbelief, the hate, and was aware she hated herself more.

'Dev Winter? Now, where have I heard that name before?' Alex mused as they shook hands. He smiled. 'Ah, yes, young Jon. He's been full of you all day. You work at the stables, I gather?'

'Not exactly,' Dev allowed, accepting the drink proffered by Colette's husband, pressed into service as a waiter.

'So, what exactly do you do?' Alex probed, and amazing though it seemed, Holly sensed vibes of hostility quivering on the air as the two men squared up to one another.

'Oh—this and that,' Dev allowed airily, sipping his wine. He raised his glass. 'An excellent Chablis,' he pronounced, neatly side-stepping Alex's bald enquiry. 'My compliments, Mr Courdrey, you keep an excellent cellar.'

'Thank you. And the name's Alex. Lucy, my dear, be a darling and introduce Dev to the others.'

It was a dismissal. Even Holly was struck

by Alex's peremptory manner, but Dev simply raised a lazy eyebrow, tossed a mocking smile at Holly and allowed the simpering Lucy to drag him away by the hand.

'If he's a stable hand, then I'm the Prince Of Wales,' Alex declared once Dev was out of earshot. 'Winter? I can't think why, but the name rings a bell. Just what does he do for a living?' he queried sharply.

Holly shrugged. 'You heard Dev. This and that.' She shrugged again, risking a sideways glance. 'A euphemistic term for a journalist, apparently.'

'With a journalist's nose for a story. Hmm. Interesting. Has he been hanging around long?'

'Here? In Houlgate, you mean? He's down for the summer, as far as I know. On holiday.'

'Holiday? A reporter on holiday?' Alex gave a snort of derision. 'I'm surprised you can stand the man at all, given the hounding the press gave your father. Surely you can't have forgotten?'

'Do we have to discuss Dev?' Holly queried, half-afraid that if Alex raked his mind he'd somehow link Dev with that disastrous summer, would cause a scene and, worst of all, upset Meryl, who was blissfully unaware of Dev's connection with the gutter press and the part he'd played in the death of her husband.

'We don't *have* to do anything,' Alex replied unexpectedly. 'You and I, Holly, can do as we choose. It's our house, our party, our life. Just tell me what you want, and I'll wave a magic wand and it's yours.'

'How about another glass of wine?' she

153

murmured, finding Alex's lightning changes of mood unnerving.

'If madam's sure that's all she wants...' Alex shrugged, casting a vain glance about for Henri. 'Madam's wish is my every command. But it looks like I'll have to fetch it myself. Stay here. I'll be back in an instant.'

He was as good as his word, was back before Holly had time to blink. It was her third glass of wine and it was beginning to go to her head. She was a bag of nerves, and no wonder, with Alex and Dev under the same roof But she'd been a bag of nerves to start with, she acknowledged.

And she barely recognized Alex in this strange mood, was beginning to wonder if she knew the man at all. He was—different somehow, more possessive, and she was beginning to suspect there were facets to Alex she'd never even dreamt about. Always a force to contend with, there was something about him tonight she couldn't come to terms with. Possessive. Yes. That was it. What Alex Courdrey wanted, Alex Courdrey bought. And it was just beginning to dawn on Holly that she was next on the shopping list.

He slid his arm around her waist, pulling her close, leading her back into the house to rejoin the others. Yet another possessive gesture, she acknowledged, finding his whole manner unnerving. The kiss, the strange glances, the loaded words—it all seemed out of character somehow.

Until tonight he'd never made any demands, had been content to let Holly set the pace.

And yes, they'd kissed—he could hardly ask her to marry him without some sort of physical contact. But it was nothing like the kiss in the garden that Lucy and Dev had witnessed.

Yet why the concern? She was a woman of the world, for heaven's sake. She'd made love with Dev, had had more men than she cared to remember in the bad days, the dark days when her father died and Dev walked away. So why behave like a skittish virgin now? She was on the verge of getting engaged, she chided silently, just a step away from marriage. Marriage, she whipped herself silently. Man and woman, body to body.

Only, it was Dev's body that sprang to mind, Dev's kisses she was craving. Because Dev had walked back into her life and was creating waves in her ordered world. Until Dev came back, she'd been happy with Alex. But you hadn't said yes, the voice of her conscience reminded her. You were going to say yes, she replied. It was all a matter of time. Time. She needed time, was aware from Alex's expression that she was running out of time. Tonight. It was crunch time, Holly. Because she knew, instinctively she'd known all day, that tonight was make-up-her mind time.

Follow your heart, Meryl had told her. And somehow Holly would have to find the strength to make that decision. Now or never. Alex or Dev. No. Not Dev. Devlin Winter wasn't in the frame. Just Alex. And in that case, she was a fool to let Dev needle her. Ignore Dev. He was nothing more than a temporary distraction.

155

The music on the stereo came to an abrupt end, the sound of laughter and voices suddenly over-loud. Alex bent his head, kissed her neck. 'Won't be a moment,' he reassured her and, for the first time in what felt like hours, Holly was alone. The relief lasted less than thirty seconds.

'Congratulations,' a low voice murmured at her side. 'If I hadn't seen it for myself, I'd never have believed it. Oh, yes, I'd heard of you, of course, heard the rumours about you and Alex tying the knot, but...'

'But what?' Holly queried coldly, staring into the diamond-bright eyes of Alex's personal assistant.

Lucy Trent's mouth formed the semblance of a smile. 'Let's just say, I didn't think you had it in you. After all, you let Dev slip through your fingers. Careless, I'd say.'

'And you haven't, I suppose?' Holly challenged, wondering just how much Lucy Trent knew about Holly's relationship with Dev.

'What do you think?' Lucy riposted gleefully, and her contemptuous gaze swept over Holly, finding fault in the dress, probably finding fault in the body beneath, Holly wouldn't mind betting. The same age, the same height, the same build, the two women were chalk and cheese.

Lucy Trent was sophisticated and voluptuous in a slinky black dress that clung to the contours of her body, leaving little to the imagination, sophisticated in a way that *she* could never be, Holly noted sourly. And yes, from a distance the

156

woman had appeal, would always have appeal for certain men. For Dev? Holly wondered fleetingly, her mind skittering away from the thought.

And Holly, the chalk or the cheese? she probed, her face almost bare of make-up, the pale grey, diaphanous dress emphasizing the steel of her eyes, the cut exquisite, the cost more than she could afford, but the whole effect pleasing. Until now.

Locking eyes with Lucy Trent, she saw herself through Dev's eyes. Holly Scott, fair-skinned, fair-haired, squeaky clean and shining. And next to the flame-haired, flamboyant Lucy Trent, totally devoid of colour. Washed out. Yes. That just about described her. Washed out. And yet, she consoled herself, clutching the threads of dignity, Alex wanted her. Dev wanted her, too, in his own warped way.

'So where's Dev now?' Holly enquired waspishly. 'Not stood you up, I hope, gone home without you?'

Lucy Trent glanced casually around. 'Oh, worry not,' she reassured, those red-lacquered talons patting Holly's arm. 'He'll be in the garden waiting for me. There's a secluded little spot down in the corner, you know.'

Holly did. Hadn't Dev taken Holly there, kissed her, almost made love to her? The knife blade twisted. The rat! Clearly the place for Dev's sordid assignations. How else could Lucy know the spot existed?

Darting her another malicious smile, Lucy drifted away in a cloud of heavy perfume.

157

She must reapply it every hour, Holly decided sourly. Though in need of some fresh air to clear her nostrils, clear her mind, she was afraid of bumping into Dev if she left the house, would hate to be accused of spying on Lucy and her conquest.

Desperate for a snatch of peace, she went upstairs. She'd look in on Jonathan, then pop to her own room to powder her nose. Her lips twisted wryly. Powder her nose, comb her hair and add the merest touch of lipstick though, on second thoughts, she'd do that first.

Unconscious of the irony of condemning Lucy Trent for a similar habit, she sprayed her wrists with perfume. Ilexia. Light and fragrant and with merest hint of spice, it was new, a present from Meryl, who'd brought it back from a shopping trip to Paris at the beginning of the holiday.

'Just a little thank-you for looking after Jon,' she'd explained. 'And when I saw the name, I simply couldn't resist it. Ilexia. Like your father's yacht, it could have been named for you.' And Holly had been touched, expensive bottles of perfume being one of the first casualties of life on a budget. And it *was* expensive, Holly acknowledged, turning the bottle over, her fingers tracing the bold French script she didn't understand. *'Pour celle que j'aime...'* Something to do with love, she decided, recalling the words of a song and she was smiling to herself as she closed the door and stole back up the hallway.

Only, reaching Jonathan's room, she caught the sound of voices and halted, darting back as

158

the door swung open. Too late, Dev's solid body filled the frame, and catching the expression on his face, Holly froze.

'Congratulations, Holly,' he sneered with cruel echoes of Lucy Trent. 'It looks like you've landed the catch of the season.'

'Don't be so revolting,' she hissed. 'And will you please keep your voice down?'

'Why? Afraid the great man himself will hear me? Or more afraid that he'll see us together and jump to the wrong conclusion? Though, on second thoughts,' he added slyly, folding his arms and watching her from under hooded lids, 'he might jump to the right one.'

'And what's that supposed to mean?'

'You know. You and me. Man and woman. Together.'

'History, Dev. Whatever you and I had, it was all over long ago.'

'That's not how it seemed last time, Holly. You and me,' he reminded. 'Man and woman. Together. Naked on a beach at midnight.'

'You might have been naked, I—'

'Was fully clothed, give or take the odd technicality? A pair of briefs, Holly. Very brief briefs, Holly. Cream lace, high-legged—'

'Don't—'

'Don't what?' he enquired mildly, too mildly. 'Don't recall every word, every gesture, every touch? And I do, Holly,' he told her solemnly. 'Each and every moment is engraved upon my mind. And you wanted me. You might have denied it, you might have backed away, but you wanted me. I know. I touched you. Remember where I touched you, Holly?'

'No!' Her cheeks burned with the shame.

'Yes!' He moved close, too close, and Holly backed away, brought up sharp by the wall behind. Logging her panic, Dev laughed. 'No escape, my little tigress,' he told her. 'No escape. Ever.' And he kissed her, briefly, insultingly, his hands slipping into the curves of her body as he tugged her into the hard lines of his. He made Holly gasp at the contact, the proof of his arousal shocking her, and then, just as insultingly, he thrust her away.

Holly felt her knees buckle, would have fallen but for Dev, his hands shooting out to hold her, steady her, his eyes locking with hers, then he swore lightly under his breath and she was back in his arms, the hatred for the moment pushed aside.

She was kissing him, was aware of Dev tugging her through a doorway and into the welcome darkness of the spare room, was aware that it was wrong, but too right to be wrong, and allowed Dev's mouth to plunder hers.

Madness, summer madness. And Dev was right. No escape, ever, because she wanted him, always had, always would. From the moment they'd met. Summer madness. Madness on the sand. And she loved him, wanted him, needed him, needed him to hold her, to kiss her, to touch her, to fill her with heat, and pushing herself into the rigid lines of his body, Holly knew that Dev wanted her every bit as badly. Madness.

A lifetime passed before Dev calmed the

160

frenzy, raised his head, allowed his eyes to lock with Holly's in the soft glow of light thrown up from the garden beneath.

'Hell, woman, you drive me crazy,' he murmured. 'The taste of you, the touch of you, the smell of you. Mmm.' He inhaled deeply, nibbling at her mouth all over again. 'Ilexia. What excellent taste in perfume, my dear,' he teased on a lighter note.

'How on earth—?'

He put his hand to her lip. 'Hush. I'm a man. I know about these things. Trust me.'

Trust him. The one thing Holly couldn't do, she realized sickly, making her way back downstairs. Ten minutes. Ten minutes and Dev had managed to turn her world upside down again. But if nothing else was clear, one thing was glaringly obvious. She couldn't marry Alex. Not yet. Not until she'd purged Dev Winter from her system once and for all. The question now, of course, was how?

CHAPTER 9

'Sweetheart. I wondered where you'd got to?'

It was a question, not a statement, and gazing up into Alex's cloudy blue eyes, Holly's heart sank. She was going to hurt him. Whichever way she looked at it, she would hurt him. And for what? So she could carry on battling with her conscience? But if Alex would only give her time...

If she could stall him, head him off...a couple of weeks, a month or two. That's all she needed. Just to get things straight in her mind. Just to be sure that by committing herself to Alex she was doing the right thing. Marriage was a solemn step. Till death us do part. And she had to be sure she was doing the right thing for all of them.

'I—popped up to see Jonathan—'

'You ruin that child,' he interrupted crossly. 'And at this hour of the night he should be asleep.'

'With a houseful of people and enough noise to waken the dead?' Holly pointed out as evenly as possible. 'And you surely don't begrudge five or ten minutes spent with my brother?'

'Fifteen. And I was worried. One minute you were here, the next you'd disappeared. And since Winter was conspicuous by his absence—'

'You put two and two together and, bingo!

162

It's nice to know you trust me,' she added, a guilty conscience fuelling the sarcasm.

'Not at all. As I said, I was worried. He's a journalist and I won't have you pestered under my roof. So if he wasn't with you, where the hell has he disappeared to?'

'Probably cosily ensconced in a dark corner of the garden with the voluptuous Lucy Trent,' Holly suggested. Since Dev hadn't reappeared, Lucy's earlier dart shot home with devastating accuracy.

'Hmm. You're probably right.' Alex grinned. 'Rather him than me,' he added. 'Given Lucy's maneating tendencies.'

'Don't you like Lucy?' Holly asked as a knife blade twisted.

'Like her?' Alex shrugged. 'She's good at her job, one of the best, and she's fun to be with at times like this. But as for liking her—' He shrugged again. 'She's had more men than I've had hot dinners. Not my type at all. Worried, Holly?' he asked slyly.

'Should I be?' she stalled, aware that her own past was a closed door to Alex and, if he regarded Lucy as some kind of slut, where did that leave Holly?

He laughed, pulling her to him and giving her a reassuring hug. 'No, my love. Believe me, I like my women a little less shop-soiled. Sweet and innocent, just like you.'

Sweet and innocent. Such innocuous little words, really. But if Alex was expecting to find his bride a virgin on their wedding night... Holly smothered an hysterical giggle. In this day and age? Not impossible, she could allow, but unlikely. But since they'd never discussed it... Her heart sank. The old double standards. Alex was a man of the world. He wouldn't be going to his marriage bed a virgin, Holly would stake her life on it. But how ironic if he really did expect Holly to be as pure as the driven snow.

The night seemed neverending, with Holly's nerves as taut as fiddle strings. But if Alex rarely left her side, Lucy Trent seemed glued to Dev's. Dev and Alex. Like Lucy and Holly, chalk and cheese. The same age, give or take a year or so, the same build, Devlin dark and devastatingly handsome, Alex ruggedly blond and with those piercing blue eyes that missed little as they darted about the room. Alex, sharp and decisive. Dev, lazily incisive. Chalk and cheese. The man she was expected to marry, and the man she loved.

Loved and hated, she amended. Loved and hated for seven long, lonely years. And since she'd managed to survive that, she could surely survive the next seven and the seven that followed? Follow her heart or her head? Holly didn't know, but she hoped and prayed that Alex would give her the breathing space she needed to make the right decision for everyone.

The music halted abruptly and all eyes turned to Alex, who'd moved to the stereo. Holly glanced round, a vague unease eating away at her. Meryl. She'd seen little of her stepmother all evening, Tom Clancy having managed to monopolize her, but since Tom was standing at an open window, glass in hand and morose expression on his face, he clearly hadn't managed to pin Meryl down. So where on earth had she got to? And then Holly saw her, Meryl's eyes brimming with silent apology as they locked with Holly's across the room. And, logging the tray of glasses—champagne flutes, Holly amended—and the distinctive bottles a flushed Colette was clutching, Holly's heart sank.

A dream, or a nightmare? she wondered as Alex beckoned her forwards, and wooden steps carried her across as everything faded—the noise, the colour, the knots of friends with their bright, smiling faces.

'Well, folks,' Alex murmured, popping the first cork, 'it's celebration time.' And he filled two glasses, allowing the froth of bubbles to subside before filling them to the brim. Passing one to Holly, he raised his glass, beaming at Holly, beaming at his guests and pausing, partly for effect, partly to give Colette and Henri time to hand round the wine. Then, reaching for Holly's hand, he drew her to his side, his gaze switching from Holly, to the roomful of people and back again.

'Friends, a toast,' he declared, piercing blue eyes fastened on Holly, refusing to allow her to look away. 'Though,' he amended playfully, 'since it all depends on Holly, I hope it is. But if I don't ask, I guess I'll never know. So, here goes. Holly,' he said solemnly, a hint of a smile playing about the corners of his mouth, 'will you marry me?'

She drew back the pretty floral-patterned curtains, allowing bright fingers of light into the room. It was the same scene she'd woken to every day for the past three weeks and yet today her eyes were unseeing, unfocused, Dev's shocked expression filling her mind.

'Will you marry me?'

The most wonderful words in the world if the right man is saying them. And as the roomful of people had held their breath, Holly had prayed for the ground to open up and swallow her. Clever Alex. Clever, clever Alex, who always got what he wanted, bought what he wanted, if there was no other way. And, by choosing to propose in public, he'd made sure that Holly couldn't refuse. Will you marry me? And Holly had closed her eyes, blocking out the man, the room, the stark realization that Alex had trapped her.

How to refuse, to let a man down gently? Embarrass him in public, make a fool of him in front of his friends? It would take a harder woman than Holly to do it. Clever Alex. But there was always later, she'd reassured herself, clutching at the straw. A couple of weeks, a month, time for the excitement to die down. And then she'd have to tell him—she really would have to tell Alex the truth.

So—she'd opened her eyes, unseeing eyes that had crossed the room unerringly to Dev, had pulled Dev sharply into focus, reading the pain, that fleeting glimpse of desolation that would live with her forever. Then the shutters had come down and the glance that he had shot back at her was full of cruel indifference.

Damping down the panic, she'd licked her lips, her gaze sweeping from face to smiling face, Dev to Alex and back again. And, as Holly had read her answer in each and every set of sparkling eyes, her racing heart had turned to stone.

'Well, sweetheart?' Alex had prompted, and Holly had woken from the dream to find she *was* living that nightmare. Because she'd caught a movement out of the corner of her eye as Lucy Trent slid possessively close to Dev, her red-taloned hand deliberately brushing the front of Dev's trousers, Dev's hand closing round to hold it in place. Something vital had died in Holly's mind—she'd nodded, smiled, heaven only knew how, but she'd forced her lips into the semblance of a smile, and then she'd turned to Alex.

'Yes, Alex,' she'd told him, tears hovering dangerously on her lashes. 'Of course I'll marry you.'

The rest of the night had been a blur: hugs, kisses, congratulations, champagne, far too much champagne on top of all the wine. No wonder her head was splitting.

Oh yes, and Meryl's worried expression. 'This is what you want, isn't it, Holly?' she'd probed softly as the two women embraced. 'You're doing it for yourself? Not for me and Jonathan, not for Alex. You're doing it for yourself?' And Holly had nodded, Meryl's smile of relief like the sun coming out from behind a cloud.

So many smiling faces. Just Dev's expression

striking a note of discord, outwardly composed but the contempt crystal clear to Holly. Because Dev despised her. But since the feeling was mutual, she had consoled herself, maybe now they were quits.

A solitary tear forced its way out from under her lashes. Holly brushed it away with an angry sweep of her hand. Not a good idea, she decided as the pain sliced through. Hell, but she needed something for that headache.

She pulled up short in the kitchen doorway. 'Couldn't you sleep either?' Holly murmured in surprise as Meryl jumped guiltily, shuffling an envelope beneath a magazine. Early-morning starts were a very rare occurrence for Meryl.

'Too much champagne,' Meryl admitted over-brightly. 'On top of all that excitement. Sit down and I'll make us some coffee.'

She turned away, filling the kettle, keeping her back to Holly. Spotting the bottle of painkillers, Holly half-smiled. It was scant consolation, but she was glad she wasn't alone with an army of little men hammering away inside her skull. She reached across the table, fingers closing round the bottle as her trailing sleeve nudged the magazine. As it began to slide away she made a grab but, reactions clumsy, she missed, instead nudging it over the edge and onto the floor along with a batch of buff-coloured envelopes.

On the point of reaching down, she caught Meryl's gasp of dismay and pulled up sharp. 'What is it?' she asked, moving swiftly to her side.

Meryl shook her head. 'Nothing. Nothing for

you to worry about,' she insisted, her exquisite face crumpling as the tears began, great, heaving sobs that filled Holly with foreboding.

'Meryl! Oh, darling.' And she folded her arms around her, holding, simply holding, reassuring, soothing, till the worst of the storm had passed. When the sobs turned to sniffs, she steered Meryl back to her place at the table, handed her a box of tissues, gave her shoulders another brief hug of reassurance and then turned her attentions to the coffee.

'Here. It's hot, sweet and black and will have you back to normal in a jiffy.'

The minutes passed. Holly didn't speak, eyeing Meryl thoughtfully and sipping her coffee, waiting, simply waiting for Meryl to pick her time. And an uninvited guest sat between them on the table—the pile of buff coloured envelopes that could only be bills.

'I—shall have to sell the house,' Meryl murmured at last.

'Oh?' Holly queried, her voice carefully neutral. Sell the house, the last tangible link with Daddy? Things must be bad.

'Yes. This is from the bank.' Selecting a crumpled sheet from amongst the pile, Meryl smoothed it out with fingers that shook. 'It seems I'm overspending,' she explained tightly. 'Have been overspending for some time, and, well, they've finally run out of patience,' she ended almost defiantly.

'But—I don't understand. We can't owe them that much, surely?' Holly queried.

'We don't. I do. My problem, not yours.'

169

'Our problem,' Holly contradicted softly. 'And we can weather the storm. However much we owe, we *can* weather the storm.'

'No, Holly. Not this time,' she contradicted starkly. 'I've been living on borrowed time for years, and well—' she shrugged, a wealth of misery in her eyes '—this is it. My own stupid fault for burying my head in the sand and expecting someone else to wave a magic wand.'

'But—why didn't you say?' Holly asked, scanning the letter from the bank and wincing at the figure that leapt off the page. 'If I'd known, we could have cut down, made a few economies—'

'Like living on fresh air?' Meryl cut in drily. 'Oh, Holly, love. Think. Who do you think has kept us going so far? You. Don't you see? We'd never have coped without your money. And you did cut down. You lived on next to nothing, for heaven's sake. You put everything you earned into the household expenses pot and spent next to nothing on yourself. And since you lost your job...'

She didn't need to finish. Since Holly's job had come to an end, things had been going from bad to worse. And, since Meryl wouldn't recognize an economy drive if it hit her in the face, it had always been just a matter of time. But if Meryl had buried her head in the sand, she wasn't the only one. So—it was all down to Holly. She'd had seven years of leaning on Meryl and now it was her turn. It was the least she could do. And once she was married to Alex, none of them would never have to worry about a thing.

And since that's what she'd envisaged all along, this feeling of doom hanging over her really was ridiculous.

It was a tense drive to the airport, Holly absurdly relieved to wave goodbye to Alex, equally relieved that she'd avoided bumping into Dev and Lucy Trent. And they would be together, Holly decided, amazed that Lucy hadn't contrived to flaunt her latest conquest in a fond farewell scene before climbing the steps of the aircraft and waving him off in a cloud of heavy perfume.

Bitch. Probably, Holly acknowledged, her lips tightening at the thought of Lucy and Dev together, Lucy and Dev kissing, Lucy and Dev making love. No! She pulled her thoughts up sharp. She was engaged to Alex now. It was high time all thoughts of Devlin Winter were banished from her mind.

'Got you!'

'Dev!'

'The very same,' he murmured grimly, snaring her wrist and pushing her back against the bodywork of the car. 'Okay, lady, talk!'

'To you? What about?'

'You and Courdrey,' he suggested coldly. 'That touching little pantomime you put us through last night. Or better still, you and me.'

'You and me don't exist, remember?' she snapped, aware of a sudden weakness in her

171

knees, of the currents of heat swirling out from the points of contact on her wrist.

'No? Well, in that case, lady, neither does this.' And he dipped his head, kissed her, briefly, bruisingly briefly, cold black eyes pinning her as he raised his head. 'Well?'

'Well, what?' Holly stalled, her stomach churning, the waves of heat running through her treacherous body.

'Don't!' he insisted tightly. 'Don't play games with me. You love me, damn it!'

'Do I? Do I really, Dev?' she enquired, angling her head to meet his gaze, that arrogant gaze that seemed to bore right through to her soul.

'Oh, yes, Holly. Either that, or you're the best little actress this side of Hollywood. And yet, why not?' he sneered with an ugly curl of the lips. 'Courdrey's clearly besotted, so he must be convinced, more fool Courdrey. And as for me—'

'Yes, Dev? As for you?' she queried with an icy calmness that was sheer bravado. Actress? Hardly, she acknowledged, but she was learning, and learning fast. Alex, Dev, the roomful of people last night. And herself. No. She wasn't fooling herself. But the truth had to be buried once and for all, for all their sakes.

'I'm a bigger fool than Courdrey, hey, Holly? Because I know. I know you, and I know the way you and your kind operate. And heaven help me, I still desire you.'

'No, Dev.' Holly swallowed hard, shook her head. Love. Desire. Need. Of all the words that

Dev could have used, he had to pick the one that carried no commitment. Desire. Nothing more, nothing less. 'Be honest at least.' she berated coldly. 'You never really wanted me. If you had, you'd never have walked away, left me, left me to pick up the pieces of a life that you helped to destroy.'

'I walked away because I cared.'

'Well, that makes two of us. Because I care. I care about Alex, which is why I'm going to marry him.'

'Oh, yes?' He twisted her wrist, glanced scathingly at the ring that Alex had placed on her finger ten hours earlier. 'Quite a rock,' he acknowledged, his voice oozing contempt. 'And just the thing for a spoilt little rich girl. Holly Scott,' he jeered. 'Every inch her father's daughter. And that's what this is about, isn't it, Holly?' he demanded tersely. 'Money. Courdrey's money to add to Gregory Scott's stockpile.'

'Leave my father out of this.'

'Why? Why the hell should I? Does the truth hurt, Holly? Can't you face the cold, hard facts of life?'

'Facts? Ha! For a journalist, Dev, there are definite flaws in some of your reasoning,' Holly flung out without thinking.

'Meaning?'

'Nothing. Nothing for you to worry about,' she retorted, dangerously close to blurting out the truth.

Dev's fingers tightened their grip. 'Just what are you saying, Holly?' he asked, his head close

173

to hers, his eyes locked onto hers, refusing to allow her to look away.

'You're the man from the gutter press—you tell me,' she countered frigidly.

'For your information, madam, I'm not, and never have been, a member of the gutter press,' he stated tersely, nostrils flaring white.

'No? Well, in that case, Dev, how would you describe your sordid occupation? Reporter? Journalist? *Gentleman* of the press?' she queried, unable to keep the sneer from her voice.

'Maybe—once,' he allowed. 'But not any more, Holly. Not any more, I promise you.'

Promises? From Devlin Winter? My, my, progress indeed. Holly swallowed hard. 'So what exactly do you do for a living these days? Nothing mundane, I hope?' And a dozen and one things flashed through her mind. The holiday he seemed free to prolong, the house that wouldn't come cheap for weeks on end at the height of the season, his expensive taste in tailoring, judging from the dinner suits—*plural,* she emphasized grimly, each exquisitely cut and styled and quite obviously made to measure.

'I—get by,' he retorted.

'I bet you do,' Holly allowed, absurdly hurt by his evasion.

'So—' Black eyes bored into her, and Holly had the distinct impression that every word, every nuance of expression had been stored in that razor-sharp mind, a journalist's mind, and Devlin Winter—ex-journalist now if Dev was to be believed—had no intentions of letting a single, insignificant detail escape his notice. 'So, madam, you were saying...?'

'I was saying?' she stalled, licking her dry lips.

'Facts,' he prompted. 'The Holly Scott version, at least. With this fortune I thee wed,' he reminded her cruelly. 'Yours—and Courdrey's. Money, Holly. Lots and lots of money. And Courdrey's no fool. He knows a bargain when he sees one.'

'Don't be so revolting. Alex—'

'Worships the ground you walk on, I suppose?'

'Naturally he loves me—'

'Oh, naturally,' he parodied cruelly. 'You and your fortune both, hey, Holly?'

'Since the fortune doesn't exist—thanks to you—hardly,' she tossed out bitterly. There, she'd said it. She hadn't meant to, but goaded beyond endurance, the words had simply slipped out. And why not? Watching the range of expressions flitting across his face, Holly was glad. She'd thrown him. And she was glad. For clever Dev Winter had worked it all out in his mind, and lo and behold, the mighty Dev Winter was wrong for once.

'What do you mean, it doesn't exist?'

'Just that. We lost it. We lost the lot when Dad died.' And she angled her head, jutting her chin in defiance. 'So you see, Dev, there's the glaring flaw in your logic. Like it or not, Alex and I belong together. Money simply doesn't come into it.'

'No? Well, that's another flaw, Holly. And I'm not sure that it paints a nicer picture.'

'And what's that supposed to mean?' she demanded.

'Come now, Holly. Don't play the snow-white innocent. I've watched you with Courdrey, I know how you react with me—'

'With revulsion,' she interrupted hotly.

'Really?' he queried softly. And before she could fathom his intentions, he'd dipped his head, brushing his lips against hers, a fleeting touch that set the blood, boiling in her veins, and Holly shivered, part need, part fear. She saw, from Dev's flash of triumph, that he'd logged each and every reaction and she closed her eyes in an effort to put the knowledge from her.

'Liar!' he said softly. And since Holly froze, refused to open her eyes, to meet that mocking, knowing gaze, he kissed her again.

'Leave me alone,' she gasped, struggling to be free, another waste of time since Dev simply tightened his grip.

'Why?' he demanded, his breath a warm caress against her skin. And again he kissed her, and fervently kissed her again.

'Why, Holly? Why fight it, why fight me? *We* belong. You and me, Holly. We belong together. We've always belonged. We'll always belong.'

'Past tense, Dev. Oh, yes, I'll allow you that,' she acknowledged tightly. 'A long, hot summer of belonging. And yes, it was good while it lasted. But it's over. It was over the day you took Daddy's money and ran. And weren't you the lucky one?' she berated icily. 'Since you got more than the rest of us. Because Meryl and I

176

were left without a penny—'

'Poor little rich girl,' he jeered cruelly. 'How did you cope? But no—don't bother replying. Let me guess. Courdrey. The house, the holiday, expensive little trifles like that ring. And you thought you had it made, didn't you, Holly? Until I walked in and created waves in your well-ordered world. And now you're afraid. You're running scared. You're terrified I'll force you to choose. Me—or Courdrey. The man you love versus a meal ticket for life. And that's what it boils down to, isn't it, Holly? Money.'

'If that's what you really believe,' she retorted sweetly, all of a sudden very, very calm. 'Look on the bright side, Dev. You've escaped, escaped the clutches of a cold and calculating golddigger.'

'So—it is the money?' he hissed, a look of sheer revulsion crossing his face.

'That's rich, coming from you,' she tossed out bitterly.

'You're so sure, aren't you, Holly?' he castigated coldly. 'You really are convinced that your father bought me off?'

'I should be,' she explained with a curious lack of emotion. 'I watched him write that cheque, Dev, a cheque clearly made out to Devlin Winter.'

'I see.' Just that. Two little words. And yet Dev blanched beneath the tan, the racing pulse at the corner of his mouth drawing Holly's gaze like a magnet.

Abruptly he pushed her away, releasing her, and Holly fought the urge to take a step backwards, instead rubbing at her wrist where his fingers had bit. And still Dev didn't move, simply stood and watched her, the pain in his eyes tugging at her heart strings. She'd condemned him. He'd taken the money and run and the knowledge hurt. But the irony was, Holly was no better than Dev. Whatever her motives, in marrying Alex she'd be crossing a threshold, living in a house of glass, and simply wasn't entitled to throw stones. Not any longer.

She took a deep breath. 'Dev—'

'No!' His hand came down hard against the side of the car as he cut her off. 'No, Holly. No more. I've heard enough. More than enough,' he muttered, but he'd swung away and the words sounded strange, slurred—didn't sound like Dev at all.

Holly felt the stirrings of panic. 'Dev? What is it? Please, Dev,' she implored as he seemed to stumble, lost his balance, put out a hand to steady himself. 'Tell me what's the matter.'

'As if you care,' he snarled, but his voice barely carried over his shoulder and Holly's alarm increased.

'Dev—'

'Leave me alone,' he insisted, beads of perspiration breaking out across his brow. He leaned heavily against the car, fumbling in his pocket for his keys.

'For God's sake, Dev,' Holly implored, clutching at his sleeve. 'Will you please tell me what's wrong?'

He straightened for a moment, wiping the back of his hand across his eyes, the pallor of

178

his skin ghostly beneath the tan. 'Nothing,' he told her thickly, looking at her, looking through her, if the glazed expression in his eyes was anything to go by. 'Nothing for you to worry about, Holly. Headache. Migraine. They come on occasionally. Legacy of the accident,' he explained as he winced in pain, closed his eyes against the sudden glare of the sun. 'I'll go home. Sleep if off. Be fine in an hour or so. Nothing to worry about,' he insisted, as he attempted to insert his key into the lock, used the fingers of his left hand to guide the key into position.

And then Holly realized. 'You can't see!' She was horrified. She suffered from headaches herself occasionally, the wrong time of the month mostly. Though she'd read about the debilitating effects of migraine, she'd never witnessed one first-hand. *If* it was a migraine. Oh, God! What if it was something else, something more serious?

'No. Be fine. Just sit here for while,' he insisted. 'It'll pass. Always does. Ten minutes, twenty. Then I'll drive home and go to bed.'

'Drive? You're in no fit state to drive,' she countered, aware of the note of hysteria in her tone. 'Dev, you can't see, for heaven's sake.'

'No.' He slumped down onto the driver's seat, but made no effort to swing his body behind the wheel. He gave a weak grin. 'But it doesn't last. It never does. Go home, Holly. Leave me alone.'

'No chance,' she contradicted, beginning to pull herself together. 'Come on.' She gripped his arm, attempting to pull him to his feet. 'I'll drive you home.'

'In that heap of decadence on wheels? I'd rather walk,' he told her with a welcome flash of the Dev she knew and loved.

'You might have to,' she told him briskly. 'I'd take you in yours, but I'm not sure I could cope with the left-hand drive.'

'I can manage—'

'Don't be so pig-headed,' she snapped. 'You're in no fit state to go anywhere on your own.'

It was a tense, silent journey, Holly driving as smoothly as she could and sticking rigidly to the limit. She was achingly aware of Dev slumped beside her, his head cradled against the headrest, eyes closed. Whenever she risked a sideways glance, her stomach muscles clenched. If anything, he looked worse, face devoid of colour, perspiration beading his brow and collecting in the hollow at the base of his throat.

She racked her brains for the little she knew about such attacks. Pain, nausea, dizziness, temporary blindness. Once the attack took hold, nothing to be done except rest in a darkened room. A couple of hours, a couple of days, if the attack was a bad one. Just rest.

She brought the car smoothly to a halt. 'Sit still,' she ordered as he began fumbling with the seat belt. 'Just this once, Devlin Winter, will you please do as you're told.'

'Yes, ma-am!' he shot back promptly and, though he winced again with the effort, he managed a half-smile.

She crossed round to the passenger side, pulling the door wide. Aching to help, to take his arm, have him lean against her, Holly resisted, allowing Dev to push himself free, to stumble the few steps up to the house, and she pinned her eyes on him, noting the way his shirt clung damply to the contours of his body, the fine lawn material strangely translucent. She had to clamp her arms to her sides to stop herself from reaching out to him.

She'd pocketed his keys at the airport and, as Dev paused, she scanned the bunch for the house key. Inside all was silent—Francine's day off, Holly assumed, following Dev into the kitchen.

'I'll make you a drink,' she said at once, checking the water level in the kettle but wondering how on earth she'd manage on the solid fuel range.

'No!' He straightened properly for the first time in what seemed like hours. 'Go home, Holly. You've done your good deed for the day,' he pronounced scathingly. 'And there's nothing you can do here. I don't need you, Holly. I don't need anyone. I just want to be alone.'

'But—'

'No. No buts. Just go. Go away and leave me in peace.'

Holly swallowed hard. 'If you're sure that's what you want...'

'I'm sure.'

Holly shrugged, fighting back the tears. 'Fine,' she conceded unevenly, placing the keys in the centre of the table, scrubbed and bare apart from a recent postcard franked Lourdes. Lourdes. Strange what your mind focuses on when your world begins to fall apart. A postcard from Lourdes. *My legs are much stronger now, thanks to you. I couldn't have managed the trip without your help,* Holly took in without thinking. Then it was Holly's turn to straighten. 'But if you change your mind, Dev,' she added softly, almost pleadingly, 'you know where to find me.'

'Sure. In the house that Courdrey built,' he tossed out with unexpected bitterness. 'Though on second thoughts,' he tagged on cruelly, 'perhaps I mean his bed?'

She swung away, fighting for control, aware of the tears hanging dangerously on her lashes. Fool. What had she expected: surely not a 'thank you, Holly, please call again, Holly, nice to know you, Holly, let's be friends, Holly' response? Dev was bitter. And Dev had every right to sound bitter.

And something else struck her as she put the car into gear and backed it carefully out of the yard. Dev was at the airport all right, but only a fool would believe he'd been waiting for Holly. After all, wasn't there the poisonous Lucy Trent to wave off on the same plane as Alex? So, might as well face it, Holly, she whipped as an icy finger touched her heart. Dev might insist it's you that he wants, but he happily spent the night in the arms of another woman. Her chin snapped up in defiance. Fine. Well, you can love them and leave them, Devlin Winter, she railed, choking back the tears. But from now on, you'll leave Holly Scott alone.

CHAPTER 10

Life went on. Doesn't it always? Holly scorned, thinking of the dark days when Dev had loved her and left her. Life had gone on. And though it hadn't been easy, she'd survived, Seven years of hell, she conceded, but life had gone on. And this time? Holly shrugged. This time she was achingly aware that a ten-minute drive would take her straight to Dev's door. Would he still want her? she mused. Would that be all he'd ever want? After all, what has he promised? Nothing. He'd given her everything, and offered nothing. Everything—and nothing. Precious little past, precious little future, with Dev, at least.

And something else she'd conveniently forgotten, though heaven knows how, she punished herself. Life doesn't go on for everyone. After all, Daddy had died and Devlin Winter, despite his flat denials, had played more than a passing part in it.

So—she was better off without him. And, if she told herself often enough, she might even come round to believing it.

The phone rang. Holly stiffened. It was too early in the day for Alex and, since Meryl was out having her hair done, she was tempted to ignore it.

'Ho-lly. Can't you hear the phone's ringing?'

Jonathan demanded, breaking off from the task in hand. He'd been sprawled out on the terrace playing 'pogs', and with the imaginary opposition no match for Jonathan's skill, his pile of counters had grown larger and larger and was now leaning more precariously than the famed tower of Pisa.

'Sorry, poppet.' She closed her magazine, taking her time as she strolled lazily across the terrace. With a bit of luck it would ring off before she reached it. At least, that was the theory. Catching sight of her face reflected in the window, she pulled a wry face.

It was Meryl. 'Holly. Thank heavens. I'm running late. My own fault really for deciding on highlights at the very last moment. And I simply didn't notice the time—'

'What have you forgotten this time?' Holly interrupted drily.

'Jonathan. He's due at the stables in another ten minutes. Could you be a darling and drop him round? Bless you, Holly. You're a lifesaver.'

Hardly, Holly allowed as her heart sank. The stables. And dangerously close to Dev. Still, she'd have to face him sooner or later. It might as well be now.

But, having braced herself for the worst, when they turned into the yard, the firmly shut door and blankly staring windows were clear indication there was no one home.

'You will stay and watch, won't you, Holly? Please, please, please,' Jonathan coaxed as Holly brought the car to a standstill.

184

Holly ruffled his hair. 'Of course I will,' she reassured him lightly, crossing her fingers that the absent tenant would stay precisely that: absent. For an hour or so at least.

They were a stable girl short, she noticed, counting the number of small heads and realizing someone was bound to be disappointed. But if leading a horse around the paddock was all that was needed... Her French wasn't up to explaining, but Holly was comfortable with horses and, in a matter of minutes, found herself setting a very sedate pace with her smiling four-year-old charge on the most docile animal in the stable while Jonathan joined the more advanced group tackling the jumps in the field.

And it was fun. And she forgot about Dev for whole minutes at a time, was laughing happily with little Thérèse when a familiar voice behind sent the blood rushing to her ears.

'Who'd have believed it—Holly Scott doing five minutes' honest work for a change?'

'I'm merely helping out, Dev,' she pointed out coolly. 'And since I work with kids all the time, believe me, it's hardly a novelty.'

'Work?' He raised an eyebrow in eloquent surprise. 'Strange, I can't imagine you joining the ranks of the human race and soiling your pretty hands on anything as mundane as work.'

Holly flushed. 'Do you have to be so revolting, so patronizing?' she snapped, pointedly turning away and concentrating fully on her charge. She didn't see him go, was simply aware that Dev was no longer there. Sure enough, when she next glanced round, there was no sign of him, just the dusty Citroën parked in front of the house. But it spoiled her day, took the edge off the fun she'd been having with Thérèse, and she was glad when one of the stable girls took over.

She drifted across to lean on the fence, and watch Jonathan going through his paces. He'd come along in leaps and bounds, literally, she realized, as he sailed across the jumps with all the aplomb of a fearless six-year-old. And Dev was right. Jonathan was a natural, would be sure to want lessons once they were back at home. More expense. And yet with Holly safely married to Alex, all the niggling worries of the past few years should be over.

'Have you time for a drink?'

Holly stiffened. Lost in thought, her body's radar system had clearly let her down. 'Why?' she queried, grey eyes shooting daggers as they locked with his. 'So you can carry on making snotty remarks about my lifestyle? Thanks, Dev, but no thanks,' she told him coolly. 'I'd rather die of thirst in a desert.'

Surprisingly, he smiled. 'You're right. The remark was out of line but hardly worth falling out over. And since I haven't thanked you for Sunday, the least I can do is offer you a drink. How does freshly squeezed orange juice sound? When you're ready, of course.' And he turned away before she could reply, leaving Holly to stand and fume.

Impossible man. Because Dev knew she couldn't turn him down. Not without seeming

churlish—or afraid. And since she was neither...
Oh, yes? Holly's lips twisted. Who was she
kidding. But she'd go.

Dev was in the kitchen, and spotting the
drinks set out on the table, Holly paused warily
on the threshold.

'It's cooler inside,' Dev explained, sensing her
unease. 'But if it helps to set your mind at rest,
leave the door open.'

Holly swallowed another sharp retort. He was
right, she was afraid but she wouldn't give him
the satisfaction of admitting it. 'Fine. We might
even catch the stirrings of the breeze,' she
allowed, slipping gingerly into her seat. It was
an uneasy silence, but since Dev had issued the
invitation, Dev could play host, dredge up the
small talk for once.

'So—' He'd taken the chair opposite and now
he smiled, raising his glass. 'Here's to friendship,
Holly. And before you start denying it, think.'

'About what?' she queried warily.

'Your reaction at the airport. You could have
walked away, but you didn't.'

'Oh, yes? And what did you expect? But silly
me,' she sneered. 'How could I have forgotten?
Join the ranks of the human race and help a
friend in need?' she drawled. 'Heaven forbid
that Holly Scott should soil her pretty little
hands.'

'Whoops. Looks like someone touched a
nerve,' he observed with the merest hint of
amusement.

'Someone did. But since he had the grace to
apologize so nicely, who am I to hold a grudge?'

187

she goaded, tilting her chin in defiance.

'A friend?' he queried softly, and this time there was no trace of amusement, just the merest hint of doubt.

Holly's surge of anger waned. Friends. Lovers. Enemies. Or ships that passed in the night? And at the end of the day, what did it matter? They had no future, not together at least. But in the meantime, it wouldn't hurt to be civilized.

She nodded. 'Friends,' she agreed. 'Which means you don't need to thank me. I could hardly walk away and leave you, Dev.'

'I think that's debatable, all things considered. I was angry,' he explained, when Holly raised an eyebrow. 'But I'd no right to take it out on you. So—' He raised his glass again. 'Here's to friendship.'

'To friendship,' Holly echoed. 'And long may it last.'

'Hmm. Correct me if I'm wrong, lady, but something tells me you're not crossing any fingers.'

'Where you and I are concerned, it would take more than crossed fingers and luck to keep the peace,' she reminded him. 'Still, you never know...'

'And pigs might fly, hey, Holly?'

'They might indeed,' she agreed solemnly, but Dev was smiling and, since the day was too nice to waste on pointless niggles, Holly began to relax.

He was looking well, she was relieved to discover, having shaken off the effects of the migraine days ago. Sunday had been interminable, with Dev never out of her mind. Having left him alone in the house, she'd been worried sick. Anything could happen, she'd thought the moment she'd driven away. She should have stayed, should have insisted on staying. He'd been in no fit state to overrule her, despite his parting shot. And though there was probably nothing she could do apart from be there, she should have stuck around.

After a sleepless night she'd been aching to phone, to ask how he was and, equally afraid that he'd cut her, nearly took the coward's way out by asking Meryl to phone. But she'd left it, finally summoning up the nerve by mid-afternoon. She was sorry she'd bothered. It was like talking to a perfect stranger. He'd thanked her politely for running him home, and equally politely turned down the offer to run him back to Deauville to pick up his car.

'It's all been taken care of,' he'd insisted, putting the phone down without a moment's hesitation. Left holding the handset, Holly had been absurdly hurt.

Facing him now across the width of his kitchen table, she smothered a smile. Friends? Some hope. But it was a definite improvement on Sunday, she could allow.

'So—' Dev topped up their drinks. 'You work with kids. Tell me about it.'

Holly swirled the orange juice round and round her glass. 'There's not a lot to tell,' she conceded carefully. 'I'm a nanny.' Past tense, she amended, but silently. Her job had come to an end at the start of the summer. In the normal run of things, she'd have found herself another by now. Only Meryl had jumped at the chance of taking Alex's villa for the summer. And why not? A whole summer of sun, sand, sea and no responsibilities, courtesy of Alex. Given the state of their finances, Holly was beginning to understand why. No responsibilities, no worries. Holly's lips twisted. And then the Catch Twenty-two—Devlin Winter living on their doorstep.

'A nanny, hey? I'm impressed, Holly. But I can't see that going down well with Courdrey. Bad for his image, having his wife go out to work.'

Holly flushed. Trust Dev to hit the nail on the head. She and Alex had come close to quarrelling more than once about Holly's need for independence. But she wasn't about to let that slip. Where Dev was concerned, information was knowledge, knowledge was power. And Dev was an expert. Bit by bit, drop by drop he'd piece his facts together and then, bingo! He'd have wormed things out of Holly that she wouldn't have known herself.

'You're back to being snotty again,' she said instead, regarding him steadily.

'And you're being evasive.'

'Oh?' Holly flushed despite herself. 'And how do you work that out?' she enquired coolly.

'Simple. The moment I mention your private life, you clam up. But you're right. I was—'

'Snotty?' she supplied drily.

Dev grinned. 'Such a quaint turn of phrase, Holly. I can't imagine where you've heard it. Working with kids, perhaps? Now why, I wonder?'

'Why, what?' Holly snapped, beginning to think there was nothing she could say to pierce his composure.

'Why work? As the fiancée of one of the richest men in the world, why the need?'

'Is this your idea of friendship, Dev?' Holly needled crossly. 'The third degree?'

'Just thinking aloud,' he admitted, not the least put out. 'Something doesn't add up.'

'You don't say,' Holly drawled. 'Well have I got news for you, Dev. It's none of your business remember?'

He shrugged again. 'If you say so.'

'I do.' She drained her glass. 'Now, if you don't mind, I think it's time I was going.'

'Ah, yes, but I do—mind, that is,' he contradicted her smoothly, and, as Holly made a move towards the door, Dev out-thought her, was up on his feet in an instant, his powerful form filling the frame and cutting off the means of her retreat.

Holly pulled up sharp. Playing games. She might have known not to trust him. But how to slip past without brushing against that powerful form and triggering a host of needs that clever, clever Dev surely wouldn't miss?

She took a deep breath. Easy girl. Don't overreact. Just stay cool, calm and in control. Calm? With six feet two inches of dynamism less than a hand's-span away? And lest the thought should lead to the deed, she clamped her hands to her sides, her gaze not quite steady as she locked her eyes onto his. And she wanted him. Even now she wanted him, wanted those sultry black eyes to travel her body, ached to feel his arms around her, to have his mouth exploring hers. Only she mustn't. She was engaged to Alex and she'd be strong. She had to be strong, for everyone's sake.

Impasse. Not a sound, not a movement, just a man and a woman alone, electricity quivering on the air between them. Dev. Every straining, solid inch of muscle familiar to her touch, every nuance of expression locked in her mind. And he wanted her. Dev's need, like Holly's, screaming out for fulfilment. But she mustn't.

Think, Holly. Think of Alex. Dear, sweet Alex who needed her, too. Dear, sweet Alex, who'd manipulated the engagement, her subconscious needled, but the thought was disloyal and she pushed it away before it could take hold.

Dev. Devastating Dev, and *yes*, his eyes were beginning to travel her body, lingering on the swell of breast beneath the flimsy T-shirt, down, down one long, long leg, up the other. Her bare skin was tingling at the almost tangible caress, so much skin exposed beneath the short, flimsy skirt that Holly was beginning to feel naked, wanted to be naked. As Dev's heated gaze reached the juncture of her legs, she felt the sudden flood of dampness. Oh, hell. Oh, God. Oh, please, God, she prayed, help me to resist, help me to be strong.

Dev smiled, and Holly's heart flipped over. Six feet two inches of sheer masculinity. Six feet two inches of man. Her man. She wanted him. And she allowed her eyes to range his body, hungrily, from the arrogant face with its aquiline nose and razor-sharp cheekbones, down to the V of his open-necked shirt, the dark shadow of hair hinting at the mass that covered a powerful chest, an eloquent invitation for fingers to touch, Holly's fingers, then down, down, and down.

Yes, he wanted her, she realized as her heart soared. Dev wanted her every bit as much as she wanted him, the need clearly outlined beneath the tightly stretched fabric of his jeans. But it was madness. She had to be strong. She had to resist.

Fighting for control, she licked her dry lips, the gesture unwittingly provocative, and a moment later she was in his arms, her own arms folding around him by reflex as Dev scooped her to him. He pulled her into the hard lines of his body, and as he ground his hips against hers, Holly felt the floodgates open.

'Hush, sweetheart,' he soothed as Holly began to moan, and his mouth covered hers. It was magic, sheer magic, the touch, the taste, the smell of him, the need of him, and her body was swaying against him, her hips describing erotic circles that heightened the tension, Holly gasping at Dev's reaction, Dev growling as he ground himself against her.

So hard. So wonderfully, wonderfully hard, and she had aroused him, teased him, tantalized as she pulled away suddenly, a moment, no more, because long, tapering fingers reached out to snatch her back.

'Witch,' Dev muttered against her mouth, and then his lips were on hers, his tongue sliding through into the sweet, moist depths, and as his mouth explored, so his hands explored, raking the lines of her spine, stealing round to brush the swell of her straining breasts.

Holly twisted back in his arms, allowing his fingers to reach the hard, thrusting buds of her nipples, another fleeting touch before Dev moved on, and down, down, into the curve of waist and hip, across the swell of hip and under the hem of her much too skimpy skirt.

As his hands and fingers stroked the soft inner flesh of her thighs, his mouth was plundering hers, his tongue sweeping through into moist, inviting corners, sweeping, darting, exploring, devastating as Holly's tongue joined in the love dance, entwining with his, the tension mounting, the need mounting.

Holly's mind and body were screaming out for Dev, hands, fingers, mouth, oh, God, how she wanted him, ached for him, needed him, and the rest of the world was forgotten. Gone. No past, no future, nothing, because she was here, now, with Dev, wanted Dev, and wonderful, wonderful Dev wanted Holly every bit as badly.

Probing fingers reached beneath her panties, slowly, oh so slowly, exquisitely slowly, parting the curls. Then he paused, and Holly's lids snapped open in alarm, her frightened gaze locking onto his, reading the message that came steadily back to her. As Dev smiled, so Holly smiled. He loved her. Surely he loved her? And surely loving Dev so badly couldn't possibly be wrong? And they belonged. They'd always belonged together.

'Oh, Holly,' he murmured almost reverently. 'Oh, my love.' And he dipped his head to kiss her, softly, tenderly as Holly rocked herself backwards and forwards against a single, stroking, probing finger.

The phone rang. Dev cursed as Holly froze, common sense welcoming the intrusion, but mind and body both crying out for fulfilment.

'You, lady, stay right there,' he instructed thickly, cupping her face in his hands and kissing her briefly. He crossed the kitchen as Holly slumped against the wall, her breathing shallow. And she watched him. And she loved him. And she wanted him. And she should go now, *now* before things got out of hand.

'It's for you. Meryl,' he explained, holding out the handpiece.

Meryl. What had she forgotten this time? Holly wondered crossly. And, since it was Colette's day off, she wouldn't mind betting there was nothing at all in the house for dinner and Meryl had only just remembered. Only she was wrong.

'Holly?'

'Something's wrong. What is it?' Holly asked, annoyance giving way to alarm as her sensitive ear picked out the pain in Meryl's voice.

'Just—something silly,' Meryl explained, clearly close to tears. 'I tripped. These wretched shoes,' she explained. 'And I've twisted my ankle.'

'Where are you?' Holly asked.

195

'At Marcel's. They've packed my foot in ice but—'

'Then stay right there and rest it. I'll be over as soon as I can.'

'Trouble?' Dev queried, coming up behind and slipping his arms around her waist, his lips nibbling hungrily against her ear.

She told him. 'Probably just a sprain,' she explained, pulling away, the need, the void, the gaping void of unfulfilment almost driving her insane. 'But I'll know better when I see her. Jonathan—'

'Will be fine. Leave him with me,' he insisted. 'Just concentrate on Meryl. You're right, it could be something and nothing. But better play things safe and have it X-rayed. Now go. I'll look after Jon.' He kissed her, briefly, too briefly. 'You're not to worry,' he added softly, cupping her face in his hands. 'I won't say a thing to Jon. If he asks, I'll say you've gone shopping.'

'But—we could be hours.'

'No problem. I'll feed him here and, if it starts getting late, I'll drop him back home and hang on there until you show. You'd better leave your keys just in case. Now go.' And he spun her round, propelling her firmly to the door, the touch of skin on skin making Holly go weak at the knees. 'And stop worrying,' he added, hugging her briefly, reassuringly. 'Jonathan's fine. You just concentrate on Meryl.'

Concentrate on Meryl. Another five minutes and they'd have been making wild, passionate love on the kitchen table, she told herself, stifling the hysteria. And cool, calm Dev was telling her to concentrate on Meryl. Oh, Meryl, she berated silently. What have you done? Oh, God, she added solemnly, aware that Meryl's interruption was simply that, a temporary halt on the long, hard journey back to Dev. What on earth have I done?

CHAPTER 11

'How is she?'

'Fine. She has slight concussion from the bang on her head so they're keeping her in for observation. Apart from that, no broken bones, just a badly sprained ankle.' Holly hooked a stray lock of hair behind her ear. 'I'm sorry. I didn't expect to be this long.'

Dev shrugged. 'No problem. Jonathan's been as good as gold. He's had cheese on beans on toast for his tea and he's tucked up in bed with a jigsaw and a book. Pop up and say hello while I pour you a drink.'

'I—'

'Don't know what to tell him?' Dev smiled. 'Since she's bound to be home tomorrow, why let him worry? And Meryl must have stayed out late before.'

Holly nodded. Dev was right. A tiny white lie wouldn't hurt, and Jonathan, being Jonathan, took the story of the party in his stride.

'You will come back and tuck me in, won't you, Holly?' he reminded her almost as an afterthought. 'And ask Dev to read me a story?'

'Well—I'm not sure Dev's planning to stay that long,' she explained lamely.

'Oh, but he promised,' Jonathan explained matter-of-factly, wide brown eyes full of trust.

She didn't want to go back downstairs, have to face Dev, make polite conversation with Dev when all she wanted was Dev touching her, kissing her, loving her. She was stalling, and Dev would know it. Even so, she headed for her bedroom, peeling off her clothes and taking a quick shower before pulling on the first thing that came to hand: a sleeveless, button-through dress that skimmed across her breasts and over the contours of her body before swirling out into a full, calf-length skirt that made a soft, swishing noise as she moved.

Reaching for her comb, her fingers brushed against the ring box, the huge diamond glinting balefully up from its velvet nest. Expensive. Ostentatious. Cumbersome on Holly's slender finger. But typical Alex. She's mine, hands off, the ring was stating eloquently.

Without pausing to think, Holly closed the box, dropped it into a drawer, hiding it away among the pile of underwear. A quick spray of perfume and then she stood before the mirror, brushing her hair, her solemn gaze coming back at her. Stalling. She'd been little more than ten minutes but Dev would know she'd been stalling. Ah, well...

She found him in the kitchen, stirring a casserole in the oven. 'Something smells good,' she murmured, her mouth dry, her tongue sticking to the roof of her mouth.

Dev straightened, tossing a tea towel over one shoulder. 'Boeuf bourguignonne. I guessed you wouldn't have eaten, and if you had, it would heat up fine for tomorrow.'

'No. I haven't eaten all day,' she acknowledged, taking the glass of wine that Dev offered, careful to avoid contact with those long, tapering fingers.

He raised his glass. 'To us?' he suggested. 'Or maybe it should be to absent friends?'

Absent friends. Meryl. Alex. *Alex*. Oh, God, she was alone with Dev in Alex's house. Not quite, she amended. There was a real-life chaperon all fed and bathed and tucked safely up in bed. Bed. Did all thoughts have to lead to bed? Bed. And Dev. Not here, she told herself It was Alex's house. She couldn't betray Alex's trust here. Not even for Dev.

'So—' Dev drained his glass. 'I'll say goodnight then.'

Holly inclined her head. Let him go. Safer that way, she told herself. But he *had* looked after Jonathan and Jonathan had set his heart on that story.

'Have you eaten?' she heard herself saying instead.

Dev shook his head. 'No,' he admitted carefully, his eyes never leaving her face.

'So why not stay, share that wonderfully fragrant casserole? I guess we can make it stretch for two.'

'I guess we can at that,' he agreed solemnly, 'since I made enough for you and Meryl. There's creamed potatoes in the pan,' he added. 'And the beans should just about have finished simmering.'

'Here?' she asked, suddenly very, very nervous. 'Or the dining-room?'

'Oh, here,' he decided. 'Much more cosy.'

Yes. Cosy. Too cosy. Just the two of them. All that was missing was the candlelight, and sure enough, even as the thought popped into her head, Dev reappeared in the doorway, candle brackets in hand. Great minds, she mocked, but silently, aware that Dev had made himself at home, had clearly raided the sideboard in the dining-room for candlesticks and candles. He placed them in the centre of the table as Holly busied herself at the stove.

'So—' she raised her glass as he slid into place opposite '—*Bon appétit.*'

Dev nodded, held her gaze for long, long moments and then took a sip of the excellent Burgundy.

'Don't worry, I brought the wine,' he explained, seeming to read her thoughts. 'Jonathan and I stopped off at the shops. I wasn't sure what food you'd have in the larder, especially on Colette's day off.'

Holly smiled. No. He'd guessed rightly that there'd be little. Or maybe he simply remembered Holly's bag of groceries the day she'd had her bag snatched.

He'd changed too, she noted, the brown-checked shirt and jeans having given way to a turtle-neck jumper and tailored trousers. And yet the whole effect was casual. Nice and easy. A bit like their conversation. Casual. Idle chatter. This and that, nothing important, nothing personal. It was all carefully peripheral, superficial, just talk, words, meaningless words that kept erotic thoughts at bay. Only it didn't work. Not for Holly at least.

She dabbed at the corners of her mouth with her napkin. 'Thank you. That was wonderful. I didn't know you could cook,' she said at last, amazed to discover that, despite her nerves, she'd completely cleared her plate.

'Just a little something I picked up in night school,' he teased. 'Along with that other well-known French speciality, cheese on beans on toast.'

'Ah, yes. I guessed that would throw you. I assume Jonathan provided the recipe?'

'And had himself promoted to chief cook and bottle washer. He's a good kid.'

'Yes.' A wonderful kid. Only Alex didn't seem to think so, Holly acknowledged silently. Alex. Face it, Holly, you're making a mistake. Marry Alex and you'll be living in limbo. But if she didn't marry Alex...Holly smothered a sigh. Given the financial mess that Meryl was in, it was academic. She was engaged to Alex, and she'd marry Alex, and as for Dev—

'I'd offer a pound if I thought you'd be honest,' he interrupted softly.

'I'm sorry?' she queried, not following.

'Your thoughts. All of a sudden you were miles away.'

'Ah.' She gave an offhand shrug of the shoulders before forcing a smile. 'Save your money, Dev. They're not worth repeating.'

He raised a disbelieving eyebrow. 'If you say so,' he allowed, but to Holly's relief, he let it go.

Cheese. A creamy Pont L'Eveque with chunks

of freshly baked baguette—so much nicer than the plastic cheese and biscuits served back home. Holly put the thought into words.

'Just laziness, I guess,' Dev concluded. 'Could you see your average British housewife queueing three or four times a day for bread? We'd need a bread shop on every corner.'

'And what's to stop the average British husband lending a hand?' she pointed out slyly. She sat back in her chair, folded her arms, a smile of amusement playing about the corners of her mouth. 'Dear me, Dev. Sexist comments from the man who's just produced a first-class meal and without a single woman in sight,' she mocked.

'Ah, yes, but I'm the exception that proves the rule, Holly. And for this meal, I had a definite woman in view. You, madam, are highly honoured.'

'And you, sir, are too clever by half,' she riposted, colouring.

'A man of many talents,' he agreed, but Holly simply smiled.

Dev made the coffee while Holly cleared away and stacked the used plates in the dishwasher. And since they carried their drinks through to the lounge, Holly perched nervously on the edge of what should have been an easy chair. She didn't know why but, all of a sudden, it seemed much less safe than the kitchen where the solid pine table had kept them firmly apart. Though she'd have been happier on the terrace, she didn't want to be out of hearing range of Jonathan.

And so the conversation went on, light, trivial, seemingly unimportant, yet the words chosen with care. A single word, a glance would be enough to light the blue touchpaper, and Holly was achingly aware of where that would lead.

Dev checked his watch. 'It's getting late. I ought to make a move. Do you suppose Jonathan's dropped off by now?'

Holly shook her head. 'A story you promised, a story he'll be waiting for. But don't worry. You can keep it short and sweet. As long as he sees you, he'll be happy.'

'Five minutes then,' Dev murmured.

Holly nodded. Five minutes and then Dev would be gone. She'd be safe. Five minutes and she'd take herself off to bed, climb beneath the duvet and spend long, sleepless hours aching for Dev's touch, Dev's kisses, Dev's body entwined with hers. Dev. Oh, God, would she never be free?

She jumped up, heading for the kitchen and the open bottle of wine. Despite the wonderful meal, they'd barely consumed a glass each. Staying carefully sober, she realized, deciding that a second glass wouldn't hurt at this stage and, carrying it back into the lounge, she stood at the open window, eyes unseeing as her mind wandered along the forbidden pathways of the past.

Dev, naked on the sand beside her. Dev, smouldering black eyes openly caressing. Dev, touching, kissing, loving. Loving and leaving, she reminded bitterly. And as for the trail of devastation he'd left in his wake... But no,

Holly dashed the tears away. Too much pain. Not tonight. She wouldn't spoil tonight. She'd simply let him go without rancour. It would be little enough thanks for Dev's help with Jonathan. Jonathan. Frowning, she glanced at the clock. Five minutes, Dev had said. But since Holly's glass was now empty, Dev must have been gone over half an hour.

She tiptoed upstairs, pausing outside Jonathan's room. There wasn't a sound and the door creaked slightly on its hinges as Holly pushed it open, the noise overloud in the silence. She peeped round, greeting Dev's wry smile with a grin. He was slumped in the chair beside the bed, Jonathan's fingers clutching Dev's, refusing to loosen their hold even in sleep.

'I didn't want to move in case I disturbed him,' Dev explained in a whisper as Holly approached the foot of the bed.

'Don't worry, once he's out, he's out for the count,' she reassured him, but she was whispering, too, and laughed out loud at the absurdity. Catching the sound, Jonathan stirred, relaxed his grip, turned over, the comfort thumb slipping into his mouth as he settled on his side.

Finding himself free, Dev stood and stretched before heading for the open door. Holly smoothed the duvet, then dropped a light kiss on the sleeping child's forehead.

'Night, night, poppet. Sweet dreams,' she murmured, wishing she could wave a magic wand and conjure up sweet dreams of her own.

Reaching the doorway, she looked back, a silent Dev beside her. Man, woman and child. A happy family grouping. Only it wasn't. It never would be, she told herself bitterly. Because Dev didn't belong in her life and never would.

Out in the confines of the hallway Dev seemed close, unnervingly close, and Holly felt the panic rise. She pushed past, intending to head for the stairs and safety, heard the sharp hiss of Dev's indrawn breath and froze, froze as Dev's arms closed round, holding and enfolding.

'No, Dev,' she said automatically, her frightened eyes locking with his.

He released her at once, the surge of disappointment knocking the breath from her body, but he made no effort to move, simply stood and watched her, his body tantalizingly close, his eyes boring through and seeing to the centre of her soul.

She wanted him. And Dev wanted her. And they were alone. Man and woman alone with the knowledge, the raw, aching need that screamed loud between them.

Holly ran the tip of her tongue along her dry lips, the gesture unwittingly provocative, and Dev swore lightly under his breath, swinging away, his clenched fingers eloquent proof of his pain, of his need, of the rigid control hanging by a thread.

Suddenly Holly couldn't bear it any more and she reached out to touch the back of his neck, felt the ripples beneath her fingers as Dev's body reacted, responded, responded for a wonderful heart-stopping moment and just as swiftly recoiled.

'Don't!' he said thickly, repulsing her. 'For God's sake, Holly, don't start something you won't allow me to finish.' And he spun round, the anguish on his face tearing her apart. 'I want you,' he said urgently, unsteadily. 'But if you don't want me, Holly, walk away now before it's too late. Go,' he repeated harshly, black eyes pools of torment. 'Are you listening, Holly? Go away and leave me in peace.'

Holly felt the sting of tears. Incapable of speech, she simply nodded, turning on her heels and heading for her bedroom door. Dev could see himself out. Safer that way. Safer this way, she consoled herself, suppressing a sob as she reached for the handle. And she'd been strong. They'd both been strong, she acknowledged, and she turned, never dreaming that Dev wouldn't have gone and—oh, hell! He was standing, watching, the misery in his eyes a mirror image of Holly's.

She stumbled back against the door jamb, dropping her lids in an effort to block the image from her mind—or bury it once and for all beneath a torrent of tears she simply couldn't control.

'Sweetheart, Oh, sweetheart, please don't cry,' he entreated her in anguish, and the gap between them disappeared as Dev closed in, pulling her roughly to him and dipping his head to kiss away the tears as Holly felt the fight drain from her body. She wanted him. Heaven help her, she'd always want him. And

207

as Dev swept her off her feet and into his arms, Holly rested her head against his chest, logged his racing heart and smiled inside. Because whatever happened after tonight, there'd be a single, precious moment of love to hang on to for the rest of her life.

CHAPTER 12

He placed her gently on the bed. 'It isn't too late, sweetheart,' he told her solemnly, pulling back for a moment.

'Isn't it?' Holly queried, and she smiled through the rainbow of tears, snapping the buttons on her dress one by one, slowly, deliberately, her eyes never leaving Dev's face. Reaching the bottom, she shook the folds of the material open, exposing the body beneath, naked but for the scrap of lace that covered the V of her legs, the equally flimsy scraps that masqueraded as a bra. And she dropped her gaze, cupped her hands around her breasts, drawing Dev's smouldering eyes down with her.

'Are you sure?' she queried softly, and smiled again, felt her body tighten beneath the reverence of his gaze. 'Are you sure?' she repeated, arching towards him, and Dev growled, was beside her in an instant, stretched out on the bed as he buried his face in her hair. Holly's arms folded round him, holding, caressing, stroking as she inhaled the special male scent of him, felt the warmth of his body against hers.

'Oh, Holly,' he murmured, raising his head. 'What have you done?' he asked softly, but he was smiling, and Holly's smile broadened.

'What have I done?' she countered saucily.

'Why, Devlin Winter, nothing at all—yet,' she told him throatily. 'But before the night is over...'

'Yes, Holly? Before the night is over?' he challenged softly.

But Holly simply smiled, reaching out, running the flat of her hand across his chest, her thumb idly brushing a nipple that hardened at her touch.

'Witch!' he murmured, capturing her hand and nuzzling the palm. 'My wonderfully wanton witch.'

He peeled the jumper over his head, muscles rippling in the silver glow of moonlight, and Holly remembered that other night in the moonlight when they'd come close to making love on the beach. Two weeks, she recalled. And what a fool she'd been trying to resist him. She loved him, for heaven's sake. He was in her blood, she lived him, breathed him, loved him and nothing in the world could ever change the way she felt. And tonight he was hers, only hers. And tonight she belonged to Dev. Body and soul. And tomorrow didn't exist. Not now. Not ever. Because the reality of all the tomorrows was too awful to comprehend. And so she'd pretend. He was here. They belonged. Tonight they belonged.

She slipped out of her dress as Dev lay down beside her, and propping himself up on an elbow, he gazed down, his expression so unexpectedly solemn that her heart skipped a beat.

'Dev—'

'Hush,' he entreated, placing a finger on her lips. 'Hush. Let me look, let me savour.' And he smiled, Holly's fears subsiding as their glances locked. 'You're very beautiful,' he told her, the single finger sweeping across first one cheek then the other, smoothing away the residue of tears. 'You're very beautiful and you're mine. All mine. Are you listening, Holly? You're mine.'

He dipped his head, his mouth covering hers, and Holly gasped at the contact, her arms folding round to cradle his head, to prolong the kiss. Dev growled as her lips parted, inviting, enticing, his tongue sweeping through into the moist, nerve-tingling depths, and Holly moved against him, felt the hardness at his groin and a gurgle of laughter rose in her throat.

'Witch!' he said again, lifting his head briefly, and then his mouth was blazing a trail, temple to temple, his lips nibbling, nuzzling, his tongue teasing, eyelid, nose, eyelid, across her cheek and back to the corner of her mouth where his tongue darted through again, entwined with hers. Holly captured his tongue and teased in turn before the laughter rose up again and Dev escaped, escaped to punish her, dropping featherlight kisses along the stem of her neck while his hands began to roam her body.

And damn the man, he knew exactly what she wanted! And he denied her. So near, so far. Hands, mouth, tongue, teasing, tantalizing, touching, briefly, far too briefly before moving on and on and round and round, ever circling, almost connecting, almost, and then drawing

211

away, a bittersweet frustration that drove Holly to screaming pitch.

But her turn would come, she consoled herself. And then Devlin Winter would beg. And she'd deny him—up to a point, of course. And she smiled at the knowledge and Dev, seeing the secret smile, ground his hips against hers, an eloquent reminder before he drew away, the thrill running through Holly like a flame.

'Not yet,' he told her thickly. 'Too soon. Much, much too soon.'

And Holly could only agree. As magic fingers circled her straining breasts, as Dev's mouth nuzzled the hollow in her throat before moving down to the V of her cleavage, she could only hope that the moment would last for ever, knew that in her heart it would last for ever. Because she loved him. And tonight, if only for tonight, Dev loved her.

'Hell, woman. I want to look—properly,' he told her, raising his head from the depths of the valley. And he slid his hands beneath her, snapping the catch of her bra and pulling the offending garment free before tossing it into a corner of the room.

'Oh, Holly. Wonderful, wonderful, Holly,' he murmured, a single finger reaching out to touch, and her nipples hardened at the touch. He raised his finger to her mouth, allowed Holly to moisten it before rubbing at first one straining nub and then the other, his eyes never leaving her face. And then he dipped his head, circling each breast in turn, fingers, mouth, tongue, Holly writhing beneath him, moaning deep in

212

her throat as he pushed her breasts together, explored the valley with his tongue while magic thumbs played havoc with her nipples.

'Not yet, my little princess,' he murmured against her ear, and he was kissing her mouth again, lips hard and punishing, teeth nibbling as Holly arched against him, a searing contact of skin against skin as her breasts brushed his chest lifting her higher and higher. And Dev laughed, sensing the frustration and yet denying her, denying them both as he pulled free. And the tiny kisses began to build, down again, round, round and round her aching breasts, the circles growing smaller and smaller, breast to breast, nipple to nipple until Dev was sucking, tugging, biting, sucking again, mouth to breast, hand to breast, stroking, caressing, kneading.

'Oh, Dev. Please, Dev. For heaven's sake, Dev!' Holly implored, plunging her fingers into the silk of his hair and raking through. A tremor ran through him as she felt the ridge of puckered skin, and she froze for a moment, no more, aware that she'd hurt him, horrified that she'd hurt him but Dev kissed her, briefly, reassuringly.

'Soon, sweetheart,' he promised smokily. 'And again and again all night long, hey, my love?'

My love! Holly's heart took wing. Tonight, if never, ever again, Dev loved her. And tonight she would believe it.

'You bet!' she told him, smiling inside, drawing his head down to hers, kissing his mouth and running her fingers, lightly this time, across the scar tissue. Such a dreadful scar, she realized, but she didn't have time to dwell on it because Dev had grown impatient and was tugging at her panties, which clung damply to her body. Holly lifted her hips to speed the process, looking on in wonder as Dev tugged at the zipper of his trousers and, shrugging himself free, stood proudly naked before her.

'Oh, Dev! Oh, my God,' she murmured, her eyes moving from his straining manhood to his face and back again. And she reached out, wanting to touch, not sure that she'd be allowed to. Sure enough, Dev jerked out of reach, laughing as Holly groaned in anguish.

'Not yet!' he cautioned and, careful to avoid the body-to-body contact that would drive them both out of control, he knelt on the floor beside the bed, kissed her mouth, the hollow in her throat where a pulse raced, feathered down to the valley between her breasts, and lower, his tongue darting into the dimple of her navel, triggering explosions that began in the pit of her belly and spread ever outwards, whirls and swirls of exquisite pain. And still he didn't touch her. No hands, no fingers, no searing skin on skin. Just Dev's mouth, lips, tongue, teeth, tongue lapping, teeth nibbling, lips caressing. And Holly writhed. And she purred. And she moaned. And she gasped.

'Oh, Dev!'

'Oh, Holly!' he echoed with a smile in his voice, and his mouth moved on, away from the curls at the juncture of her legs, down, down one creamy thigh and over her knee, a lazy glide of tongue that lapped at her instep, created currents of heat before switching to her toes, tugging at her toes and then upwards, a fresh exploration, but slowly, oh, so tantalizingly slowly as his tongue slid across the smooth skin of Holly's inner thighs, paused at the curls, nudged aside the curls and—

'Dev! Please, Dev!' she pleaded, and she was writhing with pain, with want, with need, the need for Dev to stop, the need for Dev never to stop because Holly was in heaven, heaven and hell both as he teased her body, lifting her time and again to melting point, almost. So near, so far and then, just as the explosions were primed to begin, he drew back, enough, no more, but enough to keep Holly begging for more and more and more.

Then he was stretched out beside her on the bed, his mouth plundering hers, his hands ranging her body, kneading her breasts, teasing her nipples which hardened and strained, thrust proudly at his palms as Dev growled, and then he was sucking, hungrily, greedily, Holly's reeling mind beginning to register yet another centre of pleasure because Dev's hands had moved down, and—

'Oh, God!' she gasped as a single, exploring finger plunged into the damp curls, instinct an unerring guide to the tiny ridge at the heart of her needs. And Holly was out of control, was trembling beneath him, felt the waves of emotion begin to build, a tidal wave of pleasure that surely must come to an end. Yet, the moment she reached the apex, it was Dev thrusting inside her, his magnificent body in perfect harmony with hers, the rhythm speeding as the music in her head reached the crescendo and she was lost, lost, lost, carried away into the magic strains of the night, body, mind and soul, that launched her into a whole new dimension.

'All night. You promised,' he told her solemnly, raising his head a lifetime later.

'Heaven help us both tomorrow, then,' she acknowledged, but she was smiling, and her hand trailed down to the juncture of his legs, closing round as he stirred against her, and she laughed as Dev pulled away.

'All night, maybe,' he agreed. 'But all in good time, my little wanton. I don't know about you, Holly, but right now I need a drink.' He kissed her, briefly, shockingly briefly, and then padded naked from the bedroom.

Left alone, Holly smoothed the sheets and rearranged the pillows, stacking them as back rests before slumping against them. There was precious little room for two in her bed, but they'd manage. And since sleep appeared to be the last thing on the agenda, the narrow confines were all the more erotic.

No place to hide, she told herself, bringing her knees up under her chin and wrapping her arms around them, hugging the precious seeds of happiness in her mind. She was floating on a cloud and she never ever wanted the night to end. Because tonight she loved and was loved, tonight she belonged and tomorrow—but, no, her mind skittered away. She'd face tomorrow in the harsh light of day.

Tonight she was happy, and tonight nothing would be allowed to come between her and that happiness. Only Dev. And he was at the heart of it. As he pushed the door open, Holly blushed at the memory of the wonderful things Dev had been doing to her mind and body.

'I looked in on Jon,' he explained, handing her a glass of chilled white wine. 'He's sleeping like a baby.'

'Dressed like that? What if he'd been awake?' she almost gasped.

'And pray, just what's wrong with this attire, madam?' he challenged with mock severity, a critical glance travelling the long, lean lines of his body.

'From where I'm sitting, not a single thing,' she allowed as Dev, naked as the day he'd been born, climbed onto the bed beside her.

'I should hope not,' he chided, dipping his head to kiss her mouth. 'But worry not, my love. I simply put my head round the door.'

'But if he'd seen you—'

'Why, he'd be dreaming, of course.'

'Just like me?' she queried softly, gazing shyly up at him.

'I hope not,' he told her, the expression in his eyes fleetingly serious.

'Dev—'

'No.' He cut her off abruptly, kissing her, slipping his arm about her shoulder as he drew her down into the niche of chest and arm. 'No need for words. Not yet a while.' And they lapsed into silence, Holly taking tiny sips of

217

buttery wine, savouring the taste, savouring the memory, living each and every moment of being with Dev.

'Dev?' she murmured dreamily, at long last.

'Mmm?' he queried softly.

'Have you ever been to Lourdes?'

'What a strange question to ask your lover in the middle of the night.'

'Stalling, Dev?' she challenged, but softly, not yet sure of her ground.

'Simply making an observation, oh curious one. But since you've asked, yes, as it happens. I've travelled a great deal in France, Holly, and yes, I've been to Lourdes.'

'Recently?' she queried, instinctively aware that she was pushing back boundaries and not sure she had the right to.

'Fairly recently,' he allowed, giving nothing away.

'And did it help?'

'Did it help what?' he queried, the first hint of puzzlement in his tone.

'Like being in church. The mass in Houlgate. I—I'm—not sure what I'm asking really,' she stammered.

'No. But I think I'm beginning to see what you're driving at. Been reading my mail, Holly?' he queried drily.

'Just a glance, an unintentional glance, I promise you. The postcard—'

'Yes. Carelessly left on the kitchen table.'

'And do you mind?'

'Since the postman undoubtedly read it, and since it was in full view of any one dropping by for coffee, why on earth should I mind?' he asked.

'Now you're being evasive.'

'And you're afraid to put your thoughts into words. Afraid, Holly? Of me? Surely not,' he chided softly, turning his head to look at her, his eyes sombre black pools in the silvery light of the moon. 'Why not say what's on your mind, Holly? Spit it out before it chokes you.'

She took a deep breath. 'How can I ask?' she said simply. 'It's private. Something between you and your conscience.'

'And the postman, presumably,' he teased. 'And you—if you're sure you'd like to know?'

Holly nodded. 'I'd like to know—if you're sure you want to tell me?'

She saw him nod, close his eyes, lay his head back on the pillow. 'It's a long story,' he said at length. 'But I guess it goes back to the accident—'

'Sweetheart—'

'No,' he reassured her swiftly. 'I'm not about to bore you with all the gory details. But I was lucky. I survived, thank God—thanks *to* God,' he told her fiercely. 'And for once in my selfish, self-centred life I had to do something for somebody else. And, yes, Holly, to return to an earlier question, it helps. I go to mass because it helps. I lend a hand at Lourdes every once in a while because it helps. It helps put my problems into perspective. Strange,' he added, running his fingers through his hair in unexpected distraction, 'put like that, I guess I'm just as selfish as I've always been.'

The woman, Holly remembered as the pain scythed through. When he crashed the car, he'd been rushing back to be with the woman he loved.

'Don't,' she entreated, feeling the pain, his pain as well as her own.

'Don't what? Don't say it like it is, Holly?'

'Don't punish yourself for something you couldn't help,' she said softly.

'Oh, Holly.' He turned his head, his eyes locking with hers, the moment timeless. 'If only,' he murmured enigmatically.

'If only what?' she queried, almost afraid to breathe.

'Seven years too early, seven years too late. If only the gods had been kind to us,' he acknowledged, confusing her all over again, but since he was kissing her, holding her, stroking her, the sudden urgency caught her unawares and Holly's mind closed round the precious snippets of information, storing them away.

Dev—hands, mouth, tongue, body dominating her thoughts in an instant, the tension mounting, the tempo quickening as Dev parted her legs and thrust hard against her and she cried out as the release came, wave after wave of pure, unashamed pleasure rippling through her body. Holly smiled. Oh, yes. Man and woman, perfectly matched.

'I'm sorry,' he murmured softly.

'For what?' she asked, nestling against his chest, feeling his heart racing beneath her cheek as she allowed her fingers to scrunch the thick, dark mass of hair.

'For rushing it. I meant to take my time, savour each and every moment. But damn it, woman, you drive me insane.'

'All night,' she reminded. 'And by my reckoning, Dev, that leaves another five hours. Five hours of love. And next time, Dev...'

'Yes? Next time, Holly?' he prompted with a smile in his voice.

'Next time, my lord and master, it's my turn. Understand?'

'Perfectly,' he growled. 'That's what a man likes to hear, that he can fold his arms, lie back and think of England.'

'Sorry to disappoint you, Dev, but if I've got a hand in things, England's the last thing you'll be contemplating.'

'Promises, promises,' he teased. 'I can hardly wait.'

'Ah, yes, but patience,' she pointed out sweetly, 'is a virtue.'

'And virtue brings its own rewards,' he countered, snuggling down so that Holly was lying in the curve of his body, his front curled around her back, just like a pair of love spoons. 'Face it, Holly,' he added gleefully, kissing her exposed shoulder, 'Either way, I just can't lose.'

They slept. An hour, no more, seemingly aware that the moments of the night were too precious to waste in the land of dreams, such wonderful dreams, Holly acknowledged, wriggling her bottom into the warm lines of Dev's stomach.

She felt him stir against her, his manhood

hardening and straining and she smiled inside, wriggled closer still, teasing, inciting, heard Dev's sleepy growl of pleasure and pulled away, laughed as he reached out to pull her back into his arms, and his hand sneaked round, finding a breast ripe for his touch, his fingers cupping, taking the weight almost reverently, an idle thumb teasing the nipple which stiffened at the touch.

'Now we're quits,' he growled against her ear, thrusting his hips against her bottom. 'You're hard. I'm hard. I wonder who'll break first.' And his tongue darted into her ear as he nibbled the lobe, a strange, erotic touch that sent the heat surging through her body.

But it was Holly's turn. After all, hadn't she promised? And she twisted round so neatly that the contact of skin on skin was barely broken. And now he was pushing hard against her belly and she undulated against him, her hips describing erotic circles, touching, inciting, tantalizing, teasing, drawing back for the merest hint of an instant before swaying forwards again.

Dev groaned, and Holly laughed as she caught his hands to her breasts and allowed his hands to cup the creamy flesh, to squeeze, caress, and squeeze again as he teased her nipples by pinching them lightly between forefinger and thumb.

Holly laughed again, pushing his hands away and taking the weight of her straining breasts into her open palms. And she squeezed and rubbed the nipples with her thumbs, gurgling

222

inside as Dev groaned at the sight, and then she took pity, splaying her fingers and offering her breasts. Dev didn't need a second invitation, his mouth closing hungrily around one whilst his hand captured the other, and Holly arched her back, pushing herself into him, Dev's growls of frustration music to her ears until, finally taking pity, she raised her hips, parted her legs, allowing him the access that he craved, and Dev thrust home, unerringly, his fingers gripping her shoulders, thumbs stretching down to brush the rounded upper curve of breasts. Holly pushed forward to maintain the contact, and as his hands moved, closed around her straining, aching breasts, Holly laughed, pulling free.

'Not yet,' she told him smokily, and she pushed against him so that Dev was lying on his back, gazing up at her, a smile of indulgence playing about the corners of his mouth. 'Thinking of England?' she enquired saucily, straddling him.

'What do you think?' he challenged, but he raised his arms, threaded his hands behind his head, casual, oh so casual. Holly raised an eyebrow, lowered herself into position, thrust hard against him and back, almost to the point of separation. And then she paused.

'Like it?' she enquired, moving oh so slightly against him. And then she pulled back. Paused. Held position. Then the merest, tiniest, most infinitesimal movement back again.

'Oh, no, you don't!' he growled, thrusting against her, his hands whipping round to grip her shoulders, and he pulled her into his arms, allowed Holly's hips to build the momentum and then he rolled them over in the narrow confines of the bed, and they were soaring, higher and higher, faster and faster as the momentum gathered pace, man and woman, skin against skin, body buried in body, until the release came, an earth-shattering, mind-blowing explosion that built, detonated, reformed and rebuilt time and again, and again, and again.

And finally, sated, they slept.

A lifetime later, she felt Dev stir against her. 'The morning chorus,' he pointed out wryly, opening his eyes in the half-light and smiling down at her. 'I never thought I'd dread the simple sound of birds waking up the day.'

'"It was the nightingale and not the lark,"' Holly teased more in hope than expectation.

'Don't!' he said urgently, his eyes full of sudden shadows.

'Dev?'

'I don't want the night to end any more than you but, when it does, we'll have our whole lives ahead us. That happy ending, Holly. It's ours. We will make it happen.'

'But—'

'No buts. Just you and me, for ever and ever. Trust me.'

For ever and ever. Or till Dev grows tired. A happy ending. Trust. She'd trusted him once before, she recalled. And look where that had left her. And Dev had promised her nothing.

She slipped out of bed as Dev headed for the shower, pushing aside the curtains. Daylight.

Jonathan would be stirring soon and Dev would have to go. Yes. The lark was heralding the morn. End of the night. End of the dream. Because Dev had promised nothing. She leaned her forehead against the pane of glass, felt the chill, felt the chill of dread that was touching her heart. What had she done? A night of love. So little to ask for. Such a lot to relinquish. Only Dev had promised nothing. A single precious night of love, on her part, at least. And as for Dev—Holly brushed a tear away. He hadn't been short-changed, she decided. Wish to God that she had. So much easier to hate him that way. Love. Oh, Dev. Why did you come back? Why? Why? Why after all these years did you have to walk back into my life and turn it upside again?

She heard a movement at her side and turned her head. 'Holly?' Dev murmured, puzzled by her brooding silence. 'What is it, sweetheart? Tell me what's wrong.'

'Nothing,' she said, mustering self-control with a massive surge of will. 'You'd better get dressed, Dev. Jonathan will be up soon, and heaven help us if he sees that you're still here.'

'Ashamed, Holly? Of us?' Dev sounded amused.

'No. But he wouldn't understand and Meryl—'

'Will have to know sooner or later, Holly. But you're right. It wouldn't be fair on Jon. I'll go.'

Yes. Go. And don't come back, she added silently. Because it was all or nothing and she'd

225

been kidding herself. All night long she'd been kidding herself. She loved him. All or nothing. And since Dev didn't love her... Something clicked.

'What do you mean, Meryl will have to know sooner or later?' she queried in a strained voice.

He glanced up, straightening, zipping his fly and fastening the button securely. 'You and me. We belong together. And once you've told Courdrey—'

'No,' she said softly, almost pleadingly.

'No, what?'

'You and me. We don't belong. We're back in the real world now and—'

'No, Holly!' He closed the gap between them in an instant, strong fingers reaching out to grip her upper arms. 'You love me. You want me. We've just spent the night making love, for heaven's sake. You're mine,' he added, almost shaking her. 'You belong to me.'

'I don't *belong* to any man, Dev. I'm my own woman. Holly Scott, remember?'

'As if I'm likely to forget,' he tossed out bitterly.

'And what the hell does that mean?' she snapped as black eyes continued to bore into her.

'Holly Scott. And every inch a Scott,' he railed. 'And I should have known. Oh, yes! Oh, yes, I should have seen it coming. Because you simply can't resist following family tradition, hey, Holly? Money,' he all but spat, thrusting her away in disgust. 'Courdrey's money to make life sweet for Gregory Scott's money-grabbing, avaricious little girl.'

'No. You're wrong, very wrong.'

'Am I? Then tell me, my dear,' he entreated icily, folding his arms and regarding her from under hooded lids. 'Just out of idle curiosity, you know. Why Courdrey? If it isn't the money, then it has to be something else. Love?' he suggested sceptically. 'Sex? Better than me? Hell, woman, he'd have to be good to be better than me.'

'So sure, hey, Dev? Always so sure,' she mocked, but she was crying inside, dying inside, hitting out at the man she loved, hurting the man she loved and hating herself. And it didn't help that Dev was right. It was the money. But Meryl or Jonathan notwithstanding, she'd throw it all away tomorrow if Dev really cared. If he loved her. Love. He didn't know the meaning of the word, but no—that wasn't true either, she amended painfully. His woman. His love. She existed all right, somewhere. Only maybe, just maybe, the woman didn't need Dev, didn't love Dev, didn't want Dev. And maybe, just maybe, this was Dev's way of coping. Like Lourdes and going to mass. Love them and leave them. Love Holly and leave her. Except, of course, Dev didn't love her.

'You can't climb out of bed with me and go running straight into Courdrey's, damn you,' he said bitingly.

'Why not?' she queried calmly, a lot more calmly than she felt. 'After all, this is the twenty-first century, give or take a year or

227

two. And men and women do, you know.'

'Don't—'

'Don't, what? Speak the truth, Dev? Tell me,' she entreated frigidly, lifting her chin in unconscious challenge. 'Last Saturday. The night of the party. My engagement party,' she emphasized cruelly. 'Was it your bed, Dev? Or Lucy's?'

'But we— That was—'

'Different?' she suggested softly. 'I don't see why.'

'Because it didn't matter, Holly. It didn't. count. It wasn't important. Lucy—'

'Poor Lucy,' she mocked, but the pain was all hers, was tearing her apart. Dev and Lucy. Making love. Dev and Lucy, mouth to mouth, body to body. Dev and Lucy. Hands, mouth, tongue exploring. And oh, hell, how the picture hurt.

'You really are serious, aren't you, Holly?' he asked incredulously. 'You really do prefer Courdrey—and his millions—to me?'

'What do you think?' she asked, holding his gaze.

There was a pause, the longest pause she'd ever endured, and the shadows flitted across his face, his arrogant face that she loved so dearly, and Holly held her breath, waiting, simply waiting. Because even now she was weakening. She loved him. And one word from Dev and she'd take the terms he was offering. Hell and damnation, probably she acknowledged bitterly. But one word from Dev...

'I think you're lying. The Lord only knows

why, but you're lying. But your body doesn't lie, *this* doesn't lie,' he insisted, snatching her to him, kissing her briefly, insultingly, his hands ranging her body, a featherlight touch that Holly was powerless to resist. And he raised his head, his face dangerously close to hers, black eyes seeing to her soul. 'Your body doesn't lie,' he told her. 'And you can't. You won't. I refuse to believe you can climb into bed with another man when you body's crying out to be with mine. You can't.'

'Can't I?' she challenged, shaking herself free and forcing herself to meet his arctic gaze. 'Well, I've got news for you, Devlin Winter,' she castigated softly. 'I not only can—but will—and have done. Seven years, Dev. Seven long, lonely years. And more men than you've had hot dinners. After all,' she told him confidentially, 'practice makes perfect. And last night's performance surely has to prove it.'

'You're lying.'

'Am I?' she asked, aware of the snarl of disgust that darkened his features, of the wild pulse beating at the corner of his mouth. And as something vital died in Holly's mind, she smiled. She shrugged. 'Well, if you say so...'

He turned away, leaning against her dressing-table, the angle of his head strangely appealing, and Holly stepped forwards, reaching out, heaven only knows why, since she'd finally succeeded in convincing him. Only, sensing her approach, Dev spun round, the bleak expression in his eyes stopping her dead.

'Ilexia,' he sneered, opening his fingers to

reveal Holly's bottle of perfume. And he turned the bottle over, reading the caption, the words of French that Holly had been unable to understand, reciting the words in French almost like a prayer. 'Did *he* buy it? *Did* he, Holly?' he demanded harshly, his frigid glance sweeping across. And though she shook her head, it was already too late, because Dev had raised his arm and, with another snarl of disgust, hurled the bottle at the wall. Holly could only stand and watch as the crystal shattered, spattering glass and perfume across the sheets that bore the imprints of their bodies.

'Dev—'

'No.' He cut her off with an imperative wave of the hand. 'I've heard enough. More than enough. Enough to last me for all the tomorrows,' he added enigmatically. 'But if it helps, Holly,' he told her, angling his head, his piercing gaze colliding with hers, 'I'm sorry.'

'But I'm not,' she told him softly, dropping her eyes in shame and squeezing back the tears. And if Dev chose to misunderstand, well, she guessed she'd learn to live with it. After all, hadn't she had seven long, long years of practice?

PART TWO

CHAPTER 13

'She's sixteen years old, for heaven's sake. And she's my daughter. Look me in the eye and tell me you haven't been using Holly to dig the dirt on a story and get your filthy claws into me.'

Sixteen. Dev pulled the car off the road and put his head in his hands, Gregory Scott's words running through his head like the recurring theme of a film—or a nightmare. Sixteen. Sweet sixteen and never been kissed. Hardly, he could allow, but there was no escaping the facts. Dev *had* seduced her. All summer long. Loving her, wanting her, needing her. But robbing her of her innocence. Guilty. Guilty as hell because ignorance is no defence. Guilty as charged—no, not quite, he amended. Because yes, he'd loved Holly, made love with Holly, spent long, hot summer days with Holly, long, steamy summer nights with Holly, but Gregory Scott had never once entered his mind. He'd simply loved Holly. And it was wrong. Wonderful, but wrong. The most wonderful summer of his life. Oh, Holly! What have I done? Oh, God, what have I done?

And from Gregory Scott's face, the angles and planes an aching reminder of Holly, Dev had turned, sensing Holly's presence, seeing Holly framed in the doorway, the look of disgust she took no pains to hide. Because Gregory Scott had condemned him, and Holly had listened to the words. And Devlin Winter had been proud, proud and stubborn. Holly believed. It was enough. And so the nightmare had continued. Twenty-four hours. How much can happen in twenty-four hours? Twenty-four hours ago he'd been lying on a beach with Holly, kissing Holly, loving Holly, being loved by Holly. And then the bombshell—

Just sixteen years old. And he loved her. And he'd left her. And life would go on. So—Dev straightened, glanced around, attempting to focus his mind. First things first. Shake off the jet lag, then back to London. See the boss. Have himself assigned to another job. And forget her. And he *would* forget her—in time. Time. It was all a matter of time.

Oh, yes, and the small matter of an understanding boss.

Nik Fisher's face was stormy. 'Another commission? Are you mad? This story's hot, Dev, red hot. Scott's up to his neck in pension-fund fraud and you've got a direct line to his heart—always assuming he has one, that is.' And the heavy features lightened as he laughed, his warped sense of humour detecting one of his weak, but legendary jokes.

Dev stood impassive. Normally he'd join in, anything to keep Nik happy. Only not this time. This time, he'd had enough.

Suddenly aware of the deafening silence, Nik Fisher frowned. 'Come on, Dev. You're a professional. It's just another job. And you're one of the best. And since you found the girl, did exactly as planned—'

'Not quite,' Dev amended painfully.

'No? Well, that's not what I heard. But I guess you know better.' He shrugged. 'Just good friends, huh? But good enough to take the next flight out and offer an olive branch? Though, on second thoughts,' he added, grinning like a stuck pig, 'make it a sprig of holly. Holly—get it?'

'Is that supposed to be funny?' Dev enquired deceptively mildly. For two pins he'd tell Fisher exactly what he could do with the job. And the words orifice and stuff wouldn't come close to an accurate translation. Strange how he'd never realized before just how much he detested the man. Twenty stones of pink, perspiring flesh. Twenty stones of leering, laughing lard.

The phone rang; as Fisher turned to answer it, Dev wandered over to the window. London. Grey, grimy London. Even in the middle of August there was a pall hanging over the place. And it was cold. Despite the sunshine, the temperature in the mid-seventies, after a summer of sun, sand and sea in Los Cristianos, Dev was chilled to the bone. Still, he could hardly blame the weather, he thought wearily.

'Okay.' Nik Fisher had slammed the phone down, was eyeing Dev with anything but benevolence. 'Basically, what you're saying is you've blown it. The best reporter I've got has had a six-week break at the firm's expense and hasn't a single word to show for it?'

Dev shrugged. 'Scott didn't show, as I'm sure you must know, and the girl was too young to help. She's just a kid, Nik, still wet behind the ears.'

Only that wasn't true either, he told himself. He was lying, lying to Nik, lying to himself. And the stark fact was, neither one believed him. And Holly—

'Wet behind the ears, huh?' Nik Fisher whistled under his breath. 'Like I said, if you say so. But if the girl wasn't worth pumping, what was to stop you sweet-talking the other one?'

'What other one?'

'The wicked stepmother. The young, attractive fortune-hunting model who married Scott last March and put the girl's nose firmly out of joint.' And then, incredulously, 'You mean you didn't even see her?'

Didn't see her, didn't know of her existence. Not strictly true, of course, since Dev had done his homework, spending time poring over archives, writing copious notes and committing interesting snippets to memory. And then he'd arrived in Tenerife to see Venus emerge from the waves and the rest of the world had ceased to exist. Holly. He could smell her, touch her, taste her. And oh, God, how he wanted her.

'So—' Nik Fisher was frowning again. 'You blew it. For two pins, Dev, I'd fire you.'

For two pins I'd quit, deny you the pleasure, Dev countered acidly, but silently. Aware that he was perilously close to doing precisely that, he simply shrugged, pouring himself a coffee from the jug that simmered permanently on the bench. It would be thick as treacle and bitter as hell, but he needed a drink, needed a brandy more, needed to escape from the man's oppressive presence.

Remembering in time whose office it was: 'Coffee?' he offered politely, holding out an empty cup.

Fisher shook his head. 'Go back to Tenerife, Dev. Another two weeks, three at the most and the story's ours. He's guilty as hell and we'll have a world exclusive. Your steamy nights of love with Scott's attractive daughter.'

Dev's head snapped up. 'You've been checking up on me.'

'Too damn right I have. Six weeks and hardly a phone call. Six weeks and barely a word. I wanted dirt on Scott, not a travelogue. So—what's it to be? Tenerife or Siberia?'

Another of Nik's little jokes. Only, this time he wasn't joking. Dev sipped his coffee, eyed him warily. What could he say? He was stymied. Damned if he did and damned if he didn't. Only he couldn't. He loved her. He owed her. He'd done more than enough to hurt her. He had to leave her in peace.

'I can't,' he said simply.

'Can't—or won't?' Nik queried unsmilingly.

'And what's that supposed to mean?' Dev challenged, a shiver of premonition running down his spine.

Nik smiled, only the light didn't reach his eyes. Strange eyes, almost colourless, Dev registered, as Nik, those beady, translucent pupils never leaving Dev's face, reached into a drawer, drew out an envelope, placed it squarely on the desk in front him.

'Can't—or won't?' Nik repeated, pushing the envelope across.

Dev glanced down. Spanish stamps. Tenerife postmark. Yesterday's postmark. Had clearly been opened. Was just as clearly addressed to Dev. His frigid gaze snapped back to Nik.

'All's fair in love and war,' the other man reminded him with another sly smile. 'And since you weren't here to open it yourself...'

'Since it clearly didn't arrive until this morning,' Dev bit out, 'that, Nik, is a matter of opinion.'

'Well?'

'Well, what?'

'Aren't you going to open it?'

'Since someone else got to it first, apparently not.'

'Well, don't you want to know what's in it?' Nik demanded impatiently.

'Not especially.' And definitely not with those beady eyes boring into him. Holly. For a fleeting moment of madness he thought it could be Holly. And then common sense surged. She had his home address. Why the hell would she write care of the office? So—that only left Gregory Scott. And he could well imagine what he'd have to say.

'Okay.' Fisher straightened. 'Since you won't, looks like I'll have to.' And he drew out the contents, a single slip of paper—no, not a piece of paper, Dev realized as Nik flipped it over with a theatrical flourish. A cheque. English pounds. An obscene amount of English pounds. 'Payment for services rendered?' Nik queried softly. 'Stud fees, Dev? Or a simple case of blackmail?'

Dev didn't move, hardly dared breathe. Stud fees? Given Gregory Scott's reaction, quite the reverse. Hands off, then. Off what? Dev wondered fleetingly. Holly? Or had Nik hit the nail squarely on the head? Because the story was about to break and this was Gregory Scott's less-than-subtle way of buying Dev's silence?

'Well, Dev?'

'You tell me,' he invited calmly, a lot more calmly than he felt.

'Oh, no,' Nik countered with that familiar, sly smile. '*You* tell me.'

'Nothing to tell,' Dev insisted, his calm air sheer bravado.

Fisher tapped the cheque. 'No,' he agreed thoughtfully. 'I guess there isn't—now.'

'Meaning?'

'He's bought you out. Here's the proof of it. The only question now, of course, is why?'

'Wrong, Nik. Wrong on every count.' And though Dev's temper was simmering just below the surface, he calmly reached across, filched the cheque from under Fisher's grubby fingernail and ripped it clean in half. 'Satisfied?' he queried icily, holding the scraps between forefinger and thumb and well out of Fisher's reach.

'Not wise, Dev. Not wise at all,' Fisher murmured coldly, shaking his head. And then he grinned, producing a wad of photostats from a box file on the desk, and the same obscene amount of money clearly payable to Dev stared out from a dozen pages. 'Exhibit one, perhaps?' he queried slyly.

Dev shrugged. What did it matter? Nik needed a story, would invent one if necessary. And if Dev—or Holly—got caught in the cross fire, then tough. As Fisher had eloquently stated, all's fair in love and war—in this line of work at least. But what a revolting way to earn a crust, Dev acknowledged, his lips twisting bitterly. Gutter press. And Dev Winter was no better than the rest.

'So—' Nik mused, watching him carefully. 'You'll go back?'

'No.' Dev's tone was curiously flat, the absence of emotion all the more emphatic. 'Not a cat in hell's chance. Not if exhibits two to a hundred thousand were sitting on that desk. I'm through with Tenerife.' Through with you, if you push me too far, though judging from Nik's glowering face, quitting was a luxury that could well be denied him.

Unexpectedly, Fisher smiled. 'Fine,' he murmured, slumping down into his seat. 'Siberia it is. Or in this case, the chilly glens of Scotland. Deer rustling. The wildlife man in the Scottish office has gone down with the plague or something equally revolting. The job's all yours. Oh, and this time, Dev, make sure you rustle up a good story, huh?' And belatedly aware of what he'd said, Nik grinned.

'Don't,' Dev urged, before the man could speak, could invite applause for another play on words. 'Don't even think it.' But Nik was smiling. And so was Dev. Fleetingly. Another day. Another day without Holly. But day by day, bit by bit the pain would ease and he would forget her. Only right now, the easiest way of managing that was to focus on the bottom of a glass. And the bigger the glass, the better.

A week. A week of banishment. And Nik had been right about one thing. It was cold. Cold as the plains of Siberia. But Dev was busy. He had a job to do and every waking hour was filled to bursting point. It was the nights that proved a torment. Because looking at the world through the bottom of a glass didn't help at all. Oh, yes, the alcohol worked. It took the edge off the hunger, the raw, aching need he had of Holly.

Then he'd sleep, sleep the sleep of the damned, because his dreams were full of Holly, dreams that turned into nightmares with Gregory Scott's face looming large, his words booming round and round inside Dev's head. Sixteen. And he'd ruined her life. And worse than that, thanks to her father, she really did believe that Dev had been using her. Better that way, he consoled himself. He'd loved Holly. She'd loved him. Now she would hate him. Holly was luckier than Dev, he acknowledged. She had the hate to focus on.

'Let me guess. The frozen north doesn't hold much appeal for a sun-tanned southerner?'

A woman's voice, just a hint of amusement. Dev glanced up, resenting the intrusion and

241

yet aware from her face that it was more than idle curiosity. 'Hi, Flora.' He spread his hands, waving her to the chair opposite. 'Can I get you a drink?'

She shook her head, glancing across to the noisy group who were pushing their way through to the bar. Recognizing Dev, one or two raised a hand in greeting, and he nodded, managed a fleeting smile before switching his gaze back to Flora.

'Why not come over and join us?' she suggested warmly.

It was Dev's turn to shake his head. 'Thanks, but in my present state of mind, I'd only prove a damper,' he explained with an apologetic shrug of the shoulders.

Flora smiled. 'Fine. And in that case,' she declared, slipping into the vacant chair and shaking off her jacket, 'if a girl's allowed to change her mind, mine's half of shandy.'

Dev grinned despite himself. Out-manouevred. She'd known he was simply being polite, offering the drink in the first place, that he wouldn't be keen to join the gang from work. But half an hour's small talk wouldn't hurt and then he'd make his excuses, take the long route back to his digs and then finish the night in a warm haze of malt.

Or that was the plan. Walking the late-night streets with Flora on his arm hadn't been in the frame. But Flora was undemanding and better than that, she was fun. Fun. How long since he'd had fun? A lifetime, he decided as they reached her front door. And yes, the past ten days had been a lifetime. A lifetime without Holly. Holly. Face it man, he told himself sternly. You've lost her. She was never yours to take in the first place and now you've lost her. And life has to go on.

Flora smiled up at him. 'A wee nightcap?' she offered. 'Or a coffee, if you'd rather.'

He shook his head, aware of the flicker of disappointment that crossed her face in the shadows, yet her ready smile was back in an instant.

'Why not?' he heard himself agreeing, following her inside.

It wasn't a large flat but was neat and tidy, with surprisingly modern prints dominating the soft pastel walls, and he flung his jacket over a chair as he sank down into the cushions of the low-backed settee.

'Scotch?' she enquired, holding out an almost-full bottle.

Liquid comfort. Given a choice, he'd opt for brandy any day but in this neck of the woods that was tantamount to treason, and when in Rome...

He took a long, hard slug and, aware of the girl slipping in beside him, Dev felt the stirrings of unease. He should have taken the chair, made it plain from the start that all he wanted was that drink. And the company. The company of a pretty girl, and, yes, come to think of it, Flora was pretty. Five feet six, he gauged, slim but with curves in all the right places and a cascade of dark brown curls framing her heart-shaped face. Attractive. At twenty-one and

243

clearly independent, she'd be every man's ideal. Every man except Dev.

'So—want to tell me about it?'

'About what?' he stalled, swirling the golden liquid round and round his glass.

Flora shrugged. 'Fine.' As on the doorstep, she wasn't the least put out by his rebuff. 'You'll be going home soon, I suppose?' she probed, tactfully changing the subject.

Dev shrugged. Home. Home alone. 'Who knows?' he murmured drily. 'Who cares?'

'I do, as it happens. But I don't expect that to console you.'

'Oh?' He twisted round, pushing his body back against the arm. It wasn't a bit comfortable but it put space between them and he felt safer. He swallowed a wry smile. Safe. How ironic. The famed love-them-and-leave-them Devlin Winter had finally got his comeuppance, and how!

'You're a new face, a breath of fresh air in the office,' Flora explained, sipping her drink thoughtfully. 'You've livened things up.'

'Heaven help the place normally, then,' he allowed with another fleeting grin. 'Face it, Flora, I'm hardly the life and soul of the party.'

'Not tonight, maybe,' she agreed, 'since there's clearly something on your mind. But—'

'But?' Dev queried.

'You work hard. You've a different approach. And your reputation's preceded you. It's been nice working with *The Beacon's* top reporter.'

Ex-top reporter, if Dev didn't toe the company

244

line back in London. And he wasn't kidding himself on that. Sending Dev to Scotland had been inspirational on Fisher's part; though Glasgow was hardly the ends of the earth, it had taken Dev away from his usual haunts, the wide circle of friends and host of invaluable contacts who helped Dev nose his way into a story. If he'd worked hard this week, he'd really had no choice. He was the new boy in town and he was on his own. Oh, yes. His lips twisted bitterly. And work helped to numb the pain of Holly.

'And?' he queried, smiling despite himself.

'Like I said, I'm impressed. If you stayed, you'd be running the place inside a month.'

'Maybe,' Dev mused. And he had to admit, the place was in need of a shake up.

'But?'

'Did I say but?' he found himself teasing.

'You didn't need to,' she retorted, smiling, relaxing, moving imperceptibly closer. 'It was written loud and clear on your handsome face. Like I said earlier, the frozen north doesn't appeal, hey?'

'Some parts definitely would,' he admitted, his warm, appreciative glance travelling over her. Flirting, he realized as the whisky fired his blood, dulled the nagging pain that was pulling at his heart. And why not? A bit of harmless fun. As long as they both knew the rules. And since Flora Penman flushed prettily, darting him a shrewd, assessing glance from underneath her long, curly lashes, she'd know the rules all right.

She leaned forwards, parting her lips, not so much a blatant invitation as a hint and Dev, under the glow of the spirits, felt the first stirrings of interest.

'Any parts in particular?' she enquired softly, wide brown eyes fastened on his.

Dev dropped his gaze, his eyes moving down her body, slowly this time, a long and leisurely perusal. Slim to the point of skinniness, but with surprisingly full breasts; since she'd gone out straight from work, neatly dressed in office clothes: crisp white cotton blouse that gaped slightly across her cleavage, giving a tantalizing glimpse of the curves beneath, and a severe navy skirt, straight cut and short. Good legs, he acknowledged, sweeping the shapely calves and ankles and then climbing upwards.

Reaching her breasts again, his head snapped up in alarm. 'I don't think—'

'Yes, you do,' she contradicted almost pleadingly, and Dev held his breath, dropped his gaze to the blouse she'd neatly unbuttoned, his eyes flicking back to lock with hers. Along with the whisky, it was just a wee bit of comfort she was offering, and judging from the expression in her eyes, it had taken a lot for Flora to push herself forward, make the first move. And if Dev rebuffed her...

He closed his eyes for a moment. Why not? Why not take up the offer? Lose himself in her body. *Use her,* the voice of his conscience bit. But she wanted him, and though clearly out of character, she hadn't been slow to let him know. And Flora was a woman, damn it. She knew the rules and she knew what she was doing. And she was offering. But Dev didn't have to say yes. Didn't have to say no, either, he reasoned, weakening despite himself. Give and take. Man and woman. Sex. Oh, so easy to say yes. Only he couldn't. So how to turn her down without seeming churlish or embarking on a long explanation he wasn't yet ready to share?

Sensing a movement beside him, he raised his leaden lids. 'Please, Dev,' Flora murmured, sliding into his arms and raising her face for a kiss. Dev stifled a groan, logging the fear, the hesitation, the shadow of hunger in her eyes. His heart sank. He was going to hurt her. Whatever he did, he would hurt her. And God, she was pretty. She smelt good, felt good, all soft and sensuous and inviting, and as her arms slid up behind his neck, drawing his head down to hers, the tensions of the day begin to drain away.

Their lips met. Hardly fireworks, but she tasted as good as she looked and Dev growled suddenly, gathering her to him, pressing her to him, his mouth exploring hers, his tongue teasing hers. He was vaguely aware of her fingers fumbling with the buttons of his shirt, tugging the material free from the waistband of his trousers, and she pushed the material away, rubbing herself against his chest, the lace of her bra all scratchy and strange, decidedly erotic.

Suddenly impatient, Dev pushed her blouse over the curve of her shoulders, peeling her arms from the sleeves, his sure fingers homing in to snap the catch of her bra. And then it was skin against skin, body against body and Dev knew he was losing the battle.

Without breaking the contact, he urged her back onto the cushions, his mouth beginning to explore her neck as his hands slid down, down and round. And Flora laughed as her nipples tightened, and her hands ranged his body, kneading the taut muscles of his back, sliding over the curve of his buttocks, over and round, and, as she rubbed against him, Dev hardened.

He groaned, burying his face in her breasts, his tongue lapping, his mouth teasing, his teeth nibbling the swollen nipples. Hell, but she tasted good, smelt good, felt good. And he needed her. So, so easy to forgot, to respond, to react, to drive himself into her body and lose himself, to close his eyes, close his mind and take her. And with urgent fingers tugging at his zipper, Dev felt the heat of anticipation. He wanted her, she wanted him just as badly. Not love, sex, the voice of his conscience reminded. Sex. Wonderful, mind-blowing sex. Sex with Holly. Love with Holly. Sex with Flora—No!

He pulled away, his fingers closing round her wrist, a vice-like grip that bit cruelly into her flesh. And catching the awful flash of comprehension in her eyes, he hated himself, loathed himself. He'd hurt her. Damned if he did and damned if he didn't. He'd hurt her, but the least he could do was salvage her pride, give her back her self respect.

'Too soon, honey,' he murmured wryly, back

in control and thinking fast. And he drew her back into his arms, kissing her, cradling her face in his hands and kissing her again, and then he held her against him, stroking, soothing, calming, waiting for overwrought emotions to calm. For long, long moments neither of them stirred.

'I guess I'd better be going,' he murmured at last.

'Coffee?' Flora asked, her face cradled against his chest.

Dev shook his head. 'It's late. And you and I, ma'am, are up at the crack of dawn tomorrow. Work,' he reminded, dropping another light kiss on her forehead.

'As if I could forget.' But she was on her feet now, her back turned against him as she retrieved her blouse and bra, and Dev, feeling her pain, her embarrassment, headed for what he hoped was the bathroom door.

He took his time, buttoning his shirt and tucking it down into his trousers, his strained face staring back from the glass. He'd wanted her. No. His body had been playing tricks. He wanted Holly. Always Holly. And sweet release for his body would have been torment for his soul. He'd have loathed himself. He loathed himself now. He stiffened. For the night wasn't over. The worst was yet to come, because heaven alone knew how, but he'd to go back into that lounge and say goodnight to a girl he'd just rejected. And more than that—he had to do it without hurting her.

'See you tomorrow,' he murmured at the

door, and impulsively he bent his head and kissed her.

Not surprisingly, Flora didn't respond. 'Good night, Dev,' she said instead. And then, the dry words sounding strangely prophetic to Dev's sensitive ears—or maybe it was guilt, he acknowledged fleetingly— 'Goodbye, Dev.'

CHAPTER 14

Free. Six months of freedom. Six months of hell. But he'd kept himself busy, called in a handful of favours and roamed the French countryside in search of interesting snippets to beef up into features. It paid the bills and it kept him busy. Not the high-profile job he'd had in London, but it kept the wolf from the door and more importantly, his mind away from Holly. No. He'd never manage that, he realized, but the sheer graft of work helped. As did being away from British papers.

When the story finally broke, Dev had scoured the pages of *The Beacon* for the slightest mention of his name, breathing a huge sigh of relief when he didn't find it. Poor Holly. She'd be going through hell. But she wouldn't find Dev joining the hysterical mob braying for Scott's blood and maybe, just maybe, he told himself, clutching at straws, maybe it would be some consolation.

Six months. Six long months of hell. But the right decision, he was sure of it. Thanks to Flora.

Flora. His mouth softened at the memory. 'Goodbye, Dev,' she'd murmured drily, not waiting for Dev to move away before closing the door. And though he'd had every intention of walking back to his hotel and climbing into bed, somewhere along the way he'd had a change of mind. He'd had enough. It was his life and it was high time he took control. And life on the road suited him.

Reaching the centre of the town, he spotted a phone box and checked his pockets for jetons. Might as well call Joe, see how he felt about a convent of nuns and their illicit brewery. More mileage in that than the perfume story. Dev grinned. Good old Joe. He'd taken everything Dev had offered, but published it under a by-line to stop Nik Fisher exacting his revenge. Dev Winter, Our Man In France.

Good old Joe. Poor, pathetic Fisher. Dev's grin broadened as he recalled Fisher's stunned reaction to his news...

'What do you mean, you're quitting?'

'What I said. I'm through. Finished. I've had enough.'

'You're through, all right,' Fisher had acknowledged icily. 'Through with me, through with *The Beacon,* and you're finished in the business. Understand, Dev? Walk out on me and you'll be cutting your own throat.'

But Dev had simply shrugged. Maybe, he'd silently conceded, and since Fisher had influence, he'd be on the phone within minutes blackening Dev's name. But Dev didn't care any more. He was free. Or as free as he'd ever be with the shadow of Holly hanging over him.

Without a word, he'd swung away, heading for the door.

'And where the hell do you think you're going?' Nik had demanded querulously.

'Going?' Dev had halted, not bothering to turn, half-smiling to himself 'Surely it's obvious. I'm leaving. Quitting. Walking out. You know, the sort of thing you do when you've resigned.'

'Resigned, my foot. You're fired,' Fisher had roared.

'A rose by any other name,' Dev had murmured, completely unperturbed. 'Either way, Nik, I'm off.'

'Oh, no! Not without working your notice. And since you've just had six weeks' paid leave, you'll work your ticket and stick around until October. Are you listening, Winter?'

Oh, yes, he'd been listening. But it hadn't made a scrap of difference. Paid leave. Nik Fisher's quaint description of heaven. His six weeks of bliss with Holly. Dev's lips had twisted. 'Goodbye, Nik,' he'd flung back over his shoulder, his outstretched hand closing round the handle.

'But—you can't, damn you! Are you listening, Winter? You can't. I won't let you. Damn it, man, you can't!'

Dev had turned then, smiling, though the light hadn't reached his eyes. And he'd paused. And he'd waited. And his glance had travelled the dingy office, over the shabby furniture and across the greasy, coffee-stained carpet before climbing the desk to the enormous tub of lard that was slumped behind it, and their glances had locked, forcing Dev to smother an instinctive grimace of distaste. 'Can't I?' he'd queried softly, arching a single, enquiring eyebrow. And the lazy smile had broadened. 'Well, have I got news for you,' he'd contradicted silkily, flicking two fingers to his temple in jaunty salute. 'Just you watch me...'

Easy. Easy as pie. And despite Nik Fisher's sour prediction that he was finished in the business, Dev had survived.

Humming lightly under his breath, he dialled the international code and the number he knew by heart, fingers tapping out a rhythm on the shelf as he waited for the connection.

'Joe—'

'Dev! Thank God you've called. Since he did it last night, it missed the early editions so we can still make a scoop if you fly back today. You knew the man. How soon can you be here?'

'Hey, slow down, Joe.' Dev smiled indulgently. 'I'm your man in France, remember? Why the sudden need to pull me home?'

'Scott. Did he fall or was he pushed? And you knew him, Dev, spent a whole summer shacked up with his daughter. Hell, man, you must have known the guy.'

Dev winced at the crude turn of phrase. Though it could have been worse, he silently acknowledged, Joe's command of expletives a legend in the business. And how the hell had Joe known about Holly? Dev stiffened. Fisher. Trust the man to waste no time opening his mouth. But no time to waste on Fisher. Dev's mind had moved on and, sensing the barely suppressed excitement in Joe's voice, a prickle of apprehension rippled down his spine.

'What has Gregory Scott done now, Joe?' he asked carefully.

'Gone swimming. Swimming with the fishes. He's drowned. We-ell,' Joe added with rare journalistic concession to accuracy, 'he's missing, presumed drowned. Disappeared from that yacht of his off the coast of Tenerife. The Elixir or something.'

'*Ilex*,' Dev corrected automatically. Holly. Oh, God, Holly!

'So, until the body's found, it's anyone's guess what's happened. My money's on a set-up,' Joe murmured confidentially. 'Faked suicide. You mark my words, in another few months he'll surface in Monte or Rio with the elusive Lord Lucan and under the circumstances, they'll make a good pair. So, Dev, my boy,' he ended almost gleefully, 'how soon can you be here?'

London? Was Joe mad? Head back to London at a time like this? Dev would take the first plane out, all right, but he'd be flying south, not north, and without another word, he dropped the handpiece back onto the cradle.

Holly. He had to get back to Holly. She'd be in Tenerife, he'd stake his life on it. Or on her way. Because that's where Scott was. Missing, presumed drowned. Did he fall or was he pushed? What the hell had Joe been hinting? Suicide—faked or otherwise? Murder? Or accidental death? And Dev hoped to God for Holly's sake that it was the last one.

Holly. Oh, my love. He had to get back. He had to get to the airport—Toulouse, he decided, mentally gauging the distance. He'd be there for

255

Holly. Hang on in there, sweetheart, he prayed. I'm on my way. And he put the car into gear, leaving the sleepy town behind and heading for the open road, his racing mind juggling the priorities. Money first. Head for Tarbes and call in at the nearest bank. Thank God he'd plenty saved. Time. That's all he needed. Time to sort out his finances, time to book a plane ticket, time to make the tortuous drive to Toulouse.

Holly. Oh, God, how he'd missed her, and his mind slipped, seeing Holly that very first time, rising out of the water at Los Cristianos. And since it was a private beach, her father's private beach, she was naked. Naked, and beautiful. Just like a goddess. Aphrodite emerging from the sea to capture his mind, his mind, soul and body. And he'd held his breath, convinced he must be dreaming.

But, no, she was walking towards him, hadn't seen him, was shaking drops of water from her eyes, the most beautiful woman he'd ever seen. Holly. Wonderful, sun-kissed Holly with her long, fair hair plastered to her shoulders, seawater trickling down her cleavage. High, firm breasts, dark nipples prominent—Dev went hard simply at the memory. As he had done then.

She'd drawn nearer, close enough for Dev to see the colour of her eyes. And still she hadn't spotted him, unexpectedly camouflaged beneath the shade of the single palm umbrella. Beautiful. Wonderful. Flat belly, long, slender legs, legs all the way to her armpits, he remembered thinking

256

at the time, and with that luscious tangle of curls at the apex.

And he'd stepped out, gently so as not to startle her, and she'd smiled, not in the least self-conscious. Because she'd known, as Dev had known instinctively, that they belonged. And he'd kissed her. Simply that. But it was enough. Because the flame had run through them like a brand. And she'd raised her head, her breathing not quite steady, and he'd seen the wonder in her eyes, the fear flickering in her eyes, love in her eyes. And then she'd bolted. And Dev had smiled. And waited. Day after day he'd waited. Because she'd be back. He knew she'd be back. And next time...

He closed his eyes for an instant, a mere fraction of an instant, his need of Holly so urgent he almost cried out with the pain. Then the shrill blast of a car horn dragged him rudely back to present and, too late, Dev realized the road had snaked into a bend. And he was fighting for control, fighting with the wheel, losing the wheel as the road dropped away and the bend doubled back on itself, and then he was falling, falling, falling into the blackness...

CHAPTER 15

Practice. And practice makes perfect. And she'd had plenty of that recently. Seven years of living without Dev. Seven days of living without Dev. Because he'd gone. He'd simply turned and walked away. Not a word, not a sound. All week, not a word. And then Jonathan had gone across to Branville for his riding class.

'Dev's gone. Josette says he's gone to work in Paris and he won't be back for the rest of the summer. Truly, Holly. Francine told her. But, it isn't fair,' Jonathan wailed. 'He promised. He said he'd take me riding. Why did he promise if he knew he was going away?'

And meeting Meryl's solemn gaze across Jonathan's tousled head, Holly's heart turned over. He'd gone. She'd driven him away. Was there no end to the pain, to the heartbreak? she asked herself. Holly, Dev, an innocent six-year-old boy. All down to Holly.

She crouched, pulling Jonathan to her, hugging him fiercely, holding him, drawing comfort from the child's warm body. 'I'm sorry, poppet. But these things happen—'

'But he promised—' Jonathan repeated, his brown eyes swimming with tears. 'And grown-ups always keep their promises—you said,' he added accusingly.

'I know, darling. And they do, if they can. I

guess something important came up and Dev didn't have time to explain. How about I take you riding instead?'

His face lit up. 'Will you?' he asked, and just as swiftly the clouds were in his eyes again. 'But you don't ride. Not like Dev.'

'Not as good as Dev, maybe,' she allowed, smiling despite herself. 'Since I'm bound to be rusty. But give me time to practice—'

'No!' He twisted free, his face red and angry as he hit out, fists flailing the air in front of them. 'Don't want you. Want Dev,' he insisted fiercely, and though Holly tried to draw him back, he pushed her away, turning on his heels and dashing from the room.

Holly straightened, Jonathan's unconscious choice of words running through her like a blade. Want Dev. Oh yes, she wanted Dev. Loved him, wanted him, ached for him, needed him. But she'd driven him away and this time there'd be no going back. Dev had gone for good. Damping down the pain, she forced a reassuring smile for Meryl. 'Let him go,' she advised, catching the heavy tread of footsteps on the stairs. 'He'll come round.'

'You knew, didn't you, Holly?' Meryl probed, cloudy blue eyes fastened on Holly's face. 'And you're right, of course. Jonathan's just a child and he's bound to come round in time. But what about you?' she added softly, unexpectedly. 'Will you come round as easily?'

And Holly nodded, too raw to reply, aware of a wealth of knowledge in Meryl's eyes and suddenly afraid that, once she began, she'd never be able to stop, that the whole sordid tale would come spilling out, raking up the past, the pain, the love, the need, and she closed her eyes, squeezing back the tears, fingernails digging cruelly into her palms as she battled for control.

'Oh, yes,' she told Meryl, willing herself to believe it. 'I'll come round.' And she would too, if it took half a lifetime. Seven years times seven. More than half a lifetime. But time would pass and Holly would cope. And, in the meanwhile, it was Saturday tomorrow and Alex would be flying in to spend time with his cheating fiancée. Holly's lips twisted. Shop-soiled. Yes, that just about summed her up. But how could anything so wonderful possibly sound so sordid? Oh, Dev. What have I done? What have we done? And how on earth to face Alex and pretend there's nothing wrong?

'Not wearing my ring, Holly? Not tired of me already, surely?' Alex drawled, and though the words were light-hearted, Holly's sensitive ear caught the thinly veiled annoyance in his tone.

She flushed, glancing down at her hands. She hadn't worn the ring since the night of the engagement. No, that wasn't strictly true, she amended, recalling Dev's sneering observation at the airport. But she'd hadn't worn it since. Part guilt, she acknowledged, part unease, because the solitaire diamond was heavy, it didn't sit well on Holly's slender finger and, since it was clearly worth a fortune, she was terrified of losing it.

Alex raised a sceptical eyebrow. 'Lose it?' he murmured in response to her feeble explanation. 'That's hardly likely, Holly. And what if you did? It's well insured. One ring, two, a dozen.' He shrugged. 'Once we're married, you'll have a bank vault full,' he pronounced carelessly. 'Now run upstairs, there's a good girl, and put it on. You're mine, and I want the whole world to know.'

Holly's colour deepened. You're mine. Two men, an identical claim. And they were both wrong, she insisted, pulling open the dressing-table drawer and taking the box from under the frothy pile of underwear. She was Holly Scott, with a mind of her own. She belonged to no man—yet. But she caught sight of her reflection in the glass and knew she was dangerously close to selling herself.

'Much better.' Alex flashed his approval, his warm, appreciative glance narrowing in speculation as it travelled the length of her body. 'Now, how about a drive?'

'A drive?'

'Sure. Why not? We can drive along the coast, find ourselves a secluded little cove and spend a lazy afternoon alone. Just the two of us. You, me, and a bottle of wine. Colette's already packed a bottle in ice, so grab your swimsuit and we'll head east. Or west, if you'd rather.'

'But—you don't like beaches,' Holly stalled, remembering the last time she'd been alone on a beach with a man, alone with Dev at midnight.

'I do now,' he murmured, and his glance

travelled over her again, lazily, suggestively, openly, appraisingly, and tiny hairs on the back of Holly's neck began to stand on end.

'Down to the beach? Yippee!' Jonathan trilled when Holly explained they were going out. 'I can come, can't I, Holly?'

'Sorry, kid,' Alex cut in as Holly searched for the words to let him down gently. 'Another time maybe. This trip's just for the grown-ups.'

'But it wouldn't have done any harm,' Holly protested out in the car. 'Jonathan's just a kid—'

'Exactly. Someone else's kid. And he's always underfoot. There's no privacy, Holly. We're never alone. I simply want us to be alone. There's no harm in that, surely, honey?'

None at all. In normal circumstances.

Man and woman. Newly engaged. Stretched out on a beach. Close. Dangerously close. Half-naked. More than half-naked. And exposing more of Alex's body than she'd ever seen before, Holly realized, subconsciously noting the sprinkle of gold across a powerful chest, the well-toned muscles taut from daily workouts at the gym, and reaching the bulge at the junction of his legs, her eyes skittered away. Because they were alone, half-naked and alone.

A shadow fell across her. Holly glanced up to find Alex lounging beside her, his body propped up on an elbow.

'My Holly,' he murmured, trailing the back of a finger across her cheek. 'My sweet and innocent little Holly.'

Holly felt the stirrings of alarm. Sweet and innocent? Hardly. Shop-soiled. Just the sort of woman Alex professed to despise. And why not? Didn't Dev despise her too, now that she'd given him the truth? More men than Dev had had hot dinners. Past tense, she consoled herself. She'd turned into a tramp all right, but that was in the past. Oh yes? And who was she kidding? Engaged to one man, making love with another. All night long. Only it wasn't love, on Dev's part at least. So—face it, Holly. You're a tramp. Dev's turned you back into a tramp. And how!

Alex dipped his head, brushing his lips across hers. 'My little Holly,' he murmured again, nibbling at the corner of her mouth, and then he was kissing her, his lips moving against hers, his tongue pushing through, sweeping into the warm, moist corners of her mouth. A moment later he was stretched out on the towel beside her, and Holly could feel his body heat, was shockingly aware of his hands roaming her body. She began to squirm in protest, an automatic response that Alex completely misconstrued, because he raised his head for an instant, steely blue eyes locking with hers, an amused expression playing about the corners of his mouth.

'Sweet and innocent little Holly, huh?' he queried slyly. 'But not so sweet and innocent that she doesn't know how to please a man. Still, them that asks no questions, don't get told no lies,' he murmured indulgently. 'And you're mine now. All mine. Mine to touch, to

263

kiss, to touch again. Only mine, hey, Holly?'

And she nodded, fear flickering in her eyes. He knew. He knew she wasn't a virgin and she ought to be relieved. No more lies, no more pretending. When it came to their honeymoon, she wouldn't have to lie. Honeymoon? The way Alex was behaving they'd be making love way before then, she realized hysterically, aware of his hands straying to her breasts, hating the thought of his hands on her breasts. But since she'd already proved she was a tramp, why not simply lie back and enjoy it, think of England? She felt the pain run through her. Lie back and think of England. Just like Dev. Only he hadn't. He'd responded, reacted, he'd cleverly turned the tables and he'd done things to her body she could never hope to enjoy with Alex. Because she loved Dev. She'd always love Dev. And Alex—

'Alex, sweetheart,' she protested, struggling to be free as insinuating fingers pulled her breasts away from the triangular scraps of gingham.

'Damn and—' He released her abruptly and Holly followed the line of his gaze, breathing a huge sigh of relief when she realized they were no longer alone, that Alex's anger was directed not at her but at the noisy, laughing group of teenagers who'd dropped their towels onto the sand and were racing down to the water's edge.

'Sorry, honey.' He tweaked a nipple before hugging her briefly. 'It looks like we'll have to wait. Might as well have that drink.' And he rummaged through the ice bag that Colette had packed, producing corkscrew, bottle and glasses.

Wait? Wait for what? Holly registered as she tugged her bikini top back into place. He surely didn't intend making love out here on the sand? And yet, why not? Dev had. In Tenerife. Day after day after day. And heaven knows, Dev had been a perfect stranger. She'd known Alex for months and they were engaged, so why the prudish reaction? Not prudish, she amended bitterly. That implied the sort of modesty Holly had forfeited years ago. So, just what was the word she was searching for? But she shied away, closing her mind, aware that she was dangerously close to giving Alex the truth. That she didn't love him. That she couldn't marry him, not on any terms. And all for a man who wouldn't know or care. Four lives ruined, all for the sake of Dev.

Pre-wedding nerves, she told herself sternly, pulling herself together for the short drive back. Because she *would* marry Alex, and she would make him happy. And furthermore, she'd lay the ghost of Devlin Winter once and for all.

It was a tense two days, Holly immensely relieved when it was time for Alex to go. 'Next weekend,' he promised, kissing her, his tongue darting into her mouth and sweeping on into deep and sensitive corners. And he pulled her against him, making her shockingly aware of his need, a stark reminder that they'd simply postponed the inevitable, that the scene on the beach was just a taste of what would come. Because Alex wanted her. She belonged to him now. And he would have her. And Alex Courdrey had waited long enough.

'So—' He raised his head, continued to hold her, to move his hips against hers, the force of his arousal driving the breath from her body. 'Next weekend we name the day. And make it, soon, hey, Holly? Then you can climb into bed with me whenever the fancy takes us. Next weekend,' he underlined solemnly. 'I can't wait.'

For what? she wondered, vaguely alarmed. For Holly to name the day? Or did Alex have something else on his mind? Like what, for instance? Like sex, for instance, she decided, damping down the panic. Sex. And you might as well face the truth, girl, she silently scorned. Holly Scott, tramp of the decade, was terrified.

'So Meryl and Jon are away for the night, stopping over at the Cresswells?'

'You're surprisingly well informed,' she agreed, an awful thought occurring.

'Hardly. Since Deric's my best friend, he just happened to mention it when I called. And talking of Deric, he'll be best man at the wedding. When's it to be?'

'When's what to be?' Holly stalled, following Alex inside, the unaccustomed silence deafening. No Jonathan. No Meryl. And recalling Meryl's apologetic smile as she and Jon had left earlier, Holly was beginning to see that clever, clever Alex had engineered the whole thing.

'The wedding. You have come up with a

266

date like I asked?' he queried sharply, blue eyes pinning her.

Holly flushed. 'Not exactly,' she murmured. 'But now that you're here—'

'Yes. Now that I'm here, we'll decide on a time and place and then I'll contact Lucy, set the ball rolling.'

'Lucy?'

'Of course. She's my trusty right hand. And since I'm busy working and you'll be far too busy shopping for your trousseau, Lucy can attend to all the tiresome little details.' He tossed his jacket over the back of a chair, loosening collar and tie before heading for the drinks tray on the sideboard. 'There's nothing for you to worry your pretty little head about,' he carelessly informed her. 'All you have to do, Holly, is decide on a time and place. Drink?' he added, swinging round to face her.

Holly shook her head. 'Too early for me,' she explained.

Alex grinned. 'For some things, Holly, it's never too early—or too late,' he murmured enigmatically. 'Come here.'

'Why?'

'Because I want to kiss my fiancée. Any objections?'

'And if I had?' she stalled, reluctantly allowing him to tug her close.

'Then I'd simply overrule them. Hmm.' He pulled her against him, his hands sliding down her back and over the swell of her buttocks, his lips languidly nuzzling hers. 'All alone. And you, my love, taste good enough to eat. Talking of which, we'll eat out, save Colette bothering. And later...hmm...later,' he emphasized thickly, his breath warm against her mouth, 'later, we'll do whatever the fancy dictates. You and me, Holly.. All alone.'

All alone. Alone in the house with Alex. A skittish Alex. A demanding Alex. Her fiancé. And nothing and no one to come between them.

Dinner. And Holly barely touched the exquisite platefuls of food that were placed before her. And Alex, missing nothing, reached across the table, taking her hand in his and squeezing reassuringly. 'Don't worry,' he murmured. 'Relax. Believe me, Holly, there's nothing for you to worry about.'

And that, Holly decided, anything but reassured, was debatable. But if she hardly touched the food, she was less sparing with the wine. Dutch courage, she could allow, but she had to do something to calm her frazzled nerves.

So—home time. She halted at the car, waiting for the central locking tone as Alex came up behind her. It was a warm night and she hadn't known what to wear, baulking at the usual balmy night attire, skimpy dresses with their tiny shoestring straps and plunging necklines and their unconscious invitation.

She opted in the end for the cream silk pyjama suit she'd worn to dinner at the Cresswells, dinner with Dev. And later on the beach with Dev. Everywhere she turned, reminders of Dev.

Even the picture postcard that had come in the morning post. It had been addressed to Jonathan, and though Holly had tried to avert her eyes, curiosity had beaten her, and she had read Dev's bold, sprawling script.

Sorry, pal. Guess we'll have to catch up on that ride another time hey? But keep up the practice. You're the best. Tell your mum and Holly that Dev says hello. It's been a good summer, one of the best. Just like you. Hope you can forgive your good friend Dev for running out without saying goodbye. Maybe you'll understand when you're older, Jon, but there are times when a grown-up simply has no say in the things going on around him.

Or her, Holly had added silently as the pain drove through. A good summer. One of the best. And what exactly did that mean? But hardest of all was the realization that, had it been Alex, Jonathan would have been the last thing on his mind. But Dev had cared, and cared enough, to try to make a small boy happy.

'Mmm.' Alex's growl of pleasure brought her rudely back to the present.

'Alex,' she murmured with an attempt at lightness that didn't quite come off. 'Anyone could be watching.'

'Let them. You're mine, and I don't care who knows it.'

'Maybe not,' she allowed shakily. 'But surely there's a time and place.'

'My place. Our place,' he amended thickly,

his hands sliding up inside the silky jacket, scorching her bare flesh, cupping her breasts, weighing her breasts, thumbs idly brushing the outline of her nipples, and as Holly went rigid, Alex growled, pulling her breasts free of the cups, pinching each nipple between finger and thumb. And heedless of who could be watching, he pushed the flimsy material out of the way, dipping his head, his mouth fastening hungrily on first one breast then another.

Holly froze. 'Not here, Alex,' she pleaded softly, and he laughed, obligingly released her, his warm glance slipping over her, the meaning plain. Not here, not anywhere, she added in silent anguish. But how on earth to wriggle out of things once Alex took her home?

Home. Home alone with Alex. She headed straight for the sideboard, needing a drink, any drink, the stiffer the better, pouring herself a large brandy while Alex garaged the car.

Alex. Dear, sweet Alex. Clever, clever Alex. He'd backed her into a corner. No escape, she was beginning to think, with cruel echoes of her time with Dev. Because Holly was little more than a puppet with Alex pulling the strings. He'd engineered the lot, the engagement party, Jonathan and Meryl's absence, and later tonight he'd planned the finale—a steamy love scene with Holly. Because Holly belonged to him. She was just another commodity on the market, and Dev had been right all along, Alex had made the highest bid.

He locked the terrace windows behind him

and, heading straight for Holly, took the drink from her fingers, placing it on the coffee table. 'Mmm. You taste wonderful,' he told her, cupping her face between his hands and gazing down, the blue eyes locking with hers, smoky with desire. 'Let's go upstairs.'

'How about a drink?' she stalled, wriggling free and doubling back to the sideboard.

'Sure. Why not?' he agreed easily enough. 'Scotch, please. No ice.' And she watched warily as he shrugged himself out of the dinner jacket before tossing it carelessly into a corner along with the bow tie, at the same time loosening the top two buttons of his shirt. Casual. For Alex, far too casual, though being blond, he'd never make the same impact in white as Dev—Dev.

She pulled herself up short. She really must stop thinking about Dev. It wasn't fair, on any of them. And if Dev created a stir when he walked into a crowded room, so did Alex. He had an aura, an aura of power, Holly had identified recently. Money and power. Add to that his rugged blond looks, and was it any wonder women fell at his feet in droves? And yet Alex had chosen Holly.

So, she swallowed hard, the least she could do was put Dev out of her mind and remember she was marrying Alex. Marrying Alex. Going to bed with Alex -and soon if Alex had his way. Making love with Alex- but no, her mind skittered away again.

'In here?' she murmured, handing him a glass, too nervous to recall that he'd already locked up. 'Or out on the terrace?'

'We'll stay inside. Nice and cosy on the sofa,' he declared, patting the space beside him.

Holly took it, though gingerly, allowing Alex's hand to snake round her shoulder, tug her close, was shockingly aware of his hand brushing the swell of her breast as it slid down her arm.

So—she swallowed hard. This is it, Holly. Now or never. Either it's over, and you tell Alex now, or you forget Dev once and for all.

Alex dipped his head, kissing her, his tongue trailing across the soft inner flesh of Holly's lower lip. 'Mmm' he murmured. And he cupped her face in his hands, his eyes deep, swirling pools that filled her with dread. 'Let's go upstairs,' he said again thickly. 'We can take the drinks with us, and face it, Holly, there's a huge double bed just waiting to be christened.'

'Tonight?' she stalled, grey eyes full of shadows. 'Why the sudden rush, Alex?'

'Hardly a rush, since we've known each other for months, and we have just got engaged.'

'Exactly. So why spoil things? Why rush things now when we're so close to being married?'

'Because I want you. And I've waited. And I've waited long enough. And you're stalling, though the lord knows why. Afraid, Holly? Of me? Of making love? Surely not?' he chided. 'You're a woman, a very desirable woman, and you do know what I'm saying, Holly.'

Yes. Virginal she wasn't, and gentleman through and through, Alex was hinting at what they both knew to be true. 'I thought you liked your women whiter than white, less shop-soiled?' she reminded, clutching at straws.

'Woman,' he emphasized fiercely. 'And I do. But a bit of practice doesn't hurt,' he murmured, kissing her. 'Not in this day and age. And since I'm a man of the world, I can live with that. Past tense, Holly. Now that you're mine, naturally things will be different. So—'

'We can't.'

'What do you mean, can't?'

Holly took a deep breath, her eyes darting about the room, looking anywhere but at Alex. She licked her dry lips. 'I'm sorry, Alex. Yours I may be,' she acknowledged shakily, 'but if you're thinking what I think you're thinking, tonight you're going to be disappointed.'

'You mean you won't?'

'I mean, we can't, not this weekend, at least.' And she gave a nervous little laugh. 'It's—just one of life's little inconveniences,' she explained, crossing her fingers at the tiny white lie. 'Something a girl has to live with month in and month out.'

'But—' His face was a cold and angry mask. 'But you haven't complained of a headache all day,' he pointed out sceptically.

'That's because the headache and the stomach cramps usually disappear after day one,' Holly explained.

'And that was?'

'Thursday,' she lied, crossing yet another set of fingers. Because heaven help her if Alex ever decided to keep track.

'Fine.' He reached for his glass, drained it in one, strolled leisurely across to the sideboard and poured himself another, a very large one,

273

Holly noted as the waves of relief washed over her.

Then he swung round to face her, his whole expression tight. 'I'll be over next weekend, Holly,' he reminded with chilling lack of emotion. 'And if I were you, I'd talk Meryl into taking Jonathan out someplace. Because next weekend, come hell or high water, I'm taking my fiancée to bed. Understand, my love? You'll be going to bed with me. And sleep,' he added thickly as he tilted his glass, drank the contents off in one, 'sleep is the last thing on the agenda.'

CHAPTER 16

'I've something to tell you.'

Meryl's smile broadened. 'Good, because I've something to tell you,' she trilled, rare spots of colour staining her cheeks.

Watching her, Holly felt a prickle of alarm. Her stepmother was happy, bubbly almost, had been the same all week, now that Holly came to think of it. Only Holly had been too wrapped up in her own world to notice. So, any minute now Meryl's bright smile would disappear. Because Holly was about to drop her bombshell and that worry-free future she'd privately promised was about to disappear.

'Oh?' Holly murmured warily.

'You first?' Meryl invited, a secret smile playing about the corners of her mouth.

'No.' Holly shook her head. 'You first,' she insisted, because Meryl was seething with excitement and Holly was stalling, precious little time to muster her thoughts, to find the words to soften the blow. Her lips twisted. Some hope. But Meryl was clearly over the moon and Holly couldn't take the shine off her news before she'd even heard it.

Meryl placed her coffee cup down in its saucer then glanced across, blue eyes dancing. 'I'm going to marry Tom,' she said simply.

'Tom?' Holly repeated stupidly.

'Yes. Tom Clancy. He's been pressing me for months now, and last weekend at the Cresswells I finally said yes.'

Holly didn't react, didn't blink, needing time for the words to sink in, half-afraid she'd been hearing things, or that Meryl was simply teasing. And she really did want to believe it, was desperate to believe it.

Watching the shadows chase across Holly's face, Meryl's smiled faltered. 'Oh, Holly, aren't you pleased?'

'Pleased?' Holly reached across, hugging her, the block of ice around her heart beginning to melt. 'Pleased?' she repeated, pushing back her chair and almost dancing round the table. 'Meryl, darling, I'm thrilled. It's the most wonderful news in the world.' And then something struck her. 'But—after the hysterectomy you said you'd never re-marry?' she probed carefully.

'Which was true. And still would be but for Tom,' Meryl explained. 'But he has a grown-up family already and doesn't need a son and heir, and since he's wonderful with Jonathan—'

'And Jonathan's fond of Tom—'

'Precisely.'

'But...?'

'Is there a but?' Meryl queried, eyes silently pleading.

'Dad?' Holly probed, sensing that there was, in Meryl's mind, at least. 'So that's what's bothering you? The thought that I wouldn't approve because of Dad? Oh, Meryl, Meryl,' she chided softly. 'You're young. You've your whole life in front of you. And Dad would have been pleased. Just like me. After all, you're no Queen Victoria.'

'Really, really, Holly? You really are pleased?'

'Really, really, Meryl. Believe me, it's the best news you could have given me.' Not quite, of course, she amended silently. But rule Dev out of the picture and Holly meant every word.

'So, it's a bit early in the day for champagne but—' Meryl raised her cup '—here's to future happiness. You and Alex, me and Tom.'

Holly swallowed hard. 'Ah,' she said with woeful inadequacy.

'Ah, what?' Meryl echoed. And then she forced a smile, blue eyes flecked with shadows. 'It's Dev, isn't?' she probed.

'Has it been so obvious?' Holly challenged pleadingly.

'Only to me. Because I know you, and I've watched you battle for weeks now. And deep inside I've always felt that you and Alex didn't belong together, that you were marrying for all the wrong reasons. So, if it's any consolation, Holly,' she told her frankly, 'I'm relieved. But where do you go from here, love?' she added softly.

Only Holly didn't know. Dev might not want her any more, even on his terms, and as for Alex—oh, God! Alex was flying in within the hour. What on earth was she going to tell him? How was she going to tell him?

'Off? You're calling the wedding off? Are you mad? The notice has already gone to *The Times*

277

and Lucy's got half of London working on the arrangements. Off? Don't be ridiculous, Holly,' he castigated coldly. 'Everything's booked. The service, the reception, the honeymoon. The twenty-first of next month.' he added carelessly. 'At St Paul's.'

Holly swallowed hard. And then, deciding she'd misheard, 'St Paul's? You surely don't mean the cathedral?' she queried politely.

'The one and only. Now, pour us a drink each and come and give your fiancé the kiss he deserves after a long week's absence.'

'But—' Holly felt the anger surge. 'You need more than three weeks' notice to book St Paul's, surely?' she challenged.

'Of course. Which is why I did it months ago.'

'But we weren't engaged months ago,' she pointed out calmly, a lot more calmly than she felt.

Alex shrugged. 'We were a couple. We both knew the score. It was only a matter of time. I knew you'd come round sooner or later.'

'But—you said that I could decide,' Holly reminded him, absurdly hurt that Alex had been lying, had promised her the moon and stars and then proceeded to set his own ruthless agenda. And no, it didn't hurt, she corrected, identifying the embryonic emotion for what it was. Relief. Sheer relief. Because all of a sudden she wasn't about to hurt him. She'd face him with the truth all right, deliver a massive blow to that ego. But hurt him? No. Her lips twisted. Alex Courdrey wouldn't know the meaning of the word, not beneath that heavy cloak of arrogance.

'And so I did,' he agreed offhandedly. 'But there's plenty of time to change things. If there's anything you're not happy with, just give Lucy a call and—'

'No!'

'No? Well, in that case, sweetheart, it's all systems go. Now, come here.'

'No,' she repeated, suddenly ice-cold calm.

Expressive eyebrows rose. 'Dear me,' he mocked. 'You *are* out of sorts today. Pre-wedding nerves?' he queried scathingly. 'Or, in view of my plans for this evening, another dose of premenstrual tension?'

Holly flushed. So he'd known. But it hardly mattered now. 'Neither,' she conceded coolly. 'As we're clearly both aware. And there isn't going to be a wedding. I'm sorry, Alex, but I can't marry you.'

'Sorry?' he queried with an ugly curl of the lips. 'You plan to turn me into the biggest laughing-stock in London and you have the nerve to stand there and say you're sorry? Oh, no, my dear. No one, but no one,' he emphasized coldly, 'does that to Alex Courdrey.'

Holly shrugged. Fine. He'd learn. Sooner or later. And she placed the ring box with its expensive, ostentatious contents carefully on the table in front of him.

Alex's frigid gaze whipped from Holly to the plush velvet box and back again. 'You're serious, aren't you?' he queried, as if testing the idea in his mind. 'This isn't some warped idea of a joke? You really are running out on me?'

Holly nodded, watching a range of emotions chase across his features. Dear, sweet Alex who'd treated her like a princess. Dear, sweet Alex who'd promised her the earth. Dear, sweet, *scheming* Alex who'd coaxed and teased and single-mindedly manipulated Holly all along. Scheming, scheming Alex. Ruthless Alex. Disbelieving Alex.

'You bitch!' He jumped up, bearing down on her. Holly flinched at the venom in his tone, backing across the room, coming up short against the sideboard. 'Don't think I don't know what's been going on,' Alex snarled, his hand snatching at her upper arm, fingers curling round, biting deep. 'It's Winter, isn't it, Holly? You've decided he's a better bet than me.'

'Dev? Don't be silly. He's—'

'A journalist?' he sneered.

'Well, no,' she allowed, something in his tone puzzling her. 'Not now, apparently.'

'Apparently? Don't make me laugh. You know. You've known all along, have been stringing us both along, if the truth's known, playing one off against the other. Well, for your information,' he told her almost gleefully, 'you've picked the wrong one. Sorry to disillusion you, Holly, but I'm still worth several millions more than Winter.'

'So I would imagine,' Holly retorted coolly. 'Since Dev—'

'Is the richest man in France? One of the richest men in Europe?'

'Now you're being ridiculous.'

'And you're being evasive. But you can stop

280

pretending, Holly, because I know.'

'Really? Well, in that case, Alex, you know more than me. You're talking in riddles, and this is hardly the time or place.'

'No. I guess you're right. Like making love with your fiancé, Holly. The wrong time and place,' he reminded, generous lips curling in contempt. 'Last weekend. Tell me, my dear—just out of mild curiosity, you understand. The wrong time—or the wrong man?'

'Meaning?'

'Meaning, Devlin Winter. All summer long. The moment my back was turned. Quite a cosy arrangement, really, with his house a ten-minute drive away. Not to mention the riding lessons. Quite a cunning little plan all round,' he railed. 'Who'd have guessed that sweet and innocent Holly Scott could be so devious? Or underhand. Or ruthless. Using her own brother as a cover, the perfect excuse for spending time with Winter. No,' he added contemptuously, 'I never realised what a scheming little bitch you were. Until now.'

She closed her eyes, shutting out the man but not the words, Alex's words dripping poison. And he was wrong. Right and wrong. Because if Alex's words stung, the truth was even more awful. And she'd hurt him, pierced that mask of arrogance and dented his pride. Pride. Only his pride. But she'd hurt him and worse than that, she'd betrayed him. The least she could do was let him down gently.

'No, Alex. You're wrong,' she heard herself pleading.

'And you're lying. Lying to me, lying to yourself. You and your *nouveau riche* lover.'

'Once and for all,' Holly spat. 'Dev isn't my lover.' And since Dev had gone, it was true. Dev had gone. And Holly had driven him away. And it hurt. It hurt like hell. But Alex was shaking her now and Holly dragged her mind back to the present, saw the gleam of speculation in Alex's cold eyes and was suddenly afraid.

'No, Alex,' she protested, sensing danger as he dipped his head, his breath scalding her skin, but Alex simply laughed and then he was kissing her, his lips insulting, his words insulting, and Holly closed her eyes, closed her mind, not listening to the words that punctuated his kisses.

'Rags to riches,' he almost crooned, nibbling at the corners of her mouth. And his hands slid down, finding her breasts, squeezing her breasts, hands, fingers and lips branding, branding her with hate, branding her with shame. The more she struggled, the more Alex seemed to react. 'Real fairy-tale stuff,' he sneered, grinding his hips against hers, a savage reminder that she was his for the taking. And though Holly jerked away he simply laughed, pulling her back, his mouth covering hers again, and when she clamped her lips together in a vain attempt to deny him, his tongue pushed through, darting into sensitive corners and sweeping across the soft, inner skin of Holly's lips, a deliberate invasion, a calculated insult. 'But if the guy didn't bother explaining, Holly...'

He laughed again and Holly seized her chance,

jerking her head away. 'Exactly,' she pointed out softly, afraid of Alex in this mood, caught fast and hating it but determined not to squirm, to give Alex the satisfaction of seeing her struggle, because the more she struggled, the more he seemed to enjoy it. 'And if Dev didn't see the need,' she added, damping down the panic, 'why should you?'

Alex raised his head, logging the fear in her tone, the fear in her eyes. 'Oh-oh,' he mocked. 'Something tells me that prissy Holly Scott's suddenly afraid she's missed the boat. Or should that be fortune?' he countered slyly. 'Two in fact. Mine—and Winter's.' And he shook his head from side to side, his steely gaze raining scorn. 'Careless, Holly. Very, very careless.'

'Will you please get to the point?' she snapped, completely forgetting the need to stay cool, calm and in control.

'If you're sure that's what you want?' he drawled with more than a hint of amusement. 'Devlin Winter,' he explained, cupping her chin and running the edge of his thumb along her bruised and swollen lips. 'The perfume king. The man behind the Aphrodite Empire.'

'And how do you work that out?' Holly demanded, flinching at the touch.

Alex shrugged. 'Research. The guy didn't add up, so I had him checked out.'

'And?'

'And, bingo! Oh, he was a journalist all right, six or seven years ago. Till he knocked himself up in a car smash and was nursed back to health by nuns. Nuns!' he tagged on gleefully. 'I can

283

really see Winter running amok in a nunnery. And just by way of a thank-you, he turned their cottage industry into the biggest perfumery in France. Money,' he mused with another evil smile. 'All that lovely money,' he emphasized slyly. 'Mine—and Winter's. Still, that's the way the cookie crumbles,' he jeered, pushing her away in disgust.

'You pays your money and you takes your chances. And this time, Holly, you lost. Understand?' he demanded frigidly, pouring himself a drink. And taking a long, hard slug, he allowed his insolent gaze to travel the length of her, down, then up, appraising, assessing, insulting as he lingered on the generous swell of breast beneath her now crumpled T-shirt.

'You lost,' he stated simply. 'And we're through. And if you were to come crawling back on your hands and knees tomorrow, I wouldn't give you so much as the time of day. Because we're through. Understand, Holly?' he repeated, eyes pools of hate as they fastened on hers. 'It's over. *My* decision. Because you're a cold-blooded tramp and we're through. And heaven help Winter, but he's welcome to you. Always assuming,' he tagged on cruelly, raising his glass in awful mockery of a toast, 'always assuming he wants you.'

Always assuming he wants you. Scheming, fortune-hunting Holly Scott. Tramp of the year, Holly Scott. And by giving her the truth, clever, bitter Alex had made sure that Holly had lost Dev for good. No Dev. Ever. Because whatever

Holly said now, Dev would never believe her.

'Is it the fortune, Holly, or is it the man?' Dev had asked all those weeks ago. And she'd loved him, made love with him, spent the most wonderful night of her life with him, then rejected him. Gone running back to Alex. At least, that's how Dev would see it, because, lo and behold, Dev acquires a fortune and scheming Holly Scott bounces back faster than the speed of light!

Only, it wasn't true. But how to convince Dev? She loved him. And Dev despised her. Holly Scott, tramp of the year, she underlined as the tears poured silently down her cheeks. In Dev's eyes as well as Alex's. Because she'd caught the expression on his face when she had told him. Disgust. And if he was the last man on earth, she couldn't go running back to Dev now.

But if Holly was guilty as hell, Dev had lied too, she realized, attempting to counter the pain. All summer long. Not a word, not a hint about his success. Aphrodite Perfumes PLC. Devlin Winter's multi-million-pound empire. Dev had lied. Just as he had that long, hot summer in Tenerife when he'd kept quiet about his job. Lying by omission. That summer and this.

Only, suddenly, it wasn't important any more. Nothing was. Because there'd never really been a future. Not for Holly and Dev. Because Devlin Winter, she reminded herself cruelly, had his own love. The woman he was rushing back to at the time of his accident. And Devlin Winter, she added, stacking the cards against him in an

285

effort to dull the pain, the screaming, aching void of having to live without him, Dev had had a hand in the death of her father, had taken her father's money and run, and worse, had used that money to build himself an empire. Oh, yes, Devlin Winter was damned.

And heaven help her, she loved him. All the tomorrows, she realized starkly. All alone.

CHAPTER 17

'So, what will you do?'

Holly shrugged, aware of the wealth of sympathy in Meryl's cloudy blue eyes. 'What can I do?' she stalled, reducing the piece of toast on her plate to a heap of sticky crumbs. 'It's my job. I'll simply have to work round it.'

'But you might bump into Dev?'

'Unlikely. I'm several floors up, don't forget. And the visit is bound to be brief. It's just a press call,' she reminded her. 'Dev's latest venture. The Aphrodite Beauty range. Look out, Body Shop, here he comes,' she caught herself sneering. 'Selfridges, Harrods, all the quality stores in the space of a morning. And then back to Paris to carry on counting those neat piles of millions.'

'So bitter, Holly? That's not like you.'

No. Holly swallowed hard. So bitter. Five bitter months of hell. Thanks to Alex.

Meryl stretched her hand across the table. 'Oh, Holly, Holly, what are we going to do?' she pleaded softly.

'Nothing,' Holly insisted tightly. 'Nothing at all. Just carry on as normal.' Although normality, she was beginning to think, didn't exist. Not for her.

Determined not to brood, Holly threw herself

into her work, modelling the exclusive design-label gowns she could never afford in a million years; though her lips twisted, it wasn't in bitterness. Had she married Alex, she'd have been buying, not selling, she realized, the idea vaguely amusing, and some other poor soul would be at the beck and call of the rich, pampered and all-too-often rude women with their bottomless cheque books and personal accounts. And with money no object, Holly could have taken her pick of all the top names: Chanel, Dior, Versace, Jean Muir and Holly's personal favourite, Frank Usher: less pretentious than the others, stunningly simple, beautifully cut and styled. And expensive.

Still, as Alex had eloquently reminded, you pays your money and you takes your chances. And Holly had lost. Kept her self-respect but lost. Lost Dev. Lost what had never really been hers, she'd tried to console herself. And then she'd gone back to London to pick up the threads of her life, only to discover Alex had beaten her to it.

Since Alex Courdrey was a name to be reckoned with, Holly was ostracized. No friends. No job. Only Meryl. Wonderful, wonderful Meryl who asked no questions but simply offered unstinting support. Just as she had the first time. And since history was almost repeating itself, Holly was coping, and thanks to Meryl, coping well.

The job helped, kept her mind from straying down forbidden pathways, and she crawled into bed most nights too tired even to cry herself to sleep.

'But you don't need to work.' Meryl had insisted when Holly had returned home after yet another fruitless job search. 'Not now. You've done more than your share already, Holly. You've paid the bills for years, love. Now it's my turn.'

But Holly had been adamant. She'd pay her way. She was taking charge of her life and she was determined to pay her way. Only, thanks to Alex, there'd been weeks and weeks of disappointment and no matter where she'd turned it had been the same. No jobs. Oh, there was no shortage of job ads for nannies, she'd discovered. Just no call for this nanny in particular.

Untrained, unqualified, unwanted, each and every door had been slammed in her face—quite literally, some of them. And as for those personal endorsements she could always rely on... No chance. And that had hurt too. But curiously enough, she didn't blame Alex.

Despite the January weather, it was hot in the store. As she wriggled out of the black satin ballgown and into the regulation gold and navy suit, she was glad to note it was time for her break. The job was—different, she acknowledged, and instead of waiting for the lift, took the stairs to the staff canteen, her footsteps echoing eerily in the stairwell. For once she'd been lucky, found herself in the right place at the right time with no sign of Alex. And as soon as she'd saved enough for a deposit, she'd move out from under Tom and Meryl's feet. A place of her own. Small, but all hers, she added silently, fiercely. And paid for out of her own, well-earned pay packet.

'Mind if I join you?'

Holly glanced up, smiling her assent as the younger girl scrambled into the vacant chair opposite.

'You work in Collections, don't you? I've seen you modelling the gowns.'

Holly nodded, racking her brains to place the girl but without success. 'Holly Scott,' she offered. 'But you'll have to forgive me. I've only been here a month so I don't know many names yet.'

'Suzy Bennett. The Beauty Room.'

Which would explain it. Not so much a room as the entire lower-ground floor, complete with hair treatment bays, beauty salon, perfume bars and make-up. And the one floor in the store Holly avoided like the plague. Because the slightest whiff of perfume, any perfume, brought back that awful scene with Dev when the bottle of Ilexia had been smashed against the wall.

'And have you worked there long?' Holly enquired politely.

Suzy grinned. 'Just over a year,' she confided. 'I trained as a beauty therapist but failed the course miserably. I'm dyslexic,' she added matter-of-factly. 'I soak up facts faster than a computer but just can't cope with the written exams. So, here I am.'

'Yes. Doesn't seem fair, does it?' Holly agreed.

'Oh, I don't know.' Suzy shrugged, demolishing a very large chocolate eclair with her fork.

'I like it here. Lots of toffs,' she explained cheerfully. 'And the work's practically the same. Not to mention all the free samples.'

'Now there's an idea,' Holly allowed. 'The odd free sample of the things I sell wouldn't go amiss.'

'Staff discount?' Suzy reminded.

Holly shook her head. 'Staff discount on a pair of tights is as much as I could afford.'

'Expensive, huh?' Suzy probed. 'Pity. I'm getting married in the summer and was hoping to pick out something special.'

'But it doesn't have to be a big name,' Holly reminded her, sensing her disappointment. 'Why not pop up and have a look on your next half-day? If we're not too busy, I'll show you round. After all, you are a prospective customer.'

'It's a deal. Tomorrow—no.' Suzy shrugged apologetically. 'In view of the visit of the great man himself,' she explained with a moue of resignation, 'all leave's been cancelled. Downstairs at any rate.'

'Sorry?' Holly was intrigued.

'Haven't you heard? There's a big launch tomorrow. Aphrodite World. And the power behind the throne is jetting in. It's like a madhouse down there. Any one would think the king of France was visiting. You should pop down, take a peek.'

Holly shook her head. No chance. Too much risk of bumping into Dev. As she'd told Meryl on Monday, the chances were remote. Holly worked upstairs, Dev would be breezing through the Beauty Room complete with obligatory entourage: a bevy of beauties endorsing each and every product, rat pack of reporters, camera men and assorted hangers-on. Close. Dangerously close. No escape, she allowed with a fleetingly sad smile. But tomorrow she'd avoid the lower-ground floor, and Dev, like the plague.

'You know,' Suzy mused, green eyes narrowing. 'You're wasted here. Tall, slim, pretty. You ought to be a model, a real model.'

'Too old,' Holly reminded. And tall and slim she might be, but she was hardly Kate Moss. 'Besides, I'm happy enough working in Collections.' For now at least.

Suzy shrugged. 'It was just a thought, all those posters, putting ideas in my mind. The Aphrodite competition,' she added as an afterthought. 'Surely you must have noticed?' And when Holly continued to look blank, 'Dear me, you do lead a sheltered life. The face of Aphrodite,' she explained patiently. 'And the worldwide search for a face to feature on the range. *You* don't fancy entering, I suppose?' she suggested thoughtfully. 'Staff are allowed—I checked.'

Catching Holly's horrified expression, Suzy grinned again. 'Like I said, it was just a thought. I'd have a go myself,' she confided. 'But, I just haven't got that special something. Now, you...'

'Thanks, but no thanks,' Holly murmured drily. She checked her watch as Suzy pushed back her chair.

'Back to the grind,' Suzy murmured. 'And between you and me, I'll be glad when it's this time tomorrow.'

This time tomorrow. Holly pushed her plate away, the mere thought of food enough to make her heave.

This time tomorrow and it would all be over and done with. Dev would have breezed in and breezed out again and Holly would be safe. Until next time. And there would be a next time, she was beginning to think. Because no matter where she went or what she did, sooner or later Dev would turn up. The proverbial bad penny. And she loved him. And she hated him. And Dev despised her. Tramp of the year. Tramp of the decade, almost. Only that wasn't true either, she allowed. Five months, six at the most and then she'd come to her senses, had been brought to her senses by that revolting man who'd thought that he could buy her. Holly flinched at the memory. Oh, God, how had she ever sunk so low?

'Why not stay home today?' Meryl suggested, stacking the breakfast plates in the dishwasher.

Tom had left half an hour ago, planning to drop Jonathan at school before heading into work, and Holly was all too aware she was cutting it fine, that if the tubes were as crowded as normal, she risked arriving late. And since she was still working her probationary period, she was risking the sack.

'Call in sick,' Meryl urged. 'Heaven knows, you look pale enough. I can phone for you.'

Tempting. So tempting. Call in sick. She felt sick. Wouldn't begin to feel better until Dev was safely off the premises. Two o'clock. Another six

293

hours and she'd be safe. Six hours of hell. Stay home and she'd be safe all day. Tempting, so tempting. And glancing up, she found Meryl's soft blue eyes fastened on hers and realized she simply couldn't do it.

'Wimp—or woman?' she tossed out in sheer bravado, pushing back her chair, and the look of relief on Meryl's face almost made up for the pain. Almost.

Almost there. One fifty-five. Allow an extra half-hour to be on the safe side and then she'd be safe. For now.

'Hi!' Suzy breezed across the busy staff canteen. 'Can't stop. I'm needed downstairs. You should have popped in—everyone else on the staff did. You missed a dream,' she breathed, enormous green eyes shining. 'An absolute dream but a real nice guy. No side at all,' she confided. 'As down to earth as you and me. And as for good looking...' She whistled appreciatively under her breath. 'Half the girls were ready for swooning and I can't say that I blame them.'

'You mean he's gone?' Holly queried carefully, her heart thumping so loudly that surely the whole room could hear.

'Afraid so. Half an hour ago. An absolute dream...'

An absolute dream. Holly smiled despite herself. The new, improved Dev, rich, hand-some, famous—and nothing at all to do with Holly. And though she was free, she'd never escape. There was no escape from the memories.

No escape. Back in the department, Jaqui

294

Miles was waiting. 'Oh, there you are, Holly. I was wondering where you'd got to. Madam would like some perfume,' she explained, nodding across at the middle-aged woman who was seated in the comfortable, low-backed viewing chair, fingers impatiently tapping the arm. 'I've phoned downstairs but they're rushed off their feet today. Pop down for a bottle, will you? It's that new one. Aphrodite. Oh, and have it charged to madam's account.'

Yes madam, no madam, three bags full, madam. But Mrs Saville was a valued customer, a rich and valued customer, and despite the surge of dismay, common sense told her she was over-reacting. Dev had gone.

Gone but not forgotten, she realized, emerging warily from the lift to find the entire floor simply shrieked Dev: posters, displays, competition entry forms. The face of Aphrodite. A blank. Like Holly's mind. Because Dev hadn't yet chosen the face to launch his thousand ships. Hardly, she corrected as the flight of fancy over came her. Aphrodite. And Ilexia.

Holly stopped in dead in her tracks. That distinctive smell of spice. How could she have forgotten? And as the nausea rose in her throat, she stumbled against a mirrored pillar, clutching the ornamental rail like a lifeline. Ilexia. All the tomorrows. All the hate. All the love. Love. No. She loved Dev, she corrected, but he'd never, ever professed to love Holly. Simply made love. And how!

And then she saw him. Holly froze, sure she was dreaming, that the figure reflected in the bronze-tinted glass was a figment of her imagination. But no, she felt the buzz of excitement that rippled round the floor and realized it was Dev all right. She turned, slowly, carefully, afraid that a sudden movement would catch his eye—ridiculous, really since the place was alive with movement. Dev. Oh, God, Dev!

Thinner, she decided, though the overcoat made it difficult to assess. And though he was smiling, Holly's sharp eyes detected strain in the angles of his face. Shock of jet-black hair, collar length, she noted, and longer than she remembered, the silver more pronounced now. Too many worries, no doubt. Worried about how to spend all that money, she added sourly, unfairly, and she crept round the pillar, carefully keeping out of sight as Dev headed for the bank of lifts.

And then she saw the woman. Nothing like as tall as Holly, she decided, making an instant, instinctive comparison. But slim. And pretty. Long, wavy hair. And smiling. Smiling up at Dev, whose hand cupped her elbow as he guided her across the floor. The woman paused at the open lift and Holly held her breath, watching with awful fascination as she raised her face in expectation of a kiss. And sure enough, Dev dipped his head, brushing his lips against hers as he pulled her close, hugging her. And, oh, Dev, Dev, Dev!

As the pain scythed through, Holly felt the sting of tears, dashed them away with a gesture of impatience and taking a huge gulp of air, steeled herself to glance across. They'd gone, the lift doors swinging to as Holly realized she'd escaped.

No escape. No escape from the pain. And damn Devlin Winter, but she had a job to do. Five minutes later she emerged from the staff lift, swinging through the automatic doors onto the sales floor, clutching the box with its distinctive Lalique bottle. Less a bottle than a statuette, Holly corrected, having been unable to avoid the huge display stand. A Venus emerging from the waves. Aphrodite to give her the Greek name, Dev's name.

And seeing Jaqui Miles's worried face across a sea of heads, Holly darted forwards, dodging the browsing crowds but pulling up short when she heard a familiar voice at her elbow calling her name.

'Holly?'

Doubt, wonder, amazement, but most of all, disbelief in his tone.

'My God, Holly,' he breathed. 'What on earth are you doing here?'

CHAPTER 18

'Go away,' Holly hissed, attempting to slip past. But Dev, being Dev, simply side-stepped neatly, out-thinking her, out-manoeuvring her, and bringing her up sharp against a rigid display stand.

'Will you please move out of the way?' Holly implored, careful to avoid contact with those probing black eyes.

'Why?'

'Why? Isn't it obvious? I'm busy. I have a job to do.'

'So I gathered. But why?'

'Never mind why. Just go away,' she hissed again; and, spotting Jaqui Miles bearing down on them, 'Do you want to lose me my job?'

'Holly!' Sharp. Impatient. Given Mrs Saville's clout with a cheque book, more than a hint of worry in Jaqui's tone.

'I'm sorry, Miss Miles—'

'Miss Miles—' Dev flashed her the most devastating smile. 'Allow me to introduce myself. Devlin Winter. And since Holly and I are old friends...'

'Winter? Oh, you mean—' And to Holly's amazement, the normally cool, calm and unflappable Jaqui Miles blushed to the roots of her hair.

'Exactly. And since I'm merely passing

298

through... Such a hectic tour, you understand... If Holly could—?'

'Take the rest of the day off? But of course,' Jaqui breathed as Holly's sinking heart settled somewhere near the floor.

'Now hold on a moment,' Holly bit out, catching sight of Mrs Saville's face as she rose from her chair. 'In case it's slipped your notice, Dev, I'm dealing with a customer.' And she darted away, breathing a huge sigh of relief that, for a moment at least, Dev was a good arm's length away. 'Mrs Saville. Wait! Please wait,' she called, hurrying after the woman's retreating, uncompromising, sable-draped back.

'Mrs Saville—madam.' Dev bowed, halting the furious woman in her tracks, and another devastating smile worked wonders. 'Yours, I believe,' he murmured, taking the box that Holly was clutching. And in less than an instant he was signing it. 'Lavinia. Such a pretty name,' he allowed as the woman's hard features softened. 'Compliments of Devlin Winter of Aphrodite Perfumes.'

'You think you're so clever, don't you?' Holly snapped, emerging warily from the cloakroom ten minutes later. She'd deliberately taken her time, hoping Dev would have taken the hump and gone, but no, there he was, larger than life and apparently unaware of the stir he was causing among customers and staff alike. Unaware—or completely uncaring. Arrogant. Yes, that was it. Strange, she'd never really noticed before. But then before, she reminded herself bitterly, she'd been blissfully unaware of

299

Dev's true identity. The perfume king, Alex had scorned. Not some gutter-press reporter. Or, recalling Dev's evasive reply when challenged, someone into this and that. And yet, Holly probed, had anything really changed? He was the same Dev he'd been all summer. Dangerously devastating, but still the man who'd spent hour after hour making a small boy happy.

'Allow me,' Dev insisted, ignoring her barbed remark, not to mention her scowl as he took the square woollen wrap from her fingers and draped it across the shoulders of her coat.

'Where are we going?' Holly enquired as, down in the street, he hailed a passing taxi.

'My place, or yours?' he challenged, helping her inside and, ignoring yet another glare from Holly's flashing eyes, gave directions to the driver. 'The Grosvenor. Buckingham Palace Road.'

The Grosvenor. Hardly roughing it, Holly could allow, but somehow she'd expected something outlandish: the Ritz, the Savoy, the Intercontinental.

'Too obvious,' Dev explained when Holly put her thoughts into words. 'With the launch in the news this week, they'll be crawling with reporters with an eye to the main chance, and between you and me, I find all that attention overpowering.'

'Poor little rich boy,' Holly scorned, having the grace to blush when Dev shot her a sharp, reproachful glance.

'And like most men,' he added as the taxi pulled up and the uniformed door man sprang forward, 'the small boy inside me is mad about trains. With Victoria station behind,' he reminded her, logging Holly's blank response. 'Would you believe, the hotel has its own back door to the concourse?'

'You are teasing?' Holly queried, leading the way up the canopied steps.

'Only a little,' he allowed, black eyes dancing.

Holly flushed, flouncing into reception then pulling up short. Reception. A staircase straight out of a film set. Or the lifts. The discreet signs for restaurant and bars simply didn't register.

'The tea room—or my room?' Dev challenged, sensing her sudden unease.

Since wild horses wouldn't have dragged her into a bedroom with Dev, she opted for the tea room, and whilst he didn't make a comment, there was an almost imperceptible twitch of those much too generous lips.

'So—' Cosily installed in a secluded corner, the banks of plants providing a screen from prying eyes and giving them a privacy Holly found oppressive, Dev fastened his gaze on Holly. 'To return to an earlier question, Holly: what on earth are you doing at The Store?'

'Simply earning a crust, Dev. You know, work,' she needled. 'Soiling my hands is how I once remember you phrasing it.'

'But you married Courdrey. What on earth is he doing allowing you to work in a department store?'

'Oh I see, *your* wife wouldn't be allowed to soil her pretty hands?' she challenged. His wife. There, she'd said it. And Dev didn't deny it, she noted, her heart turning to stone.

Pure guesswork, of course, but there'd been no denying the intimacy between Dev and the woman at the lift. They'd been comfortable together, completely at ease. The woman from the past, Holly decided. Dev's love. So he'd finally persuaded her. And Holly should have been relieved. He was out of reach now. Safely married. She wouldn't be tempted to yield. Her lips twisted. As if Dev would want her, she acknowledged. Tramp of the year, Holly Scott. Would any man want her now?

'Not at all,' he demurred. 'I'm all in favour of independence. But you're missing the point, Holly. I'm just surprised to find Courdrey's wife is allowed to go out to work.'

'A debatable point since I don't know the lady.'

'Meaning?'

'Alex's wife. The present Mrs Courdrey. Someone—Alex, I suppose—must have forgotten to introduce us,' she murmured flippantly.

'But—you're Courdrey's wife.' Half-challenge, half-statement, the sudden doubt on Dev's face tugging at her heart strings. And then she remembered. Dev was married. As if he'd care. Holly pulled herself together.

'Am I? And what on earth gave you that idea?'

'But—I saw the notice in *The Times*. Damn it, Holly, the twenty-first of September at St Paul's.'

'Ah, yes. Now that you come to mention it, Alex did tell the world that he'd set a date.'

'And?'

'And?' Holly shrugged, sensing her advantage, an insignificant advantage, maybe, but for once Devlin Winter was in the dark, she'd caught him unprepared. She angled her head, met his gaze full on, forced a brittle smile. 'He forgot to tell his loving fiancée, would you believe?'

'Holly—'

'I called it off,' she announced, the edge to his tone throwing her. 'Couldn't go through with it. Hence the job.'

'I see.' Just that. No reaction. Not a blink, not a smile. Just those two words.

Holly dropped her gaze, focusing on the starched white cloth with its smattering of crumbs. Afternoon tea. So very ordinary. So very English. Tiny squares of bread and butter, slivers of cucumber nestling between, smoked salmon on brown, egg and cress on white. Dainty scones with clotted cream and jam. Food. Beautifully prepared and presented but right now food, any food, would choke her. She glanced up, catching the waiter's eye, a silent plea for help, and he came across at once with a fresh pot of tea and jug of boiling water.

'Holly?' Soft, oh so soft.

'Dev?' she queried, eyes glued to the white porcelain tea pot with its craquelure glaze.

'Look at me, Holly. Please, Holly.'

And Holly did, raising her eyes, slowly, so slowly, suddenly afraid of what she'd find. Because of all the emotions in the world, Dev's pity was the one she really couldn't handle. Not today.

'Because of me, Holly? Because of us?' he asked. Softly, oh, so softly.

Not pity then. Not triumph. No muted gloating here. But what? So much emotion in those deep, dark pools.

'Was it, Holly?' Dev pressed. 'Was it because of me?'

How easy to say yes. Yes, yes, yes! I couldn't marry Alex because I love you. I love you. I need you. I want you. How easy, and how foolish. Because Dev didn't want her. Not any more, not ever, not really. Oh, yes, he'd *said* he did, so many times in the past that Holly had lost count. But it didn't mean anything, want.

Sex, was what he really meant. Good sex. Wonderful, mind-blowing sex. But that was all, she faced it, swallowing hard. Holly was good in bed and Dev had wanted her. And why not? Hadn't she had plenty of practice? Tramp of the year, she whipped herself. Tramp. And Dev knew. Because Holly had told him. And he'd reacted. Disgust, distaste, revulsion. She'd logged his reaction. And Dev wouldn't want her now if she was the last woman on earth.

'No,' she said brusquely, far more brusquely than she intended. 'Good heavens, Dev, whatever gave you that idea?'

He flinched, an instinctive response that he'd masked in an instant, strong features back in control, just those deep, black eyes brimming with disgust.

'Fine. Whatever the reason, I can't profess to be sorry. But I hoped—'

'Hoped?' Holly queried, suddenly puzzled.

'Nothing. Nothing at all. Have some more tea,' he insisted, changing the subject abruptly.

Tea. Yes, why not? That quaint English way of coping with disaster great and small.

Tea. And small talk. Small talk with a virtual stranger. And then Dev mentioned Jonathan and the tensions of the day magically disappeared.

'Thank you.'

'For what?'

'The postcard. He was gutted when you left in such a hurry. You'll never believe how much the card helped.'

'It was the least I could do. I—'

'Yes?' Holly sensed the hesitation.

'I was going to suggest dropping by. I'm in town for a few more days yet. But I guess Jon's away at school.'

How easy to say yes. Say yes, Holly. Lie. Keep Dev away from her family. She'd tried it once before, she recalled, and it hadn't worked then. So—she took a deep breath. 'No. He goes to the local primary,' she reluctantly admitted. 'So—'

'So?'

'I'll have Meryl give you a call. She finally took the plunge and married Tom, you know.'

'No. I didn't. But I'm glad.'

'Yes.' The only decent thing to come out of the summer, Meryl and Tom, behaving like a couple of lovestruck teenagers. Just one of the reasons Holly needed a place of her own. Privacy. For all of them. Despite the house with its dozens of newly renovated rooms. Dad's house, Meryl's house now, Holly amended, in trust for Jonathan. And restored to its former glory, thanks to Tom.

Nearly there. Nearly over. And when Dev called round to see Jon, Holly would make sure she was miles away. Dev. Alone? she wondered. Or would he want to bring his wife along? His wife. Nearly there. Mellow now. The earlier niggles forgotten. Just curiosity. Curiosity killed the cat, she told herself, but that wasn't about to stop her. Holly knew. And she wanted Dev to know that she knew. Safer that way. No more pretending. No more lies. No more temptations.

'She's very pretty.'

'Who?'

She took a deep breath, the words almost choking her. 'Your wife.'

Expressive eyebrows rose. 'And how would you know about my wife?'

'I saw you. At the lift. In the perfume hall. You were kissing.'

'Oh, yes. Just a little peck goodbye,' he explained with thinly veiled amusement. 'I should hate you to get the wrong idea, Holly. Because when I'm feeling romantic, I'm much more steamy, I assure you. Quite inclined to get carried away.'

'In public?'

'Well, no, not normally in public. There's the odd public beach I seem to recall, but then the lady and I were always alone.'

Holly blushed. How cruel of him to remind her. 'But that's not something you're likely to tell your wife, Dev, surely?' she needled.

'Worried, Holly? Afraid that I'll spill the beans, share all our guilty secrets?' And he moved his head from side to side in silent condemnation. 'Would *you* have told Courdrey?' he challenged coldly.

'You know I wouldn't!' Holly bit back, her chin snapping up in defiance.

'Exactly.' Point made. Grim-faced. Tight-lipped.

She'd hurt him, worse—insulted him. Holly swallowed hard. 'I'm sorry,' she murmured almost pleadingly. 'She's very lucky. I guess you both are.'

'Who?'

'Your wife, of course.'

He grinned, the expression in his eyes like the sun coming out from behind a cloud. 'Not guilty, Holly,' he conceded lightly. 'Not yet, at least. But I guess you're right. I'm the lucky one, and to return to an earlier comment, the future Mrs Winter is the most beautiful woman in the world.'

There. She'd done it. She'd finally forced the truth. And it hurt. Oh, God, how it hurt. And Holly swallowed the pain, buried the pain, would live with the pain day in and day out for the rest of her life. Because she'd lost him. He'd never been hers, and she'd lost him. Because he wasn't married yet, but soon he would be. And Holly had lost him. And, if everything else was equal, she attempted to console herself, there would always be the shadow of the past hanging over them. Her father's money. And Dev, she forced herself to face, had taken that money and run. Much better this way. Much better all round.

'So—' Holly's turn to rise to the occasion, feign an unconcern that could have earned her an Oscar. 'You've found your face of Aphrodite, then?'

'Maybe,' Dev acknowledged lightly. 'But somehow I don't see her relishing the publicity.'

'But as your wife she'll have to get used to publicity. Surely the two go hand in hand?'

'Very true, Holly. Perhaps I should ask her, call off the worldwide search.'

'And lose out on all that publicity, Dev...?'

'Ah! So I'm rumbled.' He grinned, completely unabashed, and, leaning back in his seat, he folded his arms, black eyes dancing with amber lights. Devastating Dev. Wonderful Dev. Someone else's Dev.

Holly didn't really mean to sound nosy; somehow the question just slipped out. 'What's her name?'

'Who?'

'You know very well who,' she snapped, annoyed with herself, more annoyed with Dev for playing games.

'The girl you saw me kissing, huh? Flora. Flora Penman.'

'Flora. A pretty name. You could always use it for one of your perfumes.'

'Well, no. I've tried it once before you see and, well—' He gave an eloquent shrug of powerful shoulders. 'It simply didn't work.'

'Oh?' Holly queried as tiny hairs on the back of her neck began to prickle.

'Ilexia, Holly. Surely you must have guessed by now. It was named after you.'

Ilexia. Which explained Dev's uncharacteristic surge of anger. And because Dev mistakenly thought that Alex had bought it, he'd smashed the bottle to pieces.

Holly felt the sudden sting of tears. Ilexia. Like her father's yacht, named for her. And she'd never known, never guessed. And it really didn't matter now. Nothing did.

'Thank you,' she said, simply, raising her head, meeting his gaze though the effort nearly killed her. 'I think I'm beginning to understand.'

'No, Holly,' Dev contradicted starkly. 'I don't think you are.'

Another day, another dollar. And a sluggish Holly dragged herself out of bed and splashed her face in a basin of cold water in an effort to banish the shadows. She hadn't slept at all, was sharply aware of Meryl's worried gaze crossing the kitchen with surreptitious frequency. Sleep? With Dev's words, Dev's smile engraved upon her heart—no chance.

The images had run through her mind like an unremitting movie show. Dev, on the verge of being married. Dev, kissing the girl—Flora, Holly amended, trying the name out in her mind. A pretty name. A pretty girl. Woman, she supposed, since she was clearly older than Holly. Five or six years older, she'd hazard. And attractive. Holly and Flora. Chalk and cheese. Dark and fair. And Dev, making love to Holly, making love—but no! Holly's mind skittered away, the truth too awful to face. Because she loved him. And Dev wasn't hers any more, had never been hers in the first place. But, oh, how wonderful it had been while it lasted.

'Something on your mind, love?' Meryl probed, pouring them each a fresh cup of coffee and pulling up her chair. 'Work?' she hazarded, shrewd blue eyes searching Holly's face, and then, into the loaded pause, 'Dev?'

Holly sighed. 'Dev.'

'It might help to talk, you know.'

'Yes.' And with so much buried, so much festering, the relief of pouring it all out was a luxury Holly simply couldn't afford. She took a long sip of her coffee, racking her brains for something to say, achingly aware that Meryl wanted to help, equally aware that this time Holly was on her own. She'd grown up. And she was on her own.

'You saw him, then?'

'No escape,' Holly conceded. 'I thought I was safe and then the moment I relaxed, practically walked into his arms.'

'And?'

Holly shrugged. 'You know Dev. He sent his regards. Said he'd like to pop round some time, say hello to Jonathan.'

'If you think that's a good idea...?'

She nodded. 'Sure. Why not. Jon will be over the moon. And Dev was good with Jon.' Would make a good father, she added silently, bitterly. A wonderful father to Flora's babies.

'He's the man, isn't he, Holly?' Meryl probed softly. 'From Tenerife, I mean. The man your

310

father was so angry about?'

She nodded again. Why deny it? Meryl had known at the time there was a man in the frame, and that Gregory Scott had tried to buy him off. And, despite taking the money, Dev had sold his story.

'Oh, Holly, Holly, what are we going to do with you, love?'

'Find me a man?' Holly teased, with a sudden return to humour. But catching Meryl's instinctive flash of horror, Holly raised her hands. 'Joke, Meryl. I'm through with men—for ever. Cross my heart and hope to die.'

'And Dev?' Meryl queried with a knowing smile. 'Are you sure you're through with him?'

'Oh, yes,' Holly acknowledged drily, draining her cup and pushing back her chair. 'Dev and I are through. Didn't I tell you?' she confided chirpily, grabbing coat and bag and pausing in the doorway. 'Dev's engaged to be married. And furthermore, the great man's besotted. And just in case you think he's spinning me a yarn,' she tagged on swiftly, 'I know. Believe me, Meryl,' she insisted tightly. 'I've seen them together.'

And since they didn't know they had an audience, their tender little scene was a genuine show. It was the truth. And it hurt.

Work. With all its reminders of Dev. And avoiding the lower-ground floor didn't help at all. Word had spread like wild fire and Holly, she was horrified to learn, was quite the celebrity herself.

'Well, aren't you the sly one?' Suzy murmured,

though not unkindly, stepping into the lift beside her. It had been busy in the staff canteen and with Holly the centre of attention, there hadn't been room for Suzy to join her for coffee. 'And to think you never said a word.'

'Sorry, Suzy.' Holly shrugged apologetically. 'If it's any consolation, Dev and I had lost touch. I wasn't even sure he'd remember me.'

'With your face and figure?' Suzy raised a sceptical eyebrow. 'He'd have to go around with his eyes closed. So, how did you get on?'

'Get on?'

'Sure. You know. When old Milesy gave you the afternoon off yesterday. Did he ask you out?'

'When he's happily engaged to someone else, I should hope not,' Holly scorned with mock indignation and, seeing Suzy's face fall, couldn't help but laugh. 'Never mind, Suze,' she reassured lightly as the lift doors swung open. 'Next time Dev's in town, I'll introduce you. You never know, you might just sweep him off his feet.'

'Taking my name in vain, Holly?'

'Dev!'

'The very one,' he agreed pleasantly. 'Complete with burning ears.'

'Oh!' Holly flushed. Suzy blushed. Dev simply flashed one of his devastating smiles in Suzy's direction.

'Devlin Winter,' he murmured, taking her hand. 'I believe Holly's just agreed to introduce us.'

'Suzy Bennett,' Holly supplied. 'And if you'll

excuse me, I'd better get back to work.'

'But—' A look of sheer panic crossed the younger woman's face.

'Don't worry,' Holly reassured drily. 'You're safe. He's engaged.'

'He certainly is,' Dev agreed good-naturedly. And he offered Suzy his arm. 'For the next twenty minutes, or so, I'm all yours. The Beauty Room. I never forget a pretty face,' he confided with another bright smile, 'so lead on, my dear. One or two things need sorting and I do believe you're just the girl I need.'

'You made Suzy's day,' Holly conceded when Dev reappeared half an hour later. And though she hadn't raised her hopes, she'd have been absurdly disappointed if Dev had left without saying goodbye. 'It was good of you.'

'My pleasure. She's a nice girl. Bright, too. Wasted in a job like this, wouldn't you say?'

'Just like me?' Holly challenged with an irrational stab of pain.

'Maybe,' he conceded carelessly. 'But it's my guess you're simply filling time. This time next week, next month, next year at the latest, you'll have moved on.'

'So sure, Dev? Always so sure,' she needled.

'No, Holly. Not always,' he contradicted coolly. 'And never where you're concerned. So—' He changed the subject abruptly. 'Tell me about Suzy.'

'Why?'

'Because I'm asking. And like I said, she's bright, wasted in a job like this.'

Holly swallowed a bitter retort. Because he's asking. Oh yes, the mighty Devlin Winter utters a request and the whole world bows down in instant obedience. 'I haven't known her long,' Holly explained. 'She's fun, works hard, has a nice bubbly personality. She's a fully trained beauty therapist, but failed the written exams. Naturally enough, she's doing the next best thing.'

'Why?'

'Why? Because she needs a job just like the rest of us, I suppose. You know, Dev, work. It helps pay the bills.'

'Thank you, Holly,' he acknowledged witheringly. 'I meant, why did she fail her exams? The girl's bright. Beauty and brains,' he mused. 'A rare combination for a blonde.'

'Such sexism, Dev. You ought to be ashamed of yourself.'

'Well, I'm not. Simply stating the truth.' And then, logging the mulish set of Holly's lips, he grinned. 'Okay, Holly. You win. The remark was uncalled for. I apologize. Happy now?'

Hardly. But who was she to hold out against him? 'She's dyslexic,' Holly explained, and unconsciously quoting Suzy's own words, 'She can soak up facts like a computer, but simply can't read or write. Interrogation over?'

'For now,' he agreed. 'And, since the lovely Miss Miles is hovering, I guess it's time I did a spot of shopping. I need a present,' he explained, 'for Flora. What would you suggest?'

'You are joking?' she enquired politely.

'Not at all. I know, how about a scarf? One of those woollen things you were wearing yesterday. Just the thing for keeping out the Scottish chill. Come on, Holly, show a teensy-weensy bit of interest. My money's as good as the next man's,' he reminded.

A present for Flora. A length of cord, perhaps, Holly suggested, but silently. Just the thing for wrapping round his neck and pulling tight. Very tight. Choose a present for Flora. Had he no soul? Insensitive man, having his lover select a gift for his fiancée. Ex-lover, she corrected grimly, spreading the entire collection out on the display counter. And Dev, being Dev, took his time.

'Fine. Have it gift-wrapped, will you? Now, then—' He glanced around, seemingly unaware of the crowd that was beginning to form, of the murmurs of approval, the Aphrodite name running like a Mexican wave through the curious circle of onlookers. 'Something more personal, I think. More sexy. Just the thing for a man to give his future wife. Ah, yes! Lingerie. This way, Holly,' he entreated crisply as a seething Holly trailed forlornly in his wake.

Lingerie. Was he mad? Have Holly pick out an indecent froth of lace for Dev to have fun and games with on his wedding night—if he waited for his wedding night. Holly's face was set in cold and angry lines.

'Black?' Dev queried. 'Or is that too wanton? White, perhaps? Hmm. Too virginal?' he probed, turning to Holly, rigid beside him. 'What do you think?'

315

'Since I don't know the lady as intimately as you, I can hardly hazard an opinion!'

'Oh, I don't know.' Black eyes narrowed suddenly, moving from her face, down, down over the swell of breast beneath the distinctive blue-and-gold patterned blouse, down into the curve of waist and on, skimming her hips, a slow and leisurely perusal, an intimate perusal, because every curve, every hollow was known to Dev. Dev's hands, Dev's fingers, Dev's tongue—

Holly's cheeks flamed as she pulled her thoughts up sharp, aware that Dev had noticed, that his eyes had moved lower, down her legs and up again, pausing for a tantalizing moment at the apex, gauging to perfection the junction of her legs beneath the fabric of the skirt, and despite her rigid self-control, she flooded, despised herself for the weakness.

'Ah, yes!' Dev picked out the wispiest, filmiest nightie in the collection. 'Perfect,' he breathed. 'Will it fit?'

'How on earth do I know?' Holly growled through tightly clenched teeth. And then, recalling Dev was a customer, and an influential one at that, 'What size is she?'

'Hmm.' Another intimate, assessing sweep of Holly's body. 'About your size, at a guess.'

At a guess? The man was engaged to be married and he was guessing the girl's size! Holly gave a mental shrug. Who was she to criticize? 'Size twelve, then,' she grudgingly admitted.

'Fine. That'll do nicely.'

'Colour?' Holly prompted tightly.

'Oh, I don't know. You know her colouring, you decide.'

'You wouldn't like me to select a time and place for the wedding?' she hissed under her breath. 'Not to mention the honeymoon.'

'Now there's an idea,' Dev mused. And catching Holly's look of horror, 'Joke, Holly. You had a sense of humour once, I seem to recall.'

'I had a lot of things once,' she responded bitterly, common sense and caution tossed to the winds.

'Meaning?'

'Nothing. Nothing at all. Nothing for you to worry about, Dev.'

'Oh, but I do, Holly,' he informed her tersely. 'Since I'm sure I had a hand in the loss of one or two of them. And that is what you're implying, isn't it?'

'Skip it, Dev. This is hardly the time or place.'

'No. And in that case, lady, why drag it up now?'

Impasse. Holly's face a tight and angry mask, twin spots of colour burning in her cheeks, Dev's eyes black as thunder. Because, yes, Dev was right. Loss of her virginity. He took it. Took it, then brutally discarded it. Guilty as charged. Not quite, Holly allowed, her inherent sense of fairness rising to the surface. Because Holly had given it, and given it willingly. And Dev, like Holly, had never stood a chance.

'I'm sorry,' she said softly and, risking a

317

rebuff, reached out to touch his arm. 'The remark was uncalled-for, Dev. I'm sorry.'

'Sorry? Yes, Holly, and so am I,' he conceded, the white lines of anger running from lips to nostrils beginning fade. He shook himself free. 'The black one,' he decided, barely glancing across. 'I'll pick it up tomorrow with the scarf. If you wouldn't mind having them wrapped, separately, please.'

'Till tomorrow, then,' Holly acknowledged, crying inside. Because she'd hurt him. One stupid, unthinking remark and she'd hurt him. And by hurting Dev, she was hurting herself more.

'Tomorrow? Yes, I suppose so,' he acknowledged curtly, and then he smiled, a strange, mocking, knowing curl of lips. 'But you'll be seeing me well before then, Holly,' he informed her gleefully. 'Meryl phoned. She's invited Flora and me for dinner. Tonight. And from what Meryl was saying, you're eating at home too. So, see you there, Holly. Seven o'clock sharp.'

CHAPTER 19

'Meryl, how could you?'

'Sorry, love. You know how it is.'

'As a matter of fact, no, I don't,' Holly contradicted flatly, folding her arms and filling the doorway.

Meryl gave an apologetic smile. 'I could hardly ask Dev without his fiancée,' she explained, running a critical eye over the highly polished table and reaching out to tweak a linen napkin back into line.

'Maybe not,' Holly agreed. 'But why tonight? Why not tomorrow, or Sunday, or any day in fact when you know I'm going out? And you didn't *have* to tell him I'd be here,' she added almost venomously.

'I know, love. And I'm sorry. But—' Meryl gave another little shrug. 'You don't have to stay. Have a quick drink for old time's sake and then take yourself off. A last-minute date,' she suggested hopefully. 'Dev will understand.'

Dev will understand? Oh, yes, he'd understand, all right. He'd know. He'd see straight through her and he'd know she was running away. And in that case, Holly decided, flouncing out and up to her sitting-room, she was staying put. But how on earth to get through an entire evening of watching Dev making eyes at another woman?

'Problem solved,' Meryl explained twenty minutes later when a showered and dressed Holly drifted down to the kitchen for a pre-dinner drink.

'Oh?' she murmured, holding her breath. She'd heard the phone and paused, lipstick poised halfway to her lips as Meryl's voice in the hall drifted upwards, words of regret, Holly decided from the tone, and the wild ebb and flow of adrenalin had left her confused. He couldn't come. Good, she declared grimly to her scowling reflection. But in that case, why the massive surge of disappointment?

'Dev's arriving in half an hour,' Meryl explained, and darting a shrewd, assessing glance at Holly, added, 'But he'll be alone. Flora can't make it, apparently.'

'Oh.' Better—or worse? Holly probed as a newly scrubbed Jonathan bounced down the stairs and in through the door like a whirlwind.

'Do you think Dev will read me a bedtime story, Holly?' he asked doubtfully.

'Of course he will,' Holly reassured. 'But just in case it has to be a short one, how about you and I go into the lounge and make a start now.'

Half an hour. Twenty minutes. Five minutes. Bang on cue the doorbell rang and one excited little boy, who'd barely heard a word that Holly had said, could contain himself no longer. He was up in a trice, followed at a much more sedate pace by Holly, and she stood at the end of the marble tiled hallway as Tom, hotly pursued by Jon, greeted their guest.

'Dev! Good to see you.' The two men shook hands as Jonathan insinuated himself between them and Holly couldn't help but smile as with a whoop of delight Dev swept the boy off his feet, holding him high above his head before swinging him round and down again.

'Hi-ya, pal.' Dev ruffled Jonathan's still damp curls. 'And how's the riding coming along?' he asked, producing a parcel from the pocket of his coat.

'Yippee! *Black Beauty,*' Jonathan yelled, stripping away the paper to reveal a video.

'Thank you, Dev. But you really shouldn't. You spoiled him enough last summer,' Meryl demurred, blushing prettily as Dev kissed her cheek, presented an exquisite spray of orchids.

'With you for a mother, how could he possibly be spoiled?' Dev countered, grinning. And then he turned to Holly. 'A kiss for old time's sake, Holly?' he challenged softly.

Holly froze. Playing games. Always playing games. And would the kiss for old time's sake have been so forthcoming if Flora had been hanging on his arm?

'Hardly, Dev,' she somehow managed to decline. 'Since you and I parted less than three hours ago.'

Chicken, he mouthed, and as the colour ran into her cheeks, Holly spun round, leading the way into the rarely used drawing-room. As if the comfortable but still shabby lounge wasn't good enough for the mighty Dev Winter, Holly decided acidly, careful to take a chair.

Chicken, black eyes laughingly proclaimed

321

as they locked onto Holly's and, despite her resolve, fresh waves of colour flooded her face.

Thank heavens for Jonathan, whose excited chatter filled the gaping silences when Meryl and Tom disappeared into the kitchen to supervise last-minute arrangements.

'Just a family dinner, Dev,' Meryl explained when they were seated.

'In that case I'm honoured,' Dev countered warmly. 'Having no family of my own, I've missed out on such a lot. And, since I'm a virtual stranger, it's nice to be counted part of yours.'

'Stranger? Not in this house,' Tom declared, nodding at Jonathan, who'd been allowed to stay up for half an hour's treat. 'Believe me, every other word starts with Dev and has done for months. You've certainly made an impression on my stepson.'

Let's hope the halo doesn't slip and clonk him one, Holly decided sourly, unfair of her she knew since Tom was right, Dev *had* been good with Jonathan, all summer long. Wonderful with Jonathan. Would make a wonderful father. Father. Flora. Babies. Flora's babies.

Once it had begun, Holly couldn't halt her train of thought. My babies, she told herself fiercely. My baby. Dev's baby. Oh, God! And she looked across the table and saw Jonathan and Dev with their heads close together and suddenly couldn't take any more, was vaguely aware of a range of shocked expressions as, with a mumbled apology, she scraped back her chair and fled from the room.

'Holly?' Meryl's voice five minutes later, heavy with concern.

Holly raised her head, came face to face with a stranger in the glass. So white. Crying inside. Dying inside. Wimp or woman? she asked herself, and bracing herself for the worst, slid back the bolt on the bathroom door.

'What is it?' Meryl asked, blue eyes cloudy.

Holly shrugged. 'Something went down the wrong way,' she lied. 'Sorry, Meryl, I didn't mean to worry you.'

'If you're sure? Look, why not stay up here a while? Dev won't mind—'

'No! I'm fine. Really fine. I just need a drink.'

A drink. A brandy. An evening of hell. And Jonathan helped, taking Dev upstairs for a precious half-hour's peace, allowing Holly time to pull herself together. And Meryl and Tom, with an understanding born of love, kept the conversation flowing, around her. And then Dev was back, taking his place beside her on the sofa, another mistake, Holly realized, discovering too late that they were alone on the chesterfield. And Dev took her hand, cradled it, his thumb lightly brushing her skin until Holly was finally forced to meet his gaze.

So much knowledge. So much love—no! Not love, Holly countered, attempting to pull away.

'Why, Holly?' he asked simply.

'I choked,' she explained as the fingers tightened their grip.

But Dev shook his head, simply repeated the question. 'Why?'

Why had she allowed him to walk away? Why had she made him go away? Why had she finally rejected him? Because she loved him. And Dev knew that she loved him. And Dev wasn't free. Dev loved Flora.

She licked her dry lips. 'Flora—'

The phone rang, slicing through the tension, and guessing that Tom and Meryl had popped up to say goodnight to Jon, Holly scrambled thankfully to her feet.

'Flora Penman here. Dev's press agent. Sorry to disturb you but—'

'Not at all. I'll get him for you.'

Another brandy. Another half-hour. And then Dev's taxi was at the door. Thank heavens for pre-booked taxis, Holly decided. The perfect excuse to get away. Not that Dev seemed in any particular hurry to go, but it served to bring the evening smoothly to a close.

Sleep. No chance. Too many thoughts, too many memories. Ironic really. This was her family home and, to all intents and purposes, Dev had been part of tonight's family group. Her father would turn in his grave, she decided, damping down the hysteria. Dev Winter, who'd taken Gregory Scott's money and run, had been wined and dined in style in Gregory Scott's home.

And finally on the verge of sleep, something struck her. Dev's press agent, Flora Penman's soft Scottish burr had declared. What a curious way to describe their relationship. Unless, of course, Holly mused, Dev's fiancée was the sort of independent woman who liked to keep her

324

man on his toes. Logical, Holly supposed. After all, hadn't Flora done exactly that for the past six years or so? And through the sea of tears, Holly smiled despite herself.

'Ah, Holly. You're wanted in the office. Better go now,' Jaqui Miles added thoughtfully. 'It doesn't do to keep JC waiting.'

JC. Jason Cooke. A summons to heaven in The Store—or hell, depending on the reasons. And Holly was perplexed. She'd done nothing wrong as far as she was aware, apart from taking the afternoon off with Dev, and she had been given permission, she reassured herself.

'Ah, Holly. Do come in. Sit down, make yourself comfortable. Coffee?'

The red-carpet treatment. Heaven, then. Though heaven alone knew why. And JC, of course. And Holly lapsed into puzzled silence as the coffee arrived, a steaming cafetière complete with sugar bowl, cream jug and three cups and saucers. A sharp rap at the door made Holly glance up.

'Dev!'

'The very one,' he agreed as Jason Cooke beckoned him forwards, waved him to the chair opposite.

The preliminaries over, the moment Dev was settled, Jason Cooke rose to his feet. 'I'll leave you to it,' he declared, ignoring the panic in Holly's eyes. 'Don't forget to help yourselves to coffee.'

And then they were alone. Silence. Just Holly, and Dev. Alone. And Holly sipped her coffee, risked a surreptitious glance, found Dev's thoughtful gaze fastened on her face and flushed in annoyance. Playing games.

'What are we doing here, Dev?' she asked crisply.

'Worry not, Holly. This is business. I've a proposition to make.'

'You *are* joking?' she enquired when Dev had finished explaining.

'About this sort of money? What do you think?'

Money. Dev's new god. No, not new at all, she corrected bitterly. Her father's money. The pay off that had helped start Dev off in the first place.

So—Holly angled her head, returning his gaze with her own icy stare. 'And does what I think matter?' she enquired coolly.

'Of course. Since the whole scheme hinges on you.'

'Yes.' And what a scheme. The face of Aphrodite. Holly. 'Fine. Well in that case, Dev, thanks, but no thanks.'

'Why?'

'I'm simply not interested, Dev.'

'Just like that?'

'Just like that,' she agreed grimly, holding his gaze.

Dev shrugged, pouring himself another coffee, holding the cafetière out in silent enquiry, but Holly shook her head, not trusting herself to speak. The face of Aphrodite. And she still wasn't convinced that it wasn't just some cruel hoax on Dev's part. After all, he'd found the woman of his dreams, Flora. Flora. Yes. Why not plaster *her* face across the billboards, have it adorn each and every expensive little pack, or dominate beauty counters from here to Timbuktu and back again? And Holly knew. Hadn't Dev already given her the answer to that one?

'She might not relish the publicity,' he'd teased over afternoon tea at his hotel. And yet he must have known Flora's views, knew full well she'd hate it. Just as Holly would hate it. Aphrodite. Goddess of love. Dev's love. Second-best love, she scorned silently. Well, Devlin Winter could think again. Holly Scott had her pride.

'Not a cat in hell's chance,' she insisted when Dev repeated the proposals.

She caught the flash of annoyance that he'd masked in an instant and then Dev was back in control, leaning back in the chair, Jason Cooke's chair in Jason Cooke's office, completely at home, completely relaxed, just as if he owned the place. Formally dressed as he had been last night, this time it was a steel-grey business suit. Steel grey to match the expression in his eyes. But Holly wasn't impressed.

Unexpectedly, Dev smiled. 'Come on, Holly, be fair. It's a once-in-a-lifetime chance. You're not seriously thinking of turning it down?'

'Sorry to disappoint you, Dev. But that's exactly what I'm doing.'

'You can't.' Emotionless. Polite.

'Can't I?' Expressionless. Equally polite.

'I'm afraid not, Holly. You see, there's one

327

tiny little detail you seem to have overlooked.'

'Oh?' Just the merest apprehension, the feeling she was being backed into a corner, that Dev was holding all the cards and was about to play his ace.

'You've no choice, Holly,' he told her softly. 'You pose for the photos, become the face of Aphrodite or...'

'Or—?'

Powerful shoulders were raised in a casual, offhand shrug. 'Put quite simply, Holly, The Store loses out. I pull out and this becomes the only retail outfit of its size in the world without an Aphrodite contract.'

'But—that's blackmail.'

'Not blackmail, common sense. And think of all that money, Holly.'

'Keep your filthy money,' she protested, scrambling to her feet and towering above him for once. 'I'm not interested.' Money? Take money from Dev? Money she could trace all the way back to her father? Judas money. Ha! She'd rather starve.

'Fine.' His cold glance flicked over her, missing not a thing, Holly was sure, the tell-tale spots of colour in her cheeks, the anger burning in her eyes. 'Your decision,' he acknowledged easily. 'No photos. No fee. No contract for The Store.' And those black eyes were ranging over her, not a cold and cursory glance this time, but a slow and deliberate appraisal that took in the body beneath the layer of clothes, store clothes, the standard blue and gold outfit with its discreet store logo. 'No contract, no job,

Holly,' he pointed out softly.

'I have a perfectly good job here,' she retorted with an angry shake of the head.

'Present tense, Holly,' he reminded, and though he remained seated and was forced to angle his head to meet her gaze, Dev was clearly in control.

'Meaning?'

'Like I said, no contract, no supplies, and once I explain my reasons to The Store's director...'

Guess who's out of a job? she supplied silently, aware of a pulse at the base of her throat beating wildly. 'You wouldn't dare.'

'Wouldn't I?'

No. He couldn't do it. He wouldn't. Punish Holly. But *why?* It didn't make sense. Revenge? she mused. Dev's warped idea of a joke? Holly Scott, the face of Aphrodite? Surely not. So why the offer—? Ah, yes! She folded her arms, hugged her body, suddenly chilled despite the warmth of Jason Cooke's office with its wall-to-wall opulence. Oh, yes, she acknowledged grimly, her racing mind having sifted all the evidence. She was beginning to see what he was doing.

Clever Dev. He didn't really want Holly staring out from the wrapper of every pack his company produced. He'd want the woman that he loved—Flora. Flora Penman. But this was Dev's revenge. Because he knew. Holly was cornered. He knew that Holly would turn him down. And then he'd pounce. Like Alex, he'd make certain she was unemployed and unemployable. The rat. The scheming, hard-nosed rat. Dev's terrible revenge for that night of love, for Holly's ultimate rejection. And how she'd underestimated him. Had she ever known him? she wondered hysterically, squeezing back the tears, damned if she'd cry in front of this man who'd taken her from hell to heaven and back again. Alex and Dev, carved from the same avaricious, scheming, ruthless block of stone.

Her eyes whipped across the space between them. Dev was bluffing. And in that case, he was about to find out that there was more to Holly Scott than met the eye.

'Fine. If that's what you really want.'

'You'll do it?' Amazement. Disbelief. Incredulity.

Holly nodded, swallowing a bitter smile. That had thrown him.

Breaktime. As if the anything-but-cosy hour she'd spent in Jason Cook's office hadn't been long enough. And Dev had gone. Just like that. He'd nodded his approval, had the cheek to give her a brief hug of the shoulders, and then he'd gone.

'I'll be in touch, Holly, the moment the lawyers have sorted out a contract; in the meantime, I'm sure there's no need to remind you that this is confidential.'

'In case you change your mind?' she'd hissed, pulling free of his embrace.

And for once, Devlin Winter had had the grace to flinch. 'A contract's a contract Holly.

Written or verbal. I'll keep my word, I promise you.'

'All the tomorrows,' she'd heard herself deriding as Dev headed for the door. 'Was that a contract, too, Dev?' And she'd laughed. Laughed in his face. Laughed till she'd cried. But then it didn't matter. Dev had already gone.

So, back to work. Hardly rushed off their feet even for a Monday and Holly had seized the chance of an early break, twenty minutes of peace.

Except, of course, she'd reckoned without Suzy.

'I can hardly believe it,' Suzy trilled. 'The most wonderful news in the world.'

Oh, yes. Wonderful, Holly echoed. Keep it under wraps, Dev had warned and yet Suzy had the news almost as fast as Holly. And then something Suzy said pierced the misery.

'I'm sorry, Suze, what did you say?'

'The very first Aphrodite Beauty Salon. Eat your heart out, Holly, you're looking at the first-appointed therapist. And furthermore, I get my pick of the sites.'

'You?'

'The very one. Thanks to you, of course.'

'Me! And how do you work that out?' Holly demanded, almost choking on her coffee.

'Simple. I wouldn't have had a look in but for you. That personal introduction,' she explained. 'I owe you, Holly. So, if you're ever in need of a facial...' Her voice trailed off as she took her cue from Holly's stunned silence. 'No, I guess not,' she added woodenly. 'With a face like yours, a

331

facial's the last thing you'd be needing.' She swung away, shoulders drooping.

'Suze!'

She turned, eyebrows raised in enquiry.

'About that facial,' Holly murmured brightly. 'Book me in as your very first client, hey? And not just the facial, make it the works.'

And Suzy's bright smile made up for the pain of having to pretend. 'You bet!'

Curiouser and curiouser. A man of many parts. An outer case of steel, yet a heart of pure gold—when it suited him. Like the boy in Houlgate, Holly recalled, pulling her collar up close around her neck as she stepped out of the staff entrance and into the chilly London rush hour. He'd berated Holly as a fool for not reporting the theft to the police and then, lo and behold, hard-hearted Devlin Winter had given the boy a job. And Suzy? Holly mused, struggling to make sense of it. Clearly another nice gesture from Dev.

'Holly?'

He stepped out of a doorway in front of her, forcing her to swerve.

'Now what?' she bit out, barely slowing her pace. Besides, it was too cold to stand and chat, however pleasant the company, and Devlin Winter, she acknowledged bitterly, didn't quite make the grade. Not with Holly. Not today. Even allowing for Suzy's news.

'I thought you might like to come for a drink.'

'With you?' Holly's smile was brittle. 'No thanks, Dev. It would choke me.'

332

'Why, Holly?'

'You know very well why. Do you know something, Dev?' She turned to face him then, all thoughts of Suzy and the boy and Dev's soft inner shell having vanished from her mind. 'You're no better than Alex. Not really.'

'Meaning?'

'You're a bully. You take what you want, or buy what you want, and if all else fails, you bully your way through with ruthless efficiency.'

'That isn't fair, Holly.'

'No? Well, that's life. Life isn't fair. And that's a lesson some us learned seven years ago—the hard way.'

Dev flinched. 'So cruel, Holly? It's not like you—'

'No? Well, I've changed. I've had to.'

'Thanks to me, you mean?'

'If the cap fits...' she pointed out sweetly and, not waiting for an answer, set off again as fast as the tightly fitting court shoes would allow.

She hadn't gone far when she realized she wasn't alone. Clever Dev. Goodness only knows why, but he'd been waiting for her, had guessed she'd travel to work by Tube and positioned himself at just the right spot to intercept her. And now he was dancing attendance like her shadow. Well, let him. She was going home. And if Dev Winter had nothing better to do, he could follow her down into the subway with its heaving mass of commuters, could elbow his way through to the train just like countless thousands others, and then straphang, avoiding the pickpockets and gropers, of course. Everyday life on the underground. For the workers, at least.

'Listen, Holly—' A hand on her arm, restraining, insisting, because Devlin Winter had decided he wanted to talk.

'Let go of me,' she hissed, pulling up short and uncaring of the crowds jostling past.

'When I'm good and ready.'

'Oh, naturally, sir,' Holly sneered. 'Like I said, Dev, you're no better than Alex. Well, I've had enough. I'm a grown woman now and I'll decide what happens in my life. Leave me alone. Are you listening, Dev? The contract, yes! I can hardly avoid signing on the dotted line, but nothing else—no favours, no cosy little chats over afternoon tea, no drinks, no bed—nothing. Or are you really so like Alex you'll even try forcing your way into my—?'

She pulled herself up sharp, horrified at what she'd almost given away.

Black eyes narrowed dangerously under the glow of the street lights. 'Force his way into what, Holly?'

'Nothing. Nothing for you to worry about.'

'Courdrey tried to force his way into what, Holly?' Dangerous. Cold. A chilling lack of emotion. And Dev wanted an answer, would stand here all night if necessary, but sooner or later he'd wear her down, drag the answer from her. And something—shame? pride? or a sudden insight into Dev's terrible rage, rage at Alex if she told him the truth—made Holly take a deep breath, come up with a plausible response.

'He tried to force my hand about the wedding,

of course,' she stated flatly.

'Liar!' Face blazing, eyes spitting flames.

Holly flinched.

He snatched at her wrist, pulling her against him, his face close to hers, black eyes deep, treacherous pools. 'You're lying, Holly.'

'No.'

'I know you. You're lying, covering up for that—rat.'

'No! No, no, no.' She twisted free, rubbing at her wrist where his fingers had bit, and then she angled her head, her eyes nuggets of ice as they locked with his. 'Maybe it's a case of better the bully you know, Dev,' she murmured softly.

His chin snapped up. 'Oh, Holly, Holly,' he berated. 'How could you? How could you lump me in the same class as Courdrey?'

'Class, Dev? Surely you mean muck heap,' she derided, and she was glad to see him flinch this time. 'Are you and Alex really so different?' she challenged.

'Meaning?'

'Rich. Powerful. Ruthless. You've made your mark on the world and still you want more. Always more. More power. More control, control of other people's lives. Oh yes, silly me,' she jeered, eyes stinging in the wind now. 'I almost forgot. More money. Because money gives power, the power to destroy. My life, Dev, and my father's. And all for the love of money.'

'I've told you till I'm blue in the face, Holly, I didn't break that story.'

'No?' Holly shrugged. 'Well, maybe you

335

didn't,' she conceded coolly. And since she'd scoured the pages of that scandal sheet he worked for day after day after day without coming across Dev's name, maybe, just maybe, he was telling her the truth. But he was still guilty as charged. 'Money, Dev,' she reminded him frigidly. 'My father's cheque. Or was that just a figment of my imagination?'

He blanched, the intense black of his eyes the only spots of colour in the rigid lines of his face. 'No, Holly. No.' And he twisted away, half-stumbling across the pavement, reaching the metal barrier at the kerb and clinging on almost as if his life depended on it. And though an uncaring crowd surged between them, filling the void, their eyes collided across a gaping chasm. 'No, Holly.'

No. It wasn't a figment of her imagination. And Dev knew, as Holly knew, that the cheque would damn him forever in Holly's eyes.

CHAPTER 20

Ilexia.

The distinctive fragrance hit her as she opened the cloakroom door and Holly choked back the nausea. No escape. Home, work, the staff restroom of all places. Wherever she went, so many reminders of Dev.

'Hi, Holly. Want a squirt?' Suzy's laughing eyes met Holly's in the glass, and Holly glanced down at the bottle in Suzy's hand, remembered the last time she'd seen the same distinctive bottle in someone's hand, and suppressed the pain along with the memory with a massive surge of will. She shook her head.

'No? Fine. Suit yourself,' Suzy murmured good-naturedly, dropping the bottle into the clutter of her open handbag. 'I know Aphrodite's the latest in the range,' Suzy acknowledged, snapping shut her bag and swinging round to face her. 'But as far as I'm concerned, this is a much nicer smell.' Double checking, she lifted her wrist, inhaling deeply before tagging on dreamily, 'For the woman I love today and all the tomorrows.'

'*What* did you say?' Holly queried, stunned, half-convinced she was hearing things.

'It's the motto on the perfume,' Suzy explained. 'For the woman—'

'Yes, I know. I know the words at least,'

Holly cut in sharply. 'But—I—are you sure?' she persisted, tripping over her words while her mind tripped over a million and one incredible possibilities. 'I didn't realise you were fluent in French, Suze?' And then, thoroughly confused, 'Wait a minute, you're dyslexic —how on earth—?'

'Simple. I had someone explain it, Holly.'

'Who?'

'Why, the great man himself, of course,' Suzy informed her with another dreamy expression in her eyes. 'When he autographed my box.'

Dev? Another idea of a joke, courtesy of Devlin Winter? But why? He'd named the perfume for Holly. He *said* he'd named the perfume for Holly and since it was new in the shops the month that Meryl had bought it...

Holly's half-day. Four hours of thinking, wondering, turning it over in her mind. Four hours of dealing with clients, modelling gowns. And all the time her mind going round and round in circles. And she had to know. Once and for all. So, the moment she was free she braced herself, heading down to the Beauty Room, stifling the nausea as she counted out her money.

'Hey. You're forgetting your staff discount,' the heavily made-up assistant reminded as Holly snatched the package and swung away.

'No time,' she explained apologetically over her shoulder. Easy enough to process, she knew, but she'd be expected to stand and chat, was quite the celebrity herself these days, her afternoon out with Dev common knowledge in the store.

Back to the lift, up, so long, why does it have to take so long? Out on the street Holly paused, taking huge gulps of cold, fresh air. She needed a translator, someone fluent in French. But who? She caught a sudden movement in the corner of her eye. A ripple of store flags. Flags. Word association. Flags of nations. The French Embassy. Holly shrugged. Why not? A strange request maybe, but it would only take a moment. The staff would be French, surely wouldn't mind giving her the truth. The truth. Was she ready to face the truth?

She hailed a passing cab, and since they were soon swallowed up by the midday crawl of traffic, Holly pulled the package from her handbag, scrunching the wrapper into her pocket as she balanced the box in her palm. The truth. Was she ready for the truth?

No escape. She had to face the truth, and she tugged the bottle free of its protective padding, flinching, because the faint but detectable fragrance of Ilexia wafted upwards, and steeling herself, she turned the bottle over, looking for the words, the words of French that she'd never bothered to have translated.

For the woman I love today and all the tomorrows.

'Oh, God!' Holly stuffed her hand into her mouth in an effort to halt the choking sobs.

For the woman I love today and all the tomorrows.

In English. Because this was England and

the words, naturally enough, were written in English.

He loved her. Dev was telling her he loved her. Past tense, she realized. He loves Flora now, has loved Flora for years, since before the accident. And the future Mrs Winter, Dev had told Holly less than a week ago, was the most beautiful woman in the world.

So—face it, Holly. He loved you—once. The perfume was proof of it, Dev's tribute to Holly for taking her virginity, for ruining her father. And the contract? she mused, her mind running on, her eyes unseeing as the cab nosed its way into a middle lane, came to a halt, hemmed in left, right and centre by an almost solid mass of traffic. The Aphrodite contract she'd refused to take at face value. That made sense too, now, she knew with the benefit of hindsight. And *yes,* Dev had bullied her. Because he'd known, she acknowledged, smiling despite herself. He'd known her so well, had known she'd never have signed that contract otherwise. So—not Dev's revenge, Dev's atonement.

Holly had been wrong. So very wrong.

Only it was worse than that, much, much worse.

'Holly? Darling, oh, darling!' Trust Meryl to ask no questions, simply opening her arms and drawing Holly into the house, into the lounge, the only room that hadn't been renovated and which Holly loved for its memories of her father, holding, hugging and reassuring her, and, the moment Holly's sobs subsided, pressing a large and much-needed brandy into her hand.

'Dev?' Meryl queried softly, once she gauged Holly was back in control.

Holly nodded. Dev. She loved him. She'd lost him. Could even find it in her heart to forgive him. Because he'd loved her—once. And the cheque didn't matter any more. Dev had more than atoned.

There was a rustle of paper as Meryl reappeared at her side.

'What is it?' Holly asked, glancing up at her, suddenly apprehensive.

'I've been clearing out your father's papers,' Meryl explained, a wealth of knowledge in her soft blue eyes. 'There were boxes and boxes stacked in the loft that I haven't had time to go through until now. I found this.'

'But—it's addressed to Dad,' Holly stated stupidly, taking hold of the envelope with fingers that shook. Through another blur of tears the smudged London postmark and the date leapt out at her, the date—and the name of the Los Cristianos villa where Holly's world had at the same time come to an end.

'Yes'

Oh, hell. Panic. Holly licked her dry lips, eyes darting from the faded address to Meryl's face and back again. 'I don't think—'

'Open it, Holly.' Soft, like the edges of colour around her stepmother's irises. Soft. Tinged with sadness. Soft. Sympathetic. Full of understanding.

Such a poignant, handwritten note: 'You can't buy me off a story that doesn't exist, Mr Scott,' Dev's bold, flowing script stated tersely. 'And as

341

for Holly—I love Holly. And one day I'll come back for Holly. And believe me, the taint of money will never come between us.'

Just that. Oh, yes, and the torn scraps of cheque that fluttered onto Holly's lap, clearly made out in the name of Devlin Winter.

And just as clearly rejected.

Apologize. How to apologize to the man you loved, the man you'd sat in awful judgement upon, damned for all time?

Taxi to Victoria then—or Tube? Quicker by taxi, she argued. But the Tube would give her time to muster churning thoughts. So, underground it was, and sure enough, just as Dev had claimed, the hotel had its very own back door to the station.

'Mr Winter? I'm sorry.' The receptionist was pleasant but firm. 'I'm afraid he's given strict instructions that he's not to be disturbed.'

Do not disturb. Do not pass go. Go straight to jail. Hardly, Holly allowed, but at least she'd managed to retain her sense of humour.

'Writing paper and envelope? Certainly, madam. On the desk to your right.'

So—pen poised. How on earth to begin? Hard enough face to face but... Dear Dev, sorry, it looks like I've been wrong all these years. Holly's lips twisted. Not evenly remotely funny, she decided, and taking a deep breath, began to write straight from the heart:

All the tomorrows, Dev. I loved you then, I love you now, I'll love you always. And knowing that you loved me once will live with me through all the tomorrows. Thank you, Dev, for giving me something precious to hold on to. Holly.

She tucked Dev's note and the scraps of cheque inside and sealed it quickly before she could change her mind. Having handed it in at reception, Holly turned to leave, bumping straight into the girl—woman, she corrected automatically—who'd just breezed in through the revolving doors.

'Oh. I'm terribly sorry.' A soft, Scottish burr, a pretty face, not quite as tall as Holly. Slim. Attractive. Definitely attractive, and looking at Holly with a quizzical smile.

'No, *I'm* sorry,' Holly murmured, tears welling. Sorry about so many things, and she dashed away, pausing at the top of the steps to glance back in time to see Flora Penman waved on to the lifts. Do not disturb. Except for Flora. And face to face she was even more lovely than she had been at The Store. And it hurt.

The doorbell. Ignore it. Meryl and Tom would have a key and Holly simply couldn't face so much as the milkman collecting his money.

Only it rang and rang and rang, wearing Holly down until, with a muttered curse that would have made the devil himself blush, she headed for the top of the stairs. There was a dark figure outlined in the frosted glass of the door below. The milkman. Holly might have known and then—

Voices, a key in the lock, the door swinging open, swinging shut behind his familiar figure. And watching from her vantage position at the top of the stairs, Holly stopped breathing. Leastways, she was sure that she had, since her heart began to kick wildly in her breast as the truth began to dawn. Only, Holly didn't know, not any more. A million and one reasons, she told herself, a million and one emotions running through her mind. Hope. She couldn't bear it. To raise her hopes and then have them dashed cruelly to the ground. No, much better not to hope in the first place.

'Holly?' Just a hint of uncertainty reverberating round the marble-tiled hallway, but then Dev was in a strange house and couldn't even be sure that Holly was home.

She stood quite still, waiting, wondering, until, almost as if sensing Holly's presence, Dev glanced up. Nothing. Holly didn't breathe, didn't blink, and then Dev moved, releasing her from the spell and Holly turned, dashing back up the corridor to her sitting-room as Dev took the stairs in a series of leaps and bounds.

'Oh, no, you don't!' he insisted, inserting his foot into the door jamb as Holly attempted to slam it behind her.

'How did you get in, Dev?' Not, what are you doing here, Dev, or, why have you come? she noted with a touch of hysteria.

'Meryl. We met on the doorstep. And being a diplomatic lady, she immediately made herself scarce with Jon, and the words riding lesson, McDonald's and movie floated back as they

344

reached the corner of the street. So—' He angled his head. 'We're alone.'

'Yes.'

Holly remained standing, eyeing him warily, her arms folded tightly across her chest, an instinctive gesture of protection that Dev surely wouldn't miss. And since Holly was clean out of pride, she didn't care any more.

Why had he come? To rub her nose in it? To demand the apology she still hadn't offered, she realized, thinking back to the note she'd left. To gloat, gloat because stupid, blinkered Holly loved him still? Surely not, she mused as the pain scythed through. Dev wouldn't. Because every damning charge she'd laid at his feet had been wrong. He was everything Holly had said he couldn't be. So—not revenge. It simply wasn't Dev. But why had he come?

'I got your note.'

'Yes.' A figment of her imagination perhaps but Dev seemed to have moved imperceptibly closer. And since it wasn't a large room in the first place, Holly fought the urge to take a step back.

'Holly.'

'Yes?' Not a figment of her imagination. Dev *had* moved, was close, much too close for comfort. No coat, she noted, vaguely aware that Dev must have received her note the moment Holly had left, and since she'd been in the house less than twenty minutes, he must have followed at once by taxi. But why?

'Holly?' Jacket discarded now, his hands were reaching for her shoulders, and Holly closed her eyes. So close. Close enough to touch, to kiss, and the last of her resistance drained away as Dev caught her to him and she was kissing Dev, holding Dev, wanting Dev, madness, she knew but it didn't matter. Nothing mattered. Only Dev. Because she loved him.

As the kiss came to an end, Holly glanced up, suddenly shy under the blast of Dev's solemn gaze, and seeing the fear flickering in her eyes, Dev smiled, dipped his head, touched his lips against hers, setting on fire all over again.

'I'm a fool,' he murmured thickly, cupping her face, dipping his head, his lips tracing the outline of her mouth, a long, slow, sensuous trail, tantalizing, teasing until Holly couldn't take it any longer and she raised her hands to the back of his neck, running her fingers through the silk of his hair, instinctively avoiding the ridge of damaged skin, urging his head down, urging his mouth to meld with hers.

'Holly, Holly, Holly,' he murmured, and then all the restraint was gone because he was kissing her, as Holly was kissing him, kissing her, touching, setting her on fire, magic hands, magic fingers, tongue, lips, hands ranging her body, his mouth nuzzling the hollow at the base of her throat as his fingers tugged at the buttons of her blouse, snapping the buttons before tugging it free of the waistband of her skirt.

Holly gasped, gasped as his fingers homed in on her breasts, pulled her aching, straining breasts free from the cups of her bra, and she glanced down, seeing his dark head against her breast, loving his head against her breast, his

346

tongue teasing her nipples, nipples tightening, hardening, stomach muscles clenching as she pushed herself against him. And Holly felt the strength of his arousal and she wanted him. Because Dev wanted her. Wanted her.

Despite the need, the screaming, aching need, Holly froze. He wanted her. She'd been here before, she thought with awful clarity. Dev wanted her. Nothing more, nothing less. Easy lay Holly, tramp of the year Holly, she emphasized cruelly. Because Dev knew—hadn't she told him so herself? And Dev was no less human than the rest. He wanted her, simply wanted her body. Because Holly was good in bed, and why not? After all, she'd had plenty of practice, and Flora—

'No!' Twisting free, twisting away, plucking at the edges of her blouse and pulling them together in an effort to cover her shameful nakedness.

Dev swore eloquently under his breath, then twisted her round to face him, iron fingers on her shoulder, branding, scalding, eyes blazing as they locked with hers.

'But why, Holly? Why?' Sheer incredulity. Why? Why not, was what he really meant. 'We're good for each other, we need each other. Why, Holly, why?'

But she simply shook her head, incapable of speech. Want. Need. All Holly needed was love, and love, she recalled, remembering Flora's smiling face, was the one thing Dev couldn't give her. Not any more.

He touched her again, she recoiled as if stung.

'Leave me alone!'

'But—you *love* me!'

Statement of fact, Holly agreed silently, bitterly. But not *carte blanche* for Dev to do what he liked. Or the perfect excuse for Holly to yield. Oh, no. She was through with being a tramp. She wasn't giving in to the needs of her body, not even for Dev.

'You love me, damn it. The note—' He ran his fingers through his hair, an unwittingly appealing gesture of distraction, and Holly felt her knees turn to water. She'd hurt him. She loved him. She'd no choice but to hurt him. 'You *said* you love me.'

Doubt. Disbelief. Deny him, Holly. So easy to deny it. Only it simply wasn't true and Dev knew—no, she amended. There were shadows in his eyes. He didn't know. He wasn't sure. And she didn't have the right to deny him. She couldn't lie. Not now. Especially not now.

'You said you loved me.' Almost toneless, the hint of accusation that didn't quite mask the pain, Holly's pain as much as Dev's. She loved him. She'd hurt him. How could she possibly deny it now?

'You *know* I love you.'

'But—*why*, Holly, why?'

He really didn't understand, did he? she realized, dropping her gaze and twisting away, turning her back and fumbling at the buttons of her blouse.

She needed a drink. Her lips twisted. She

348

didn't keep so much as a glass of water in her sitting-room. There'd been no need, since Holly spent most of her time at home in the lounge downstairs, playing games with Jon, watching TV with Jon, and once Jonathan had gone to bed, she'd spend a pleasant hour with Meryl and Tom over a glass of wine before heading back to her own room. Because until Meryl had married Tom, that's what she'd always done, and all Holly's attempts at diplomacy when Tom moved in had been soundly blocked by Meryl.

'You're part of my family,' she'd insisted firmly. 'Always have been, always will be.'

'But—you need time alone, time to be together,' Holly had argued.

And Meryl had smiled, blue eyes twinkling. 'Believe me, Holly, we get plenty of that.'

A moot point, since they cavorted around the house like a pair of teenagers, but Holly had been touched, falling in with Meryl's wishes, but determined to find a place of her own as soon as she could and give the newlywed couple time alone.

So—'Why did you come, Dev?' There, she'd said it, and her voice, she noticed with a touch of pride, hardly wobbled at all.

'I came because I thought we had a future, Holly.'

'And how could you possibly think that?' she asked incredulously, leaning back against the window sash, needing something solid to support her.

She caught the shadow of pain that crossed his

349

features, the bitter twist of his mouth. 'Oh, you know, this and that,' he allowed, the sneering tone slicing through her. Because Dev was back in control now and being human, he was simply following Holly's lead. Tit for tat. She hit out at Dev, Dev hit back at Holly.

'You know, things like your response when I touch you, kiss you, the expression in your eyes when I arrived just now, the note you chose to deliver personally this afternoon. Why go to all that bother, Holly?' he whipped with a vicious snarl of the lips. 'Since I've waited seven long years for you to acknowledge the truth, another twenty-four hours wouldn't have made any difference. You could have saved yourself a wasted journey, popped it in the post. And was it really worth the effort?' he scorned. 'Not even a grudging apology, my dear. Just a few trite lies. A declaration of love that isn't worth the paper it was written on.'

'No! That's not true.'

She caught the flash of contempt he didn't bother to mask and as the pain scythed through, she darted across, coming to a halt before him, close, dangerously close. Because she loved him. And even now, just one tender word from Dev would be enough. Love? She'd never have his love, she acknowledged, but oh, God, how wonderful it would be to feel his arms around her. One last time. Just one last time, she argued in her mind. But no, she saw the hatred shining out from Dev's chill black eyes and the idea withered clean away. Dev didn't want her. Not now. And who could blame him?

But he deserved the truth. She wanted him to have the truth.

'No more lies, Dev,' she said softly, pleadingly, aching to reach out and touch him, run her hand along the angle of his jaw, feel the tactile rasp of stubble beneath her fingers. And achingly aware of how close she was to doing precisely that, she clamped her hands to her sides, just the message in her eyes betraying her inner turmoil.

'Lies, Holly? For your information, madam, I never lied. And as for you—' Cold, black eyes flicked the length of her, down then up, a cold and calculated insult before coming to rest on her face. 'As for you,' he informed her icily as Holly struggled not flinch, 'I simply don't know what to believe, not any more.'

'I never lied, Dev.'

'No? I don't suppose you did. Simply play-acted all summer long. Last summer, Holly,' he emphasized cruelly, 'and those touching little scenes with your lover.'

'You were my lover, Dev.'

'The one and only, hey, Holly?'

'Believe it or not, yes.'

'With your self-confessed track record, Holly?'

'Cruel, Dev. So cruel.'

'I'm simply being honest, Holly. Which is more than I can say for you. And to think, Flora was quite concerned that you were so upset. Little does she know—'

'Flora? *Flora?*' Holly emphasized with sheer incredulity. 'Oh, that's nice, isn't it?' she jeered as the anger surged. 'And to think, I had you down for a gentleman. Fine gentleman you turned out to be, discussing gullible Holly Scott back behind her back. Had a bit of fun, Dev? Been telling tales out of class? Had yourselves a laugh, hey—you and your loving *fiancée,*' she spat.

'My *what?*' Dev challenged as Holly's anger fizzled out as fast as it had blazed.

'You heard.' Sniffing now, because she was crying, dying inside and she no longer cared that Dev would know she was crying for him. She loved him. Dev could choose to believe it or not.

He moved in behind, touching her again, just the lightest of touches but Holly shivered, attempting to twist away, was shockingly aware of Dev's fingers brushing her neck, brushing aside the swathe of hair, even more aware of his warm, fragrant breath on tingling, over-sensitized skin.

'Don't. Don't touch me, please,' she insisted as her blood began to boil.

'Why, Holly? Don't you like it?' he murmured, his lips dropping tantalizingly light kisses along the stem of her neck, and as Holly slumped against him, his hands slid into the curve of her waist, tugging her close, so close she was aware that she'd been wrong. And how wrong! He wanted her. She could feel just how badly he wanted her.

'Don't you like it?' he challenged again, and his hands moved upwards, a lightning brush of breasts that were aching to be touched, to be kissed by Dev, to be tongued by Dev.

'You know I like it. Just as you know I

love you,' she admitted woodenly. 'Don't, Dev, please.'

'But you want me, Holly.'

'Yes.' Fingers clenched, nails digging deep into her palms. God help her, but it was true.

'And I want you.'

'Yes.'

'And you do know how much I want you, don't you, Holly? *Don't you?*' he said again and he pushed himself against her, slid the flat of his hands down to the plane of her stomach and urged Holly back against him, the hardness unmistakable, Dev's need unmistakable, Holly's need unmistakable as her legs turned to water and she was moaning, was aware of Dev stroking, his fingers pressing into her groin as she moved her hips, ground against him, and it was madness, and she was powerless to stop it.

No escape. No escape from Dev—ever. She belonged to Dev body and soul and he could take her, use her, abuse her, discard her, go back to the woman he loved, as long as he always came back to Holly. His terms. Because she loved him. Because she needed him, only him. And if that made her a tramp in the eyes of the world, well, she guessed she'd learn to live with it. Because she loved this man, body and soul.

'I *love you*,' she insisted fiercely, twisting round in his arms, needing to feel his lips moving against hers, needing that hardness pressing into her groin, and she went damp at the thought, was aware of Dev's fingers, magic

353

fingers stealing under the hem of her skirt as his mouth claimed hers. Mouth, lips, fingers, touching, tasting, teasing, and thank heavens she was wearing stockings, she decided as her mind soared skywards. Much less practical than tights but oh, so sexy, allowing Dev's long, slender fingers to stroke the tingling flesh of her thighs, to stroke, to tease, to slide nearer and nearer, upwards until he reached the hem of Holly's damp panties.

Dev's probing finger touched and he realized, his growl of satisfaction in her ear warming her all over again, and then his finger had slipped inside, homing in on the ridge that held the key to her centre of pleasure and Holly was in heaven, moving against him, back and forth, aware of the waves of pleasure, equally aware, as Dev held back, that the tidal wave of pleasure would be deferred because Dev wanted Holly, Holly and Dev together, and this tiny, exquisite taste of bliss was just a foretaste of what would come. And soon.

'I love you, Dev.'

'All the tomorrows.' He cupped her face, smiling down at her, black eyes dancing with amber lights. 'My Holly. My love. I love you, Holly.'

'No!'

She couldn't believe it. For Dev to lie—now of all times. And the anger, the pain, the betrayal were suddenly too much for Holly to take and she pushed him away with a massive surge of strength.

'No.' she said simply, dying inside, grey eyes

354

full of silent condemnation. And she shook her head from side to side. 'No, Dev. Don't lie. Don't pretend. Be honest at least. You love Flora. I know, you see.' she explained tightly as the knife blade twisted. 'I've seen you together. You and Flora go back a long way. You and Flora belong. And yes, you can take me,' she acknowledged with poignant disregard for pride or self-respect, 'even now, I want you to take me. But don't ever, ever lie to me again. Understand, Dev? No lies, no pretence. Only the truth.'

And into the screaming silence Dev's loaded words:

'I love you, Holly.'

CHAPTER 21

He darted towards her but she waved him away with an imperative stroke of her arm.

'No! No, Dev. Don't touch me. Ever again. Leave me alone. Are you listening, damn you?' she snapped, crumbling now, the anger just a front. As the tears slid unheeding down her cheeks, she backed carefully away, was brought up short against the settee. She lowered herself onto the cushions, holding another cushion to her chest, holding, hugging, watching, watching the shadows chase across his face through a scalding sea of tears.

'I love you, Holly.' Curiously flat. No heat. No emotion.

'You love Flora.'

'And what on earth gave you that idea?'

'You. The accident. The woman you were rushing back to.' The most beautiful woman in the world, she remembered, her chin snapping up at the memory. 'The future Mrs Winter. And, yes, Dev,' she acknowledged fairly, 'she's very pretty.'

'Wrong, Holly. She's more than pretty. She's the most beautiful woman in the world, always has been, always will be.'

'Yes.' She swallowed hard, inwardly flinching. He was being honest at least.

'Holly?'

'Dev?

'When are you going to marry me, Holly?'

Another strange idea of a joke? she wondered, not even vaguely amused, not even angry any more.

'Soon, Holly. Please, Holly. All the tomorrows, Holly.' And then he was kneeling at her feet, not touching, simply looking, black eyes full of pain, full of love. Love. For Holly.

'What are you saying, Dev?' Holly asked as the fire began to glow in her veins.

'You know what I'm saying. I'm telling you I love you, only you, only ever you. Today and all the tomorrows, Holly.'

'And Flora?'

'Does Flora matter?'

'No.' Not a pause, not a moment's hesitation. And though Holly didn't understand, it was true. 'No. Dev,' she repeated softly. 'Flora doesn't matter.'

'I love you,' he said solemnly, cupping her face and kissing her mouth. 'And now I'm going to prove it. And you know what that means, don't you, Holly?'

'Bed?' she queried with an impertinent tilt of the head.

Dev nodded. 'Bed!' he growled, scooping her up into his arms and striding over to the open doorway at the far side of the room. 'All night long.'

Later, hours later it seemed, Dev raised his head. 'About Flora.'

'Hush, love.' Holly pressed her finger to his

357

lips. 'You don't have to explain.'

'Maybe not,' he agreed, taking the finger into his mouth and nibbling playfully. 'But that isn't going to stop me.'

'But a gentleman should never kiss and tell,' she pointed out pertly, her fair hair spread out across the pillows. And she was happy, oh so happy.

'Very true, my love. And in that case, maybe I'd better not bother.'

She hit him with the pillow. 'Devlin Winter, there are times when you make me want to scream.'

'Frustration, huh?' he enquired smokily. And he stretched out a finger to touch the nipple that was already hardening beneath his heated gaze. 'This sort of frustration?'

'No, not that sort of frustration.' And then, as finger and thumb came together to tweak the rigid nub and Holly writhed against him, 'Of course that sort of frustration. Dev!'

'Just testing,' he explained, not a bit repentant. 'Which brings me neatly back to Flora. You'd spotted us together,' he acknowledged, smiling broadly. 'Misread a completely innocent hug between friends after a job well done, and changed the colour of your eyes to the most delicious shade of green.'

'I was jealous.'

'Positively eaten up with it, I'd say,' he agreed solemnly. 'Interesting. Most revealing. But if you'd stopped to think for a moment, you'd have worked it out for yourself With Flora's help, of course.'

358

The phone call, Holly realized. The night Dev had come to dinner. 'Press agent, huh?'

'Guilty as charged. And I couldn't believe it when you didn't pick it up. I was so sure that I'd been rumbled. Do you mind?'

'That my husband-to-be is a highly successful business man with a string of attractive women at his beck and call? Oh, I guess I can learn to live with it,' she teased. Then, 'Wait a minute. The scarf you forced me to choose I can live with, Devlin Winter. But that indecent froth of lace—'

He grinned. 'All yours, Holly.' And he dipped his head to breathe against her ear, 'But I was saving it for the honeymoon.'

'I can't think why,' she countered saucily. 'Since I've no intentions of wearing clothes, any clothes, on my honeymoon.'

'Not even during the day, Holly?'

'Not even then, Dev.'

'Hmm. Well, then I guess we'll have to compromise, my beautiful little wanton. You put it on. I'll take it off. Deal?'

'Deal!'

More kisses, languid, lazy, the urgency over—for now. Holly propped herself up on an elbow, gazing down at him, her grey eyes suddenly dark with shadows.

'Since you've explained about Flora—'

'Sweetheart, I know what you're going to say, but don't. There's no need. Don't punish yourself. It doesn't matter.'

'But it does. I saw your reaction.' More men than you've had hot dinners, she'd declared, hitting out, punishing him, punishing herself more. Because the grain of truth had been inescapable. 'You were disgusted, Dev.'

'Yes. Because of me,' he explained, kneeling beside her, cupping her face, his eyes full of strange urgency. 'Because of what I'd done, Holly,' he insisted, refusing to allow her to look away. 'I hated myself for what I'd done to you—taken something precious—your innocence. I thought I'd ruined you.'

'I—'

'No.' He cut her off with a kiss. 'No more words, no more explanations. It's over and done with. I was the first and I'll be the last. And that's all that counts, my love.'

My love. So much love, she thought, nestling her head in his shoulder. And since her bed was only a single, she began to wonder just how they'd adapt to a double. The bigger the better, she decided. All that space. All that room. Room to kiss and chase, play hide and seek. Hardly, she corrected, her lips curving into a smile of satisfaction, and glancing down, seeing the secret little smile, Dev guessed that her thoughts had taken an erotic turn and stirred against her.

'I know what *you're* thinking,' he murmured into her hair.

'And I know what *you're* thinking,' Holly gurgled, reaching down to touch him, to run her fingers the length of him, loving the strength of him.

'Your turn?' he queried huskily.

'My turn,' she agreed smokily, and she

pushed him back against the pillows, her fingers kneading the taut flesh of his shoulders, kneading, caressing, moving across the powerful chest with its dark mass of hair that simply ached for fingers to scrunch, Holly's fingers.

She laughed as her thumbs brushed against his nipples, felt his nipples harden, tiny tips of pink peeking out though the curls, and she dipped her head, teasing first one then the other with her tongue, her hands against his shoulders, barely restraining, she knew, but pinning him.

'My turn,' she reminded him when Dev growled and seemed about to stir, and she urged him back against the pillows, sitting astride his legs, her hands caressing his body, each and every inch of him, *almost* each and every inch of him, because Holly was in control.

Dev was writhing, and Holly was denying him, so near, so far, trailing her fingers the length of his thighs, reaching the top and trailing away again, threading the curls, stroking the base of his belly, almost touching, almost, and yes, just the merest brush of a finger, and away again.

'You can't, woman,' Dev groaned in anguish.

'Oh, yes, I can, Dev,' she retorted pertly.

And she did, driving Dev to fever pitch and yet still she denied him, denied herself just as badly, such exquisite pain, until Dev couldn't take any more and he snatched at her wrist, guided her fingers—not that Holly had need of guidance but yes, she'd got the message—and she smiled as she made the connection he craved, felt the surge of power in her palm and smiled inside. Because she loved him. Because he loved her.

'Do you think Tom and Meryl would mind if we raided their wine store?' Dev murmured yet another lifetime later.

'Since it is a special occasion,' Holly conceded. 'And since Meryl's in open collusion, apparently, I guess they'd be disappointed if we didn't. But don't you think you ought to put some clothes on?' she asked as he padded naked and shameless to the doorway.

'Why? We're alone. And if I read Meryl's hints correctly, we're going to be alone all night. All night, Holly,' he emphasized smokily. 'I hope you're not feeling sleepy?'

'Never felt more awake,' she agreed, leaning back against the pillows and drawing her knees up under her chin. And she smiled. And she was still smiling when Dev returned ten minutes later with glasses and wine on a tray, and an assortment of cheese, fruit and biscuits.

'Hungry?' he asked.

'Only for you,' she replied. But she was teasing. And she was more than hungry, having eaten nothing all day and very little in the week that Dev had been back in her life.

'There—was a time—a very brief time,' Dev explained with a strange look and a strangely tender kiss, 'when I thought that Jonathan was mine—yours and mine. But he isn't.'

'No.'

'But he could have been.' Statement, Holly

noted, not question. Dev knew. But how on earth—?

'These.' He nudged aside the curls at the juncture of her legs, his fingers tracing the barely discernible silver puckers of skin that feathered the base of her stomach. 'My baby, Holly?'

She nodded, her eyes suddenly bright with unshed tears. 'A beautiful little girl,' she acknowledged. 'Oh, Dev, she was perfect. But she came too soon. I lost her.'

'Oh, God, Holly. I should have been there.'

'How could you have been there? You didn't know. You weren't to know,' she reassured him fiercely, cradling his head to her breast, rocking him, soothing him. 'And everything was fine until that last dreadful story hit the billboards. And I needed you—'

'I know, darling. I know.' Dev's turn to hug, to reassure her. 'Believe me, Holly, the moment I heard, I was on my way—'

'The accident? You were coming back for me—?'

More kisses. More love. A lifetime of reassurance. So much to explain but a lifetime ahead of them now and since the needs of the body seemed particularly pressing...

And when they came up for air—

'Such a lot of wasted time.'

'No. All the tomorrows,' Dev reminded. 'You, me, and our babies. Lots of babies, Holly.'

'But a little girl first, hey, Dev?'

'As long as I get to choose the name. How does Flora grab you—?'

'Devlin Winter—'

'I know. I'm impossibly frustrating, but—'

She cut him off, her lips moving against his, her tongue tracing the outline of his mouth, loving the feeling of power. Her man. And he wanted her. And she had roused him, would go on rousing him for a lifetime. A look, a gesture, a secret smile, her tongue peeping out from between her barely parted lips and he'd know what she was thinking, would read her face across a crowded room, and he'd know that she wanted him, and soon, that the moment they came together and touched, they'd ignite.

The knowledge would heighten the tension, the raw aching need would heighten the tension, and they'd skirt the edges of the need, keeping distance between them, till the need became unbearable, and then, and only then, would they make their escape, barely making it home before clothes were frantically discarded, and they'd most definitely not make it to the bedroom.

'Talking of Flora—'

'*Were* we talking of Flora?' he teased, refilling Holly's glass.

'How did she know it was me she'd collided with in the foyer this afternoon?' Holly quizzed him, the thought having only just struck her.

'Ah yes. Cunning little gadgets called photographs, my love. Dozens of them. Had you cared to visit my hotel room—my hotel sitting-room, I hasten to add—for afternoon tea last Wednesday, you'd have rumbled me days ago.'

'More fun this way?' Holly challenged. More fun, more pain, but infinitely more honest since the shadows of the past had been banished once and for all.

'More fun,' he agreed. 'But never again, Holly. Because now that I've found you, I'm never letting you go. So—' He kissed her, cupping her face in his hands, kissed her again, a wonderful buttery taste of wine and man. 'Just name the time and place, Holly,' he commanded fiercely. 'And for pity's sake, woman, make it soon.'

'St Paul's?' she couldn't resist teasing.

'Ouch! I guess I asked for that. But if that's what you want...'

'No, Dev. I just want you. For ever and ever and all the tomorrows.'

'No escape, then,' he acknowledged, his attempt at mock despair woefully inadequate.

And Holly laughed, urging him back against the pillows again, sliding her hand across the taut planes of his body and down into the tangle of curls at the apex of his legs, searching, seeking, the thrill running through her when she found him hard and ready, and she moved in beside him, body to body, face to face, barely needing to guide Dev inside, simply enjoying the touch, the feeling of power, the stirrings of desire and then they were moving together... And when she opened her eyes to find him gazing down at her, Holly smiled.

'No, Dev,' she told him smokily. 'No escape from Devlin's desire. Ever!'

This Large Print Book for the Partially sighted, who cannot read normal print, is published under the auspices of

THE ULVERSCROFT FOUNDATION

R